LET'S BE REAL

(THE NURSE NATE SERIES, BOOK 2)

BREA BROWN

WAYZGOOSE PRESS

CONTENTS

1
EVERYTHING CHANGES

AFTER A YEAR OF THIS, IT STILL FEELS ODD TO BE THE ONE sitting in the parent's chair, on the other side of the endless stream of questions.

"Crawling and cruising okay?"

"How about standing?"

"Any signs of walking yet?"

"Doing well with the sippy cup and eating with her hands? How about exploring with the spoon?"

"Any adverse reactions to solid foods?"

"Regular bowel movements and wet diapers?"

"How many words would you say she's regularly saying?"

"Reacts, as expected, to sound?"

"Pointing at things? Using both hands equally during play?"

"How does she sleep?"

"How many teeth does she have? Let's take a look!"

Of course, I'm ready for the questions; I wrote down the list of words Georgia (who's the smartest one-year-old ever, naturally) already knows. Documenting her bowel movements and wet diapers for the week before to get a more accurate picture of her habits was my next step, but Betty vetoed that.

And I realized she was right, of course. Sometimes I get carried away, though. Thank God I have a wife who keeps me in check.

That's right. *I* have a wife. And a daughter. And a dog.

If someone had told me two years ago that this would be my life, I would have punched him (because I'm sure it would have been my brother, Nick) for joking about one of my biggest dreams. But it's true! I'm married to someone I'm so in love with that sometimes simply looking at her is like a kick to the 'nads. And don't get me started about my baby girl. Most days, I can't think about her without tearing up.

I just realized it kind of sounds like the best things in my life make me miserable, but that's not the case at all. Maybe that means I'm a masochist. There's definitely a case for that, based on my history. But it's more that I don't think crying or feeling strongly about things is negative. Sure, being kicked in the balls isn't my favorite experience, but it's an effective reminder of what's most important in life. I'm okay with occasional discomfort for a good cause.

Anyway.

This pediatric clinic, where I spend every weekday as a family nurse practitioner, is one of the few places I won't be judged for letting my inner helicopter parent show. Dr. Reitman understands parents. More importantly, as my boss for the better part of the past decade, she understands *me*.

Plus, I'm nothing compared to some of the folks who come through here with their kids. I'm downright chill when measured against that yardstick.

After Dr. Reitman receives her answers and pokes and prods at a less-than-enthusiastic diapered Georgia, she nods at me to dress the shivering baby. While I do, she steps across the room to strip off and dispose of her gloves, then keys some things into Georgia's electronic medical chart.

"Well, what's your medical opinion?" I ask lightly.

She smiles but keeps her eyes on the monitor while she clicks the mouse and types. "She's amazing, as I would expect any child of yours to be."

I laugh and pull the one-piece summer romper over my daughter's head, threading her arms through the appropriate holes and snapping the garment closed between her legs. "Well, naturally. But is she on track, physically and developmentally?"

"You know she is. She's perfect."

"Well, *I* think so, but it's good to get an impartial second opinion."

"I'd hardly call myself impartial." She turns and leans against the keyboard platform, crossing her arms over her chest. "But I'm giving you my professional opinion, anyway."

"Thanks."

"And now for a more personal opinion." She nods at my efforts to jam Georgia's chubby feet into her sandals. "You're a natural at that."

"Makes sense, considering my vocation."

"There's a difference between giving kids shots and lollipops all day and being a parent."

"True. But this stuff has always come easy to me. It's why I was one of the only high school guys who didn't mind his mom volunteering him for babysitting gigs. It was decent money and easy work. Got paid to play."

"And change diapers."

"Meh. Poop is better than puke. And both are better than blood. It's all part of life." Holding a dressed Georgia against my side, I say, "Honestly, the hardest part about the past year has been the lack of sleep. And time. Everything seems to take forever to do. But I've loved every minute of it, especially since this little darlin's started sleeping through the night —finally."

"Ah, yes. Isn't that magical?"

"The best. I'd totally taken for granted going to bed and getting up eight hours later, with no interruptions. I've caught every germ that's floated anywhere near me for the past twelve months." Turning to Georgia, I rest my forehead against hers. "You're a little health-wrecker, aren't you?"

She giggles and grabs my nose, then kicks her feet, narrowly missing a sensitive target.

In my peripheral vision, I catch Dr. Reitman's wistful smile. "This is what I'm going to miss the most. You know, seeing parents with babies is like watching two people in a new, exciting relationship; one based on unconditional love, as opposed to romantic love, which fades."

At first, I squirm at my divorced colleague's reference to fading romantic love; then what she said before that registers. "Wait. What? Why would you miss it?"

Fingering her stethoscope around her neck, she answers, "I'm retiring, that's why."

"What?! When? Like... now?" I gently pry Georgia's soft fingers from my nose, as if I'll be able to make more sense of what Dr. Reitman is telling me if my schnoz isn't being baby-handled.

The doctor laughs at my incredulity. "Not today, no. But soon. Very soon. At the end of the year."

"No!"

"No!" Georgia parrots, demonstrating one of the words on her list.

Dr. Reitman chuckles, but I'm too distraught to admire my daughter's cuteness.

As my boss moves toward the door, I say to her back,

"But... but... you're still so young! It's not time for you to retire yet."

Head hanging, hand on the door's handle, she says down at her feet. "You're too sweet, Nate. But I don't feel young." She spins to face me. "And sure, it may be an earlier retirement than some doctors take, but I have my financial ducks in a row, and I'm ready for the next phase of my life. I want to spend time with my daughters, as adults, before they get married and start families of their own."

I rub my jaw. "Yeah. I get that, but... take some vacation. We could manage without you for a couple of weeks."

She lowers her chin and shoots me a skeptical glare. "I take a long weekend and get calls from you guys, plus come back to an unbearable patient load and overflowing email inbox. I can't imagine being gone for two weeks!"

"Greenbrier will send a sub from somewhere else in the network," I say, referring to the medical group of which our clinic is a member.

Her eyes sparkle. "They're doing one better; they're assigning a new doctor here full-time. He starts Monday."

"See? You'll have a backup! It won't all fall on you anymore."

"None of it will fall on me. Because I'm outta here."

I'm not fooled by her flippancy. And I don't want to make it any more difficult for her, either. Plus, she's not asking for my approval. She's simply giving me the courtesy of a one-on-one notification.

Swallowing my selfish disappointment, I bounce Georgia. "Well! That's... I mean, I'm happy for you. We're happy for you. Aren't we, George?" I ask, using the nickname that's not as popular at home as it is here.

She chooses not to respond but continues to gum her fist.

"We are," I reassure Dr. Reitman. "You've earned it."

She nods curtly. "Thank you. Oh, and mum's the word, okay? You're the first one I've told. I plan to make an announcement during tomorrow's morning meeting, but since you're on vacation this week and won't be there... I thought it was only fair to tell you now."

"Yeah, yeah. Absolutely. Man. Everyone's going to be... I don't know. It goes without saying we're going to miss you."

"Then why say it?" She winks, opening the door behind her and backing into the hallway, then points at Georgia. "She's cutting some new teeth. You know the drill. Get that baby home and give her a cold washcloth to chew on. Alternating doses of acetaminophen and ibuprofen if she seems uncomfortable or spikes a fever."

I shoot off a sloppy salute. "You got it, Doc."

"See ya Monday," she says over her shoulder on her way to her next appointment.

I stare at the empty doorway for a few seconds, then say to my daughter, "Well, that su-stinks," as I carry her out for one last parade in front of her avid fan club, comprised of my co-workers.

* * *

IT WAS difficult not to say anything about what I'd learned as I said goodbye to my co-workers at the end of Georgia's appointment, but I focused on their fawning attention instead, and managed to keep my promise to Dr. Reitman. Sure, there were twinges of guilt as I left, but it's not like I'll be allowing them to operate obliviously for long. They'll find out the news tomorrow in the morning meeting. Here's hoping the doctor won't betray my short-term treachery.

Great. Now I'm going to worry about that for the next twenty-four hours.

I have to tell *someone*, though. I'm going to burst if I don't say it out loud and discuss it with someone older than an infant or more human than a Corgi.

Betty hasn't set down her luggage before I've blurted the news to her. Never mind that she's just returned from a three-day training seminar out in California.

She blinks a few times, then advances farther into the living room after placing her purse and rolling suitcase in the hallway to deal with later. "Uh, okay... Hello to you too. I had a nice trip. It's good to be back on the ground again in the great state of Wisconsin, though. Thanks for asking."

When she comes to stand next to me, I look up the length of her body from my position on the floor, where Georgia and I have been playing with thirty (give or take) plush toys—and Reba the Wonderdog—while dinner cooks. "Sorry. I... I found out this morning, and I can't stop thinking about it. I've been dying to tell someone all day. George doesn't count. Because she's a baby."

Ignoring the endearment she tolerates as one of my "things" (either it's finally growing on her, or she's given up), Betty joins us on the floor and kisses my lips, then smooches the baby, leaving faint lipstick smudges all over our daughter's cheeks and forehead. "Oooh, I missed you so much," she says, eyes squeezed closed and nose buried in the toddler's hair. She pats Reba on the head and thanks her for keeping an eye on us while she's been away. After our reunion is complete, she says, "So, the good doc's retiring, huh? That's allowed, right?"

"Of course! But like I told her, she's still so young."

"Brown-noser."

"It's true!"

She laughs at my defensiveness. "Okay, okay, calm down. You're going to stroke out."

As I rein in my emotions and take a deep breath, Betty

coos at Georgia and asks her how our daughter-daddy time went while wiping the lipstick from the baby's skin. Then she turns back to me. "About the check-up... Details."

My impatient hand-wave receives a raised eyebrow, so I grudgingly elaborate, "It was fine. She's on track with everything. And somewhat ahead in her language skills."

"That's because you talk to her like a grownup."

"There's no need to talk down to children. It's condescending. And you're welcome, by the way, since my way is working." Something that's not working grabs my attention. I reach over and gently pull Georgia's thumb from her mouth, hoping Betty won't notice.

Fail.

"Where's her pacifier?" she asks, searching the floor around us for the ubiquitous device.

I avoid my wife's eyes while I distract the baby with an ultra-soft monkey that I make dance in front of her and kiss her nose. Georgia's giggles, unfortunately, don't deflect Betty's attention from her question.

After squirming under her expectant stare for a few torturous seconds, I casually say, still putting on my show for the baby, "She's too dependent on those things during the day."

"She's one. And it's better for her teeth than sucking her thumb. We've discussed this."

"Yeah, but... We're slaves to those things! I'm sick of panicking at the idea of not having one with us at all times. I find them in my pockets at work! Which is kinda gross, when you think about it. Something she puts in her mouth is riding next to my junk?"

Betty pushes on my shoulder. "C'mon. Be serious."

"I am!"

"But if you take away her pacifiers—"

"I'm not taking them away. I left one in her crib. She can have it during naps and at bedtime."

Sighing, Betty shifts her attention from my face to Georgia's, which is partly obscured by her hand, since she's plunked her thumb in her mouth again.

I pull it out, this time faster and with a silly, "Ew! What's in your mouth?"

"So, you're going to walk around behind her all day, doing that? Yanking her thumb from her mouth?"

"She'll stop. She just has to get used to not having the binky."

"This is unnecessary stress," Betty mumbles.

"What was unnecessarily stressful was keeping track of all those things, especially when we were in public, and she'd carry it in her hand half the time, then drop it somewhere, and we'd not only have to find it but then find a way to sterilize it, because... yuck!" I shiver.

"Now she'll put her fingers in her mouth, which are so much more sanitary..."

"Yeah, yeah. Whatever. I can keep her hands clean. At least I always know where they are."

Fortunately, she laughs at that. While taking a turn pulling Georgia's thumb away from the baby's face, she says, "I wish we'd talked about it before you made the decision to do this."

I swallow. "Well, you were away. And I thought this week, when I was home with her, would be a good time to implement it. I'd hoped she'd be broken of her binky habit by the time you got home."

"Is this your first kid?"

I chuckle. "Yeah. I guess this is one of those times it shows."

She pauses, then searches my face and narrows her eyes. A slow smile spreads across her face. "You're so darn cute."

"Why, thank you."

"And back to Dr. Reitman's retirement... I'm sorry. I know this isn't going to be easy for you."

My grin fades. "She's the only doctor I've ever worked for. Unless you count the ones on duty at Urgent Care, which I don't. Because they don't ever feel like the boss of me, you know?"

"What are you, seven?"

I choose not to acknowledge the dig. "At UC, nobody's in charge. There's no permanence. Most of the time, we don't know the patients and never see them again after that. We refer all of the major decisions back to their primary care physicians. The doctor on duty is more of a figurehead."

Betty stifles a yawn. "Are you going somewhere with this?"

"She's the only boss I've ever had. That's what I'm saying."

"Did you think that was never going to change?"

"No, but..." I exchange the monkey for a fleece lion from the carpet next to me and mumble down at it, "I never thought much about it."

The oven beeps to let us know our dinner is ready. She pats my shoulder and stands, resting Georgia against her hip. "I had to get over a nearly debilitating fear of flying, thanks to my department head's obsession—I'm sorry, *focus*—on continuous professional development. And now I'm racking up the frequent flier miles like a boss, going to and from all these stupid conference and training sessions. What's the worst you're going to have to deal with? Learning someone else's handwriting? Suck it up, Nathaniel."

If I didn't know her like I do, I might be offended by her apparent insensitivity. But she's talking me down from the ledge in her own way. And it's working, as usual. Plus she's speaking from experience. It seems like every other week, she has a new supervisor at the pharmaceutical company. The woman who runs the marketing department right now, as a matter of fact, has been there less than six months.

I follow Betty into the kitchen and remove the honey mustard chicken breasts from the oven while she straps Georgia into her high chair and sets the table. Reba assumes a supervisory position between the table and the door, licking her chops at the chicken-scented air that wafts around her.

Poking the meat to make sure it's done in the middle, I say, "I know it's going to be okay. Well, I *don't* know that, which is why I'm freaked out. And it's awful that I'm worried more about myself than Dr. Reitman's happiness."

"Mm-hm."

"I know what to expect from her, that's all. Each day when I go to work, I know exactly what's going to happen."

"Well, the same things are going to happen. You're still going to get barfed on, peed on, pooped on, bled on, snotted on, cried at, and exposed to millions of germs."

"Ha-frickin'-ha!"

"It's true!"

I place servings of chicken, rice, and asparagus on our two plates, then prepare one for Georgia, who's performing a drum solo with her plastic spoon on her high chair tray. "Those things are the variables in my day. The constant is how the team works to deal with those things. The doctor isn't an interchangeable cog in the machine. And neither am I, I hope."

"Nobody's saying you are." She sighs but steps up behind me. Threading her arms between mine and my body, she joins her hands in front of my midriff and rests her chin on my shoulder blade. "You're borrowing trouble. Sure, the new doctor will be *different*, and it might take some time to develop routines and learn exactly what to expect from him or her. But why are you assuming it's going to be a bad change?"

"I'm not!" I lie, continuing to dice a quarter of a chicken breast into tiny baby bites.

Betty withdraws. I drop the knife and fork and spin, grabbing her before she can retreat to her place at the table. She shrieks and laughs into my chest while returning my embrace. Georgia giggles at our antics and kicks her feet against the footrest on her chair. Deciding no chance of dropped food is worth enduring this chaos, Reba escapes.

My arms tightening around Betty, I bury my nose in her hair, inhaling apples and airports. When she realizes I'm not laughing, she quiets, matching the intensity of her hug to mine.

"Hey," she muffles into my t-shirt. "You okay?"

Since there's only one correct answer here, I kiss the top of her head, letting my lips linger there. "Yeah."

After a few more seconds, I let go and turn back to Georgia's plate, blinking away emotions I don't understand enough to verbalize. It's God's little joke that I'm able to experience complex feelings but seem biologically incapable of isolating and categorizing them, much less verbalizing them any better than a child half the time. Right now, I feel icky. And the fact that there's no logical reason for it only makes it worse.

By the time I deposit Georgia's plate on the tray in front of her and take my seat across the table from Betty, I'm able to muster a faint smile and a light, "Your turn. Tell me all about the seminar."

2

BONDING

WHY DO I SUBJECT MYSELF TO STUFF LIKE THIS? SURELY there are better ways for Dad, Nick, and me to bond. I can think of a thousand examples in a nanosecond, none of which include the words "stifling," "loud," "crowded," "dangerous" (yet somehow boring at the same time), or "baseball." Of course, I can think of worse activities, too (football, four-wheeling, steam room... *shiver*), so I guess I should shut up, eat my ten-dollar hot dog, and keep in mind this will all be a hazy memory I can wash off in the shower in a few hours.

Plus, as Nick so eloquently put it when he told me he had the Brewers tickets, "It's a yearly Bingham tradition, dillhole! Aren't you the one always sniffling about traditions like an estrogen-overdosed eunuch?"

He was lucky he was miles away on the other end of a phone line, not physically in my presence, when he said that. I merely gritted my teeth and said, "Fine. What time should we be at your place?"

"'We'? There's no 'we' here, bro. No wives or kids allowed. This is man time."

It was worth a shot. Because that's another reason I *hate*

this tradition, especially this year: it steals a weekend after-noon away from my girls. With Betty traveling so much lately, I'm particularly stingy with our off-time. It's bad enough that in the summer I have to sacrifice much of that time to the never-ending yard work and maintenance that comes with homeownership.

I don't dare say any of this to Nick, though. It wouldn't make a difference, *and* I'd have to listen to his merciless taunting as a result of speaking up. Not worth it.

So here I sit. And you'd think my thoracic surgeon brother or psychiatrist father could spring for luxury suite tickets, where we'd be served all-you-can-eat-and-drink refreshments in an air-conditioned environment, away from the sweaty, stinky stranger I'm currently sitting next to. (Nick doesn't smell that great, either, come to think of it, so I'm surround-ed.) Also, we wouldn't have to fear for our lives every time a foul ball sailed our way (approximately every 3.6 seconds here on the first baseline). And don't forget the sunburn. Because at this time of day, there's no such thing as a shady outdoor seat in this ballpark. Yeah, I'm having a delightful time.

"Can you drop the pathetic face for ten minutes and at least *pretend* you're having a good time?" Nick asks after Dad slides past us for the fifth time to go use the bathroom. (He should get that prostate checked.)

"I'm not wearing a pathetic face. This is my face-face."

"You look like you're sitting in a port-o-john at a summer music festival, instead of enjoying America's favorite pastime."

"Pardon me. I'm just not in the mood for this today."

"You love baseball!"

"I love *playing* baseball. Watching it? Not so much."

"What's the difference?"

"You know, it really is a wonder you made it through

medical school. I need to remember to pray harder for your patients."

He ignores my jab and squints toward the player at the plate, who's been up there, fouling off every pitch for what feels like the past hour. "Listen. This is important to Dad, all right? Stop being such an ass-face."

"If you have a problem with my face, I can leave. That would be awesome." I take a second to fantasize about that new, never-been-opened Jennifer Weiner book waiting for me on the coffee table.

Nick glances at me, then smirks. "You are so whipped."

"What?"

"She has you wrapped around her finger so tight, it's sickening."

"If you're referring to my *wife*, you are mistaken."

"No, I was referring to someone with smaller fingers."

"I love my kid. You should try it sometime."

"I love my kids just fine. When they're sleeping. I'd love them more if they'd sleep somewhere other than my bed. The rest of the time, they're hanging off my wife's tits or making noise."

"And getting all of the attention. Let's not forget that."

"I'm pretty sure that's included with the other stuff I mentioned."

"That's why you should be spending more time with Heidi when you can, not sitting in hot ballparks or hanging out at golf courses or whatever else you do to waste time."

"You have no clue, bro. You have one kid. And a wife who has aspirations that don't involve shooting out another kid every year."

I sigh. "That's the kind of wife you wanted."

"Uh... no."

"Well, that's the kind of wife you married, knowing full-well that's what *she* wanted."

"The woman I married was fun. The woman I'm married *to* is a walking milk machine and baby dispenser."

"Nice. That's your *wife*. The mother of your children!"

He snorts. "As if I need a reminder." Leaning closer, he says, "She used to do this thing during sex—"

I tense, not liking where this is going, especially because my lizard brain immediately and explicitly supplies the information to which he's referring.

"I can tell by that faraway look in your eye that you know exactly what I'm talking about."

I do, and it *was* amazing, but the last thing I want is to experience that sense memory and picture my former fiancée doing it to *him*. "Get to the point."

"Yeah, well. Lately, she just lays there, and it's like I'm on the clock, only there to provide the sperm. Plus she's too tired to do anything fun. Half the time, she doesn't even shave her legs. And with the damn co-sleeping... God, my own kids are cock-blocking me! Heidi and I have to have sex in one of the guest rooms and sneak back to bed—*our* bed."

"Hey, at least you have that option. And I don't ever want to know which room is your special sex room, m'kay?"

"It's the—"

"Shh!" I push him away. "Just put some more effort into things. Maybe if you spend more time with Massimo and Cruz, Heidi will be less tired and more apt to, um, play with *you* later."

"I work hard all day, man. Sometimes fourteen-, fifteen-hour shifts."

"She works 24-hour shifts, seven days a week."

"Well, aren't you the little feminist?" he says with a sneer.

I keep my eye on the action on the field (more to avoid

being beaned by a rogue ball than because I'm interested in the game) as I reply, "Yes, I am, thanks. But that's not why I said that. I said it because it's true."

"Can you pretend to be a man for once?"

"I'm all man, trust me. And because I'm more evolved than you are, I get more action than you do." It doesn't escape me that this is the first time in our lives I can say that. Also that it's a very *un*evolved thing to say. To keep the irony going, I add, "I'm simply too classy to talk about it."

Also, to be honest (but not to talk about it too much, especially to my brother), I'm still not getting "it" as much as I'd like, but what guy is? It's physically impossible—unless you're a porn star. Then it's work, and that's too depressing for words (that's what I tell myself, anyway). There aren't enough hours in the day. And in my case, there aren't enough days in the week when my wife and I are in the same house. That's life, though. It's only a small part of life, too. So, what's the point in dwelling on it?

Nick's not buying it, anyway. "Whatever. Your wife's never home, so the only action you're regularly getting is with your hand. Some things never change."

The crowd around us roars as the team's slugger smacks one out of the park. Reflexively, Nick and I jump to our feet and cheer (talk about biological impulses), but I use the opportunity to punch him in the shoulder—hard. He punches me back—harder. Bastard. I slap the back of his head, knocking his ball cap askew. He wraps his arm around my neck, pulls my head down, and rubs his knuckles against my hair. A few people around us laugh, assuming we're clowning around and celebrating the home run.

Dad interrupts our tussle by returning to our row with more beers (great... so he'll be getting up to use the bathroom again). Nick lets go of my head to receive his cup of amber liquid. With one hand, I smooth my hair while downing my beer.

"What'd I miss?" Dad asks, flipping down the shades over his prescription glasses.

Your oldest son's a massive douche, and you failed as a parent.

Instead of answering, I keep gulping.

Nick has the game play-by-play covered, anyway. Somehow during his complaining about his sex life, he registered every pitch, hit, and out. I guess he's not as dumb as he looks and sounds. I remain silent while they discuss ERA and a bunch of other stuff I don't care about.

Then Dad turns to me. "Natey-boy? You've been awfully quiet today. Something on your mind? Everything okay with you and Betty?"

I manage a small smile. "Everything's fine, Dad."

"Because it's not easy," he says to both of us. "Especially when the kids are young. It seems like all you can do not to drown in the work and responsibility of it most days. Talking to each other and building your relationship seems like extra work you don't have time to commit to. But it's a must, not a luxury."

Nick sighs and rolls his eyes, but I'm more interested in—and concerned about—the knowing tone behind the sermon than I am in its application to my life.

"You can't get out of the habit, guys," Dad continues. "One day those kids'll be gone, and you'll be left with nothing if you don't cultivate your marriages."

I swallow, then ask the briefest form of the question with a simple, "Dad?"

He smiles and waves away my concern. "Ah, don't mind me. Just a rambling old fart. Didn't mean to bring you guys down. Anyway, this is our man day! Who's ready for another beer?"

* * *

LATER THAT NIGHT, I lie next to Betty, catching my breath, almost as sweaty as I was at the baseball game.

She chuckles and snuggles up to my side, poking her fingers through my chest hair. "Whoa, Nathaniel. That was quite the performance."

Noticing the goosebumps on her arm, I pull the covers over her but leave my torso exposed and my leg poking out so I can cool off. I try to laugh off her compliment. "Is it *that* noteworthy when it doesn't suck?"

She rises on her arms and looks down at me, then slaps lightly at my chest. "You know that's not what I meant. But you pulled out all the stops tonight." Sighing, she drapes herself over me, resting her head on my chest.

I rub her shoulder with my thumb while debating whether to say anything further. My gut tells me to leave it at the show-stopping, multiple-orgasm-inducing masterpiece and go to sleep, but since when have I ever listened to my gut, especially when it's speaking sense?

Injecting as much of a casual tone as possible, I say, "I should go out of my way more often to show you I appreciate you. Or something. So you don't think I take you for granted."

"I know you love me, dork."

"Life gets busy, though. And the focus is always on something else. Work, the house, the baby, the dog." I lift my head from the pillow and look around the room. "Where is she, by the way?" When I don't see Reba staring back at me, I relax. It creeps me out when I realize the furry voyeur's been in the room with us during sex.

"She's under the bed," Betty answers, sounding unconcerned.

"Anyway," I say, determined not to get off-track, "Sometimes being around my brother—and my dad—reminds me of how I *don't* want to be. And how I *do* want *our* life to be. Like it was when we were first married." Realizing how that sounds, I immediately clarify, "Not that I don't love Georgia! I do. She's everything I—" Like a sap, I puddle up and can't finish, due to my tight throat.

Betty kisses my pec. "I understand what you're saying, you crazy fool."

My quick bark of laughter clears my throat. "How? I'm explaining it so wrong."

"Yes, but you don't have to explain it well, because I get you." She raises her head and looks me in the eyes.

I nod and sniff. "Good."

Her hands roaming, her eyes sparkling, she bites her bottom lip and smiles. "Do you really want it to be like it was when we were first married?"

I swallow loudly, both at what she's saying and what she's doing. "Yes," I croak.

Between kisses placed on my torso and a playful flick of her tongue against my nipple, she says, "I'm so glad to hear that."

"Yeah?"

"Yes. Because..." She straddles me and guides my hands to her hips, then slides them closer together across her belly. "Remember how that was?"

"Oh, yes."

"Remember how *I* was?"

"Uh-huh."

"Well, I'm exactly like that again. Exactly."

My heart goes from racing to stopped.

She nods when she sees my understanding and presses my hands harder against her. "I'm pregnant, Nathaniel."

I breathe out so hard, it moves her hair. "You are?" I whisper.

When she blinks and nods again, a tear shakes from her eye and lands on my abs—if you can still call them that. Whispering back, she asks, "Are you glad?"

Am I? I don't know. I mean, yes! Obviously, I am. I love her, and I love any and all children we have and will have together. But am I ready for another one already? Georgia is such a big responsibility. I can't say that, though. It's bad enough thinking it, like she adds a bunch of chores to my daily to-do list. That's so... clinical. And not how I feel at all. At the same time, I can't imagine adding another baby to our already-hectic routines, and since we don't know how much more traveling Betty has for work...

She's waiting for my answer. How long have I been freaking out down here? It seems like too long.

From my temple, she wipes a tear I didn't realize had leaked from the outside corner of my eye. "Is that a happy tear?" she asks with a wobbly smile.

I bob my head. "Yes. Of course." Wrapping my arms around her, I pull her to my chest and fill my kiss with all of the feeling I'd be sure to misstate if I tried to express myself in words.

After a few seconds, she breaks away and touches her nose to mine. "You had me worried for a second. Your face... You looked terrified."

"I love you so much it scares me sometimes."

Nice line, Bingham! Bonus points for it being the truth.

My wife obviously agrees. "You are on fire tonight, Big Guy."

BAD ATTITUDE

MORNING HIGHLIGHTS EVERY INSECURITY LIKE BLOOD under a UV ray. It doesn't help that Georgia and Reba have conspired to get me up before dawn this morning. Neither of them seems particularly grateful I'm giving up my own sleep for their comfort, either. Reba has nagged me from Minute One, scratching at the back door to go out, then yapping at it to come back in. I'm regretting removing that doggy door, but one too many nightmares about Georgia crawling through it and disappearing forever made that one of my first Daddy DIY projects.

Now the dog insistently presses her cold nose against my bare feet while I try to finish preparing a cantankerous baby's breakfast. If I were any good at multitasking, I would have filled the dog's dish as soon as I put her outside, before committing to the human food prep. But I can't think with a baby grousing in the background. I need to plug up her cry hole first. A pacifier would come in handy right now, but no. I'm committed to Georgia's de-pacification, if that's a thing.

Snapping, I nudge the dog away with my foot. "Reba! Knock it off! I can only do one thing at a time!"

Naturally, this induces panic at the thought of how stressed out I'll be, trying to keep two kids and a dog and a wife—not necessarily in that order—happy.

"Oh gosh, oh gosh, oh gosh," I mutter, setting the bowl of sliced bananas and Cheerios on the high chair tray and plopping into the nearest seat before my narrowing vision renders me blind.

Tucking my head between my knees, I close my eyes and breathe through my nose. A piece of cereal bounces off the back of my neck, serving as Georgia's review of this restaurant's service. Reba slithers between my face and the floor and licks my nose. I'm sure she's merely continuing her pleas for food, but for a second I'm okay pretending she's consoling me. I unwrap one of my hands from around my lower leg and blindly pat her. "It's okay," I gasp. "Everything's fine."

Georgia disagrees. Screeching like a deranged pterodactyl, she launches more food at me, this time slimy slices of fruit that stick to me.

Simultaneously straightening in my seat and swiping at my skin, I bellow in the baby's direction, "No, no!"

The screeching and shelling stop. Her lower lip quivers and pooches. Then her mouth opens, but as she sucks in every last air particle in the kitchen, a terrifying silence ensues.

"Oh, no. No, no, no." I stand and pluck her from her throne, pressing her head to my shoulder. "I'm sorry, I'm sorry, I'm sorry."

Too late.

Her unholy keening summons her mother (and kills the hearing in my left ear—hopefully temporarily).

"What the hell's going on in here?" bed-head Betty asks, blinking, yawning, stretching, pouring the dog some food, and glaring at me. (See? *She* can multitask.)

"I yelled at Georgia."

"Yeah, I heard that part."

"I may have overreacted."

"Ya think?" She stows the bag of kibble in the pantry, then reemerges. "Have fun fixing that."

As she tightens the belt on her bathrobe and lurches toward the refrigerator, our daughter pulls her wet face from the side of my neck and reaches for her mother. "Mama!" At least, that's what I assume she says. (I'm lip-reading at this point.)

At first, it appears Betty's going to be the strong one, but as soon as she turns and sees the pathetic picture we make, she tilts her head and laughs, the corners of her mouth pulling down in a fake frown. "Oh, my gosh! Look at you two! Come here."

We meet halfway across the kitchen. "Not you," she says to me as she extracts the baby from my arms. "You deserve this for being a big, fat meanie." Backing away, she flinches and yanks her bare foot from the floor when it makes contact with one of the discarded fruit slices. "I either stepped on a piece of banana or a slug. Either way, you're cleaning it up."

While I hunt down the rogue food with a paper towel, she rocks Georgia back to serenity, her quiet susurrations next to our daughter's ear doing the trick nearly instantly. Soon, only the occasional wet baby hiccup and smack of lips and tongue against thumb punctuate the slurp-crunching coming from the dog.

"Now," Betty declares, placing Georgia back in position for eating and gently pulling the digit from her mouth, "we're going to behave like civilized people, even if it *is* ungodly early on a Monday morning."

I exhale loudly in front of the coffeemaker.

"Sounds like some of us got up on the wrong side of the crib this morning," she continues, while coaxing Georgia to resume eating. "Look! Daddy made you this super-inspiring breakfast of slimy fruit and bland cereal circles. I don't know what you have to be so mad about."

I turn my head and poke out my tongue at my wife, which makes her laugh.

"And you!" she directs at me. "What's *your* deal? It's not like you to yell at your precious little girl. I thought she could do no wrong."

"I'm tired, that's all. And I don't like messes. And she and Reba are being unreasonable."

"You expect a toddler and a dog to be reasonable when *you* can't manage it most days?"

Ignoring her jibe, I haphazardly scoop grounds into the filter basket, clicking it into place in the machine. "Plus, Dr. Reitman's replacement starts today." Of course, I just remembered that awful fact, but it serves quite nicely as a scapegoat for my testiness.

"Ah-ha! I see now why we're being treated to Grumpy Nate this morning."

"I'm not grumpy!"

"Totally convincing."

"Shut up," I grumble at the brown liquid streaming into the carafe, fantasizing about the moment it flows into my "Murses Do it Better" mug, then down my throat.

"You did *not* just say that to me. Anyway, maybe you'll like this new guy. What's his name again?"

"Dr. Chancellor. And I'm sure I'll like him just fine."

"Then why so doom-and-gloom?"

I don't answer her while the coffeemaker finishes its job. This morning is proof that nothing good comes from conversation before that first sip. Finally, the machine sputters its last drops, and I pour two steaming mugs of heaven.

Despite being unsure I want to continue to be in anyone's

company, I deliver Betty's beverage, take a seat at the table, and wrap my hands around my cup while I wait for the coffee to cool. "It'll be fine... eventually. But these first few months are going to suck."

Betty blows on the hot surface of her drink and looks at me through her lashes. "They sure will, with that attitude."

"It's going to be weird, answering to *two* doctors. Which one has the most say? The more established one we've always obeyed or the new guy who's taking over? Is it disloyal to take the new guy's side, or is it smart? If he doesn't like the way we do things, do we immediately change to satisfy his whims, or do we defend our procedures and systems, because we obviously do things a certain way for a reason?"

"You're anticipating a bunch of issues that may never crop up."

I laugh bitterly. "You don't know doctors."

"I know neurotic murses. Is that close enough?"

"No. Not from the same kingdom, much less species."

"That's some science thing I'm supposed to understand, right?"

"If you passed sixth grade, yes."

She kicks me under the table. "Listen, bucko. You have to be nice to me. I'm carrying your spawn."

I clench my teeth and flare my nostrils, determined not to react to the burning in my shin or the panic rising from the not-so-under-the-surface place where I pushed it a few minutes ago. Her reminder isn't helping.

It *does* help me remember this whole conversation is only happening because I lied about the real reason for my bad mood. Therefore, I only have myself to blame. That's not a helpful realization, but it still counts somewhat. Her statement also requires a specific reaction from me, one I have to work hard to deliver.

I smile and grab her hand. "You're right. I'm sorry." Since we fell asleep without doing much more talking last night, I say now, "So, a winter baby, huh?" I wait eagerly for her answer but feign nonchalance, rubbing my chin and swirling the coffee in my mug.

"When I plugged my info into the online calculator after taking the test Friday morning, it said early March."

My shoulders relax when I realize she's only known our "exciting" news for three days, one of which while she was out of state. "Dr. Gannaway will be able to give us a more definite date. How are you feeling so far? Any nausea or other nastiness?" I ask, keeping it light. "You were so lucky with George not to have any of that." At the mention of our first-born, I glance over at her to see she's still engrossed in her cereal.

Betty looks down into her coffee and shrugs. "Okay. I guess. I'll have to give up this stuff, huh?"

"A cup a day isn't going to hurt anything."

She chuckles. "Good. Because I don't think I can make it without caffeine this time. I don't feel awful, but I'm tired. I didn't even hear Georgia wake up."

"Likely story."

"I'm serious! I was out of it."

"I was trying to be quiet so you could get a couple more hours of sleep, but these jokers..." I jerk my thumb in the direction of the dog and the baby, both of whom are perfectly civil now, of course.

"Your yelling is what woke me up, actually."

"Well, I'm an asshole. You knew that and married me anyway. Deal with the consequences."

She laughs and finds herself on the receiving end of one of Georgia's cereal bombs, which amazingly almost lands in her mother's open mouth. Sweeping the small circle from the table into her palm, Betty stands and says, "Well, on that note, I'm pulling rank and cutting in the shower line. Deal with *that*."

Without protesting, I sip my coffee while Betty fake-flounces from the room. When she's gone, I say to Georgia, "Seriously. That hook shot was impressive, but you have to stop throwing food. I don't care how cute you are."

The theme of the day, kids, is lying.

* * *

WE'VE REALLY ROLLED out the cot paper for this guy. In the staff room, the table we usually reserve for school fundraiser packets, "for sale" notices, church activity fliers, and takeout menus has been cleared, wiped, and clothed. Assorted pastries, their gelatinous fillings shining like patent leather under the fluorescent lights, rest in the middle of the table on a platter, complete with quaint paper doilies. A gallon of orange juice sweats next to a stack of plastic cups. The coffee urn—we busted out the urn!—squats nearby, belching its fragrant steam. And above the table, hanging across the top of the whiteboard we use for notes in meetings, hangs a custom-printed banner that reads, *"Welcome, Dr. Dan!"*

Oh, buh-rother. Could we look any more desperate?

I wipe my sweaty palms on my Batman scrubs and dispense a serving of coffee into my travel mug before taking a seat in the second-to-last row of folding chairs facing the whiteboard. (Want to strike that balance between too eager and too apathetic.) Feet spread, I lean forward and brace my elbows on my knees, ready to meet the man of the hour. My new boss. Whatever.

We cut two appointments off the schedule this morning to accommodate this meet-n-greet. That's two time slots we couldn't afford to slash, either, considering our bursting patient loads. But nobody asked me what I thought about completely disrupting the day's routine to make a big deal about some dude who puts on his scrubs one leg at a time, like the rest of us.

Actually, I sit down and put on my scrubs two legs at a time. Because that's safer. And more efficient.

But I'm an open-minded guy. I'm willing to give this Dr. Chancellor a chance.

It would be better if he were on time, but since I'm the only one here besides Beulah, the office manager, who's fluttering around as if she's expecting the Queen of England, I guess there's no rush.

"Here. Put this name tag on," she says, holding the already-labeled and peeled sticker out to me.

I look at it like it might be germ-laden, and I'm about to object when I realize that would make me look like an uncooperative a-hole. So even though I'm wearing my official name badge, as usual, I take the label from her and press it to my pec. Checking the time on my phone, I ask, "Where is everyone?", careful to soften the edge in my tone.

"Dr. Reitman wanted the front office folks to be out there to greet the doctor when he arrived."

"And the nurses are...?"

"Powdering their noses, I guess. I hear this guy's a looker."

"Oh, for crying out— Well, that explains why I'm the only one in here." The words are no sooner out of my mouth when the two RNs, Janet and Mary-Kate, come through the door, giggling like a couple of high schoolers. "Has everyone lost their minds but me?" I grouse, less under my breath than I intended.

Beulah tilts her head down and looks at me over the top of

her glasses. "What crawled up your posterior and died this morning? Dr. Reitman wants us to give Dr. Dan a warm welcome, so you better cheer up and find that sweet smile all the mommies go gaga over." She hands name tags to the arriving nurses, neither of whom questions the superfluousness of the stickers but eagerly affix them to their scrubs.

"First of all, nothing's wrong with me except that I'm sitting here, twiddling my thumbs when I could be working, getting ready for today's patients or seeing patients. Second: 'Dr. Dan'? Third: if I were *Dr. Dan,* I would appreciate everyone treating my first day as business as usual, so I could see what an efficient and professional practice—presumably—I'm now calling mine. And fourth... ew. Just... no."

Janet flicks my ear on her way past me to a chair on the back row. "We call you 'Nurse Nate,' so what do you have against 'Dr. Dan'? It's what he wants the patients to call him. It's easier to say than Dr. Chancellor."

Before I can continue the name debate, Mary-Kate taunts, "You're not going to be the only guy around here anymore. Relieved? or threatened?"

"Neither. Right now, I'd describe myself as 'annoyed.' Or 'impatient.'"

She laughs as she takes the seat directly behind mine. "Yeesh. I haven't seen you this crabby since... Well, never mind. A long time. Is that sweet baby girl keeping you awake at night again?"

"No. Although she did get me up super-early today," I say, taking the out. Anything's better than people thinking I'm *jealous* of Dr. Tardy.

That does the trick, and I might as well not be here anymore as they trade their own stories about infant-induced sleep deprivation.

After a few minutes, Mary-Kate pats my shoulder. "It's only

temporary. And it must not be as traumatic as we all think it is at the time, because as soon as you're no longer walking around in an exhausted haze, you think, 'We should have another baby!'"

"Sometimes the exhausted haze is part of that decision," Janet cracks.

Fortunately, there's enough cackling from the others that nobody notices when I fail to muster a laugh at the subject matter that's the best explanation for my irritability.

The ladies are still yucking it up when the rest of the staff members parade in, a tall, blond, tan dude following closely, walking next to Dr. Reitman. He pauses at the door and motions for her to enter first. She smiles tightly but complies.

Lynette, the clinic's lead receptionist, sits next to me, like she usually does in our morning meetings. But instead of complimenting my scrubs or asking about Georgia or Betty, she keeps her eyes glued to the front of the room... and Dr. Chancellor. (I refuse to call him Dr. frickin' Dan, thankyou-verymuch.)

I poke her in the side of the knee. "Psst. Good morning."

She moves her head slightly toward me but only mutters a quick, "Hey," then, "Shhh. He's about to talk."

Oh, Lord. Not Lynette, too!

I slurp my coffee, which earns me the first direct look from my friend since she walked in. "Do you mind?"

"Yeah, I kind of do," I hiss. "I've been sitting in here forever, waiting for you guys. What the heck took so long?"

She shrugs. "Dr. Dan wanted to see how everything was organized up front before we came back here. He loves my color-coding system. Called it 'rad.'"

Thinking she must be joking, and sure he didn't use *that* word, I laugh.

She pulls her head back. "Just because you don't appreciate what I do..."

"What?! You know I do! But 'your' color coding system is standard in all medical practices. If Dr. Chancellor called it 'rad,' he's either being a smug, sarcastic a-hole or patronizing you. If you'd like me to start patronizing you, you're out of luck."

"Seems like you've taken the smug, sarcastic a-hole option already."

"Hey!"

"All right, everyone. Let's get started," Dr. Reitman says with a quick clap of her hands. "Today we welcome Dr. Dan Chancellor to the practice. As you all know, Dr. Chancellor—"

"Dr. Dan," he says, taking a tiny step toward his colleague to correct her.

"It's easier for the kids to say," my Bat-signal-covered ass.

I snicker when it's obvious Dr. Reitman is thinking something similar—perhaps even more profane—at being interrupted. She clears her throat. "Dr. Dan. Right. As you all know, Dr. Dan is going to be taking over the practice when I retire at the end of the year, but in an effort to make the transition as smooth as possible, we'll be co-leading this clinic's operations from now until December. As the months go on, I'll be taking on a lighter patient load, while Dr. Ch... uh, *Dan* gradually increases his. The rest of you will be doing your usual stellar jobs and helping him become acclimated to the practice. It's all pretty straightforward. Any questions?"

She stares straight at me, but I quickly look down and fiddle with the spill guard on my travel mug. I'm afraid if she looks at me like that for too long, I'll erupt with a huge, whiny "WHYYYYYY?", and that wouldn't be very professional.

Dr. Reitman waits a few more seconds, clasping her hands behind her back and rocking on her feet. "Okay. Hearing none,

I'll turn it over to Dr. Dan." She nods at him, then sits in one of the chairs in the front row.

To my dismay, my co-workers greet the new doctor with applause. I join in so I don't look conspicuously dickheaded. He fans his open hands in front of him, as if to tamp down our clapping. Only too eager to oblige him, I wrap my hands around my mug and extend my legs, crossing them at my ankles.

"Good morning, everyone. In case you're having a hard time keeping up on this Monday, I'm Dr. Dan Chancellor—Dr. Dan to all of my patients... and friends, which I'm sure we're about to become. A little bit about me: I'm a graduate of the University of Wisconsin, where I got my undergrad degree what feels like forever ago..."

Bitch, please. The man's not much older than I am, probably Nick's age, thirty-seven tops. And he knows he looks good. Barf.

"...after which I attended med school at Johns Hopkins in Maryland, where I specialized in pediatrics...."

But somehow missed the class about being on time.

"Kids are my passion..."

Said every pervert ever.

"...they're our future..."

Sing it, Whitney.

"...I can't think of a more important job than the one we will collectively do here in this clinic every single day...."

No pressure.

"...which brings me to something I want to emphasize right away. You and me are a team...."

You and I. Or how about 'we,' dude? I guess grammar wasn't a big emphasis at ol' JH, either.

"...there's no hierarchy here. Without you, this place couldn't function, and I couldn't do my job. As far as I'm concerned, that makes us equals..."

What is this egalitarian nonsense?

"...so there will be no 'pulling rank.'"

Riiiiiight...

"And each of us will do what needs to be done to treat each and every patient. If you see something that needs doing, and you're qualified to step in and do it, you do it. A phone's ringing and poor Lynette's already on another call with three calls on hold? You pick it up. A patient has had an accident in the hallway, and you're not already busy with something else? You put on your janitor cap and clean it up. The dishwasher needs unloading in the break room? Your mother doesn't work here; *you* do. You see a need, you make it your responsibility. No one person is greater than that ideal. Including me."

An appreciative chuckle ripples through the room.

Nice one. I can totally see this guy risking his manicure on a puke slick in the hallway.

"Hey, dude," he interrupts my skeptical inner grumbling and squints to read my ID badge and/or name tag. "Nate, right?"

I straighten my legs and scoot my butt toward the back of my seat. "Yes."

He laughs. "No need to get all stiff and formal, Batman. You're the clinic's FNP, right?"

For some reason, I'm suddenly hesitant to admit something I'm normally pretty proud of, but I reply, "That's right."

"Big deal."

"Excuse me?"

He smirks. "You heard me. FNP, MD, PhD... they're all just letters, man."

"Okay... Well, sure. But—"

"No! No buts. The only butts I care about are the ones that need medical attention."

While he and the others titter at his cleverness, my

chuckle is born more out of nervousness and hides my extreme efforts not to lose it as this guy insistently flicks my last nerve.

Finally, when the laughter stops, and he focuses his eyes on mine, as if he's waiting—nay, daring—me to respond, I say, "With all due respect, I worked *my* butt off to earn those letters."

"And that's great. But what do they mean?"

Trusting he knows they literally mean "family nurse practitioner," I dig deeper to try to answer his question. "They mean I'm qualified to diagnose and treat and make recommendations regarding patient care."

"They help you to better, more fully *serve*, in other words."

"Exactly."

"They're a privilege."

"Yes! Absolutely."

"Don't forget it."

I swallow. "I... I don't?"

"You sound unsure."

My pulse stutters, and my eye twitches. "Actually, I *am* unsure why you've singled me out."

He tousles his hair. "Dude, I'm sorry. That wasn't my intent. I guess my point is that in some practices, there are certain people who are top bananas. Your doctors, your nurse practitioners, blah, blah, blah. But my philosophy is that each person is every bit as important as the next, regardless of the initials—or lack thereof—after someone's name. You dig?"

Oh, I 'dig' all right. I dig this guy's grave.

Leaning back in my chair, I prop my ankle against my knee and shake my foot. "Everyone in this room will tell you what a team player I am, Dr. Chancellor."

He puts his hands in front of his chest. "Peace, man. It's Dr. Dan, and I didn't mean to ruffle your feathers. I simply want everyone to be clear—"

"I think we get it," I say, standing and earning my incredulous co-workers' stares. "I have a patient in ten minutes. And I *see a need* for someone to unlock the doors and man the front desk, so I'll be heading that way." I peel the sticker from my chest, crumple it, and drop it into the trashcan by the door on my way out.

4

EVENING CATCH-UP

IT'S HARD TO TELL WHO'S IN A HIGHER DUDGEON WHEN
Betty and I convene at home after work. I'm the last to arrive,
since I was recruited by Dr. Chancellor to help tie up some
paperwork before I left. ("Hey, we have to keep up with this
stuff, right, or else it turns into a huge mess. Most of it's in
your handwriting, anyway. You don't mind helping Mindy so
nobody has to stay too late, do you?")

Eff him.

And honestly, eff Mindy. She'd get her work done if she
stopped talking about her boyfriend du jour for ten seconds
and concentrated on what she gets paid to do—coding and
filing. Next time I have patients backing up and need to
perform a diagnostic blood draw on someone, is she going to
step in and stick the person for me so I don't have to skip
lunch for the six thousandth consecutive day?

Oh, wait, that's right—most of my co-workers can't do *my*
job. Something or other about some pesky letters. I'm so glad
nobody needs a certain set of letters after their name to tran-
scribe patient notes. That means we're *all* qualified to do
Mindy's job.

And eff me for thinking something so elitist. I never felt that way about any of my co-workers before today. Ever. Because Mindy blabbing about her boyfriend's motorcycle never made me late for dinner until now.

For once, though, I don't even get one word of complaint out before Betty launches into her tirade. And there *is* a definite hierarchy in our house: the pregnant lady gets to vent first.

"You are not going to *believe* what she's done now."

She, she, she? Who the hell are we talking about?

I mentally flip through a list of potential female trouble-makers. Reba? Nope. If she were the subject of Betty's wrath, she'd be hiding, not sprawled out on the couch, twitching through her latest doggy dream. Georgia? No way. She's an angel. Plus she's in her favorite place, glued to her mom's hip, chewing on a teething ring and looking content with the world. Heidi? No. Despite having both slept with me—and that will never cease to be awkward—Heidi and Betty get along surprisingly well. They're not BFFs and don't spend a ton of time together (fortunately; we don't need them comparing notes or anything untoward like that), but that also means they don't have a chance to get on each other's nerves. Not to this extent, anyway. My mom? Nah. Mom loves Betty and never gives her any trouble, especially since Betty's such an improvement on...

Frankie.

Yep. Only one person puts that irate glow in my wife's eyes.

"Unless her latest settlement check bounced, I don't care," I make the mistake of saying. Out loud. My filter is officially shot.

Betty's eyes widen. "This is about so much more than money, Nathaniel."

Carrying Georgia and what appears to be a paperback

book, she follows me down the hallway as I pull my shirt over my head. In the bathroom attached to our bedroom, I peel off my pants and throw my scrubs, socks, and underwear into the hamper. As a rule, I strip and shower as soon as I get home, before I touch Georgia. I'm a stickler for hand-washing, obviously, but I don't feel truly clean after dealing with germy kids in various states of wellness until I've done a full-body cleanse.

I can't resist a tiny bit of sugar, though. While the water heats, I lean forward and kiss the top of my daughter's head. "Hey, sweet girl. What's got your mom so riled up?"

"Since you ask..." Betty thrusts the powder blue book at me, something I now see bears the name Francesca Pembroke in gold-foiled, flourished cursive. "Read the dedication."

Holding any work of Frankie's elicits a nearly physical reaction from me, but I resist the urge to throw the tome into the toilet and instead do as my wife says. Because I like her. And I want to keep living, despite the day I had and what I fear is in store for me every work day for the rest of my life. Survival instinct is a strange, illogical beast.

Clearing my throat, I turn to the dedication page and read aloud, as dispassionately as possible:

"'To N and B. Thank you for forcing me to own my talent and for helping me prove to myself that I can do anything. FML.'"

I snort at Frankie's initials: *fuck my life*. That she did. Temporarily, thank goodness.

Before stepping into the shower, I return the book to Betty. Sticking my head into the hot stream of water, I say, "News flash: Frankie's a bitch. Next headline?"

"You don't understand."

"Obviously not."

"One of my co-workers pointed out this dedication to me today. Everyone at Quimby-Rex knows about it. They drew names to see who got to show it to me. Fricking hilarious, huh?"

"They work for a pharmaceutical company. Throw them a bone that they don't know how to have fun without drugs."

"This isn't funny!"

When Betty and I were newlyweds, the most stressful thing in our life wasn't unexpectedly expecting our first child or selling Betty's house or merging our two independent lives into one. The most stressful thing was our lawsuit against Frankie. It was the source of the majority of our arguments. I wanted to close the Frank Lipton chapter of my life; Betty wanted an official court decree to state that Frankie had to let go of the part of her author brand that included me. Knowing her friend as well as she did, Betty feared we would never be free of Frankie unless a judge told her to leave us alone. She was probably right. We'd most likely be dealing with something worse than a lame dedication in a book (I'm thinking an unflattering book based on our experience, then adapted into a made-for-TV movie) if there weren't a court order forbidding it.

But we *are* only dealing with a lame dedication. And there's a reason Betty and I don't talk much about Frankie—it upsets Betty, which angers me, and those two things are likely Frankie's main objectives when she pulls crap like this. When we react as expected, she wins.

And Frankie's won enough. Our lawsuit earned some media attention (Frank Lipton was kind of a big deal in the indie publishing world for a day or two), so as soon as she settled the case with us and was out from under legal action, a big-name publisher snatched her up and offered her a huge deal, republishing all of her old books under the name Francesca Pembroke, to capitalize on her famous spy thriller-writing father's name. I only know because it was all over the Internet, and she made the rounds on morning news shows, becoming quite the media darling.

Good for her. I honestly don't care. I'm glad she's gone from my life, other than that monthly reminder of her when her settlement check clears our bank account.

It's been harder for Betty, though. While Frankie was merely a chapter or five in my memoir, she was volumes of books in the series of Betty's life story, the one constant in a sometimes chaotic upbringing and early adulthood. And I get that. But at some point, no matter how difficult it is, you have to banish someone to the past forever, no matter how big a part of your history she is. You have to move on and build new relationships, trusting that not everyone is a duplicitous, self-serving jerk who's going to put everything you've ever said and done into a book for the whole world to read and judge.

Betty's not there yet. So I wait.

Now she rants, "And she gets around the terms of the settlement by using our initials, but everyone who knows her and knows us knows who those initials belong to."

Again with the talk of initials. Please, God, what did I do to piss You off so badly today? You've been tormenting me since four a.m. Mercy!

While I lather and rinse, Betty pauses, but her voice is full of emotion when she says, "As if it's not bad enough that I lost my best friend, I have to be publicly humiliated over and over again by her. First during the court proceedings, when she called into question my professionalism and accused us of carrying on together behind her back—"

"Everyone knew she was lying. That's why we won. And those records are sealed as part of the settlement, so nobody who would possibly believe her can read her lies."

"It doesn't matter that she was lying. That she would say

those things, for the record... Like our friendship didn't mean anything."

I turn off the water, open the shower door, and grab a towel. Betty lowers herself to the closed toilet seat and stares at her knees while she distractedly rubs the back of Georgia's chubby hand. Georgia rests her head on her mom's shoulder.

Drying off and wrapping the towel around my waist, I take the baby from Betty and smother her from forehead to toes with gobbly kisses that elicit breathless giggles as she grasps handfuls of my damp hair. After a while, Betty's laughter harmonizes with her daughter's.

"You two are a sight."

I set Georgia on her feet on the floor and insert my index fingers in her fists to give her some support while she practices walking. She's taken a few wobbly steps here and there, but it seems like someone's always too willing to carry her, so she's yet to string a series of strides together into true walking. With another baby on the way, we need to remedy that.

I walk her back and forth from the bathroom to the bedroom to give Betty some thinking space, but when she seems suitably distracted watching Georgia and me from the foot of the bed, where she's moved to keep a better eye on us, I venture what I hope is a wrap-up to this particular conversation.

"You know, if *I* wrote books, I could pen a thousand passive-aggressive dedications to Frankie. 'Thanks for introducing me to the love of my life.' 'Thanks for my beautiful daughter and growing family.' 'Thanks for cheating on me and showing me your true self before I made the biggest mistake of my life—which is saying something—and married you.' 'Thanks for my daughter's college fund. We're thinking Dartmouth.'"

"Dada, Dada, Dada," Georgia chants as her legs give out beneath her.

I toss her gently into the air, catch her, and kiss her nose. "That's right! Mommy rescued Daddy from the evil novelist's mind-controlling skinny jeans, and we lived happily ever after!"

Finally, that earns from my wife the deep chortle I've been waiting for. She rises from the mattress and converts our hug into a group one. "I love you guys."

"We love you too. Don't we, George? Mommy's the best!"

"Da best!"

Betty ruffles the baby's hair, then takes her from me. "C'mere, you smart little booger. Let's go put dinner on the table while Daddy gets dressed."

"I'll be there in a minute," I promise, watching after them as they retreat down the hall. Betty murmurs something against Georgia's head, then kisses her chubby cheek.

That's my family. And without that fateful blind date with Frankie—and everything that followed—who knows what would be?

My eyes land on the blue book Betty's abandoned on our bed. I stare at the glossy cover until it blurs. Then I sweep the volume onto the floor and kick it under the bed, where it deserves to rot with the dog hair and dust bunnies.

* * *

HOURS LATER, our tiny orator slumbers peacefully in her crib while I deliver a foot rub to Betty on the couch, under Reba's supervision. I can tell the dog approves by the way her eyes droop as if she's the one on the receiving end of the massage. Eventually, she drops her head to her paws and grunts as she settles in for her evening nap. I'm sure she's exhausted—and maybe dehydrated—from generating that puddle of slobber on the floor while she watched us eat our pork chops.

Betty taps her pen against the notepad propped against her knees. "I'm forgetting something," she says, referring to the weekend get-together we're hosting at her parents' cabin to celebrate Georgia's birthday. We scheduled it to coincide with the neighborhood association's Fourth of July fireworks display on the lake.

"You have the dog sitter lined up for Rebes?" she checks.

Our furry friend loves Georgia like she's one of her own litter (oh, gosh, I hope she'll be okay with the new baby, too), but she's not a fan of anyone else's kids, and she absolutely fuh-reaks around fireworks. Even the lame firecrackers people on our street set off put her on edge.

"Lynette will be here sometime Friday night, after we leave. Remind me to get the guest room ready."

Betty puts a check mark on her list but scrawls the new item and sighs. "This list is getting longer, not shorter."

I rub harder. "Why don't you put that down and relax for a minute? Stop worrying so much. It's only my family. It's not like it has to be perfect."

It will be, though. Betty will see to it. She goes into public relations mode when we host anything, and no detail is too small to get exactly right, especially if it relates to Georgia. She's determined to be the nurturing mother hers never was.

"It's already not going to be perfect, since my parents can't be bothered to be there."

Rub, rub, rub... That's the extent of my input on this topic. The son of psychiatrists, I can't help but get overly passionate about the legacy Betty's mother and stepfather have handed down with their unconventional parenting—and now grand-parenting—methods. If you can call absenteeism a method.

I made the mistake early in our marriage, while Betty was

pregnant with Georgia, of bluntly stating the consequences of her lax upbringing—worst case scenario, of course, because that's how this dumbass rolls. I was mostly giving my wife an out for her unplanned pregnancy in college and her first child's resultant adoption. She, however, misunderstood and thought I was predicting she'd be a cold, standoffish mother, and suffered a panic attack that nearly required medical intervention.

Since then, I've learned to keep my yap shut when the subject of her parents arises. She tends to fill in what she assumes (usually correctly) I'm thinking anyway.

"I thought they'd like being grandparents," she says now. "It's all the fun without any of the responsibility. And I know you think they're in denial about their age and their mortality, and being grandparents doesn't fit with their carefree, jet-setting self-images, but... I don't know. Georgia's their granddaughter! Well, my mom's, anyway. Shouldn't biology take over at least *some* of the time? I thought it was in our DNA to feel a certain tenderness toward blood relatives!"

I want to pipe up and correct her on this point, possibly cite some research I read a few years back, but no! *No, no, no! Rub harder, Bingham, and save your scientific lecture for another day.*

She pulls her foot from my grasp. "Ow!"

"Sorry," I mutter.

Folding her legs, she tucks her feet under her knees to protect them from my clumsy paws. "You know what Mom said when she finally returned my calls and emails about this weekend? 'We'll have to play it by ear, Elizabeth. I'm not sure about Witt's schedule.' Play it by ear." Betty snorts. "Right."

Worst answer you can ever give my wife. Betty doesn't play anything by ear. The woman is hard-wired to plan. Everything. I like planning as much as the next guy—maybe more. But I definitely believe the lack of structure in Betty's upbringing created a strong desire for order; since she didn't have anyone else to provide it for her, she learned to do it herself. She learned it well. I'm not saying "spontaneity" isn't in her vocabulary, but it's definitely not a nice word, according to her.

"Anyway," she continues, "I guess that *is* a definite answer. It means they won't be there."

"We'll have fun anyway."

"We'll have *more* fun without them. But that's not the point, Nathaniel. The point is, their granddaughter is a year old, and they've seen her once. The time we Skyped from the hospital doesn't count. In person, holding her: one time. That's pathetic." She rests her palm flat against her belly. "And now..."

I cup her knee in my hand when she can't continue.

After some fierce blinking and throat-clearing she says, "Geez. I'm so emotional this time! I don't remember crying this much with Georgia."

You don't contradict a pregnant lady, so I resume my earlier vow of silence. But she *did* cry this much with Georgia. She cried all the time. When she was happy, when she was sad, when she was mad (often, considering what we were going through with Frankie), when she was hot, when she was cold, when she had indigestion...

I was so used to it that an old lady told me off in the grocery store when she witnessed Betty sobbing and not only assumed it must have been my fault but was incensed that I was standing idly by, not trying to console my engorged wife. Not that I blamed the stranger for getting the wrong idea. Who blubbers over a throwback cereal flavor? Betty did. "Frankenberry was always my favorite! Sometimes I'd eat it for breakfast, lunch, and dinner on weekends. Waaaaaaaaah!"

The lady didn't hear that part. She happened upon us much later, after I'd decided to ride out the tears by double-checking our progress with the grocery list on my phone.

"Shame on you, young man! She's upset, and all you can do is stick your nose to that silly phone! Tell her you're sorry!" She stopped just short of hitting me with her purse.

I started to defend myself, but it was too much work—and frankly, less embarrassing to simply take the blame and end the episode. Then Betty seemed to remember where we were and quickly composed herself, apologizing to the woman and sheepishly explaining that the cereal—not her husband—was the cause of her emotion.

The lady rubbed Betty's arm and commiserated about "those pesky hormones!" before returning to her own business, grabbing some Malt-O-Meal, and leaving us—without apologizing to me, I might add. But whatever.

Dealing with uncaring parents is something worth crying about, at least. Although, thinking back, that may have been what she was upset about in the cereal aisle. Damn. I wish I'd realized that then.

"I'm sorry you had to eat Frankenberry for every meal," I blurt now.

She sniffles. "Huh?"

"Frankenberry. One time, you mentioned you ate it for breakfast, lunch, and dinner some weekends. I assume it's because you had to fend for yourself, and—"

"Man, I love that stuff! I'd give anything for a bowl right now."

I stare at her.

She flutters her damp eyelashes at me.

Stifling a sigh, I stand and dig my keys from my shorts pocket. "I'll be right back."

* * *

THIRTY MINUTES LATER, with a mouth full of unnaturally pink

cereal and tiny, hard marshmallows, Betty says, "You're the most amazing man on the planet. Thanks for this. So good!"

I smile as I settle into the couch cushions with a book. "Glad I could help."

"Mmm-hmm!" She swallows. "I was mostly kidding about you going out to get this. I felt bad after you left."

"You're worth it. And it's nice to be appreciated." Flipping to my bookmark, I mutter, "Somewhere."

She slurps her milk, then nearly chokes on it when she gasps. "Oh, my gosh! I completely forgot to ask you about the new doctor!"

I pat her on the back. After she regains her breath, she sets her cereal bowl on the coffee table and asks, "What's he like?"

"I regret to inform you that my worst fears are being confirmed on an hourly basis. The guy's a douche. All about equality and using first names only—"

"Sounds super-douchey so far."

Countering her sarcasm, I insist, "He is!" I recap the disastrous morning meeting and hit the highlights of the rest of the day, ending with the part about helping Mindy before being allowed to go home.

"As if my job isn't demanding enough, I now get to be the catch-all man and pick up other people's slack."

"It'll calm down. He's just asserting his authority. At least he's doing it in a cheerful, beneficial way."

"He's doing it in a controlling, subversive way."

"Hmm. Well, I know all about new bosses, so I can tell you they have one thing in common: they come on strong but lose momentum quickly, especially if it's obvious their big plans aren't working quite the way they envisioned."

"Does that mean your presence will no longer be required at every marketing boondoggle that comes to your boss's attention?"

She laughs. "Maybe someday. The thing is, *she* doesn't have to go on these things, so it's going to take a while for her to tire of sending the rest of us on them. But she will. The cost will start to chafe, if nothing else. But on that note... I'll be traveling all next week."

I drop my head to the back of the couch and moan.

"Don't think about it," she advises.

"Sure. No problem."

She takes my book from my hands and snuggles up to my arm. "I know you miss me when I'm gone."

"I do. I can't sleep if I'm fully covered in a silent room."

"I don't snore! And I don't hog the covers, either!"

I laugh at the familiar argument. "I'm going to record it one night. You obviously need proof." I kiss her nose.

"Nathaniel?"

"Hm?"

"It's going to be okay, right?"

New baby, new boss, more traveling, more overtime...

"Sure," I answer. "Why wouldn't it be?"

5

NOT-SO-HAPPY BIRTHDAY

HER BIRTHDAY WAS NEARLY TWO WEEKS AGO, BUT GEORGIA'S too young to know or care. All she knows right now is that she's surrounded by her favorite people and covered in pink, gooey frosting. She has clumps of cake jammed between her fingers and smashed into her dark hair, and she's loving it.

I've told my inner nurse to take the weekend off and stop worrying about sugar intake and intestinal distress brought on by too much junk food. Witnessing the pure joy on my daughter's face makes that task surprisingly easy. Keeping the camera steady during my laughter has been much more difficult.

"Hey, George," I call from my vantage point a few feet away on the cabin's back deck. "Over here." She looks straight at me and hams for the camera. "Dada!" she squeals, spreading her fingers and waving her hands, flinging cake and icing onto everything and everyone within a five-foot radius of her high chair.

Nick, Heidi, and my parents duck and throw up their hands to protect themselves from the flying food. Massimo giggles and wipes frosting from his face, then pops it in his mouth. Cruz flinches at the noise but looks on with his usual glassy stare.

Betty laughs next to me. "Georgia Lou! Eat it! Like this." She mimes licking her clean fingers. "See? Look at Mommy."

"Mamamamamama."

When Betty's instruction receives no results, she steps closer to the high chair and dips her finger into the decimated pile of cake, then eats the bite. "Mmm, yummy."

"Yum!"

"That's right." Betty leans down to our daughter's level and polishes off another finger-full. "It's delicious."

"'Lisses."

"Yep." Another bite goes into Betty's mouth. "Amaz—" She screeches when Georgia decides she'd rather pull her mom's face in for a wet, sloppy, open-mouthed kiss, using Betty's hair as hand-holds.

"Oh, my gosh, this feels so gross!" Betty groans.

"Hold that pose!" I say, keeping the camera rolling. "You two are adorable."

"You put your face down here and see how adorable it is."

Handing off the phone to Nick, I say, "Okay," and join them. I snatch a mouthful of the dessert directly from the tray without using my hands and gobble it in Georgia's face. "Mmm, almost as sweet as you!" I muffle, nearly nose to nose with her.

She lets go of Betty's hair and drags one of her slimy hands down the front of my face. Everyone laugh-moans.

"And here's where Nate flips out," Nick intones.

I cross my eyes to follow a blob of icing as it drops from the tip of my nose. What's to flip out about? Is this unsanitary? Yes. But it's also wonderful. I turn my head to look at Betty, who's laughing as hard as I am. We break down harder still after getting a good glimpse of each other.

"You have a little something..." Betty points to my upper lip.

I lick it. "Thanks. Your hair!"

She pats her crusty bangs. "It's a new thing I'm trying. You like it?"

"It looks good enough to eat."

"Your phone's about to die," Nick says, reminding me we're not the only three people on this deck.

After a final, cakey kiss to Georgia's chubby cheek, I straighten and retrieve the device from my brother. "Dang it," I mutter. "We haven't opened gifts yet. I better go plug this in for a while."

"Wait!" Dad raises his pint glass of beer and says, "A toast!"

Nick flaps his lips. "Here we go."

Dad ignores him. "To the best family a guy could have. When we're all together like this, it's humbling to think that two crazy aspiring shrinks started it all."

Mom shifts in her chair and lowers her wine glass. "Jim, don't."

"No, no, no! I need to say this. I need everyone here to know how much they mean to me and that... I'm sorry." Overcome with emotion, he stops.

I exchange worried looks with Betty. Nick clears his throat. Heidi giggles nervously.

Dad takes a deep breath. "I'm sorry for my part in this coming to an end. But I want you all to know, it's not my choice. It would never end, if it were up to me."

I try to catch my mom's eye to prod her to do her usual job of translating Dad's sometimes enigmatic statements, but she continues to stare intently at her lap, refusing to elaborate or clarify, so I ask what nobody else seems brave enough to ask. "What are you talking about? Are you... sick?"

In the fading light, tears glisten in Dad's eyes. "Heartsick, Natey-boy, that's all."

"Why? What's going on?"

"Maybe your mother should answer that. Yvonne?"

After a withering glare at Dad, Mom sets her wineglass on the table next to her and lifts her chin. "I certainly wasn't planning to announce it this weekend, but I guess there's never a good time. And it's not like it's the end of the world, no matter what your father says."

"But?" Nick prods.

"Your father and I have decided to divorce."

"What?!" I nearly choke on my spit, which is interesting, considering not a drop of saliva has made it through my stingy glands since Dad started his weird toast.

"Oh, come off it," Nick says. At first, I assume he's talking to our parents, urging them to stop kidding around. Then I realize he's directing his statement to me when he adds, "Like we haven't seen this coming for years."

"*I* haven't!"

"Figures. You're so clueless sometimes."

"Clueless? There'd have to be clues to miss for me to be clue*less*. But of course, you're so much smarter than the rest of us."

Betty leans forward to block my view of Nick. "Guys. Come on." To Mom and Dad, she directs, "I... I have to say, I'm surprised, too. And sad. I'm so sorry."

Mom shrugs. (Yes, shrugs!) "Like Nick said, this has been a long time coming."

"Longer for some of us than others," Dad says.

"Yeah!" I agree.

"Have we seemed happy to you, Nathan?" Mom asks, sounding genuinely interested in my answer, like the consummate therapist asking, *"How does that make you feel?"*

"You haven't seemed *un*happy! You've just been... you guys."

"Well, being 'us' hasn't been pleasant for a while."

"You don't fight, though. You... you—"

"We're roommates and business partners who get along extremely well," Mom admits. "That doesn't make for a happy marriage, but it can make for an amicable divorce."

My stomach churns. "I... I can't... I..."

Heidi sniffles a few feet away. "Oh, my gosh. I've known you guys forever. I can't believe this is happening."

"You supposedly knew all about this, Nick, but you didn't think to let your wife in on it?" I ask. "Typical. Although I guess that would require a conversation that didn't revolve around your golf handicap."

"Why are you so mad at me, bro? I'm not the one getting the divorce. I'm not the one with the younger boyfriend on the side."

I focus my baleful attention on my parents once more. "No! Tell me that's not true. Mom?"

Her silence is plenty elucidating.

"You have to be kidding me," I mutter. "And how did you know about *that*?" I demand of my brother.

A pale, sweaty Nick replies, "I didn't. I was joking. Shit, Mom."

"Now, boys," Dad says, "don't gang up on your mother. It takes two people to make—or break—a marriage. We each made our contributions to this failure."

"Spare us the psychobabble," I say, crossing to the deck railing, where I stand with my back to the others. I stare wordlessly at the sky, despairing at the dramatic nosedive the weekend has taken.

The youngest attendees—possibly feeding off the vibe coming from their parents, possibly simply because they're up later than usual, waiting for the start of the fireworks—are starting to get whiny and restless. It's like they know they're witnessing the downfall of the Bingham family.

Well, hey. At least it's going to be an *amicable* downfall.

Amicable, maybe, but not mutual. Dad is obviously heart-broken and wants to try to salvage their marriage; Mom's the one who wants out. And why? Because she's bored? Because her life isn't as exciting as she though it would be as she approaches retirement? Because Dad can't make himself twenty years younger and compete with her new boyfriend?

I lean farther over the railing, bracing my elbows on it, ready to hurl into the landscaping below. Remembering my dying phone in my hand and the drying cake on my face, I abruptly spin and stride across the deck to the back doors.

"I need to charge this," I say, though I'm no longer sure what I could possibly want to commemorate with a photo for the rest of this night.

The first fireworks whiz and bang overhead, sending Nick's kids instantly into orbit and startling Georgia into the type of slow cry that builds like a tornado siren, eventually reaching max volume and holding there until the storm passes—or she passes out.

Betty rushes to lift our daughter from her cake-crusted high chair. Heidi edges past me with one boy under each of her arms and disappears into the house.

When Betty catches up to me with a howling Georgia on her hip, I reach for our daughter. "Here. I'll take her inside and give her a bath."

"Let's go together," she suggests.

I nod my assent, and we walk side-by-side into the house... where we come face-to-face with Witt and Kitty.

* * *

BETTY STOPS in the middle of the living room. "Mom! Dad! What are you guys doing here?"

"Well, hello to you, too, Elizabeth." Kitty releases a tinkly laugh usually reserved for awkward run-ins during intermission at the opera.

Betty shakes her head. "Sorry. We weren't expecting you, that's all. I thought you said—"

"I said we'd have to play it by ear, and we have. I hope we haven't missed all the fun."

The back door opens behind us, and Nick bursts into the room.

"Screw me. Thanks for leaving me out there with Mr. and Soon-to-be-Ex-Mrs. James Bingham, assholes."

If Kitty's forehead weren't so full of pig toxin, her eyebrows would shoot to the top of her head at that statement, but her O-shaped mouth is the only indication of shock at my brother's unconventional entrance.

Witt clears his throat. "I'll be, uh, taking our bags upstairs."

"Nate and I are in the master bedroom," Betty informs him.

He smiles coldly. "That's fine. I'll move your stuff into the hallway, so you can choose a different room." At the bottom of the stairs, he stops. "Did you know you have cake on your faces and in your hair? And why are all the children crying?" Without waiting for an answer, he tromps to the second level.

Nick steps around Betty and me. "Oh, hey," he says to Kitty. "Ummm, two of those crying kids are mine, so I'll, uh..." He disappears down the hallway that leads to the first floor rooms.

"Is everything all right?" Kitty asks, taking in her surroundings.

By all appearances, one of the fireworks skipped across the

lake and detonated in here; or we've spent the day hosting a child's birthday party.

Betty bounces Georgia more vigorously to try to get her to calm down. It's more likely she'll cause her to throw up. "Well," she begins, but doesn't seem to know where to start. Instead, she wimps out. "I'd better get Georgia's bath going." She follows in Nick's footsteps, leaving me alone with my mother-in-law.

"Nate, it's good to see you again," Kitty says after several awkward hours... er, seconds.

I smile weakly as I walk around the room, pushing toys and baby equipment into a large pile in the corner. "Yeah. Um, it's good to see you, too. I'm glad Witt's schedule allowed it."

"We can only stay the one night..."

Long enough to displace Betty and me, thanks.

"...but we figured that was better than nothing." She nods at the back doors. "Did your brother say your parents are outside?"

I half-turn, as if I need to check to be sure. "Uh, yes. They are."

"And did I hear right that they're soon to be divorced?"

That's still too fresh for me to comment on matter-of-factly, so I step around her into the kitchen portion of the open-plan area, grab a towel from the counter, and rub it over my face to clear it of cake and hide any of my visible emotions from Kitty's view. "They just told us."

"At a child's birthday party? That timing seems a bit off."

I lob the towel in the general direction of where I got it and sigh. "I don't think they planned it that way." I don't want to defend them, but it's a reflex, one that comes from a lifetime of explaining them to friends and acquaintances.

"How terribly uncomfortable. I'd go out and say hello, but... it's been a long day, and..." She edges toward the stairs.

"It's okay."

"Are they staying the night? Perhaps I'll see them in the morning."

I shake my head. Mom and Dad's decision to drive back to Green Bay tonight suddenly makes more sense than it did when they first announced it upon arriving in the early afternoon. They obviously didn't want to have to share a room or explain why they wanted separate rooms.

Kitty clicks her tongue. "Pity. Oh, well. I'm sure we'll see them again sometime."

That's hardly a sure thing, since we hardly ever see you.

She points to the kitchen counter, near my left elbow, where a large box with a huge bow sits among the dirty dishes and leftovers. "We brought Georgia a present. A professional mani-pedi kit, complete with foot bath."

What every one-year-old wants!

"Oh. Thanks. She can, uh, open it tomorrow, so you can watch her. I don't think anyone's in a partying mood, anymore."

With a casual wave of her hand, she begins her climb upstairs. "Whatever you think is best. Tell Elizabeth I said good night."

"She should be back any second," I say to Kitty's retreating back.

"Never mind. I'm too tired to wait."

"Right. Of course."

When she's gone, I spin in a circle and assess the damage around me. Pots, pans, half-empty alcohol bottles, and the untouched sheet cake we never had a chance to cut or eat, plus paper plates and plastic cups, litter nearly every inch of the granite kitchen counters. Toys cover the living room floor. Outside on the deck, the high chair still sits, covered in cake and icing. Also out there waits an even bigger mess, in the form of my parents.

It's quiet down the hallway, where it seems Betty, Nick, and Heidi have the kids under control. I'd only be in the way back there.

On impulse, I grab the notepad and pen by the landline phone in the kitchen and scrawl on the top sheet, "Went for a walk. —Nate." I prop the notepad on the back of the couch nearest the hallway entrance and slip out the front door.

\

6

FALLOUT

IT'S DAMP AND CHILLY ON THE WOODEN DOCK. I WISH I'D thought to snag my hoodie, but that would have required going upstairs and facing Witt and Kitty as they evicted us from our room. Then I would have been expected to take our stuff to a different bedroom. The only one left is the one I shared with Frankie the first time I ever came to this place, for a weekend of snowmobiling—and finding out I was the alter ego of a chick lit author.

Sleeping on this dock sounds like a better option. The mosquitoes can eat me alive, and I'll never have to face any of the things currently scaring the shit out of me.

That's right. I'm scared. I'm thirty-five years old, and I'd say I want my mommy, but she's likely too busy right now counting down the minutes before she can be with her boyfriend.

How much younger is he than she is, anyway? Mid-forties? Or Nick's age? My age? *Younger?* Oh, gosh, I can't think about that.

I spread my knees farther apart and hang my head lower, spitting into the lake, feeling the bile build and my stomach contract as it begs for me to expel that cake I ate off Georgia's high chair tray, like an animal.

"Damn it," I whisper when it's obvious my iron gut— usually my friend—isn't going to allow me the relief I want. The cake remains stubbornly lodged like a sugary rock. Well, not exactly. It rolls around from side to side in there, mirroring the thoughts doing the same thing a few feet higher, in my head.

Thoughts of babies and douchey doctors. And parents who pretend like they were never anything more than business partners. Not to be outdone by in-laws who show up unannounced at the worst possible time, of course.

My eyes and nose sting and my throat aches with the pent-up tears I refuse to shed. Eff crying. Crying isn't going to solve anything. It's only going to make me feel like a weak, self-pitying jerk. Or a pregnant woman having a meltdown in the cereal aisle.

Hollow footfalls on the dock startle me. I stiffen and blink away any evidence of my emotions. My new companion stands next to me, then lowers himself to the spongy wood and dangles his legs toward the water.

"People were worrying about you," Nick says. "Something about you falling into the lake and screaming at a water moccasin."

"Shut up. That happened one time. And if you'd come face-to-face with one of those things, you would have screamed, too. Its eyes were evil."

I shudder at the memory from less than a year ago, when all of the Binghams stayed up here for a week soon after Georgia was born. Other than losing my footing during a hike, falling into the lake, and meeting Mr. Snake, it was a great week.

"I didn't know it was possible for a man's voice to get that high." He stops. "Oh, that's right. We're talking about *you*."

"You're hilarious."

He doesn't refute my statement but chooses to stare across the dark water instead.

"Were people really worried about me? I left a note."

"You can't be trusted in the wilderness."

"Lake Ridge Estates, a master-planned community, can hardly be called 'the wilderness.'"

"For you, it may as well be. Anyway, I knew you wouldn't wander far, so when I saw you sitting down here, I took the opportunity to get out of that house for a few minutes and get some fresh air."

"Are Mom and Dad still there?"

"They were leaving when I volunteered to come look for you."

"Good. I'm glad they're gone. I don't want to talk to them."

"Real mature, bro."

"And what they're doing is mature?"

"Maturity is irrelevant in their situation."

"How can you be so calm about this? Is it because you supposedly saw this coming? And for how long? How long have you known that everything I thought about our parents is a lie?"

He flaps his lips. "Damn, you have a flair for the dramatic."

"Just answer the questions."

Swinging his feet, he grips the edge of the dock next to his legs. "Raging about it and acting out isn't going to change it, is it? It's not going to improve things, either."

"No, but I want to go on the record about this."

"It's been noted in your chart, dingleberry."

"Don't call me that."

"And stop acting like I was keeping some huge secret from

you, because I wasn't. When I said it was a long time coming, I meant I'd noticed things. Dad's been saying weird stuff for the past couple of years."

"Dad's been saying weird stuff our whole lives. I was suddenly supposed to attribute his ramblings to the collapse of our parents' marriage?"

"I did."

Lifting one foot fully onto the dock and wrapping my arm around my knee, I half-turn to get a better look at my brother's face. His smug expression makes me want to punch him. "Good for you."

"I'm not bragging about it! I'm being honest."

"Why didn't you clue me in?"

"I didn't have any proof. It was only a hunch."

"And that part about Mom having a boyfriend?"

He raises his hands in front of his chest. "Hey, that was a total guess, bro. I was joking."

"At a time like that? It wasn't funny!"

"You know how I am. I say stupid shit when I'm nervous."

Since he has a point, I merely pull at my leg hairs and sigh. "What the hell?" I grumble, referring to the entire situation.

"Pretty much."

We sit in silence for a while, swatting at mosquitoes, each of us lost in our own thoughts, before Nick says, "Your in-laws are as weird as ever."

I laugh. "Yeah, well, they're looking pretty normal right now next to our parents."

"Oh, God. You're right."

We stare at the intermittent bubbles that betray the presence of little fishies—and other things—under the glassy, black surface of the water reflecting the night sky.

Then Nick asks, "Do you think we're going to screw up our kids?"

"In one way or another. The fun part is finding out how."

"Well, my kids are going to have to share the dysfunction with at least one more sibling."

I push on his shoulder. "When are *you* guys expecting?"

"January." Righting himself, he studies my face with narrowed eyes. "Why do you say it like that? Who else do you know?"

I spread my hands and smile sheepishly. "Surprise!"

"Oh, get outta here. For real?"

"Yep. We haven't told anyone yet, because..."

...I haven't been able to say it out loud.

...if we don't announce it, it's not true.

...I feel like a big, fat jerk for being so ambivalent.

"...it's still early. We found out last week."

"Delightful," he says dully. "Well, it probably is, for you." He picks a splinter of wood from the dock and pitches it into the lake.

I could kiss my brother for making me feel better about myself. At least I don't sound like I've been handed a death sentence when I talk about *my* impending bundle of joy.

"It is for you too."

"Yeah, I guess. It'll be fun when they're all slightly older."

"Try to have fun with it now." At his raised eyebrow, I allow, "I'm not saying it's easy. But what's the point in being miserable, waiting around for better times?"

He nods. "True. What if there *are* no better times? What if we get to be Mom and Dad's age, and things just fall to shit?"

"Nice thought."

"Well? It happens. All the time. It happened to our own parents. Maybe it's hereditary."

"All the more reason to enjoy the present, I guess," I reply, trying out this "optimism" thing I see so many others practicing.

"This conversation is getting too deep and touchy-feely for me, bro. If we're going to keep at it, I need beer."

We stand at the same time, but neither of us seems in a hurry to return to the cabin.

I shove my hands in my pockets. "Nothing's ever going to be the same."

Nick sighs. "It's not going to be that different, either. It's not like we're eight years old, and we'll have to spend every other weekend at Dad's depressing bachelor pad."

"But think about holidays and birthdays and cookouts and—"

"The only difference will be that they arrive in separate cars and go home to different houses."

Leave it to Nick to oversimplify everything. "I'm not sure."

"You don't have to be. Whatever's going to happen is going to happen, whether or not you worry your stupid ass off about it."

He hooks an arm over my shoulders and pulls me toward the house. "Come on. Let's get plastered."

"Let's not and say we did."

The last thing I want is to pack up and drive home tomorrow with a hangover, but it would be nice to be inside, away from the bugs, in bed, under the covers. Maybe I can stay there for the rest of my life. Do you think anyone would notice?

* * *

About twenty-four hours later, I'm still in a major funk, but life refuses to come to a halt to allow me the serious brooding I require.

"I can't believe you're going to be out of town all week," I grouse at a scuff mark on the white baseboard, my head half hanging off the foot of the bed.

The mattress shakes under me as Betty heaves our rolling suitcase onto her side of the bed and unzips it. She removes our weekend clothes and tosses them toward the hamper, making room for her traveling work wardrobe. "Believe it."

"When is this going to end?"

"When we run out of enriching conferences to attend. Or my boss gets in trouble for spending the entire year's training budget in a span of three months." Her light tone turns defensive. "Anyway, the second half of this trip is a legitimate meet-up with the ad agency in charge of the next product roll-out in December. An anti-depressant. Sexy stuff."

"You have all that fancy video conference equipment at the office. Why don't they ever use it? Why do you have to travel to New York to talk to some stuck-up ad people about which beautiful-yet-tortured-yet-hopeful-looking actors to use in a commercial?"

When she doesn't answer, I turn my head and tuck my folded arms under it, resting my ear against my forearm while I watch her expertly—too expertly—roll her panties, slips, and wrinkle-resistant sheath dresses into loose scrolls she can unfurl and hang in hotel wardrobes sitting in rooms identical to all the other rooms she's stayed in lately. It takes me back to a time I don't want to remember, watching Frankie perform a similar routine on Sunday nights. Only I become heavier, not lighter, with every item that goes into this suitcase.

Finally, after selecting the perfect pair of shoes for each chosen outfit, sliding them into satin drawstring bags, and tucking them into the side of the case that will become its bottom when standing upright on its wheels, she stops moving and meets my eyes. "I'm aware all of my traveling makes things stressful around here."

"That's not why I hate it; I can handle the extra work. I miss *you* when you're gone, not the extra set of hands you provide in the morning or evening. And Georgia misses you."

"What about Reba?"

"To be honest, she likes having your side of the bed."

Betty raises her head. "You let her sleep in my spot when I'm gone?!"

"It's less lonely that way."

"That's kind of pathetic."

I offer her my hand to shake. "Hi, I'm Nate. Have we met?"

She cracks a smile, then goes back into motion, zipping the suitcase and setting it on the floor. She drags it to the wall by the bedroom door, where she can quickly grab it in the morning on the way to the airport for her early flight. Then, kicking off her flip flops, she crawls across the bed and rests her chin on my shoulder.

Before she can get too comfortable, I roll to my side and scoot so I'm more fully on the mattress, my face lined up with hers. Tentatively at first, then more firmly, I drag my fingertips across her lower belly. "I don't want to be a single parent with two kids. I *can* do it, but I don't want to do it."

She kisses my forehead. "You won't have to. Hopefully, this will all be over by then."

"And if it's not?"

She sighs. "Then we'll figure out something else. We're a team, remember?"

"I seem to remember making a promise to that effect, yes. I've lost a ton of sleep in the past few months, though."

"Get used to it, Nathaniel. Oh, that reminds me!" She rolls onto her back, then sits up and grabs a stack of slick, shiny booklets from her bedside table.

I prop my head on my hand and grin at her as she returns

to sit cross-legged, her back against my belly. "What do you have there?"

"A few ideas I've bookmarked in catalogs and magazines. For the nursery."

My smile fades, but I'm careful to keep my tone light. "Ah. Yes. The nursery."

"I guess we'll have to move the desk in here. And we can sell the guest bed? Or take it apart and store it in the attic until Georgia's ready for a full-sized bed. Whatever. Anyway!" She flips to a dog-eared page in the middle of a catalog. "What do you think about this crib for a boy?"

"Why, you little sexist," I joke, lowering my eyes to the page to conceal my lack of enthusiasm for this topic. Sure enough, it's a crib. But it doesn't say "boy" or "girl" to me. It screams, *"Peeing, pooping, crying, hungry, not-sleeping creature-holder."* I push the booklet away. "I don't know. It looks like a wooden crate."

She tilts her head and studies it, then laughs and wrinkles her nose. "Ew. You're right. I didn't see it before, but now I can't unsee it. It's like a chicken coop. Thanks."

"No problem. I'm here to help." Absently, I grab one of the interior design magazines from her lap and thumb through it, looking at but not seeing the high-sheen furniture and elaborate murals. Who lives like that?

"Which wall are we turning into the mural of our solar system?" I hold up the current page for her to see. "Gosh, that's fugly. Give the poor kid a gravity complex before he can even walk."

"You said 'he.'"

"Yeah, so?"

She nonchalantly flips to another folded-back page and holds it at eye level for me. "You want it to be a boy?"

"Not necessarily. I was just... I don't know. You're the one picking out 'boy' cribs!"

"That was one of many. Look. This one's more unisex."

"Why can't we get the same model we got Georgia? I already know how to put that one together."

She pushes the booklet farther under my nose. "They're going to be individuals."

"Oh, geez..."

"I like the color scheme in this picture, too."

"Do we have to decide all this right now?"

"No. Nobody's making any decisions. I'm trying to distract you from other stuff."

I flip the magazine in my hands onto the comforter next to me, roll back to my stomach, and say, "I appreciate the effort."

"But?"

You're stressing me the hell out!

This is one of the things I need to be distracted from.

I don't give two shits about cribs and color schemes.

Filter, filter, filter! "That's not your responsibility."

She rests a hand on the small of my back. "It was worth a try, though. You want to talk about it?"

"No. Thanks anyway."

Sex. Sex is what distracts men from their problems.

Filter, Bingham!

She rises from the bed, collects the glossy publications into one pile, and returns them to her nightstand. "I guess I'm going to call it a day, then. Early start tomorrow." She disappears into the bathroom, where I hear her use the toilet, then run the water to wash her hands and brush her teeth.

I haul myself up and sweep back the covers with a flourish. I should be ashamed at how quickly I can transition from *Life sucks!* to *Let's get it on!* but I'm a guy. It might be biologically impossible to feel shame about that. And who am I to argue with biology?

By the time I've taken off all of my clothes, I'm raring to go. I slide under the sheets and close my eyes, imagining what's to come, plotting my moves. Maybe tonight calls for something different. Nothing too out there, mind you, but I'm definitely not feeling the usual choreography. Sticking to a script is how married people fall into the complacency trap and find themselves filing for divorce in their early sixties.

Boop, boop, boop. Whoa, whoa!

Whew. Almost lost my mojo for a second there, thinking about that.

Back to the good stuff. I ruminate a few more minutes about Betty's soft, milky skin and the way that hollow at the base of her throat is always so warm and smells so good. I wiggle my shoulders, tensing then relaxing them to get good and loose. When she gets out here, I'm going to try that thing I read about it in *Cosmo* (shut up), and have been debating for a while whether I can pull it off. I can. I've got this. I'm—

The bathroom door clicks and squeaks. I open my eyes and follow Betty's progress across the room. She checks one more time to make sure her boarding pass is in its usual compart-ment in her suitcase, then shimmies out of her shorts so she's only wearing a t-shirt and panties. Reaching behind her, she unclasps her bra, which she pulls through one of her sleeves and drops on the floor with a contented sigh that hardens my nipples. Dear Lord, this is going to be amazing.

She turns off the lamp on her bedside table and slides into bed, still wearing more clothing than she needs, but I don't mind undressing her. It counts as foreplay, right? And when she lies on her side, facing away from me, I don't let that discourage me, either. I wait for her to settle and still, give it a five-count (cool guys don't pounce), and make my move, curling around her and pressing my hardness against her so there's no question what she does to me.

Her muscles tense under my hands. "Nate..."

"Yeah?" I kiss her neck, edging my nose closer to that sweet, fragrant spot.

"I'm so tired."

"Oh, yeah, baby. Me too—" I freeze. "Wait. What?"

She falls against me, pushing me away with her shoulder. On her back, she reaches up and lifts my hair from my forehead. I watch her lips as she says, "I'm zapped. And I have to get up early."

Okay, fast and dirty it is, then. I'll do that new thing some other time.

"What's ten more minutes?"

She bites her bottom lip to try not to laugh.

My erection falls exponentially, but I'm not ready to give up yet. "C'mon. We always have sex before you go on a trip."

"I know. I'm sorry. I'm just tired and... and gassy."

Bwoooooooop. The end.

I scoot away from her and lie on my back, staring at the ceiling.

"I shouldn't have eaten all that birthday cake today," she says. "But there was so much left over, and I didn't want it to go to waste. *You* won't eat it this week while I'm gone."

Oh, I don't know. I could eat some feelings right now.

Without looking at her, I reach across and pat her head. "Never mind. Don't worry about it. I got ahead of myself, I guess."

"I'm so sorry. I'll make it up to you when I get back."

"Don't be silly. There's nothing to be sorry about or make up. You're allowed to not be in the mood..."

...and ruin my night.

...and remind me that life really does suck right now.

She drops the most un-erotic kiss ever on the tip of my nose. "Thanks. You're so sweet." Showing me her back once more, she subtly edges farther away from me, like she's worried any contact with my naked body will give me the wrong idea. "Good night."

I stifle a sigh. "Good night."

Worst. Weekend. Ever. (And I've had some bad ones.)

7

DR. DOUCHE

I MAY NOT BE GETTIN' BUSY AS OFTEN AS I'D LIKE AT HOME, but at work, I'm busier than ever. For nearly a month, the clinic has been buzzing with patients complaining of the usual seasonal problems: summer colds, swimmer's ear, poison ivy, infected bug bites, hay fever, and sunburn, as well as diagnoses of food poisoning thanks to Aunt Velma's unrefrigerated potato salad at the family reunion and follow-ups and referrals for sprains and breaks. I run my butt off from the minute I greet my first patient each morning until I wipe down the final exam room each evening—and sometimes after that, depending on what petty task Dr. Chancellor asks me to perform.

"If you see a need" has become the bane of my existence. In addition to the needs I'm taking care of by myself at home more and more often, I see many needs at work on a daily basis, ones that used to be regularly filled by co-workers paid to take care of them but that often remain neglected long enough now that I have no choice but to step up and take care of them myself.

Like now, before the morning staff meeting, I'm balancing

a cup of coffee on a fiberglass clipboard in one hand while I click the mouse with my other hand to print my schedule. Because I *need* to see what's ahead of me today, but nobody's gotten around to printing it yet. And I'd wait patiently, but already two days this week, nobody printed the schedules in time for the meeting. So... I'm seeing a pattern here. And a need to do it myself.

Which is fine. The letters after my name don't make me above printing something. But it would be less galling if the knot of coffee-guzzling people in the hallway behind me weren't having such an inane conversation about a certain TV show they fanatically tune into each week.

"I swear, I saw man parts!" Mary-Kate says in a stage whisper while I click "print."

"I thought I did, too!" Lynette nearly shrieks. "But I figured I was just imagining things."

Dr. Douche drags liquid through his lips with a loud slurp, then says, "Well, it's about time. They show female nudity constantly. I'm not sure why there's such a double standard in movies and on shows like that. If you're going to show naked people, be equal opportunity about it."

"Amen!" Lynette booms.

"It's because men sit on boards that make those decisions," Janet supplies, while I wait for the printer to finish warming up and spit out my request. "Hey, Nate, are you printing the schedules?"

I bite the inside of my cheek, keeping my back turned to her. "I'm printing *mine*, yes."

"Can I get a copy please?" she asks. Before waiting for an answer, she turns back to the others. "And there's something sacred about a penis, or something. Which we all know is ridiculous. I mean, how many do we see and handle here every day? It's just another body part, like a finger."

Mindy giggles. "I don't know about that. Your view may be skewed to the clinical side since you've been a nurse for as long as you have."

"Not that long. I'm not that old, you know. But I also have a son, so..."

"Yo, Nate!" Dr. Douche shouts. "Print copies of mine and Pat's schedules too, while you're at it over there."

I clench my teeth and click the mouse button harder with each command I give it. When my left hand tires from being held in an unnatural position for too long, the clipboard wobbles. I slide it onto the counter next to me before I spill coffee everywhere.

"Anything else I can do for anyone?" I fling over my shoulder.

Silence greets my snarky question, followed by the doctor asking, "Did you happen to catch *Valkyrie* last night, or do you record it and watch it on the weekend?"

Retrieving the papers from the printer, I keep the three sets of schedules separate by cross-stacking them, turn to my colleagues, and reply, "I don't watch it at all. It's not my thing. If I wanted to see more blood than I do every day, I'd pick up some shifts in the ER."

Mindy rolls her eyes while receiving the printouts from me on my way past her toward the staff room.

When I double back for my mug and clipboard, Lynette explains, mostly for our newest co-worker's benefit, "Nate prefers sitcoms, rom-coms, and the occasional family drama."

I nod and return the group's indulgent smiles. "That's me. Life's dark and messy enough. I like to laugh and feel good in my spare time." Tucking the plastic board under my left arm, I down a large swallow of lukewarm coffee.

Dr. Douche nods as if I've just presented him with a challenging case study. "What's your favorite show right now? My wife recently binge-watched a comedy about a nanny with amnesia."

"*Nanesia*," I say, turning sideways to skirt the group and get to the staff room door. "Great show. Hilarious."

"It seemed pretty absurd to me," he counters, following me and leading the others.

"Well, it's hardly realistic," I say, finding myself defending my choice. "But that's kind of the point. The suspension of disbelief is part of the draw. Isn't that what you do with that gory Viking show? Or do you really believe Vikings had dragons?" I refresh my coffee just enough to make it drinkable, slide the carafe back under the filter basket, and take my first sip, regarding him over the rim of my cup.

"I like both *Nanesia* and *Valkyrie*," Lynette declares while I find the nearest empty seat and occupy it. "For different reasons."

"You like the man candy in *Valkyrie*," I say with a knowing smirk, settling my clipboard in my lap.

She laughs. "That's part of it, for sure. But the story is good too. Intense stuff."

"I just can't stop thinking that the women on that show are people's daughters." I shiver. "It grosses me out."

"Your wife is someone's daughter, too," Dr. Douche says.

Jamming my tongue against the back of my throat, I barely prevent coffee from spewing through my nasal passages. Spluttering, I eventually swallow the mouthful and glare at my boss through watering eyes.

He chuckles and wiggles his eyebrows. "Just saying. Some daughters are hotter than others."

Everyone else laughs at his sexist comment. Even if I didn't find it offensive, I'm too busy trying to breathe non-caffeinated air to join in.

From behind me, Beulah, having just arrived, taps a handful

of paper towels against my shoulder. I grab them and cough into them.

"What in heaven's name are you talking about in here?" she demands, like a mother who's walked in on her kids flipping through a lingerie catalog. Underlying disapproval overpowers her outwardly amused tone.

"TV shows," Mary-Kate answers.

"Well, this isn't a fraternity," Beulah says with a sniff as she takes her usual seat. "Let's keep it professional."

Chastened, even though I wasn't the one being crude, I focus on recovering from my near-aspiration.

Dr. Douche nods contritely at the office manager. "You're right. My apologies. The conversation got away from us." He clears his throat and glances toward the door, then says on his way through it, "I'll go see what's keeping Pat so we can start the meeting and get this day going."

* * *

I'm a single parent—again—so I needed to leave five minutes ago to rush home and shower before picking up Georgia at daycare by the six o'clock cutoff or risk a late charge (and absentee dad reputation). On days like this, I find myself scampering past Dr. Douche's office door, channeling my inner Ninja to escape his notice. Sometimes it works. Today... not so much.

"Nate!" he calls when I'm already a good ten feet down the hallway—so close to freedom, yet so far away.

My hesitation seals my fate. If I'd kept running (not distinguished, but effective), I could have said I didn't hear him in my rush to get home or in the slamming of the heavy metal staff exit door. But at the sound of my name, I pull up, like a chump. When he pokes his bleach-blond head through his office doorway, I'm still in view, unable to realistically claim ignorance of his summons.

The clock ticking in my head, I plaster a smile on my face. "Hey, Dr. Chancellor. What's up?"

His smile is equally forced when he joins me in the hallway. "Now, Nate. How many times do I have to tell you to call me Dr. Dan?" His tone suggests a playfulness his clenched jaw tells me he's not feeling.

"Uh, yeah. Sorry."

Not sorry. It's approximately the one-hundredth time I've apologized about it with no intention of changing my behavior. Most of the time I get around it by not saying his name in front of him. But that's generally because I'm afraid I'll slip and call him Dr. Douche, the name I exclusively use for him in my head and in conversations with Betty.

And now I pretend the name reminder was his sole purpose for flagging me down. "Well, good night! See you tomorrow." I take one, two, three steps toward the door.

"Wait! I need to talk to you about something."

Feigning interest, I face him fully, noticing we look like a pair of dueling medical men, me in my rubber ducky scrubs, him in his lab coat. "Oh?"

"Yeah, you mind stepping in my office?"

It's a true test of my acting skills when I assume a regretful tone to say, "Oh, man, I wish I could, but I'm already running behind. My wife's out of town, so I need to pick up my daughter from daycare, and—"

"This will only take a second."

Since standing in the hallway arguing an inevitability is only making me later, I acquiesce and follow him into his office.

Man, I hate this room. First of all, it's about the size of a coffin, which actually makes me smile sometimes when I picture Dr. Douche jammed in here, the walls closing in on him, day after day. But then I imagine him marking off the squares on his calendar until he can move into the spacious, well-decorated office Dr. Reitman currently occupies, and I seethe. Plus, the pocket size of this space hasn't stopped Dr. Douche from making it a shrine to his accomplishments. Sure, he has less room for things like patient charts, but he's carved out precious shelf and counter space for diplomas and sports trophies. Apparently, he's a Frisbee golf enthusiast.

The other reason I hate this office is that I'm never in here for anything good. For all of his talk about positivity and affirmation, he's not a fan of bestowing any of those things on me. Not that I care or need his approval. But it's painfully transparent he thinks I do and is withholding it to make a point. I caught him glancing at me once when he was praising Lynette —probably for replacing the toner in the copier, or something equally mundane—like he was ensuring I was a witness to a benevolence he's never extended to me. What a pathetic moron.

The other day, he pulled me in here to ask why I haven't adopted a more "professional" dress code, to set me apart from the registered nurses. I explained that I've invested a fair amount of capital in my collection of novelty scrubs, which the kids—and I—like. They're conversation pieces and a fun distraction for the tots who are nervous or feeling particularly unwell. Then I capped off my defense with, "Anyway, I wouldn't want anyone to think I was putting on airs or pulling rank, because of a few silly letters after my name." That shut him up, and I was thrilled I actually thought of it then, rather than hours later in my car on the way home, when I usually come up with my best zingers.

As usual, it's nearly impossible to breathe in here. I can't wait to escape. "What's up?" ...*this time?*

Clearly not in a hurry, he sits behind his desk and rocks in the chair that's about three sizes too big for this room. He steeples his fingers under his chin and half-closes his eyes, as if studying me.

I glance over my shoulder, shift from foot to foot, and widen my eyes expectantly.

Finally, he says, "You know, Nate, it pains me that we seem to have gotten off on the wrong foot."

Poker face, don't fail me now. "Have we?"

"You know we have, dude. Let's not play games." He says it lightly, yet the threat is implicit.

"I don't have time to play games. What with my patient load, on top of my added responsibilities around here lately, *and* being a busy husband and dad... What you see is what you get."

He chuckles. "Yeah. I hear what you're saying, though."

"Which is?"

"You resent some of the changes I'm making around here."

"It's your show. Not my place to resent anything. I do what I'm told." Jabbing a thumb over my shoulder, I say, "I really have to go, if that's all you needed."

Hands resting on his desk, he sits forward. "Here's the thing, Nate. I'm not going anywhere. And neither are you... for now."

Sweat seeps under my arms and pops along my lower back. My heart picks up the pace, and my mouth dries. "What's that supposed to mean?"

"The patients love you. The parents love you. Your co-workers love you. Dr. Reitman loves you. I see that. I get that."

"I love what I do, and I'm good at it. That's what people respond to. If you want me to apologize for that, then—"

"No! Absolutely not. That's the one thing you don't have to be sorry about."

"Meaning?"

"You and me, man." He waves his hand back and forth between us. "We need to get right."

I swallow and take a second to filter and moderate the thousands of furious responses that want to jump from my lips. Finally, his words still echoing in the room—or is that just my ears?—I choose, "You and *I*."

"Pardon me?"

Yeah, what?

"It's 'you and I,' Dr. Chancellor. You and I need to 'get right.'" I bend the first two fingers on each of my hands up near my head on those last two words.

Oh, shit... Not the air quotes! What am I doing?

He stares me down. I shove one of my smart-ass hands into my pocket and grip my keys, the jagged metal pressing into my fingers, keeping me focused on something other than blurting a retraction.

Finally, he smirks across the desk at me. "The take-away is the same, though."

I bob my head a few times, screw my mouth to the side, and say, "Yeah, well, the thing is, I'm okay with things the way they are right now."

Liar!

He snorts. "Well, I'm not."

"I guess that's something for *you* to work on then. Good night, Dr. Chancellor."

Before he can detain me any longer, I stride into the hallway, resisting the urge to sprint. Barely.

"It's Dr. Dan!" he shouts to my back.

I let the slamming door serve as my response.

8

DEPRESSING DINNER

IT'S ONLY AS I'M TROTTING INTO GEORGIA'S DAYCARE WITH minutes to spare that I remember I agreed to meet my Dad for dinner tonight.

"Fuuuh-dgsicle!" I hiss at the realization, while scanning my thumb to release the lock on the inner door to the nursery.

Through the narrow window, I spy Georgia sitting on her teacher's lap. She's the only remaining child, and she nearly launches herself from Miss Heather's arms when I enter the room.

"Dada!"

Now *this* is what it's all about.

"Hey, George. Sorry I'm late." I lift her and blow raspberries on the sliver of chubby tummy peeking through the gap between her ruffly top and her baby capris, then hold her close for a real hug. She wraps her arms around my neck and rests her head on my shoulder. "Dada."

Miss Heather smiles and holds the clipboard for me so I can sign out my daughter without setting her down. Then she hands me the backpack that holds Georgia's extra clothes and security blankie. "She had a great day. She loves water play. Her wet things are in a plastic bag in her backpack."

"Great. Thanks." I poke Georgia in the ribs so she'll lift her head, and I can see her face. "Water play, huh? You a little fish?" I suck in my cheeks and purse my lips. She pokes her fingers in the creases in my face. "Sish! Sish!"

"That's right. F-f-f-fish."

"Fuh-Sish!"

"Close enough. Wave goodbye to Miss Heather," I say as I secure the straps on her carrier.

"Bye-bye!"

With a limp wave of my free hand to the teacher, I leave the pick-up room with my cargo and stride down the hallway toward the exit, careful not to bump the carrier against my leg or swing it too widely with each step. Some kids endure the Tilt-a-Whirl rides of their lives as their parents transport them to or from the parking lot. After years of observing this terrible technique from others—and experiencing sympathetic motion sickness as a result—I've made a conscious effort to avoid copying it.

At the car, I hoist the seat through the back driver's side door and click it into its base. Out of breath, I announce, "It's time to go have dinner with Pop-Pop."

"Pop-Pop! Gamma!"

My fingers linger on the clasp connecting her two shoulder straps as I adjust it to its correct position across her chest. "Not Gamma. Just Pop-Pop." I clear my throat and clench my teeth. I agreed to meet Dad in a moment of weakness, but it's the last thing I want to do after the day I had.

Plus, who wants to take a baby to a pub? Not this guy. I've seen respectable families at The Cheesehead with young kids, but still... It would have been better if, in the end, I'd never remembered this stupid dinner. Dad deserves to be stood up, anyway. But I did remember, and it's too late to cancel or change the venue now. In fact, he's probably waiting for us already, wondering if I'm going to show.

It's time to stop pouting and move on.

I kiss Georgia on the nose. "You're all set, co-pilot."

Behind the wheel, before I turn on the car, I tap a text to Dad to let him know we're running late. Fifteen minutes later, I find a miracle of a parking spot on the street directly in front of the pub.

"It's our lucky night, George. Now, before we go in, I have to warn you. Pop-Pop might be sad. Of course, he'll be happy to see you, but you should be on your best behavior. Maybe a few extra cuddles and some of your cutest tricks are in order, too, all right?" I put the car in park, take out the keys, alight from the vehicle, and open the back door... to be greeted by the sight of a sacked-out toddler.

Slumped as far sideways as her secure seat straps will allow, her mouth glistening, Georgia looks like she's trying to imitate my fish impression. Her long lashes rest against her cheeks, twitching every few seconds as her eyes pinch more tightly closed, then relax again while she dreams.

"All righty." I guess forgetting the diaper bag won't be as big of a problem as I thought. As long as she stays asleep.

Walking into a pub with a baby is weird. Walking into a pub with a sleeping baby is worse. I'm mentally telling myself, *"Take that poor kid home!"* and I see the sentiment reflected in the faces I pass on my way to the far corner booth, where Dad's seated. I hate that he always insists on sitting so close to the bathrooms at this place. But he's decided over the years that this particular booth is "ours." As I approach, the server leaves a full beer on "our table" and takes away an empty glass. Oh, boy. Dad has a head start on me.

I wedge the carrier into my side of the booth as carefully as possible so as not to jostle my sleepyhead, and Dad says, "Aw, look at that angel! All tuckered out from a busy day at school, huh?"

I wish I could crawl in there with her and instantly transport us home to bed.

"You drinking tonight, Natey-boy?"

As soon as I'm sure the baby seat's not going anywhere, I plunk my arms on the table and shoot my dad a long-suffering look.

He laughs. "Kidding!"

"I'm sure I'll want to before the end of the night, but I've already reached Stage Four of bad daddydom today, so I'll pass on the buzzed driving."

"You couldn't be a bad dad if you tried." The grin fades from his face. "Watching you with her... It makes me proud. Makes me sad sometimes, too. Because I realize you didn't learn how to do any of that from me." He sticks his nose in his beer glass and gulps half of the dark liquid in one go.

"You weren't a bad father. Things were different back when Nick and I were little."

Yeah! Dads didn't take their babies to bars.

"Only because we wanted them to be that way." A stifled burp makes him close one eye and tamp a fist to his chest. "I was hands-off because I would rather focus on my career than hang out with my boys. That's what it boils down to."

I puff out my cheeks. "Feel better now that you've unburdened yourself of that?"

"No."

"Well, maybe you'll feel better after we eat. What are you having?"

"I'm not hungry."

I study him as if I'm sitting across from a stranger. His neat, trim hair is thinning on top and grayer than the light brown it used to be, but it shines under the recessed light above our booth, and it looks soft and clean, so at least he's still bathing. I recognize a few of my own features in his: a bigger version of the same straight nose and a mouth that knows how to smile but doesn't come by toothy grins naturally.

There are differences, too. Nick and I have our mother's eyes, which droop slightly on the outside corners, even when we're happy. Dad also wears wire-framed glasses, the lenses of which are speckled and smudged and glint with the slightest movement of his head. His chin is longer and pointier than mine, and his version of a five o'clock shadow would take a week of five o'clocks for me to achieve. Occasionally, he grows out what Nick and I call his Freud beard, but it hasn't made an appearance in years, not since the last time, when it came in snow white and he tried to color it to match his hair, and we gave him hell for it.

Tonight, it's as if someone coated his cheeks, chin, and neck with olive oil and threw a vat of sea salt at him. Underneath the stubble, the skin along his jaw and throat sags, like the weight of sadness is dragging his face into his chest.

For the first time ever, he not only looks his age but truly old.

"You need to eat something," I say.

He lifts his nearly empty glass. "I'm drinking bread."

"Beer-cheese soup would be better than an all-beer meal."

"Fine, if you'll stop nagging me. You know, that's one thing I don't miss about having a wife."

Mom isn't a nag, so the inaccuracy highlights the devastating truth behind the rest of his statement.

After we order, and I check to make sure Georgia's still zonked, Dad says, "Thanks for agreeing to come to dinner with me. I know I'm not one of your favorite people right now—"

"You're not my least favorite."

He chuckles. "I'll take it."

Nudging the condensation on my water glass with the side of my finger gives my eyes somewhere to focus other than his face when I ask, "Why, though? I still don't understand. And how could you let this happen? Why didn't you fight for her?"

"Your mom's not the type of woman who would respond to that. As for how, I ask myself that every day. It just... happened. It was done before I realized what was going on."

"That's a cop-out."

With a raised empty, he signals our server for another drink. His wedding ring clinks against his glass as he sets it down again on the heavy wooden table. "Believe what you want to believe, I guess. I truly thought everything was fine. I had no complaints, that's for sure. The practice is thriving. We're on track, financially, for retirement in a couple of years, if we want to quit working. We were having more sex than ever—"

"Hello! Please."

He laughs. "We were! And it was good! Turns out she was probably thinking about someone else every time."

"Dad, seriously." I gulp my water. "There are some things I don't need—or want—to know."

"I'm simply trying to lay out the evidence for you. The red flags weren't there, as far as I was concerned."

"She says you were business partners and roommates."

"I never had a roommate wake me up from a dead sleep to—"

"Okay! Got it. You thought everything was fine because she was boinking your brains out?" I stifle a shiver.

"Isn't that the definition of 'fine' for a guy?"

And now it's suddenly clear how close to the paternal tree Nick's apple fell.

"Did you and Mom ever *talk*?"

Tapping his chin, he considers my question. "Sure we did. We talked about the practice. And you and Nick. And the grandkids. And..."

"Did you ever talk about your feelings?"

His snort shakes his side of the booth. "We deal with other people's feelings all day long. The last thing we want to do is talk about them at home."

He has a point there. But I'm not giving up. I need reasons. I need answers.

"When was the last time you went away, the two of you, for vacation?"

"We took a cruise for our thirtieth wedding anniversary."

"That was almost ten years ago!"

He grunts. "We were busy."

I rub my forehead. "Yeah, busy becoming strangers who have a series of what amounts to one-night stands."

"You *do* blame me."

"No!" I pause and think more carefully about it. "Not exclusively. I blame you both. You're supposed to know what the hell you're doing by now."

He nods and stares at the ceiling. "Ah. Yes. I see now." Lowering his chin, he smirks across the table at me. "You're waiting for that magic age when you wake up and have it all figured out. And you thought your mom and I had gotten there; had been there for a while. So, doing the math, you esti-mated you only had about ten more years of always second-guessing yourself, of wondering if you're on the right track, of constantly questioning your choices and your life."

I shake my head, but damn it if he isn't right.

He flicks his fingernail against his glass. "Hate to break it to you, but it doesn't work that way. As a matter of fact, the more you think you have life figured out, the more at risk you are of losing everything. Complacency is the enemy."

My cheeks flame. "You know what the enemy is? Idiocy. Immaturity. Selfishness. Effed-up priorities. Apathy. *Those* are the enemies."

"They all fight in the same army. And they're stealthy."

"Give me a break. Don't tell me you didn't see the warning signs. Don't tell me you had no idea what was happening until it was too late. You're psychiatrists, for crying out loud!" Georgia stirs and whimpers next to me, so I reach over and jiggle her carrier but keep my attention on my dad. "You knew there was a problem, and you ignored it, like an idiot. Like the patient who has all the symptoms but thinks if he never goes to the doctor to get the diagnosis, the disease will magically go away on its own and won't kill him. And then, when you were forced to face the facts, you still opted for no treatment, like... like... a coward!"

"Quality of life is a huge factor."

I suck in a big breath through my nose before responding, but come up short, when something horrible assaults my olfactory system.

Dad tilts his head and wrinkles his nose.

"You smell that too?" I ask him. The scent wafts stronger toward me. Intentional sniffing is no longer required. A gentle pop and gurgle to my left confirms my dreaded suspicions. Red-faced Georgia grimaces back at me. "Oh, shit."

"I'll say." Dad waves his hand in front of his face. "Good grief. Take her to the bathroom."

I drop my head back against my shoulders. "I don't have any diapers with me."

"What?"

I 'fess up about forgetting our plans to meet for dinner

until I was already at Georgia's daycare, sans diaper bag, figuring she'd be okay for an hour or two.

"Talk about a rookie mistake," he mutters on a cough.

Our server arrives at the table with our food. He sets down the plates and starts to ask us if we need anything else but trails off and steps backward. "Oh, my gosh. What reeks?" He turns in the direction of the bathrooms a few feet away. "I'm so sorry!" he says to us. "I'll have someone take care of that right away."

Rather than admit I'm—albeit indirectly—responsible for the stink, I'm perfectly content to encourage his incorrect assumption. "Thanks. Uh, can I get a to-go box first?"

Pinching his nose, he nods and rushes away.

I pull my wallet from my back pocket, but Dad waves me —and the stench—off. "I've got this. Just go. I'll box up your food and drop it by your house later."

He may have been a lousy husband, but in this moment, he's the best dad a guy could ever have.

9

THE BOYFRIEND

GEORGIA'S DINNER TABLE PERFORMANCE PRETTY MUCH SUMS up my feelings about Dad's side of his and Mom's sorry breakup story. I learned more about my parents' sex life the other night than I ever thought I'd know in my worst nightmares. In fact, my dad may have triggered in me a raging case of erectile dysfunction.

I guess we'll find out tonight when Betty gets home.

I'm making her famous meatless lasagna as a surprise. She makes it better than I do, of course, but the inferior taste will be outweighed by the fact that she doesn't have to cook after being away from home for the past three days. And since the smell of cooking beef makes her want to hurl right now, this is the perfect meal.

Georgia happily blows raspberries in the seat of the grocery cart I'm pushing through aisle after aisle, as I collect the necessary ingredients to make the Italian dish. I laugh at the earnest expression on her face and her flyaway dark hair. "You take your music seriously, don't you?"

She mixes in a few "Dada"s and "Mama"s with her bubbles.

"Nice." I wipe some drool from my knuckles before grabbing the portabella mushrooms I'll need for my sauce. "Hey, don't let me forget the ricotta cheese. I used cottage cheese in a pinch last time, and it wasn't as good."

"No!"

"That's what I'm saying. It was inferior lasagna, and only the best will do for your mommy tonight."

"Mamamamamamamamamamamama."

"The one and only." I toss some spinach in the cart. "Let's make this Florentine, shall we?"

"No!"

"Yes."

"Sesh."

We turn into the pasta aisle. "I'm glad we agree. Because folic acid is good for mommies, right?"

"No!"

"You're right. It's good for babies *inside* mommies. Way to catch that inaccuracy." I hold up my hand for a high five, then grab her arm and force the celebratory gesture when she merely stares at me.

"No!"

"Hey, who's the medical professional here?"

"Gamma!"

I laugh. "She thinks so, but that's debatable. See, psychiatry—"

"Gamma!"

"Oh, never mind. I'll explain it some other time. Right now, I have to concentrate, because I can't remember the brand name of the lasagna noodles your mom likes." I bend over to inspect the boxes on the shelf in front of me, grabbing one likely candidate for a closer look. "She says it makes a difference, although I'm not sure how-ow-ow-ow..."

I startle and jump away when someone pokes me in my side. Placing myself between the weirdo with no social boundaries and my child, I swing the rectangular box of uncooked pasta like a weapon and face my molester. "What the hell?"

Mom steps into my view, laughing. "Wow. You were on your own planet."

"Mom? What are you doing here?"

"Grocery shopping."

I sigh. "Really."

"You don't look happy to see me." Her pout lasts two seconds before relaxing into a grin.

"I'm surprised, that's all. You don't shop here. You don't even live around—"

A guy I assumed was merely another shopper passing by stops next to Mom and places a proprietary hand on the small of her back. She has the grace to look embarrassed, but not as embarrassed as she should.

"Oh," I grunt.

She smiles tightly. "Nate, this is Ryan. Ryan, this is my son Nate and my gorgeous granddaughter, Georgia."

Ryan barely bothers to give us a cool nod before holding up a bottle of fruit juice and saying to Mom, "You ever tried this stuff? It's awesome."

"If you like high fructose corn syrup and chemicals," I mutter.

He rotates the bottle to read the ingredients, then lifts one shoulder toward his ear. "You gotta die of something, I guess."

"You have a while before you have to worry about that, I'd wager."

Mom chuckles nervously. "Um, anyway! I'm glad we ran into you..."

I'm not.

"...because I was going to see if it would be okay if Ryan and I took Georgia for ice cream tomorrow afternoo—"

"No." I consult my grocery list with shaky hands.

"Why not? You and Betty could spend some time alone, or—"

"I'm working at Urgent Care tomorrow, and Betty's been on the road half the week, so I'm sure she'll want to spend the day with Georgia."

"Well, we won't have her long. An hour or so—"

"I don't think so."

"Nathan!"

The cart handle vibrates in my hand as I edge past her, scooting the back wheels sideways on the industrial tiling. "I have to go. I want dinner to be waiting for Betty when she gets home, and I'm already running behind."

"I'll call her tomorrow, then. Maybe she'll want to take a nap, and we can take Georgia off her hands."

"Whatever. Bye!"

"Gamma!" Georgia wails as I push the cart like someone on that stupid grocery shopping game show from the 80s. Gamma's quickly forgotten as I take a corner fast enough to simulate G-forces, and Georgia giggles at the sensation.

Over my dead body is that home-wrecking, kiddie-juice-guzzling, barely post-pubescent walking set of abs taking my daughter for ice cream. He already takes my mom places I don't want to think about. He can't have Georgia. He doesn't want to hang out with a baby, anyway. After all, he graduated to the big boy playground equipment last week. No lookin' back!

I make a beeline for the checkout lanes, then perform a quick about-face when I realize I'm not finished with my shopping. "You almost let me forget the ricotta cheese, George. Geez, I ask you to help me with one thing..."

In front of the dairy case, I stare at the foggy doors, trying to catch my breath, panting away nausea and muttering to my one-year-old like a crazy person. "Shi—ipwreck. That guy's young. What did she say his name was?

Ryan? Yeah, he's totally a Ryan. It's like Reynolds and Gosling found a way to make a baby and named him after both of themselves."

"Baby!"

"And she knows I shop here. What the heck was she think-ing, parading up and down the aisles with her boy toy?"

"'Oy!"

"Sure, she had no way of knowing I'd be here now, but why risk it? Unless... oh, Lord. He must live around here. He's one of our ding-danged neighbors, isn't he? Maybe she met him when she was visiting us. He was playing in his tree house when she walked by, or something."

"Twee, twee, twee!"

A throat clears behind me. I glance over my shoulder and see a woman with more kids than food in her cart.

She nods toward the door with the milk behind it. "Do you mind if I slip in there and grab some things?"

Well and truly flustered now, I scoot out of her way. "Sorry. Gosh. I'm... I was just... Where the heck is the ricotta cheese, anyway?"

After pulling what seems like the store's entire stock of Vitamin D milk from the glass-fronted fridge, she reaches into the neighboring case and grabs a red, white, and green plastic tub. Handing it backward to me, she says, "There ya go."

I take the container from her. "Thanks. I'm making lasagna tonight. For my wife. Because I'm married."

Oh, my gosh. What the heck, Bingham? Shut up!

I wish, however, my mother had said something similar to Ryan the first time she met him. We wouldn't all be in this predicament, having awkward run-ins in the grocery store, muttering at ourselves in front of the milk, or blurting our marital status to fertile strangers over tubs of soft cheeses, if she had.

"My wife's pregnant," I continue my verbal incontinence, sweating at my inability to shut up.

The dairy case stranger smiles uncertainly. "That's nice."

"We're super-happy about the new baby, too. Another one like this?" I palm the top of Georgia's head. "Who would say no to that?"

She clears her throat and titters. "Well, she's darling, but... No more for me!"

I laugh, too, and gesture to the cart. "Right. I see that. That's a lot of kids you have there. But they're cute. And well-behaved."

"I bribed them before we came in here. You have a nice night now." With a final, parting shake of her head, she brushes past me and hurries away.

Slumping, the handle of the cart digging into my elbows, I set the cheese in the seat next to Georgia's rubbery thigh, deflate with relief, and blinking, say up at her while she smacks my head, "Wow. I am losing my mind. Losing it, George."

Looking at the time on my phone straightens my spine and makes me squeak. "Oh, crap. Your mommy is definitely going to be home before this dinner is ready. Dang it."

"Mama, Mama. Dang it!"

* * *

It's okay that the food wasn't ready for Betty's homecoming; she was too tired to eat and went straight to bed without dinner. I didn't even have time to tell her about running into Mom and Ryan at the grocery store or give her a heads up about the pending ice cream invitation I wanted her to turn down if Mom called while I was at work today.

The few minutes I saw Betty, pale, drawn, and quiet, seemed more like a dream than reality. In a surreal end to a surreal day, I put Georgia to bed by myself and waited for the lasagna to finish cooking. Then I immediately transferred it to airtight plastic containers, which fogged with their molten contents.

When I joined my wife in bed a couple of hours later and curled myself around her, she didn't stir. So much for testing that theory about Dad murdering my libido. Not that I was in the mood. If Dad hadn't killed it, Mom surely finished the job in the pasta aisle. I might need to make an appointment with a mental health professional sooner rather than later. Finding a local one who doesn't know my parents is going to be the trickiest part.

After a restless night, the last thing I wanted to do was work a Saturday in Urgent Care. One good thing about today's shift, though, was that it was too busy to allow for the obsessive introspection in which I specialize. Plus, it was refreshing to be around different people than usual (in other words, no Dr. Douche), so by the time I return home after my shift, I don't care that my weekend is starting twenty-four hours later than it usually does, and it's pouring rain. I'm simply glad it's here. And I'm ready to make the best of it.

Whistling as I walk into the house, sifting through the mail, I have the urge to bellow, "Honey, I'm home!" But I resist. Because the living room is empty, and the house is quiet. I saw Betty's car in the garage, so unless she and Georgia are out for a walk in this monsoon weather, it must still be nap time. At 5:30. Whatever. It's not like we have to keep a rigid schedule on the weekends. I prefer to, because it makes Mondays easier on everyone, but since I'm off this Monday, I have the next two days to straighten everything out.

I pitch the junk mail in the trash and carry the bills into the guest room, where I keep a small desk for the odious task of household bookkeeping. Slapping the envelopes on top of the closed laptop, I exit the room. Next stop: the shower.

As I advance down the hall, I peek into Georgia's room, the door of which is open. Her crib is empty. The rest of her room looks like a rock star with a plush toy fetish had an orgy with some groupies after a concert. Muttering about the chaos, I resolve to straighten it after my shower. For now, I simply close the door so I don't have to see it.

I creep closer to the mostly closed door of the master bedroom, anticipating the sweet scene I'm about to encounter: Betty, Georgia, and Reba curled up together on the bed, sleeping longer than usual due to the gloomy weather, the rain tapping on the skylight above them. Instead, when I nudge the door open and peer inside, the only one on the bed is Reba, and she has her worried gaze trained on something on the floor.

That something is Betty, surrounded by her thirty (give or take) favorite pairs of shoes, which she seems to reorganize every other month.

Bemused, I look down at the top of her head. "What are you doing?" The laugh dies in my throat when she tilts her head up to show me her pink-rimmed eyes and cherry-red nose. "Oh, my gosh. What's wrong? Where's Georgia?"

"She's with your mom, who called and wanted to take her for ice cream. It was convenient, considering, so..."

Her reply raises more questions (*Was ripped Ryan with her? Did I forget to mention you weren't supposed to accept that invitation? How long have they been gone?*), which race through my head, distracting me from the most pressing issue that seems to be at hand. I shove those other things from my mind and kneel down next to her, balancing on my toes. I rub her shoulder. "'Considering'? Are you okay?" *Please be hormones, please be hormones, please be hormones...*

She crushes my hopes with a terse shake of her head and a bite at her lip. Rising on her knees, she crawls closer to me and presses her face against my shoulder. I cup the back of her head in my hand and nearly fall backward onto my ass when she mumbles, "I'm losing it."

Something tells me she's not speaking about her mental state, although that doesn't seem to be in peak condition right now, either.

In case the first declaration wasn't painfully clear enough, she adds, "The baby."

"Oh, no." Regaining my balance, I use the wall next to me to clamber to my feet, pulling her up with me. I wrap my arms around her and rest my chin on top of her head. "Are you sure?"

She nods against my throat. "Yes."

"How do you know? Spotting is normal in most—"

When she lifts her head, I can tell by the sadness in her eyes that what she's experiencing is far from normal.

"Oh. I see. We need to call Dr. Gannaway, then. He may want to see..." I censor my inner nurse before he says something insensitive. My throat won't physically let the words pass, anyway. Lamely, I finish, "...you."

"I've already been. He confirmed it. Said there wasn't anything we could do. Said that unless I spike a fever or show other signs of infection, I can just let things... happen."

I walk her to the bed and push her gently to a sitting position on the side of the mattress, then swing her legs up. "You need to rest."

"No. I'm fine. I'd rather keep busy." She scoots toward the pillows, though, rolls to her side, and pulls the covers over her shoulder. Reba rises, hops down from the mattress, and slinks under the bed.

"Why didn't you call me?"

"There was nothing you could do. I didn't want to ruin your day."

"But—"

Our baby died, and she dealt with the horrible experience alone, while I went obliviously about my day, peering down throats and up noses. Ordering blood tests. Prescribing antibiotics. Joking with one kid to distract him from the stitches I was putting in the heel of his hand.

I sweep her hair from her forehead with my finger. "You shouldn't have gone through any of this alone. I should have been here with you."

"I wasn't alone. Georgia and Reba were with me. And then your mom called—"

"Does she know?" Telling Nick our news was tantamount to sending out detailed conception announcements to the rest of the family. Betty was none-too-pleased at the congratulatory calls from Mom, Dad, and Heidi. While suffering my wife's silent treatment afterward, I called everyone back, stressing that we wanted the information to stay in the family for a few more weeks. As far as I know, they've honored our wishes. Thank goodness.

Betty shakes her head. "I didn't want to tell anyone else before you." Now, she covers her eyes with one hand and squeaks, "I'm sorry, Nate. I'm so sorry!"

Ringing ears, the dry-yet-watering mouth, the churning stomach. I'm going to throw up.

No! Man up, Bingham.

Instead of puking, I do what I do in most situations and blink back tears. Then I climb over my wife's legs and curl up behind her, the yin to her yang. "Don't be sorry. Please don't apologize."

"You must be so disappointed!"

Guilt. It's worse than a kick to the stones.

"Shhh. We're both disappointed, right?" And I realize it's true. I am. Crushed, in fact. I must not have been as ambivalent about this whole thing as I thought. Awful way to find out.

She sniffles, her breath hitching as she says, "I... I feel like it's my fault."

"It's not." I assume that's an accurate statement, because she's not an alcoholic or a drug user (or she's hiding that well) and doesn't engage in any of the risky behaviors that are sometimes attributed to miscarriage. Most of the time, miscarriage isn't caused by what the mother does or doesn't do, anyway. It's the body's way of ending a pregnancy that wasn't right, from the beginning. It's simpler to reassure her with two words, however, than say all of that other stuff.

"Because..." Reaching back, she rests her hand on the side of my face. "I... When I found out... When I took that pregnancy test in the hotel bathroom... While I waited for the result, I wasn't sure what I wanted it to say. I might have wished for it to be negative. Until it came up positive. And I didn't feel as happy as I should have. I kept thinking about everything else. You. And Georgia. And how much I travel with my stupid job. And how does a newborn fit into all that? It doesn't! So, I sat there, staring at the test, feeling ill. And exhausted, thinking about... everything."

"That's natural, though. I thought the same things at first."

"You did?"

"Sure." *And then some.*

"That's why I didn't tell you as soon as I got home. You were freaking out about Dr. Reitman's retirement, and I was tired, and I knew if I told you right then I wouldn't be able to say it without crying and asking you how we were going to manage. I wanted to be happy when I told you. That's why I waited. And even then I was sort of faking it."

I assume she means her happiness about being pregnant, not the other thing she was doing at the time.

"I was so scared," she whispers.

"Aw, Betts." I drag her hand to my lips and kiss her fingers.

"It knew I wasn't sure."

"That's not how it works."

"Still." She chokes and hiccups with the effort not to break down.

I pull her more tightly to me and kiss her behind her ear. "Hey," I murmur. "Go ahead and cry, all right? Let it out."

"I'm afraid I'll never be able to stop."

"Yes, you will. And you'll feel better, I promise. Take it from a pro. Well, semi-pro. Imagine how rich we'd be, though, if I got paid to cry."

She almost laughs, but the full-force tears hit her instead.

I hold her until she falls asleep.

Despite my reservations about Georgia hanging out too much with Gamma and "Great Uncle Ryan," I had to concede it was in everyone's best interest that she spend the night with Mom, wherever that happens to be. I didn't have the energy to dicker about logistics. I've adopted a "Don't ask, don't tell" policy (which we all know sucks and is the epitome of mental laziness), figuring Mom won't take her granddaughter anywhere unsafe or inappropriate. Ryan's parents' basement—because that's surely where he still lives—is undoubtedly lovely and not littered with dirty socks and used condoms.

Oh, shit. I have to stop thinking about stuff like that.

After all, the whole purpose of asking Mom to take Georgia for the night is so I can focus my attention and energy and every single brain cell on Betty, not on worrying about everything else.

So far, I'm obviously doing a bang-up job.

Betty wakes up at about eight o'clock and transfers to the couch, where I deliver a steaming plate of vegetarian lasagna, a heating pad, a blanket, a pillow, and a stack of books to her.

Then I turn on *Mildred Pearce,* one of her all-time favorite movies, and cue up a couple of other Audrey Hepburn and Lauren Bacall films for later.

When she simply stares at the lasagna and presses the heating pad more firmly to her midriff, I say, "A couple of bites, okay?"

She shakes her head more firmly. "I can't."

I whisk the plate away and replace it with a large glass of water. "Drink this, then. We'll try a protein bar later, if you feel up to it."

She nods her agreement with that compromise and snuggles farther under the blanket but only makes it through half of the movie before falling asleep again, her hands wedged between her cheek and the pillow. Reba lies in front of the couch, her version of "standing guard."

I turn off the TV and retreat to the bedroom and Betty's ravaged shoe collection, thinking carefully about the most logical order to stack her footwear on the floor racks ringing the walls of the walk-in closet. Work shoes most accessible, then sneakers, then formal heels brought out only occasionally for special events. Everything organized by color, of course.

Let's make sense of something.

I'd do the same to Georgia's room, too, but it's easier, for once, to simply keep her door closed, trapping in her sweet baby scent. The stuffed toys can enjoy their debauchery for one more night. Going in there would remind me too much of our loss.

Stripping our bed and remaking it with fresh linens is a must, however. In my haste to console Betty earlier, I broke my post-work protocol and not only held her while still wearing my germy scrubs, but I lay on the bed in those scrubs, too. *Shudder.* Betty's body will have a hard enough job healing in the next couple of weeks; she doesn't need to add a nasty bug to the equation. The least I can do now is prepare a clean place for her to recuperate.

When I'm finished with that task, I cram the dirty sheets in the washer, which already holds a couple of small soiled items from earlier, soaking in cold water. I want to stare at them for a while, to wallow in the grief and disappointment I haven't allowed myself to indulge yet, but there's still work to be done. A lot of work, before the night is over—and possibly throughout the next few days. I have to stay focused. I have to be the caregiver my wife deserves. I can't afford to get emotional. Not yet. If I do, I won't be able to handle the hard things ahead.

I return to the living room to find Betty still lying in the same position she was in when I left nearly an hour ago but blinking sleepily into the middle distance. Reba stands, shakes, stretches, and yawns.

"Hey," I murmur. "How are you feeling?"

Wincing, Betty pushes herself into a sitting position. "I need to get to the bathroom."

There's no urgency in her tone, but her sweaty face tells a different story, so I rush to her side, nudging Reba out of the way with a gentle but firm foot.

"Here, let me help you."

Betty meekly pushes my offered arm away. "I'm okay. Just groggy. And crampy. I have to pee... and stuff."

"You might be light-headed from blood loss, too." I hold out my arm again, this time more insistently.

She grips it, leaning hard enough on me to contradict her claim that she doesn't need the support. Reba follows us down the hallway but stops on the threshold to the bathroom, where she paces.

After settling Betty on the toilet, I detach and go into Nurse Nate mode when faced with the definitive evidence that not only was Betty pregnant, but she's not anymore, and her body is trying its damnedest to evict its temporary, tiny resident. As I help her clean up, I'm professional, I'm solid, I'm her rock... until she hiccups, and I look up from my work in time to see her face crumple.

"Oh, Betts." I quickly drop the towels in my hands into the trash bag I brought in here for this purpose and cross to the sink. "Honey... it's okay."

"It's not okay!"

"That's not what I meant," I reassure her while I scrub my hands.

"I know!"

After a cursory drying on the hand towel next to the sink, I step in front of her and pull her head into my belly, stroking her hair.

"It keeps coming," she whimpers. "I hate that you're seeing this."

"It's gravity, that's all. You were lying down, and now..."

"It's so awful."

I realize she's not talking about what's happening to her, physically, but I stick to the medical facts, anyway. "Your body's trying to... get back to normal."

"I hate it."

"If your body didn't do this, you'd get extremely sick. And a doctor would have to go in and do it for you."

"Yeah, yeah. But..." She lifts herself slightly and looks down into the commode. "Oh, gosh," she moans, covering the opening with her body again and pressing her hand to her forehead. "I'm going to be sick."

"Okay."

When you're a nurse, you have things in your house that would seem weird to anyone else, but man do they come in handy sometimes. Enter the sickness bags I keep in one of the vanity's drawers. I grab one now, shake it open, and hand it to her. She breathes into it, but nothing happens.

After a few minutes, the color returns to her cheeks, and she sets the bag aside. "False alarm," she says with a wan smile.

"Everything you're going through is normal, okay? I know it looks horrific, but you're not losing as much blood as you think. Trust me. If I thought you were hemorrhaging, I wouldn't hesitate to call 911. Don't be afraid or worried."

"I'm not." She rocks in place and pants as another cramp hits her. "I'm not scared. I'm just... so sad!"

Her shoulders shake, and her chest heaves. Then a keening escapes her, raising the hair on my arms and neck and making the dog whimper. When she closes her eyes, the tears flood down her cheeks. "What are we going to do? Throw our baby in the garbage?" She flaps her hands toward the bag next to the door. "Flush it down the toilet?"

I'd already planned to make a trip to the clinic later, when Betty's okay to be left alone for a while and I can bear the heartbreaking task.

"I'll take care of everything." I punctuate this with a long, hard look to communicate what "everything" entails, without going into gruesome detail. I sound like the mastermind in a murder plot. Lightening my tone, I add, "All you have to do is heal, all right?"

"I'm so sorry!"

I kneel in front of her and grasp her shoulders, then run my hands down her arms before transferring them to her bare hips, squeezing hard enough to get her attention, so she'll look me in the eyes. "Stop apologizing. Do you hear me?"

She nods and wipes her nose on the back of her hand, something that would normally repulse me but in this moment makes me love her more, somehow.

"This is nobody's fault. It's sucky biology, that's all. It's a reminder that when everything goes right, it's a damn miracle. You, me, Georgia... we're all walking miracles, right?"

She takes a deep, shuddering breath. After a mighty sniff, she straightens her shoulders. "You're right. I promise to pull it together."

"You're doing fine," I reassure her with a pat to her knee. "And you'll be feeling better, physically, soon. If not, we'll need to take a trip to St. Vince."

"I'm sure I'll be fine. I'm in good hands here, right?"

"I'm not taking any chances with you."

"I don't know what I'd do without you," she whispers.

Before she starts crying again—or, more likely, I do—I hand her one of the pairs of postpartum panties she still had under the sink from when she was recovering from Georgia's birth. "Let's start with getting dressed and settled back in bed, where you'll be as comfortable as possible."

She slides the underwear up her legs, and I busy myself in the medicine cabinet, pretending to look for the bottle of ibuprofen. With the cabinet door blocking her view of my face, I take a minute to close my eyes and collect myself. It's going to be a long night.

* * *

THE NEXT MORNING, she wakes me with a kiss to my forehead. I squint at the clock. The sun was lightening the sky from black to navy to gunmetal when I fell asleep. By my calculations, I slept for about three hours. In my clothes. On top of the covers. Poised for a disaster that had already struck.

She moves the open book from my chest, sets it on her bedside table, and rests her head in its vacated spot.

"How are you feeling?" I ask, drawing her closer to my side

and cupping her bottom in my hand. I bring my other hand up to touch her forehead for an imprecise temperature check.

"Better. Sleeping helped. I'm getting hungry."

"I bet you are. When's the last time you ate?"

"I'm not telling you. You'll get mad."

"You want me to whip up some eggs for you?"

She shivers against me. "No. Not eggs. Pancakes? No, waffles. And sausage."

"Coming right up."

When I move to rise, though, grunting at the stiffness in my muscles, which must not have fully relaxed all night, she holds her position, refusing to release me.

"A few more minutes."

Slackening under her once more, I kiss the top of her head. "A few more minutes. Then you need to eat."

"I need this more."

"Me, too," I admit, closing my eyes.

I jerk awake to find that "a few minutes" has turned into two hours, and Betty's not in bed with me anymore.

"Shit!" I hiss, scrambling to my feet and rushing to the en suite bathroom, only to find it empty. "Damn it." I jog down the hallway, looking in rooms as I pass them, verifying my suspicions that I'm alone in the house. Not even the dog seems to be around.

The dog.

Reba. She was so resistant to leaving Betty's side last night that I had to carry her outside to do her business before bedtime. Then she peed as close to the back patio as possible and ran right back to the door, nudging it with her nose, eager to return to her mistress.

With this memory in mind, I yank the back door open to find the two girls warming themselves in the mid-morning sun. My heart slows.

"There you are," I state dully.

Reba rolls onto her side and presents her belly for a "good morning" rub.

Betty shades her eyes and turns toward me. "Hey."

"You were supposed to wake me up."

"I did. Then you fell back asleep. And something tells me"—she nods at my wrinkled clothes—"that you got hardly any sleep last night, so I didn't want to wake you again."

"But your waffles!"

"I had some toast. But if you still want to make me some waffles..."

My stomach growls at the thought of the warm, crispy-on-the-outside, soft-on-the-inside treats.

Before I fix breakfast, though, I check, "And... everything else? How's your bleeding?"

She reaches down to scratch Reba's belly, since it's obvious I'm in no hurry to do it. "Nothing too alarming, I guess. My inside lady parts are pissed off right now. They can join the club. When's Georgia coming home?"

I struggle to catch up. "Uh, I don't know. I didn't discuss it with Mom yesterday. I wasn't sure—"

"I want her to come home."

"Yeah. Okay. I'll call Mom while I'm making breakfast."

She nods her curt approval, then rises from her chair and stretches her arms over her head. "I'll call her. I need to call work, too."

"I can do that for you."

With a sad smile on her way past me into the house, she replies, "It's okay, Nathaniel. I don't need a nurse's note."

I follow her into the kitchen, grabbing her hand when she keeps walking away from me. She glances over her shoulder at me, then faces me fully.

"No traveling for the next couple of weeks," I say.

"No traveling."

"No work at all this week."

With a raise of one of her eyebrows, she says, "That's my sick time for the whole year! How about... two days off?"

"Three."

"Fine."

"And you can work from home Thursday and Friday."

"That's not—"

"Do it for me. Please."

"Working from home isn't 'taking it easy,' though. Trying to keep track of Georgia while on conference calls is—"

"She'll be going to daycare, as usual, all this week."

"That's silly, though, if I'm home."

"You'll be recuperating."

Her jaw sets. "Are you going to take the week off, too?"

"I will if you want me to."

"No. That's okay."

Pulling her closer but still holding her at arms' length, I look down into her eyes, light blue ringed with darker blue, like her daughter's. "Are you sure?"

"No offense, but if you're here hovering over me, fluffing my pillows, force-feeding me chicken soup, and inquiring about my bleeding every hour on the hour, I'll have to kill you."

My shoulders droop, and I avert my eyes. Around a sudden tightness in my throat, I try to joke, "Well, if my life depends on it, then I'll go to work."

"Oh, geez. I'm sorry." She clutches at the front of my shirt and kisses my chin. "That sounded so bitchy and ungrateful."

"No, I understand. I get carried away sometimes." I attempt a small smile so she knows I'm okay.

"That's what makes you so incredible, though. You genuinely care. But I hate feeling so needy." She plucks at my t-shirt collar. "And if you're home all week taking care of me, it will be a constant reminder of what's happened, and I need to allow myself to forget, even if only for a few minutes or hours at a time."

When she peeks up at me through her lashes, I swallow and nod. "I get it."

"You need that too, you know? Going to work and focusing on patients more removed from you will do you some good."

"Yeah. You're right. As long as you're feeling okay, I'll try to keep our schedule as normal as possible. But only if you promise to rest. For real."

"I promise."

"Pinkie swear." I let go of her and stick my right fist between our faces, baby finger extended.

She sighs and rolls her eyes but links little fingers with me. "Pinkie swear. Dork." Suddenly, she drops her hand, her face whitens, and her eyes fill.

"No, no, no. What's this?"

"I can't go through this ever again."

Overcome with my own emotions, I can't say anything for a while, can only press my forehead to hers. Finally I say, "Don't worry about that, all right? The chances of it happening again are..." *Where you going with this, Bingham? Because you know the statistics, and they're not going to provide a bit of reassurance right now.* "Don't worry about it, okay?" I finish lamely. "There are no guarantees, but—"

"You'll still love me if I never get pregnant again, right? And it's okay if Georgia's an only child?"

I pull my head back. "Of... of course!" I grab her hands and squeeze. "What do you...? What are you saying?"

"It's terrifying enough loving someone as much as I love her. And you. I don't know if I can handle caring that much about anyone else. I didn't even know this baby, but I feel like a piece of me died, and..."

After she trails off emotionally, I stare down at the backs of her hands, smooth and translucent, the blue veins visible but not raised. My thumbs rub furiously against her knuckles. "It's all so fresh, that's all. It just happened. It's *still* happening. We can't possibly make a decision like this right now. We need time to think about—"

"No. I don't need to think about it any more than I already have. It's all I've thought about. I want to ask Dr. Gannaway to write me a 'script for birth control when I go to my follow-up with him this week. Then maybe we should discuss something more permanent."

I swallow painfully, and my testicles rise closer to my body, as if trying to hide from what she's proposing. Breathing away the panic threatening to overwhelm me, I say, "I... I always figured we'd have more than one, you know?"

She nods. "I thought so too. But thirty-five isn't the new twenty-five when it comes to reproductive health. Maybe my body is trying to tell us something. I can't help but think that."

"We're not that old. And younger people have miscarriages too."

"Maybe if I were in my twenties, though, I'd bounce back easier. This... It's too hard. I thought I was a strong person. But I'm not." She starts crying again.

I'd do anything, say anything, to make those tears stop for good.

"Nothing is more important to me than your happiness. Nothing. What you want is what I want. Please don't cry."

I fold her in my arms and press her to my chest, which she nods furiously against. "I'm sorry."

"Nothing to be sorry about. Shhhhh."

"I want you to be happy, too."

"I am happy. If our family is complete, I'm good with that. More than good with it."

After a few sniffly seconds, she whispers, "Thank you," and pushes away from me, wiping her face as she walks toward the bedrooms, presumably to make those calls she mentioned earlier.

I stare after her, wondering what the hell just happened, what I've done, and what I've agreed to, and realizing how much it sucks to be thanked for lying.

11

CO-WORKER CLASH

I'VE BEEN TRUE TO MY WORD THIS WEEK, AND SINCE BETTY'S biggest complaint has been fatigue, I've given her some space by going to work every day. I've also been determined not to hover when we *are* together. It means that I have to trust she'll tell me if and when she needs something, but considering her aversion to feeling "needy," that's not a given.

It's been a draining week, so I'm not particularly chatty when Lynette sidles up to me in the file room and asks, "Are you going to the Brewers game this weekend?"

I keep my eyes on the chart in my hand and continue to review a patient's history, one that includes chronic intestinal discomfort and several visits to our office in the past year. "No." Tapping my pen against my lips, I consider my options regarding this patient.

"What do you mean, no? Dr. Dan reserved a luxury box for the whole office and our families! It won't be the same without you and Betty and that sweet Georgia peach."

"Yeah. Whatever." I look up at Lynette. "Hey, does Dr. Reitman have any openings this afternoon? She needs to see this kid and possibly refer him to a specialist."

Without waiting for an answer, I walk toward the reception desk, where I can consult the schedules for myself.

Lynette follows. "Dr. Reitman's always booked. But I'm sure Dr. Dan has some availability. What time were you thinking?"

I walk backwards so I can be heard by my friend without saying too loudly, "I'd prefer Dr. Reitman."

"I know. Everyone knows. But that's not happening on such short notice."

As I push through the swinging door to the front office, I face forward once more and grumble some unkind things about Dr. Douche pitching in on filing and coding in all of his free time.

"You never answered me," Lynette says, taking a seat at a computer and pulling up the afternoon schedule. Multicolored entries crowd for attention in the columns for Dr. Reitman and me. Dr. Douche's column is an expanse of white, dotted by two light blue rows, which signify fifteen-minute well-child checkups.

"Where's the rest of his schedule?" I ask.

"That *is* his schedule."

"Is he out after one o'clock?"

"No..." She looks over her shoulder at me and purses her lips.

I let loose a breath I didn't realize I was holding. "Wait a second. Why are Dr. Reitman and I busting our"—I swallow —"butts, skipping lunch breaks, when he has so many openings?"

She shrugs. "He's new. Everyone asks for you and Dr. Reitman."

"Yeah, but..." I laugh somewhat hysterically. "We're booked! Double-booked! Before you double-book us, shouldn't he be—I don't know—*single-booked?*"

"Lower your voice," she mutters from the corner of her mouth, glancing nervously at the children and parents in the waiting room on the other side of the Plexiglas window.

I flap my patient's chart against my leg and run my hand through my hair. "This is unbelievable. What does he do all day?" *Besides think of ways to annoy the shit out of me.*

She pops from her chair, smiles nervously at the now-staring onlookers, grabs the back of my scrubs, and drags me through the swinging door into the hallway, where she pulls me farther into the staff room and closes the door behind us.

"What is your problem?"

"*My* problem?"

"You've been weird all week. Weirder than usual, which is saying something, since you've been a grump ever since Dr. Dan started."

I roll my eyes at the too-familiar moniker and snort.

"See? Like that! Are you moonlighting as a chick lit author again?"

"What? No!" I try to side-step her. "I don't have time for this. I'm double-booked, remember?"

She snags my arm, knocking the folder in my hand loose, sending it to the floor, where some of the top-punched papers rip from the clasp holding them in place.

"Oh, geez. Thanks!" I snap, dropping to my knees to clean up the mess.

Crouching next to me, she collects the papers closest to her and holds them out for me. "I'm sorry. But the last time you were this testy, you were dating that nutjob Frankie and living a double life. Is everything okay?"

I haven't breathed a word about the miscarriage to anyone at work, because I never told them there was a baby to lose. Part of that fell under the traditional practice of waiting until the second trimester to tell people, which coincided with

Betty's wishes. But thinking about the biggest reason I never even hinted at our news nearly buckles my knees under the guilt. Anyway, my uncharacteristic secrecy has been a blessing, in a way—telling our families about the miscarriage was bad enough. But on the other hand, I can't use it to explain my behavior this week to my co-workers. And it doesn't apply to my behavior in previous weeks.

"I'm exhausted!" I say now. "Look at my schedule! And Dr. Douche"—*yeah, I said it out loud. Eff it.*—"sits in those meetings every morning and hears Dr. Reitman and me gasp at our bloated schedules and doesn't say a damn word! So much for 'chipping in wherever you're needed.'"

I don't even attempt to put the papers back in the patient file in the right order. I plan to delegate that. Maybe I'll dump it on Dr. Douche's desk, since he seems to have plenty of time.

Lynette stands and towers over me, a first, considering her petite stature. "It's not my job to defend him."

"Then don't!" I rise but find the closest folding chair and collapse into it, stretching my legs in front of me. I slap the patient file into the chair next to me and rub my eyes. "Listen. I'm sorry about how I've been acting. And I'm sorry about how I acted out there."

"Everyone could see you."

I drop my hand and blink to return my vision to normal. "I lost my temper, and it was unprofessional. I'm sorry."

"Are you going to tell me what's going on? Why aren't you going to the ballgame this weekend?"

"I don't want to spend a single extra minute with him, much less an entire sporting event."

"Nice. I would think you'd want to spend time with the rest of us, though."

"It's a package deal, and he's a dealbreaker."

"Why do you hate him so much, anyway?"

"I don't hate anyone."

"Okay, strongly dislike."

"The feeling is mutual. It's not like he's dying to be best buds with me and I'm being a jerk about it for no reason. He goes out of his way to make my life miserable."

"How?"

"I don't have time to present the evidence, okay? Just trust me. He corners me for uncomfortable lectures about my attitude..."

"It does suck lately."

"...He calls me out in front of everyone at staff meetings..."

"That was one time!"

"...He talks down to me..."

"He's... tall?"

I put my chin to my chest and glare up at her. "Seriously? And anyway, he's not much taller than I am."

She laughs. "Fine. You guys clash. Big deal. Do you think I agree with Beulah on everything? The woman is obsessed with having everything in triplicate, like this is 1963. But I don't act like a jerk to the rest of you and shun extracurricular activities and make scenes in front of patients in the front office."

Since I have no defense for those charges, I simply say, "And now I find out that while he's making me stay late, keeping me from time with my family, so he can make a point about how nobody's more important than anyone else in this office, and the letters after my name don't excuse me from grunt work like filing and coding—which, no offense, but yes, they effing do—he's not even carrying a full patient load! Even though I'm double-booked and never take a lunch break longer than the time it takes to choke down a packet of peanut butter crackers, sometimes *while* I'm also using the bathroom!"

She wrinkles her nose. "Ew. That's nasty."

"That's necessary. Meanwhile, Dr. Douche is playing Words

with Friends and raking his desktop sand garden between well-child checkups? You've got to be kidding me!"

"You shouldn't call him that."

"Oh, puh-lease. Defend him all you want. He's nice to you. You're perky and funny and non-threatening. And cute. And he thinks everything you do is 'rad.'"

"If you're insinuating what I think you are..."

"I'm not insinuating anything." *Yeah, I'm pretty much coming right out and saying it.*

"He's married!"

I bend my legs, brace my hands on my knees, and push myself to my feet. "That doesn't mean shit. Trust me."

"Nate!"

"I have patients to see. Lots of 'em." Snatching the file that started this whole thing, I foist it on a pale-faced Lynette. "Move this one to Dr. Chancellor's schedule. Three o'clock. Put a note in the appointment that I'll be happy to consult if he needs further information, but I'd like *his* professional opinion before referring the patient to an internist. Thanks." I stride to the door, open it, and say on my way out, "Enjoy the game tomorrow."

12

THE DIRT

THE LAST THING BETTY NEEDS—BESIDES THIS COLD Georgia's contracted, thanks to my inability to go home and shower immediately after work before picking her up from daycare—is for me to burden her with everything going on at work. But I need a release, so as soon as dinner's over, and the baby's in her crib for the night, I announce, "I'm going for a jog."

Betty looks up from her magazine, her brow furrowed. "Okay. Is everything all right?"

"Yeah! Great. Awesome."

"Oh, boy. You desperately need that jog, don't you?"

"Yes."

"Anything I can help with?"

"Nope."

"Anything I should be worried about?"

"Absolutely not. Which is why I'm going to get some perspective out there"—I point to the front door and the neighborhood beyond—"and not by moping around in here."

She turns a page and returns her attention to finding out how celebrities are just like us. (*They have douchey bosses! They go for jogs when they feel like they're about to lose their minds! They lose babies! Their parents suck!)* "Sounds delightfully mature. And noble."

On my way past her on the couch, I lean down to kiss her cheek. "Not sure how long I'll last out there. It's hotter than Hell."

"Mmmm. Don't overdo it."

I *am* regretfully out of shape. Somehow, jogging doesn't fit conveniently into a two-income household where the incomes are derived from jobs that require frequent overtime.

"I won't," I promise. At the last second, I can't resist adding on my way out the door, "I have my phone, if, you know, you need to call me... or something."

She shoots me a barely tolerant glare. "Go. We'll be fine. I taught Reba how to dial 911 in all my spare time this week."

She's joking, but that would actually be awesome.

Without thinking much about which route I'm going to take, I set off deeper into the maze of streets that wind through the neighborhood. At dusk, I'm more comfortable sticking to sidewalks on low-traffic, residential roads.

The deeper into our neighborhood I go, the larger the houses become, and the fewer cars and people I see. Wealthy folks don't venture far from the air conditioning (or pool) on sweltering summer nights. As I pass homes with immaculate landscaping and impossibly green grass mowed into pretty patterns, splashes and children's delighted screeches meet my ears, and smoke from grilling meat tickles my nose, but I don't see anyone. They're all behind their privacy fences.

With one notable exception. My brother's house comes into view, giving me my first human sighting in blocks and a good enough excuse to slow to a stop and catch my breath. Nick brings his shiny green-and-yellow riding mower to a stop, pulls up on the brake, and slumps over the steering wheel.

"Well, well, well. Look who's finally decided to do something about those love handles."

Ignoring the dig, I wipe my forehead on my shoulder and retort, "Don't you have people to do that grunt work for you? What will the neighbors think?"

He flashes his middle finger at me. "I don't give a shit what anyone else thinks. This gets me out of the house two times a week."

"You mow your lawn twice a week? That's anal."

"It's called survival, bro."

"You know, you're not under house arrest. You can leave your house at any time to go do things that are more enjoyable than yard work."

"Yeah, but yard work is Heidi-approved. If I go out to do fun things, I get the cold shoulder. If I'm lucky." He sits higher on the padded seat of his mower. "Anyway, you call your chosen escape 'fun'? No thanks."

"I'm not escaping. I'm decompressing."

He laughs. "Oh. Okay. I'll have to remember that one next time I want to watch the game at The Cheesehead or hit the links. 'Sorry, Babe, I need to decompress.'"

"If you call Heidi 'Babe,' I don't blame her for making your life miserable." I check my phone, then slide it back in my pocket when I see I haven't missed anything.

He lifts his chin. "What's going on at your house right now?"

The question sounds like a challenge to produce something interesting, so naturally, I resist playing that game. "Georgia's in bed, and Betty's reading on the couch."

"Lucky bastard."

That brings to mind all the ways I don't feel lucky, but I swallow them down, dismissing them as ungrateful. "Yeah, I am," I say quietly, crouching down to re-tie my left shoe.

He clears his throat. "How's Betty doing, anyway?"

"Physically, okay. Dr. Gannaway checked her out on Monday and said everything looked like it was progressing normally. She has another follow-up with him in a couple of weeks, to be sure."

"I'm glad she's okay, but I'm sorry about... the other thing."

I stand and wipe my face on the front of my t-shirt. "Yeah, me too. You know, it happens all the time... to other people. And you take for granted that it's one of those common complications. Until it happens to you. Then it's, like, one of the worst things you can ever imagine. Makes me feel like an insensitive jerk for not being more sympathetic in the past when I've heard about it."

"What're you gonna do? Walk around dabbing your eyes, lamenting the plight of others?"

"I guess not."

"'Cause they're not doing that for you." He picks at the steering wheel. "You're expected to get over it. You get up each day, you drive to work, you deal with patients and co-workers, and you come home to bills and yard work and car mainte- nance and everything you had to deal with before, only you have to do it with this horrible weight on your shoulders. And it gets to the point that you start to forget why you feel so shitty, so you stop to question it, and you remember, 'Oh, yeah,' and it hits you all over again. You're supposed to be the same person, but you're not. You're never going to be the same."

I drop the bottom of my shirt and stare at him.

He shrugs at my unspoken question. "Heidi had a miscar- riage. Before Massi. Way before. Right after we were married."

"Oh."

"Yeah. She was about a month pregnant when we tied the knot. Oops." He wiggles his eyebrows. "Sorry. Not sorry."

I can't help but laugh, but I stop quickly. "Man, I *am* sorry. Why didn't you say anything?"

Rubbing the back of his neck, he answers, "I dunno. We just didn't. It wasn't a conscious decision. It... it never came up. I guess we wanted to forget it happened."

"Yeah. I get that."

He swings his leg over the mower and stands, stretching his lower back. "What are you doing, anyway? It's Friday night. Don't you have a bubble bath and one of those pink books you love to read waiting for you, as a reward for getting through another week?"

"I needed to blow off some steam. Sweat it out. Work has been a bitch."

He laughs. "Yeah. I bet. I almost forgot you're working with Dan Chancellor now."

My head snaps up. "What do you know about him?"

"For one thing, he has a huge reputation for being 'difficult to work with.'"

"Where'd you hear that?"

"Everywhere, bro. You can't be part of the medical community in this town and be a dick and keep it a secret. I know that from personal experience, unfortunately. And you don't have to pretend you don't know how people feel about me."

I wince. It's true that on more than one occasion when meeting other medical professionals for the first time, they've flinched after hearing my last name, and I'm often asked, "Any relation to Nick Bingham?" then promptly ditched when my answer is affirmative. I don't take it personally.

Nick's toned it down quite a bit in recent years, but it's hard to bounce back from a bad reputation. Fortunately, his infamy had everything to do with his personality and nothing to do with his job performance. He's still the top thoracic surgeon, based on referrals, at St. Vince. For that, I'm proud of him. I'm also proud of him for realizing before it was too late that he needed to get over himself and treat his colleagues with more respect.

"What have you heard about our beloved Dr. Dan?"

"Nothing earth-shattering. But Greenbrier can't find a landing spot for him to save their lives. Yours is his fourth pedes clinic in the past five years."

"A ray of hope," I mutter, wondering how long it'll take before Greenbrier decides his placement with us was a mistake.

He shakes his head. "Uh-uh. This is it. From what I've heard, they think they've finally figured it out. He can't work with other doctors. Especially guys."

"And he hasn't been let go because?"

"Ha! It must be nice to live in your nurse-y world and not have to worry your little head about all the political back-stories."

"Meaning?"

"He's the grandson of *the* Dr. Chancellor—on the Green-brier Board of Directors. His favorite grandson, in fact. Trust me, he would have been gone by now if he wasn't. Why do you think he likes to be called 'Dr. Dan'? Wants his own identity, or something stupid like that."

I slap my forehead. "Oh, my gosh. I'm so dumb. I never put that together."

"Yeah. Anyway, so they finally found a single-doctor clinic where the doctor was retiring, meaning Dr. Dan wouldn't have to play nice with anyone else."

"Except for the other staff members."

"He doesn't have a problem with nurses or admins, though."

I raise my hand to shoulder-level. "Hello. Meet me."

He chuckles. "Oh, man. For real?"

"Yes! He hates me!"

"Why? You're just a—"

I open my eyes wider, then blink a few times, waiting for him to finish that gem.

"Uh..."

"What? Because I'm 'just a nurse'?"

He scratches his jaw with the back of his thumb. "No offense, but yeah. It's not like he has to feel threatened by you. You guys aren't doing the same job."

"You're right; we're not. I'm doing much *more* than he is. And getting paid much less. And having much less say in important decisions. And being submitted to frequent dress-downs, sometimes in front of other people."

"Seriously?"

"Well, once. But it was the first time we'd ever met, so it didn't get things off to a good start."

"Not cool. What the heck? Everyone loves you. Trust me, I hear all about it every time I say my last name to someone who also knows you. It's annoying."

I'd smile if I didn't feel so much like puking. "Not him. He's making my life miserable. And then I find out today that he's seeing about four patients each day, while Dr. Reitman and I are still double-booked."

"What a douche."

"*Doctor* Douche. That's what I call him, anyway."

"Oh, well, *now* it makes sense why he hates you."

"Not to his face, numb nuts."

Nick puts his hand on his hip and stares into space. "Wait a minute. What's going to happen when Reitman retires? Isn't the whole point of this transitional period for patients to get to know the new doctor and transfer over to him?"

"Yes! Exactly! But nobody wants to go to him, and he's apparently not in any hurry to force the issue."

"And if you're double-booked now, with two doctors supposedly in residence, you're screwed when December rolls around."

"Tell me about it. No, don't. I can't think about it right now. Anyway, eventually people won't have a choice. Right?"

"People always have a choice. They'll take their kids to Urgent Care or the ER, if nothing else."

"Nah..."

"Uh, yeah. Think about it. Who's Georgia's doctor?"

I gulp. "Dr. Reitman."

He laughs. "Shit. Talk about putting all your eggs in one basket. Anyway, after she retires, are you going to start taking your precious angel to see Dr. Douche?"

"Hell, no!"

"Why do you think *they* would?" Oblivious to my rising panic, my big brother continues, "Let's say they call because little Johnny's running a high fever and complaining of his ear hurting, but you're booked solid for the next week, and they're told, 'Dr. Douche can see Johnny this afternoon.' They have the same reaction you did—because I hear his bedside manner is pretty lame, too—and say, 'You know, I'll take my chances with a walk-in clinic, thanks.'"

"Eff."

"Yeah. And if you're booked so far out that they have to call a month ahead to get in for a well-child check, they'll give up. You'll be losing patients left and right."

I close my eyes and rub my chin. "This is bad."

"Could be. Of course, if Greenbrier notices one of its practices is performing at half capacity and is losing patients to other clinics, you won't be allowed to operate like that for long."

"True."

"Yeah. They'll shut you down."

"What?"

"Don't be naïve, bro. Greenbrier loves to pretend they're all about letting practices operate autonomously... until there's a problem. If they have to step in and work to keep a place open, forget it. They'll either shut it down or absorb you guys into another clinic."

"Oh, no."

"Yeah. And you'll be pariahs. I've seen it happen before. Nobody likes to take on a bunch of losers and try to make them part of a team that's already thriving and has a good system going." He looks at his watch and hops back on his mower. "Good talk, man. I need to finish this before it gets dark."

"Yeah," I reply distractedly. "I should be getting back home, too."

"Tell Betty I said hey."

"Will do."

As he starts the mower and lurches into motion, I step back onto the sidewalk and turn toward home, more worried than ever. Something needs to be done about Dr. Douche. Now. The question is, what? And how?

13

PLOTTING AND IMPLEMENTING

THIS SITUATION IS IMPOSSIBLE. I'VE WRACKED MY BRAINS ALL weekend, trying to think of how to fix this or avoid the disaster that now seems so inevitable it's scary. Given all of the factors, it may be that doing nothing and watching the result unfold is the most viable option. I don't think I can do that, though. I can't sit by, knowing what I do, and watch my friends' careers, at a practice we love, implode because of one entitled jerk's reign.

I could go all the way to the top, right? But that will only draw more attention to the problem and possibly hasten the end. This rescue mission needs to be at the grassroots level, but how do I get people on board? My co-workers love him. And it's no secret I don't. Laying out the facts for them will look like I'm finding new ways to trash their beloved Danny Boy. I have to be subtle. My approach needs to be nuanced.

Subtle and nuanced: not my strong suits.

And the worst part about the whole thing is that we're stuck with this guy. Therefore, no part of my plan can include plots to oust him, because the only way that's happening is if and when the practice collapses after Dr. Reitman's departure.

The success of the clinic hinges on his involvement, doing things *his* way—or letting him believe that's happening—with a smile on my face.

Because the bottom line is, I love my patients. I used to love my job, full-stop. And I still love ninety-nine percent of my co-workers, despite their disagreeing with me. Maybe especially because of that, in the case of Dr. Douche. After all, our clinic is one of the most popular in the Greenbrier system because we're cohesive. We're warm and welcoming. We're a family. And my colleagues are simply continuing that trend with their blind acceptance of our newest family member.

And why wouldn't they love him? Not only does he frequently praise their work, but he jokes with them, asks after family members, discusses their favorite TV shows, and funds expensive outings or hosts extravagant parties at his own home. Based on their experiences with him, they must assume he's the same with me, even if they never witness it. After all, they never experience him *mis*treating me, either. He's been careful about that since our disastrous public introductory clash. All subsequent dressing downs have been after hours or in his office, with the door closed.

Plan B, of course, is quitting. That's always an option.

But it's not, truly. If I follow quitting to its logical conclusion, the only difference in the end of the story is that I watch my co-workers' suffering from a distance, from the safety of wherever my new job is. I get away but leave them to perish. I couldn't live with myself if I did something that selfish. We're in this together, to the end, even if they don't realize how near the end is.

At the heart of the problem is this: patients and parents aren't warming up to Dr. Douche. Part of that could be due to his over-familiar (when he's not being insufferably condescending, that is) approach to bedside manner. Kids know the difference between friendly and fake. And their parents feel it, too. And it turns them off.

But since he hasn't encountered that many patients yet, all is not lost. We can turn this around if we nip it in the bud. That means I have to find a way to introduce him to patients and parents and control the introductions and the tone of the interactions so everyone walks away liking each other. Most importantly, they have to like him as much or more than they like Dr. Reitman and me, so they'll be open to making an appointment with him next time they call.

That last part is so counterintuitive that it makes me physically ill to contemplate.

In this morning's staff meeting, instead of staring mulishly into my coffee like I have during every staff meeting for the past month, hoping to fly under the radar and not draw the bullying attention of Dr. Douche, I wait eagerly through the usual discussions and announcements, my leg bouncing as my opening approaches. When Lynette hands out the schedules, delivering to me the rainbow-colored, full-to-bursting hard copy of mine, I barely glance at it before saying, "I have a proposal."

The previously buzzing room stills. All eyes land on me.

I hold up the piece of paper that looks like a unicorn barfed on it so that everyone can see. "Does anyone else think our scheduling system has become... unsustainable?"

Nervous glances all around, some muttering, some sighing, some fidgeting.

Before people can get too anxious about the possibility of radical change, I say, "I'm not talking about the software we use or learning a new color coding system, or anything like that. But..."

My co-workers stare expectantly.

I glance at the man who holds the power to make or break

us and clear my throat, then continue. "Dr. Chancellor needs to be given the opportunity to get to know more patients."

"Are you dissatisfied with your workload, Nate? Is that what you're saying?" Dr. Douche inquires with a smirk as he inspects his fingernails while leaning against the wall by the staff room door.

"No!"

Geez. I should have known he would have turned it around on me, no matter how I worded my proposition.

Swallowing and forcing myself to lean back in my chair, to appear more relaxed, more casual, less like my whole career depends on this working, I appeal to the entire room. "Our patients take their cues from us, though, right? The ones they know and already trust. Maybe we're not doing a very good job so far reassuring them that the changes coming to the clinic are positive, that they're going to love Dr. Chancellor just as much as they love Dr. Reitman."

"But not as much as they love you, right?"

I meet his challenging gaze. To everyone else in the room, those who haven't been privy to the after-hours pissing matches and behind-closed-doors dress-downs, his expression could be construed as teasing and playful. I see the steel behind his eyes, though. I see the muscle twitch in his jaw as he works hard not to clench it and let on to the others how much he despises me.

"They love me because they know me. They trust me. Most of them have known me their whole lives. They know what to expect from me, like if I tell them something's only going to hurt for a second, and if they hold still they'll get a reward, that's exactly what happens, as long as I have control over things."

He stifles a yawn, but I don't let his unimpressed reaction deter me from finishing.

"And the times when I can't quite deliver on a promise, they know it hurts me as much as it hurts them and that I'll do whatever I can to make it up to them. It's taken *years* to build that. We have four months to get there with you. We need to get on it."

"Okay. Fill up my schedule," he says to Lynette. "Balance it out. Take double-bookings from Nate's schedule and slide them over to mine. Done." He straightens and claps his hands once. "So, how'd you all enjoy the game Saturday? That ninth inning was something else, huh?"

"Hang on!"

He swivels his head back to me.

I force a chuckle. "Um. Sorry. But I don't think it's going to work if we force people to go to you instead of Dr. Reitman or me, especially if they show up for their appointment and find out we've moved them to a different doctor without any warning."

Finally, the woman I need to back me up speaks. "Nate's right. We'll need to be selective about this transition. We can isolate the ones we feel would be most open to change and approach the parents individually, checking with them first to make sure they think that would be okay."

Dr. Douche throws up his hands. "They're all going to have to switch eventually. What's with all the mollycoddling?"

"People like to feel they have a choice," I explain. "And in this case, they do. They can find a new doctor for their kids, at a new clinic, one they don't feel makes unilateral decisions about their children's medical care without checking with them first."

Shit. I didn't want to be that blunt. Not yet. Damn it.

Instead of conveying my panic by rushing on, I take a deep breath and carefully consider my next words. Nobody else seems to be eager to follow my downer statement, so I still have the floor when I figure out how to continue. "It's not going to come to that, obviously. We have to be smart how we handle this, though."

"And you don't think my suggestion is smart?"

Locating some shred of diplomacy, I concede, "It's efficient. And that's good. But..."

"Don't patronize me. If you have a better idea, let's hear it. The doors open in five minutes. Let's go." He claps his hands like I'm a dog he's urging to do its business more quickly in the cold.

Must not blow up. Must not tell him to go screw himself. Must stay in control.

"I was thinking we could team up."

He raises his eyebrow and purses his lips. "Go on."

Knowing full well how miserable I'm about to make a large portion of each week, I nevertheless obey him. "Maybe on Mondays, Wednesdays, and Fridays, you can shadow me. On Tuesdays and Thursdays, you can shadow Dr. Reitman. That way, patients and their caregivers will still have a familiar face in the room, but they'll also be getting to know you."

"And this is supposed to solve our bursting caseload problem how?"

I gulp. "Well, it doesn't, at first. But if everything goes according to plan, the next time those parents call to schedule appointments, when Lynette or any of the others tell them you have openings, they'll be more receptive to taking those, rather than waiting until Dr. Reitman or I have openings, because they know you." *And hopefully like you, although that's a huge "if."*

He rubs his chin.

"It's a solid plan, Dan," Dr. Reitman says. "Let's at least try it for a month and see how it goes."

"It's horribly inefficient for three of us to do the work of two people."

"The way things are now, though, two of us are doing the work of three, without any sign of things changing," she points out, saving me from being the bearer of that uncomfortable fact. "And this clinic runs on one doctor and one FNP, under normal conditions. Bursting caseloads are the norm."

"What about the patients I already have on my schedule?"

"You'll take care of those alone as planned, of course, but when you have blanks in your schedule, it's smart for you to team up with Nate or me. The alternating day plan will help us keep track of which patients you've met and which ones you still haven't seen."

He waves both hands at us. "Fine. Whatever. If that's what you think is best, Pat. I'm not convinced, that's all."

"Let's try it."

"Well, it's time to start, and it's a Monday, so I guess that means I'm Nate's right-hand man?"

As the rest of the group disperses, I step up to him and hand him my schedule. "I'll have Lynette make another copy of that for me, and we'll get started. You can take the lead, after I make introductions," I offer, ignoring the stabbing pain in my chest at the suggestion.

He grumbles something under his breath I can't quite make out as I leave the room, but I don't have time to stop and ask him to repeat himself. It's best I remain as ignorant as possible about his thoughts and feelings anyway.

* * *

WHAT'S MORE exhausting than working a double-booked schedule with minimal breaks? Working a double-booked schedule with minimal breaks alongside someone I detest *and* having to pretend I like him and he's a great guy, all the while serving as interpreter between him and the patients I know so well. I've been the recipient of countless nervous glances by parents, and more than once I've had to step in and mediate.

I try to keep quiet and let him do his thing, but his "thing" is overwhelming, especially for the shy kids or the ones feeling particularly ill. He's a fan of hokey tricks like making sound effects when he checks reflexes, showing up to appointments wearing a red clown nose, and pulling quarters from behind ears. When a little person has an ear infection, they're not only in pain but their anxiety levels are elevated. The last thing they want is the doctor "finding" a foreign object anywhere close to the site that's causing them so much distress.

After six weeks of this, I'm starting to think it's hopeless.

Worse, I'm beginning to believe Dr. Douche is an incompetent buffoon, something I was naïve enough not to consider before.

And worst of all, I worry the patients are associating me with him now and hating me as much as they hate him, because I introduced him to their lives.

Every day, I check Dr. Douche's schedule with more anticipation than my own, praying he'll have more appointments, especially on the days of the week he's paired with me. But he continues to chug along with his three or four appointments per day, usually with brand new patients, kids I fear we'll never see again.

Now we're suffering through yet another painful—more for the adults than the child—visit. I wish I could tune out while Dr. Douche lectures Beau Chomsky's mom about the importance of avoiding allergy trigger foods like honey and peanut butter until the toddler reaches a certain age, but I have to pay attention to what this guy's saying, which means I have to be a witness to the major offense his delivery is causing.

Mrs. Chomsky folds her arm over her breasts and rolls her eyes. "I have three older children, Dr. Chancellor. I—"

"Call me Dr. Dan."

"Uh... Okay. Dr. Dan. Beau's not my first child."

"That's hardly relevant, though. We make new discoveries and find new information every single day. Best practices from as recently as five years ago could be completely different now."

"I get that, too," she replies, taking his patronizing tone in stride. "But none of those allergies run in our family. I'm careful when I introduce new foods, because of Beau's lactose intolerance, but he's a picky eater, so I feed him what I can get him to eat. Otherwise, he won't eat at all. Which is why we're here today. I need advice about what to *add* to his diet, not what to take away."

"He wouldn't be as picky if you had introduced a wider variety of veggies before you resorted to sweet fruits and sugary proteins, like peanut butter."

I rub the back of my neck and blush when Mrs. Chomsky shoots an appealing look past Dr. Douche's arm at me. I've known her—and her kids—since I was brand new at this clinic.

Once she brought in her then-three-year-old, Michael, with a smallish jelly bean shoved so far up his nose I thought we were going to have to send them on to the ER for more drastic intervention. Most parents would have bypassed our office and gone straight there to begin with.

Not her. She was matter-of-fact about it and trusted us to get the job done. She straddled Michael on the exam table while one of my fellow nurses held his head, and I palpated the outside of his nose to move the candy farther away from his sinus cavity and down into his nostril. As he screamed and struggled against us, she cooed above him and told him it would be okay. She may as well have been talking to me, too. My adrenaline was coursing as I forced myself to focus on the job and not what could happen if I failed or did something to make it worse.

And when his nostril finally gave birth to that sugary nugget, she gathered her son to her chest and laughed, chiding him for being "such a goof." It was only afterward, when I felt her trembling as she thanked me with a hug, that I realized how terrified she'd been too, and how relieved she was and grateful to me for being the one to solve the problem.

As I've advanced through my career and furthered my education, she's continued to bring her brood here. Since I've become an FNP, she bypasses Dr. Reitman and specifically requests me. And now I've exposed her to Dr. Douche and his condescension. I wouldn't blame her for feeling betrayed.

There's nothing *technically* wrong with the advice the doctor is giving her right now, though, so I don't have much justification to step in and intervene. Of course, judging by the murderous look in Mrs. Chomsky's eyes, it might be a life-saving gesture to speak up. But how do I do this without making things worse between the doctor and me than they already are?

I clear my throat before the situation comes to blows. "Hey, Dr. Dan, why don't you dig up that tip sheet we have for expanding picky eaters' palates?" I suggest brightly, ruffling Beau's hair. "I don't know about you, but I'd get sick of eating the same thing every day, no matter how much I like it. That happened to me with pizza in college. It's only recently that I've been able to eat it again, that's how burned out I got. Saddest story ever, huh?"

Dr. Douche shoots me a look that implies he thinks I'm the biggest idiot on the planet, but he rises from his rolling stool and walks to the door. "I'll be right back."

As soon as the door closes behind him, Mrs. Chomsky asks, "What's the deal with that guy?"

"He's new." I offer the same explanation I've given to more people than I've cared to count in the past several weeks.

"Well, he's treating me like a moron. Like I'm a bad mom. I don't appreciate it."

Not having an answer for that, I simply say, "You can go ahead and get Beau dressed again, if you'd like."

As she tugs the toddler's clothes on, she vents, "I don't bring my kids in here for every little sniffle, you know? I brought Beau today because I'm legitimately concerned about his eating. I've done extensive research already, so I'm aware of the basic strategies for dealing with a picky eater, but his lactose intolerance makes this tricky. I came here for reassurance, but now I feel worse, like I've been doing everything wrong. With all of my boys."

I want to die when she looks up from buttoning Beau's shorts and blinks away tears.

"You're doing fine!"

"Not according to that guy!" She flaps her hand toward the closed door. "For all I know, he's out there calling child services because I let my two-year-old eat peanut butter."

"He's not."

Oh, gosh, he'd better not be making a liar of me right now.

"He's just…" I sigh. "He has the knowledge, but he needs to work on his delivery, that's all. It's easy to regurgitate the facts, but sometimes you have to take other factors into account, and some doctors aren't as good at that as others."

"Does he have his own kids? Not that you have to have kids to be a pediatrician, but… Does he have any clue how it feels to constantly second-guess yourself and wonder if you're doing everything wrong and ruining your kids?"

I'm brought up short when I have to admit, "I… I don't

know." If he has children, he's never mentioned them around me, nor does he have pictures of them in his office. And since I go out of my way not to socialize with him outside of work, I've never met his wife—or kids, if he has any. "I don't know him that well."

"But you want me to trust my family to him?"

I gulp. "He's more than qualified, if that's what you're worried about."

"Anyone with the education he has would be qualified. That's not what I'm talking about."

"I understand."

She hoists Beau onto her hip and slips his diaper bag onto her opposite shoulder. "I don't want to see him again. Next time I make an appointment for one of the boys to see *you*, that's who I want them to see. Period. Or I'll find somewhere else to take them."

I nod. "Okay. That's fair. I'm sorry."

After a perfunctory knock on the door, Dr. Douche re-enters the room with a stapled packet of papers in his hands. "Here we go. Sorry it took so long. Lynette had to show me where these—"

Mrs. Chomsky turns sideways to edge past him through the door, snatching the pages from him on her way out. "Thanks. You saved me some ink and paper from my printer at home, I guess. Totally worth today's co-pay."

I grasp the ends of my stethoscope and pull down.

"What the heck did you say to her?" he demands, plunking his hands on his hips.

Shaking my head, I chuckle and look at my feet. "You're something else," I mutter.

"Excuse me?"

"You heard me," I reply, lifting my head, my lips tightening and nostrils flaring.

"How is this my fault? I left to get that tip sheet, and I came back to find you with an enraged parent—"

"I was trying to repair the damage you did."

"Because I told it to her straight? Her kid's going to suffer physically and developmentally if she doesn't get a grip on his poor eating habits."

"A diet of peanut butter and jelly isn't the end of the world. And even if it were, there are nicer ways of tackling the problem. She came here for solutions, not judgment."

"I'm not a fan of sugar-coating my advice."

"There's a difference between sugar-coating and speaking to people with basic respect."

"The line is so thin..."

"It's our job to find it, *Dr. Dan*, and toe it. Every day. Every visit. Every patient. It's not that hard, if you have any clue at all. Which I'm beginning to think you don't."

Now I push past him. "Let's go. We have so many more parents to offend today."

14

GO, PACK, GO!

I MAY NOT BE GETTING ALONG ANY BETTER WITH DR. Douche, but things have markedly improved with my other co-workers, thanks to my tireless efforts to stop taking it out on them that our new boss is possibly one of the worst people to ever take the Hippocratic Oath. It's not their fault, after all. I wouldn't say I'm sucking up to them, but I *am* employing many of the same tactics I used to get back in their good graces after I broke up with Frankie and tried to re-enter the normal human race.

New in my repertoire are the framed pictures of each woman, Photoshopped with their celebrity crush and placed around the clinic like hilarious Easter eggs. You could always tell the exact minute one of them found theirs, due to the high-pitched shriek, followed by uproarious laughter. I must say, I found some ingenious (Rated G, of course) poses for maximum entertainment value. My favorite was the one of Dr. Reitman being "dipped" by Colin Firth on the red carpet of a movie premiere.

I also organized an impromptu Wellness Week. On the first day, in addition to the daily healthy recipe, I placed a basic pedometer in everyone's mailboxes. For the rest of the week, we competed to see who had the most steps at the end of each day. I awarded cheesy, fitness-related prizes like resistance bands, Day-of-the-Week exercise-themed socks, and terry cloth sweat bands to the daily winner. It was hilarious to see my co-workers with more sedentary jobs speed-walking laps through the halls between tasks to try to increase their step counts and compete with the rest of us, or trick those of us normally on our feet all day by volunteering to bring stuff to us, or urging us to "take a load off" in order to limit our steps and boost their own.

At the end of the week, I arranged for three massage therapists to set up chairs in the break room during the lunch hour, as a reward for all of our hard—but fun—work.

That week went a long way to reminding people I'm not all that bad and showing them how sorry I am for being less-than-fun to work with lately. But now the true test of my devotion has arrived. After turning down every single one of Dr. Douche's endless invitations to extracurricular activities to date, it's time to put aside my gigantic urge to strangle him with my stethoscope every time we're in the same room together and say yes to the green and gold postcard invitation (what are we, six?) I found in my mail slot in the staff room.

Of course, the Chancellors have been Packers season ticket holders for generations (lah-dee-dah. Like that's a huge distinction around here), but their row can't accommodate everyone from the clinic plus families, so Dr. Douche has splashed out and rented a luxury booth for all of us to attend a game. Not just any game, though: the match-up two weeks from now against the Bears. Even I recognize that's a big deal.

You'd think everyone had received a million-dollar winning lottery ticket in their mailboxes, not a card featuring a digitally manipulated Aaron Rodgers telling us to "R-E-L-A-X and enjoy the game on Sunday, October 15." I want to rip mine up and stomp on it, but I smile widely and say, "Great! I've always wanted to see what those suites looked like."

"And go to Heaven," Lynette gushes. "You have to remember to ask the attendants if you can go to Heaven."

"Pretty sure it's not up to anyone at Lambeau."

She laughs and swats my arm. "No, silly! It's a special outdoor VIP area, with an amazing view."

Free frostbite! Weeee!

"Georgia will love it."

I chuckle nervously.

"You *are* coming, right? Not even *you* can turn this one down."

"You know how much I *love* football."

"It's not about the game, you doofus! It's the atmosphere! The food, the drinks, the company!" She nudges me.

I swallow and grin. "Yeah." Flapping the card against my palm, I add, "I can't wait to tell Betty."

That evening, after Betty stops laughing, she says, "Oh, my gosh. Well, you know... babies are unpredictable. Georgia could come down with a raging case of diarrhea the morning of the game."

"I already used that one to get out of the luau."

She winces. "Teething?"

"The kid should have about six rows of teeth by now. To hear me tell it, we're raising a shark, not a child."

"Puking? Green snot? Low-grade fever? It could happen."

I run my hand through my hair and sigh. It's not just that it's football. Or a Packers game, specifically. When I was dating Frankie, her obsession with our hometown NFL team became a symbol of everything wrong between us, everything wrong in my *life* at that time. But at some point, I have to get over it. It's only one game. Nobody's saying I have to become a mega-fan and paint myself green and yellow every Sunday (and sometimes Mondays and Thursdays) from September to February.

Plus, this is for a good cause. I'm rebuilding relationships with my colleagues... and showing Dr. Douche that he's not going to break my spirit. I might be dying by degrees on the inside with every minute that passes, but nobody at that game is going to know I'm not having the time of my life. I will own this group outing.

"I can't believe I'm *wishing* an illness on my daughter. No. We're going. And we're going to have fun."

"That's the spirit! You don't have to watch the game, you know. Drink your ass off. I'll be your designated driver."

The thought of getting drunk in front of all of my co-workers—and my daughter—to endure an afternoon is not only ridiculous but repugnant. Yet still tempting, considering the circumstances.

Especially now that we're here.

It's like a John Deere convention. Who the heck decided these colors go together? And which came first, the tractor or the team colors? *"Let's see... When I think of guys rolling around in the grass, I see... dark green and mustard yellow! Yes! Plus, wouldn't it be funny to convince people to wear these colors? Not just once a week, but get them so crazed about this team that they choose to wear clothes with this color combination* all the time? *Hilarious!"*

Thanks to my football-loving brother and his family, we're properly attired for this shindig. Georgia's decked out in a hand-me-down baby track suit of Massi's, which sports a big, white G on its onesie chest. The person whose name graces the back of my jersey (Nick's jersey, more accurately) retired quite a few years ago—I think. Heidi gave Betty a choice between Favre and Rodgers. "Eenie, meenie, miney, mo" netted her the younger of the two legendary quarterbacks. I drew the line at bringing Nick's cheese wedge headgear, though. "Let's not get too carried away," I said, pulling the rubber hat off as soon as Betty plunked it on me.

When we arrive in the suite, our host strides over, snagging the arm of a live-action Jessica Rabbit on his way. She murmurs an "Excuse me" to Beulah and smiles coolly at her husband, then Betty, Georgia, and me, as they stop in front of us.

"Nate! You made it!" Dr. Douche announces entirely too loudly. "And this must be your lovely wife and daughter. It's so good to finally meet you," he gushes at Betty.

I make the formal introductions, and he fusses over Georgia to the point of embarrassment, as if she's a reticent patient he needs to charm. To my infinite amusement and pride, she merely blinks at him, then pushes her hand against his face to create more room between them.

Betty laughs nervously. "Georgia Louise!" To the couple, she explains (lies) with a slight blush, "It takes her a while sometimes to warm up to new people."

Dr. Douche smirks. "Takes after her old man, huh?"

I lift the baby from Betty's arms. "Aw, George! C'mere." I kiss her cheek, then whisper near her ear, "I love you. You're the best." After settling her in my arms, I smile at the couple before us, holding out my right hand to the woman I assume is the lucky Mrs. Chancellor. "And this must be?"

Dr. Douche flinches guiltily. "My wife, of course. Sorry."

I'm sure she is, most days.

"Veronica, this is Nate, the practice's FNP."

"The clinic's rock, more like it!" She shakes my hand. "I've heard so much about you."

Oh, I can only imagine.

In the interest of not making this afternoon more awkward than it needs to be, I simply nod and smile. And fib. "I'm glad we could finally make it to one of these things. You know, when you have a little one, it's always something."

Veronica pushes a piece of red hair behind her ear and ducks her head with a sad smile. "We wouldn't know, actually."

"Veronica and I haven't been blessed with children of our own—yet. Right, Sweetie?" he consults her, as if he needs to check. "We still haven't given up hope, though."

She crosses her fingers in front of her face. "Here's hoping that latest round of IVF does the trick."

Betty fidgets next to me while I wish a trap door would open in the floor under our feet and spit us out in the parking lot next to our car, where we can get in, look at each other, shrug, and say, *Well, that sucked. Let's get out of here.*

"Oh. I— We had no idea," Betty finally says.

Dr. Chancellor waves away her chagrin. "How could you? It is what it is. All in good time. Our lives have been so hectic up until now, anyway. And we have the children at the clinic to lavish our attention on, right? Well, I do, anyway." He glances at his wife, whose mouth twitches upward in a lame attempt at a brave smile.

"Anyway, she's a doll!" Veronica says, referring to Georgia. "All that black hair! Was she born with that or has it come in recently?"

"Part of the standard package," Betty answers. "You should see us trying to tame it in the morning. She looks like a Who!" At their blank stares, she clarifies, "From Whoville. You know —Dr. Seuss?"

"Oh, yes! Is that what they're called? How funny!"

"That's what Georgia's going to be for Halloween this year," I say.

"What a great idea!"

"Betty's," I admit. "She's the clever one."

Dr. Chancellor takes a step back. "Well, come in and make

yourselves comfortable. Get some food and something to drink. The bar and buffet are over there. The game should be starting any minute now."

"Great. I'm glad we made it in time."

"You did. Barely. Everyone else is already here, so I'm going to find a seat." Before we part ways, he says, "And Nate..."

I wait.

"Good of you to join us."

I search his face to try to judge his sincerity but can't in the few seconds I have before I'm required to give some response, so I simply reply, "Right. Thanks for the invitation."

Veronica and Betty have already settled into a comfortable conversation about TV shows, laughing like they've known each other for decades (how do women do that?), so I carry Georgia toward the buffet to survey our choices.

On the way, we're intercepted by Lynette, who grabs the baby's chubby hand and holds it up for a high five. "Give me some skin, Georgia Peach."

My daughter giggles and reaches for one of her favorite people. I relinquish my hold on her and watch as she lays a sloppy open-mouthed kiss right on Lynette's mouth.

Lynette laughs and dabs her face.

"We're still working on her form," I explain. "But the sentiment behind it is sweet, right?"

"I had no idea she felt that way about me. Listen, Peach, I don't normally swing that way, but for you... Well, come back and ask me in twenty years or so."

"This conversation has taken a disturbing turn."

Lynette pulls a face. "Hasn't it? Sorry. I don't have romantic feelings for your daughter."

"Good to know." I edge closer to the buffet and take a plate, ready to keep myself busy with food that I hope will make the next couple of hours bearable.

"But don't be surprised if I'm still single in twenty years and have given up on men. All the good ones are either taken or... taken."

In my peripheral vision, I study her, wondering if she's referring to what I said all those months ago when I intimated that Dr. Douche had the hots for her. Maybe it's the other way around? Or mutual? Or something? Her wistful expression, however, is too fleeting and aimed at the floor, not at anyone in the room, so I shake it off and return my attention to the shrimp cocktail. It's none of my business, anyway. And no matter how strongly against extramarital shenanigans (that's right—shenanigans) I am, I'm not about to lecture a friend about it.

"Anyway!" she says brightly. "You made it!"

"Why does everyone keep saying that, like we had to cross the frozen tundra to get here or something?"

"Because you never come to any of these things."

Ooh... beef brisket. Dr. D., you little suck-up.

"You act like there have been a hundred of 'these things.' I've missed, what? Three? Four?"

"Four. The fireworks in July, the baseball game in August, the pool party/luau that same month, and game night last month."

"I had legitimate reasons for not being at most of those. Georgia's birthday weekend at the lake conflicted with the first one."

When I stop speaking but keep moving along the buffet, she follows me. "And the others?"

"I'm pretty sure Georgia was sick."

"Which time?"

"The pool party thing. Maybe."

She flaps her lips. "Whatever."

I hold my loaded plate out of reach of Georgia's flailing

arms and, lowering my voice, move closer to Lynette. "Okay, fine. I didn't want to go. To any of them. Happy?"

"I'm glad you're at least being honest."

"Well, we're here now, and this is everything I thought it would be." *Overrated and a complete waste of four hours of my Sunday.* "Great food. Nice shirt, by the way," I add nodding down to her chest, which she puffs out, pushing the words "52 Shades of Clay" closer to me.

I back away.

She laughs. "Vintage."

"Clever. Goes well with the invitations we got from the good doctor." Instead of heading for the theater seating in front of the windows, I set my plate on the empty highboy table near the catered food and perch on one of the four chairs around it. When I realize I don't have anything to drink, I hop down and remedy that, returning to find Lynette and Georgia still standing by the table, picking food from my plate.

"Excuse me, but get your own."

"I was feeding your daughter."

"She ate before we left the house."

"Well, she's acting hungry."

"She's a bottomless pit. But she doesn't need to eat any of this stuff."

"A pinch of brisket isn't going to kill her."

Betty appears on my other side. "What are you two squabbling about over here?"

"How excited I am to be here."

Betty narrows her eyes. I widen mine in direct proportion to hers, daring her to call me out on my bald-faced lie. She doesn't take my silent challenge but merely smirks while the other occupants of the suite start cheering and clapping.

Lynette hands Georgia to Betty. "Game's starting, guys!" she says, rushing to an empty seat next to Janet.

Chewing, swallowing, then drinking, I watch as Betty sways to rock Georgia, who rubs at her eyes. They droop, and she finally gives up trying to keep her head up to look around. Nuzzling into her mom's chest, she shivers as Betty runs her fingers through her hair.

Great. This is interfering with nap time. It's going to be fun in our house later.

While I mentally fret about disrupted schedules, Betty says, "Dan and Veronica are saving two seats for us."

I look around her to verify this horrifying fact but keep my expression neutral while I continue eating. "That's nice, but..." I wipe my hands and face on a napkin, then wiggle my fingers toward the baby. "Before she gets too comfortable, hand her over. I'll stay back here and hold her while she naps; you go ahead and enjoy the game."

"Are you sure?"

"Yeah! I can still see what's going on." *Not really, but I don't care.*

"We can take her over there and sit."

I shake my head. "Nah. The cheering will keep her awake."

Once again, Georgia's transferred to my arms, and I hold her close, one ear against my chest, the other covered by my hand to block out as much of the ambient noise as possible.

Betty tucks her hands in the butt pockets of her jeans. "Okay, then. I guess I'll go sit with the Chancellors. Dr. Reitman's over there, too. I haven't had a chance to talk to her since her retirement announcement."

I wink. "You do that. She asks about you all the time."

Her face falls. "Does she... know?"

As I'm about to ask what she means, I figure it out for myself. "No. Nobody here does."

"Oh. Good. I was worried about that but forgot to ask you earlier. I don't want people feeling sorry for me."

Despite the familiar crushing sadness that makes me want to run to the bathroom for a quick weep, I smile. "They already do, though. Because you're married to me."

She laughs at the ceiling, drawing the attention of some of the people nearest to us in the back row of stadium seats, namely Dr. and Mrs. Chancellor. Veronica waves us over. "Hey, guys, you're missing the game!"

I jerk my chin toward a sleeping Georgia, yet again my hero.

Veronica mouths an *"Awww!"* but claps her hands when Betty accepts her summons.

Before tuning into the game—and another conversation with the doctor's wife—Betty turns and blows us a kiss over her shoulder.

"You guys are too cute for words," I hear Veronica gush.

In the noise of the suite, I can't make out Betty's low reply.

* * *

THE PACKERS SLAUGHTER THE BEARS, so I want to leave before the end of the fourth quarter to beat the traffic, but Betty told me not to be *that* guy. Now that the final second has ticked off the clock, though, I can't get out of here fast enough to salvage what's left of my Sunday.

So when Dr. Douche says, "Hey, we have the suite for another hour, if you guys want to hang out and wait for the crowds to clear," I nearly tackle Betty from behind in my rush to butt into the triangle created by her, Veronica, and my nemesis to say, "That's a great idea, but we need to get Georgia home." I lift her slightly on my arm. My sweet little Howdy Doody blows raspberries at the others.

"Wouldn't you rather stay here, where it's warm, than sit in a cold car in a line to get out of the lot, though?" he persists.

Rather than give him an outright, "No," I wave off his (unfortunately valid) point. "It won't be that bad. Come on, Betts." I hold out her coat for her.

She looks me up and down, rolls her eyes, and sighs, then turns to Veronica. "I'll call you to firm up plans for next weekend." To both Chancellors, she says, "It was so nice to meet you, finally. Thanks for inviting us. We had a great time."

Speak for your damn self. Kiss, kiss, hug, hug. Let's go.

Keeping with my act until the end, though, I grin and gush my appreciation, too, then guide my girls toward the exit.

Conversation is impossible as we make our way with the crowd to the car like a couple of cows in a loud, drunk, obnoxious herd, but as soon as I slide behind the steering wheel, Betty's ready to start our post-game debrief.

"That was fun. Makes me wish we'd gone to some of the other things they've hosted."

I shiver in front of the vent, which blows freezing air at our faces while the car warms up, but I say nothing.

"I like Veronica. We're going shoe shopping next weekend. You're not working at Urgent Care next Saturday, are you?"

"No."

"Oh, good. I'll text her right now and tell her we're on." She whips out her phone as I whip out of the parking space, only to stop short ten yards later, stuck in gridlock as we all bottleneck to the lot's exit like a bunch of 'roid-raging galoots attempting to push over the goal line.

We'd be home by now if we'd left when I originally wanted to leave, but I don't so much as mutter a single complaint to that effect. I can't get a word in, anyway. Betty's busy filling up the car with Veronica's life story. The woman obviously has no sense of privacy.

I hum and grunt my way through the conversation, barely listening while I watch out for drunks, high on their team's latest victory. I'm waving a perfect example of one of those guys into the line of cars in front of me, where I can keep an eye on him and not worry about him rear-ending us, when Betty declares, "You know, today was so much fun. I'd almost forgotten what that felt like. We should get together with people from the clinic more often."

I rub my upper lip and stare at the taillights of the drunk-ard's SUV. "Hmmm. I don't know about that."

"Yes! We're having a Halloween party, and all of your co-workers are invited."

"What? No! That's—" I stifle Mr. Negative and try to stay calm. A reasoned rejection always works better with Betty, anyway. If I'm too vehemently opposed to one of her ideas—like painting the living room gray—she views changing my mind as a challenge. If I give her alternatives, rather than simply saying "no," she generally backs off and acts like what-ever she ends up doing was her idea in the first place. "You know, it's pretty late notice for a Halloween party. Why don't we schedule a game night for sometime next month?" *Or in the month of Never.*

"Nah. There's plenty of time for people to plan and prepare."

"Plan and prepare what?"

"Their costumes, silly!" She rubs her hands together. "This is going to be so much fun! I'll print up some sweet invitations as soon as we get home, and you can distribute them at work tomorrow. I'm thinking the weekend before Halloween would be best." She claps her hands. "This'll be great, you'll see."

Georgia joins in and chants, "Padd'cake, padd'cake!'"

Still not displaying my panic—although I'm starting to sweat in this stifling jersey—I clarify, "I'm inviting everyone? Including him?"

"Especially him! And Veronica. Duh! By the way, you don't

get to tell me who I'm friends with. I like Veronica, and I'm going to hang out with her. The fact that our husbands can't stand each other has nothing to do with her and me."

"I never—" I take a deep breath through my nose and exhale slowly. "You deserve to have a best friend again. Other than me, that is."

"Thank you." Sliding off her shoes, she props her feet on the dash. "She's the first person I've felt has the potential to be my friend since I lost my best and only girlfriend in the whole world."

"I'm sorry Frankie let you down and wasn't as good a friend to you as you were to her."

She bites her lip, her smile guilty. "You mean, when I stole her boyfriend?"

"I wasn't her boyfriend anymore!"

"Okay, so when I lusted after her boyfriend?"

"You did?"

"Constantly. From the minute I met you."

"You never told me that."

"Didn't want you to get too full of yourself."

"Ha! Well, I was terrified of you."

"And I was fully aware of that. Made me want you even more."

"Geez. That's kind of sick."

"What can I say? I'm a complicated woman. Now, focus. Halloween. We need to brainstorm costumes."

What have I done?

15

MONSTER MASH

I'M NOT GOING TO LIE; I HOPED AS I CREPT INTO THE STAFF room early the next morning, before the daily meeting, that Dr. Douche would have somehow beat me to it, that when I went to insert the invitations into everyone's mailboxes, there would already be a cheesy postcard waiting in each slot, announcing a Halloween party on that same night at the Chancellor residence. Or better yet, somewhere swanky, so it would be less of a contest which gathering people would choose to attend. Or best yet, that I could concede defeat without giving people the choice, dumping Betty's fliers into the shredder and turning them into bright orange confetti before anyone saw them.

But alas. The mailboxes were empty and ready to receive the invitations.

Don't get me wrong. I love Halloween—for the kids. We always dress up at the clinic, and it's fun to see the reactions of the patients when their favorite cartoon character or action hero walks into the room instead of some boring nurse. I also enjoy handing out candy at home, making a big deal over each of the costumes, going over the top with my feigned fear at the scary ones or fanning myself and swooning at the pretty ones. And now, as a father, watching my own child participate (or, more accurately at this age, forcing her to) adds another level to the entertainment.

I've never been a fan, however, of the adult Halloween costume party. It strikes me as sad when grownups dress up—usually in flimsy, sexually suggestive costumes that cost them a fortune—to parade in front of each other and compete to see who's the most ingenious (or the dirtiest-minded). To me, Halloween—like Trix—is for kids. The only time an adult should be dressing up on—or around—that day is if he or she is doing it to entertain a child or group of children. When your audience is a group of adults you're trying to impress, it's just...

"Pathetic," I say to Betty as I adjust the hairy potato sack (basically) that comprises my Barney Rubble costume. "And not fair. *You* don't even have to change your name for the night."

Yes, Betty is the Betty to my Barney. Because what's worse than a lame adult Halloween costume? A couple's costume.

She pats my butt on her way out of the bathroom. "Nice legs, Barn."

I peer down at my bare gams and feet, then call after her, "At least let me wear shoes!"

"No!" she shouts from Georgia's room, where she's getting the baby up from her nap and changing her into the Seussical garb she's collected over the past few months. "Put on your wig."

"I'm not wearing that dead animal on my head. It itches and makes me look like an idiot."

"It's part of the costume! Barney Rubble has blond hair."

"He's trying something new tonight," I improvise, combing and finger-styling my medium brown hair into its usual shape. "A dye job. Maybe he's having a midlife crisis."

"You're such a killjoy! Now get in here and help me with this. Bring the hair gel."

I snatch the hair product and walk my furry self into Georgia's room, laughing as soon as I get a good view of her outfit, a Peter Pan-collared, bright yellow dress, striped tights, and curly-toed shoes. "Georgia Lou Who! You're so whimsical." I tap the tip of her nose and say to Betty while handing over the gel, "You did a great job, hon."

The only things that saved our daughter from completing our Rubble family were a) her unruly black hair and b) her gender, although I don't think either of those things would have mattered, if not for c) Betty already having everything to make her a Who, none of which will still fit next year. Therefore, we're a blended family. Stone Age meets stoned fantasy.

The baby bucks on the changing table and squeals.

"Now if only her hair will cooperate," Betty says, squirting a large glob of gel into the palm of her hand. "Hold her steady, will ya?"

Wrapping my hands around Georgia's waist, I hold her in a sitting position, keeping her in place and entertained with funny faces while Betty runs her gel-coated fingers through our daughter's baby-fine, black locks.

After Betty achieves the perfect curvature on the horn in the middle of our child's head, she steps back to inspect her work. "Meh. It's not exactly as I imagined, but it'll do. Maybe hair wax would have worked better."

"She looks hilarious. And adorable," I reassure the artist, hoisting Georgia from the changing table.

Betty adjusts the bow in her own hair, then flinches and gasps. "Oh, no! Where's my bone?"

Seeing her in that costume, I want to grab myself and tell her it's right here, but I'm wearing a dress and holding our daughter. And... things still haven't resumed in that department of our marriage, so it seems wrong to make jokes about it. Like I'm putting on the pressure. And I'm not. I'm determined to give Betty all the control where that's concerned.

Instead, I answer, "Check under the bed. Maybe Reba took it."

She rushes past me. "She better not have!" After a few seconds, her head pops back into view in the doorway. "Hey, while I'm looking, can you make sure Georgia's overnight bag is ready to go?"

I salute the general. "Ten-four."

She'll only be over at Nick's for a couple of hours, and she'll be sleeping most or all of that time, but we're nothing if not paranoid... er, *prepared*.

Setting Georgia on the floor, I give her a gentle pat to the butt and say, "You stay here with me, all right? Losing a prop bone is one thing, but you're irreplaceable."

Before I can move away, she pulls up on my legs, gripping my leg hairs in her rubbery hands. I hiss but bear with the agony until she achieves balance and lets go. Then I back away carefully.

"There you go! See? Walking is easy!"

She lurches forward a few steps before dropping to her hands and knees so she can follow me more quickly as I crisscross her room, shoving things into the same backpack she uses for daycare. As she babbles, I provide the running commentary to her soundtrack. "You're going to Uncle Nick's for a couple of hours, so you can sleep in a quiet house. And Mommy and Daddy don't have to worry about people being too loud while you're sleeping."

"Nonononono!"

"Don't worry; you'll get to make an appearance at the party, make your rounds, mingle and all that. But at bedtime, Uncle Nick and Aunt Heidi are going to take you home for a while."

I stuff about seven more diapers into the backpack than she'll need for the amount of time she'll be gone. Zipping her bag, I hang it on the bedroom doorknob, where we can quickly grab it later, then turn back to the baby to finish telling her the plan. "And then, when everyone here leaves, I'll come pick you up, and bring you home. See? No biggie. You like it at Uncle Nick's. Being with Massi and Cruz is like having brothers."

I clear my throat at the sudden realization that they're the closest thing she'll ever have to siblings and rush ahead before I can dwell too long on it. "They're better than brothers. Because if you ever get sick of them, you can go home. Or send them home, if they're here. Trust me; having a brother is overrated. Cousins! Now that's where the real fun is."

She stares up at me, concentrating so hard on what I'm saying that a string of drool slides off her lower lip and drizzles onto her hand on the floor. Blinking, she pushes herself into a sitting position and shoves her fist into her mouth, gnawing on it. The ski slope of her hair quivers.

"George, you look ridiculous. Ridiculously cute!" I bend down to pick her up. "Come here, you little Who. Everyone will be here in a few minutes." I pinch her toes and jiggle her foot. "I'd give my left nut for shoes like yours right now. My feet are freezing."

"Stop whining about your feet and help me set out the food."

Whirling, I face Betty, who's standing on the other side of the doorway in the hall. "Stop spying on us! We were having a private conversation."

"Whatever." She holds up the white plastic molded into the shape of a femur. "Found my bone. Now we can party."

Can't argue with that logic.

* * *

NOW THAT GEORGIA, Nick, and Heidi have officially left the premises, I can relax somewhat but not completely. Still crammed into our cozy house are more than a dozen people, wearing a wide variety of costumes that run the gamut from clever (Beulah's Hawaiian Punch: grass skirt, lei, and boxing gloves) to funny (Janet's torso wrapped in what appears to be a giant box of wine, complete with hip spigot) to surprising (Lynette's revealing Cleopatra) and everything in between, so it's a bit hot and crowded. So much for those cold feet of mine. But at least I'm no longer worried about someone stepping on my child.

"In between" is where the couples' costumes rank. Of course, there's Betty and me, as the Rubbles. The other Binghams capitalized on Heidi's bulging belly and came as the title character and her boyfriend from the movie *Juno*. And the Chancellors are the leg lamp (her) and "Fragile" crate (him) from *A Christmas Story*. Too bad it's not the other way around; it would have been nice to have another guy showing as much leg as I am. Fishnets would have been a bonus.

I crack open my first beer of the night and survey the food supply on the kitchen table. Nothing needs to be replenished or freshened, so I lob my bottle cap in the recycling bin, lean against the nearest counter, and chug most of my beverage in a few long swallows, stopping only to breathe—and belch.

"Excuse you!" Lynette says, slink-lurching into the room and opening the fridge to retrieve another hard cider. "If you were a real cartoon character, your lips would have gone all wavy with that one."

"A real cartoon character? Are you drunk?"

She wobbles on her gold platform sandals. "Maybe a tad tipsy. But you know what I mean. Is that what you're going to wear at the clinic on Wednesday?"

"Uh, no. Most of the kids wouldn't know who I was."

"That's so sad!"

"Right? But I'd feel a bit under-dressed in this anyway."

"Same here." She swigs and swallows. "But you and Betty look adorable together, as usual." She peels at the label on her bottle, then mutters, "I wish I had someone to bring as my Mark Antony." The beads in her wig click when she shakes her head, as if to clear it. "Anyway! What have you decided to be at the office?"

"I was thinking about digging out my Super Mario costume from a few years ago. It would be new to most of the kids." *And it's full coverage and requires shoes.*

"Ooh! Maybe I can be Princess Peach! That would be fun! Easy to do, too. All I need is a crown and a pink poofy dress. And one of those wand thingies."

"A scepter?"

"Yes! That." She points to me with her bottle. "So, what do you say? Do you care if our costumes go together?"

I step forward, grab a stuffed olive from the relish tray on the table, and pop it in my mouth. "I don't care," I muffle from the empty side of my mouth while surveying the trays for my next bite. "The kids will think it's funny."

"They'll love it! You're right; that costume you have on right now wouldn't be good for work. It might make the kids—and parents—uncomfortable."

"It would make *me* uncomfortable. I feel very exposed."

"What, are you going commando under there?"

When I roll my eyes and don't answer right away, she shrieks, "You are!"

"No, I'm not. I'm wearing underpants." I smile with my lips against the mouth of my drink.

"Prove it."

After drinking, I answer around a stifled burp, "What?! Hell, no. I'm not going to lift my... my dress for you!"

"It's a tunic."

"Whatever. It's staying down. I'm flashing enough leg."

"Aw, you're shy. It's not like that thing is revealing. It does nothing for your figure. Except show off your runner's legs."

"Great. That's the look I was going for." I laugh and drain the rest of my beer.

"I never realized how hairy you are."

"Hey, I'm nothing compared to my brother. He's yeti status."

She splutters, and one of her ankles rolls, sending her staggering across the kitchen and collapsing against me.

"Whoa!" I catch her, thankful the bottle in my hand is empty, or we'd both be soaked. As it is, she sloshes a good amount of her cider against her off-white, strapless, linen shirt. She's not wearing a bra, I suddenly notice. And now it's embarrassingly obvious. To me, anyway. But it hardly registers before I realize she might be hurt.

"Are you okay?" I ask, still laughing, not sure how else to react. "You rolled your ankle, maybe."

"I'm fine," she replies, leaning heavily on me to regain her footing, then pushing her wig from her eyes and straightening it. "I... I might be drunker than I thought."

"Maybe. Here. Hand me your drink for a second." I take the bottle from her and set it on the counter behind me, putting my empty next to it. With two free hands, it's easier for me to help her more firmly to her feet. Hands wrapped around her upper arms, I bend at the knees to peer into her cat-painted eyes. "Okay? Can you put weight on it?"

She nods meekly. "I think so."

"I won't let go until you're sure." My palms slide higher on her arms, resting level with her bare shoulders as she gradually puts her full weight on both feet.

She shoots me a shaky smile. "It's fine."

"Doesn't hurt at all?"

For some reason her eyes fill, but she manages a terse, clacking head shake and a whispered, "No."

As I'm about to let go, a movement over my friend's shoulder competes for my attention. Betty stops short in front of the fridge, one hand on the handle, her wide eyes on us.

"What's going on?"

"It's okay," I answer. "Lynette just sort of... fell."

"These damn shoes," Lynette says with a nervous chuckle and a sniffle.

"Yeah, maybe I'm better off in no shoes, huh?" I joke nervously.

Betty continues to stare at us. "Uh-huh. So, now. How'd that 'sort of' happen?"

"We were standing in here, talking..."

"Alone. Away from the rest of the party," Betty points out with her signature eyebrow lift.

I swallow. "Um, yeah. I was drinking a beer and grabbing something to eat, and Lynette was getting a drink, and we were talking about the costumes we're going to wear to work next week."

"You mean, you're not going to wear that?" Betty inquires, nodding at Lynette's revealing get-up. "The nipples are a nice touch."

Lynette blushes.

"Betty!"

She yanks open the refrigerator. "You know what? Never mind. She tripped and fell against you and spilled beer on her tits. If I had a dollar for every time that happened to me, out of the blue..."

"I really didn't mean to," Lynette mumbles. "Listen, I should go."

"No!"

Both women snap their heads toward me.

"She's in no condition to drive," I explain to Betty, when she looks like she's going to break one of the bottles in her hand and go for my jugular.

She laughs mirthlessly and hip-bumps the fridge closed. "Are you proposing a sleepover, then?"

Before I can answer, Lynette says, "I'll, uh, ask Janet or Mary-Kate to take me home. I'm not feeling very good right now anyway."

"I'm not feeling so hot myself," Betty replies, keeping her eyes locked on me as Lynette edges past her.

When the two of us are alone, Betty stares at me for the longest time, until I say, "Whatever you're thinking, that's not what was happening."

Her eyes narrow, and her jaw sets. "Then you're in deep shit, Nathaniel. Because I was giving you the benefit of the doubt. My bad."

She whirls and chirps in a light, happy voice obviously intended for the benefit of everyone else in the house, "Get your butt out here! We're going to vote for best costume and play a game!"

I close my eyes, pinch the bridge of my nose, and do as I'm told.

16

FOR BETTER OR WORSE

I VAGUELY REMEMBER LYNETTE LEAVING, THEN THE REST OF us voting for best costume (the Chancellors won in a landslide, although I voted for Beulah), and laughing our way through three rounds of Apples to Apples, but as soon as Betty and I are alone again, it's like our guests took all the air with them when they left.

Wordlessly, I change into street clothes and—my beer long since dissolved in my blood or gone down the toilet—drive to Nick's to get Georgia. By the time I return to the house and settle the baby for the night, Betty, still dressed as Mrs. Rubble, has finished with the kitchen cleanup and started on the living room. I join her, but the only sound between us is the clanging of glass against glass and the rustling of the bag Betty's using to collect the bottles.

Finally, after several minutes, the living room is clear of everything but the decorations Betty so gleefully installed what feels like a long time ago but was less than twelve hours earlier. I take the trash bag from her and into the kitchen. Its contents aren't going to fit in the neat cubby usually reserved for our week's worth of glass, so I prop the sack next to the blue stack of containers and return to the living room.

"I trust you, you know," Betty's voice rings through the high-ceilinged room. "Maybe that makes me an idiot. But I do. Trust you."

"And you should. I did nothing wrong."

As if I haven't said anything, she continues, turning away from me and fingering the metatarsal of a plastic skeleton hanging above the fireplace. "When you say you're working late, I believe you're actually working. And I picture you there alone."

"Betts—"

"And when you two isolate yourself from the rest of the group every time we're in a social setting with the people from the clinic—not just tonight—I don't think anything of it, because you're friends. And of course, you're going to have female friends, because you work with a bunch of women. I've never questioned that. But maybe I've been naïve."

"Nothing is going on. Nothing happened tonight."

She turns to face me, her chin trembling, her lower lids pregnant with tears. "Is that what your mom said to your dad? Did he believe it, too, because he needed to believe it?"

I barely have enough oxygen for breathing, much less talking.

"Have I been as clueless as every other person I've seen in this situation and thought, 'How could they not know?'"

"This is all interesting evidence of how much you trust me," I finally say.

She swipes at her eyes and looks down at her bare feet. "Maybe I only thought I did. Maybe I don't even know what 'trust' feels like."

"You've misinterpreted something innocent, and now

you're questioning everything based on that bad information. That's not fair."

Her head rises slowly. If irises could turn red and pupils shoot lasers, hers would be doing it. "Fair? Fair?! How fair was it to walk in on what I walked in on earlier?"

"You mean when I was making sure my drunken friend and co-worker hadn't hurt herself in my home?"

"While she rubbed her nipples against you."

"She fell! Her breasts just... came along for the ride."

"And you didn't look at them or notice them or..."

"This is ridiculous."

"That would be a yes."

"I'd like you to listen to yourself right now."

"Screw you." Her chest heaving, she spins away again, leans against the mantle at her standing chest height, and rests her head on her folded arms.

I walk up slowly behind her and reach out tentatively, not making contact with her shaking bare back the first couple of attempts, like I'm worried touching her will hurt. Finally, I rest my palm on her shoulder blade. She doesn't shrug me off, as I half-expect her to do, but she continues sobbing into her arms.

"I'm worried about you," I murmur.

"Sure, turn it around on me," she muffles.

"I'm not turning it around on anyone."

"I know what I saw."

"Yeah. I've been replaying it in my head all night, and I get that it didn't look good."

"I needed this party. I needed this night. I needed to have a good time and find the fun person I used to be. I didn't need to watch you fondle your cute, fun, funny, *young* co-worker, who's so obviously in love with you, it's pathetic."

I hold the breath I was going to use to object to the word *fondle* when the last thing she's said registers. "Excusemewhat?"

I say with what's left of the air in my lungs when I finally exhale.

"Everyone knows it but you," she says. "And like an idiot, I've dismissed it, because I knew—well, *thought*—it was an unrequited crush. When Veronica brought it up while we were shopping a couple of weeks ago, I laughed—laughed!—about it and blew it off. And she said, 'You're a much cooler wife than I am. I've made Dan leave practices for less obvious flirtations.'" Betty pivots her head to the side and sniffles but doesn't face me or lift her cheek from her arms. "And I thought, like a smug moron, 'Well, she and Dan obviously don't have what Nathaniel and I do.'" She breaks down again, her shoulder heaving against my hand.

No longer giving her the choice, I pull on her to turn her around.

"You're basing all of this on something Veronica Chancellor told you?"

"And what I've seen tonight. And in the past, but wasn't smart enough to recognize."

Must not explode. Must not shoot the messenger. I love the messenger.

"It has nothing to do with 'smart.' You can't see something that's not there, that doesn't exist. Lynette is like my *sister*. My *little* sister."

"If you had a little sister, she wouldn't be rubbing up against you in next to nothing."

"She fell."

"Or holding your baby and following you around, pretending you're a happy family."

"She loves Georgia. Everyone at the clinic does! Does that mean they have the hots for me? Is Dr. Reitman saying, 'I love you with a burning passion' every time she asks me about our daughter?"

"You're making it sound absurd."

"Because it *is*."

"This thing with Lynette isn't. It's real. And you know it."

"You know what's real? How drunk Lynette was tonight. Real drunk. You know what else is real? How manipulative the Chancellors are, weaseling their way into friendships so they can plant seeds of doubt in good, solid, loving marriages."

"Is that what this is, Nate? Is this what a good, solid, loving marriage looks like? Do either of us have a clue what that *would* look like? Who are our role models? Your parents, who are getting a divorce after your mother's screwing around with someone young enough to be your little brother? My parents, who basically have a business arrangement and never show each other any affection? Your brother and Heidi, the sperm donor and the incubator?"

"We're our own role models. Or we were, until..." I stop, trying to trace back to when things started to sour, trying to identify a catalyst. Was it the stress of being new, sleep-deprived parents? No. Was it her traveling for work? Not really. Is it the tension at work creeping into my home life? Somewhat. Is it the sadness neither one of us wants to talk about but can't shake? Most definitely.

"Until what?" she asks, obviously trying to pull from me an answer she already thinks she knows. "Say it. God, just say it! I know you're thinking it. You think it every day, even if you don't allow yourself to admit it. So say it. It will be a relief to hear it out loud. Because seeing it on your face and knowing you're feeling it but don't want to say it to me sucks."

"I have no idea what you're talking about."

"You blame me for the miscarriage."

Yet again, I momentarily forget how to breathe. On a choked whisper, I ask, "Have you lost your mind?"

"Have I?"

"Maybe!"

"What else am I supposed to think? You're so distant and withdrawn. I'm supposed to believe it's a coincidence that you started acting like this a week after... that?"

"Yes."

"Bullshit."

"C'mon, Betts... Please."

"You can't stand to be around me. Every time there's a chance we'll be alone, you find something else to do, somewhere else to be. Jogging. Working late. Meeting up with your dad. And when you are here, I'm lonely. You're always so far away..." She pauses then says quietly to her feet, "I heard you with Georgia earlier. I heard you talking about siblings."

"I was telling her how lucky she was not to have brothers like Massimo and Cruz!"

"But you don't believe that."

"Yeah, I do. Those kids drive me nuts. They're cry machines."

"Not them specifically; brothers or siblings in general."

"I was babbling to a freaking toddler!"

"You're upset that I don't want more kids."

I open and close my mouth several times on the reflexive lie that has the power to fix all of this. Or make things worse. Infinitely worse.

"I knew it," she murmurs.

"'Upset' isn't the right word."

"Screw you and your semantics."

"You want me to lie and say I'm happy about it?"

"That's what you said when we first talked about it."

"No, I didn't. I said I was 'more than good' with the way things are, with you, Georgia, and me. Because to not be good with it would be ungrateful. But I did expect us to have a bigger family. And until recently, you were on board with that."

"Until recently, I hadn't bled my baby into a toilet."

I rub the back of my neck and blink away vertigo. "We should talk about this some other time, when we're both calmer. And have had some sleep, which I'll get in the guest room." I turn to leave but pause on the threshold to the hallway to face her once more. "You know, it was my baby too. My disappointment too."

She looks marginally chastened, but as she averts her eyes toward the floor, she says, "I wish 'disappointed' was the worst I was feeling."

I let her have the last word. Because what else am I going to say? I could clarify and say disappointed isn't close to the worst emotion I experience every time I think about it, which is nearly constantly, but this isn't a contest to see who's hurting the most. Plus, itemizing our grief would only escalate the argument, and I need it to be over... for now.

17

DILEMMA

I don't consider myself an egomaniac. As a matter of fact, when I had to pretend like I was an author with an ego, it was one of the most discomfiting exercises I've ever taken part in. But even the most insecure, self-conscious, and humble of us has an inexplicable desire to see him or herself replicated, to a certain extent. That's why we reproduce. It's science—depending on which study you read or believe.

Betty has her tiny clone; I was patiently waiting my turn. But now, that opportunity is gone. And I'm a tad more bitter about it than I would like to be.

The craziest thing about it is that when I took for granted that we would have more children after Georgia, I was in no hurry to make that happen. I wasn't ever one of those guys who was like, "We're going to keep trying until we have that son I so desperately need to prove my masculinity." After all, having sons hasn't made my brother more "manly," whatever the hell that means. If anything, he's been nearly displaced by two pooping, whining, breastmilk-guzzling terrors.

And when Nick and Heidi recently found out they were expecting another boy, my brother—the idiot—made the mistake of telling me Heidi cried at the news. Worse, he added, when I simply stared at his profile, wondering how he could be so insensitive, "I'm bummed, too. You know, I look at you and Georgia... You have something with her I'll never have with my boys."

I wanted to punch him in the penis. Not because he was wrong, but because he's just so... so... clueless. I might buy that fathers and daughters have a special bond that fathers and sons don't have, but it goes both ways, if only he'd take advantage of it.

My anger is more basic than that, though. I can't help but think how arrogant it is to look at the ultrasound of any healthy baby and allow yourself to feel disappointment about something as petty as a reproductive organ. And how could he admit that to me, of all people? Girl, boy... I'd give anything to see Betty's belly swell with another person we made together.

Maybe he thought I'd reached my admittedly low limit for football when I rose from the couch and left the room. Maybe he thought it was weird when I left his house entirely a few minutes later without saying goodbye. Maybe he never noticed at all.

And when I stormed into my own house a few minutes later, my jealousy and rage still fresh after the short walk home, I didn't dare tell Betty what was wrong. Because I'm supposedly "more than good" with the decision we've made not to have any more kids. What man isn't okay with it after his wife looks at him the way Betty looked at me and pleaded with me the morning after she went through such a horrific experience?

Plus, Betty's not "more than good" with it, either. I've witnessed the longing on her face when she doesn't think anyone sees her watching Heidi lumber through her third trimester those rare (becoming rarer and rarer) times we hang out with my brother and his wife. For some reason, though, Betty—the strongest, most determined person I know—has decided the risk outweighs the reward, to the point that she feels she has no choice. And because she's so resolved, there's no changing her mind.

Last night after our fight, my fitful sleep was filled with dreams of babies with my face, babies who dissolved through my hands like paste when I tried to hold them.

It doesn't take a mental professional—or a mental professional's kid—to figure that one out.

Although Georgia isn't making a peep, and she'll sleep hours later than usual due to the break in her routine, I rise and shower in the bathroom across the hall as soon as the guest bedroom window starts to brighten.

When I shuffle into the kitchen in search of coffee, I'm surprised to see Betty sitting at the table, her chin resting on the rim of a steaming mug. Since the coffeepot is empty, I assume she's chosen the herbal route this morning.

Without lifting her head, she murmurs, her head bouncing with each thrust of her chin against her cup, "We've confused the hell out of Reba. She paced in the hallway half the night and whined next to our bed the other half."

I bite back my snarky replies and any nonverbal reactions to this news by busying myself at the coffeemaker, being extra precise as I measure the grounds. After adding water to the reservoir, I peek out the window and watch Reba while she patrols the perimeter of the yard. She doesn't appear in any hurry to come back in here. I don't blame her.

As I'm watching the coffee stream into the carafe, Betty says behind me, "I know nothing's going on between you and Lynette."

My gaze unfocused, I merely nod my acknowledgment of her statement.

"That's not to say she doesn't *wish* there were something going on between the two of you..."

I close my eyes and sigh.

"...but it's not fair to be mad at you about something that's out of your control. I... I walked in here last night and saw what was happening and flipped out. I'm sorry."

"You're forgiven. Of course."

"I do trust you. I know you'd nev—"

"Do you?" Slowly, I turn and cross my arms over my chest.

"Yes! I'm just feeling really vulnerable right now, I guess," she says to her tepid tea. "I'm sorry, okay?"

"Let's get some things straight, all right? You leveled some major accusations at me last night."

"I'm—"

"Let me finish. Please."

"Okay."

"I have *never*, not for one nanosecond, blamed you for that miscarriage. Not only would that be medically inaccurate, but despite our misgivings about the timing of having another baby, we wanted that baby. And loved it." I have to stop to clear my throat, but I power on as soon as I can. "And were devastated by what happened. Both of us. To suggest otherwise is not only unfair but insulting."

She hiccups a sob but covers her mouth with her fist to suppress any other interrupting noises.

I draw in a shaky breath and run my hand through my hair. "I also don't appreciate someone who barely knows us saying things to make you question our relationship. You should be careful around someone like that."

Anger replaces the grief in her eyes. "Because I'm such a bad judge of character, right?"

"No!"

"Yes. You don't trust me to pick my own friends. And

you're being hypercritical of Veronica because you don't like her husband. Because he's supposedly been a jerk to you. For the record, he's always been charming and nice to me. He hasn't said or done anything around me to hint at what you've described the past few months."

"Oh, so that means those things haven't happened?"

"I didn't say that!"

"This is so typical."

"Typical? What's typical?"

I chuckle mirthlessly and turn back to the coffeemaker, willing it to brew faster. "It would figure he'd find a way to charm my own wife, like it's not bad enough he has all my co-workers on his side."

"I'm not taking sides!"

"Well, you should be. Mine." Sick of waiting, I remove the half-full carafe from the burner and pour a cup for myself, then return it to its base to finish dispensing the rest of the pot.

"I'm always on your side," she claims. "I only said he was charming and nice. I didn't say that means he's a great guy to work with or a good doctor or—"

Careful not to spill, I spin, my hands wrapped around my hot mug. "He makes my life a living Hell and has treated me like dirt from the moment he laid eyes on me."

"So, his biggest flaw is that he's mean to you?"

I sip thoughtfully, then reply, keeping a tenuous hold on my temper, "No, his biggest flaw is that he's a quack, and I'm worried about the kids under his care. Coming in at a close second is that he has the potential to ruin everything with his bumbling incompetence. Patients and parents don't like him. He's going to drive away half of our patient base, to the point that we won't bring in enough revenue for Greenbrier to consider us viable."

She sucks in her cheeks and lowers her chin, obviously still skeptical, so I continue, "He could punch me in the balls and spit in my face and call me names and force me to stay late to help with insurance coding every single day, but as long as he was good at his job and could pull his own weight, I'd be okay with that. I'd happily find another clinic and get as far away from him as I could. Don't you think that's what I'd rather do? Don't you think that's what I *would* do, if it were only about me not getting along with some egotistical pinhead?"

"I guess..."

"I would! But it's not about that. I can't put in for a transfer and leave, knowing full well what's going to happen if both Dr. Reitman and I go at the same time. My co-workers— my *friends* won't have jobs for long. I have two months to turn this guy into a medical professional that at least half of the parents can not only tolerate but can trust their kids to! And I don't care if everyone else fights me the whole way, as long as it eventually gets done."

Betty clicks her tongue. "Oh, Nathaniel..."

Oh, no. Oh, nonono. Not the sad eyes and the tender utterance of the nickname only she's allowed to use. Uh-uh.

"I didn't say any of that to make you feel sorry for me. I don't need your pity. It would be nice to have your support, but whatever."

I dump the rest of the coffee that's only upsetting my stomach and push away from the counter. What I need right now is to get out of here. Since we're expecting our first big snow of the year this week, it would be a good time to have snow tires installed on both cars. That should take all morning, at least. Then I have some gutters to clean. I stride to the garage door and yank it open.

"You do have my support. Always," Betty says to my back.

I pause, then say, "It sure as hell doesn't feel like it," before exiting, careful not to slam the door and wake the baby.

* * *

THIS GUTTER JUNK perfectly reflects my attitude: stinky, sour, soggy, and overdue for disposal. I wish someone could scoop my crappy mood from my head and dump it on the compost heap.

While I'm on my last stretch of gutter, close to the downspout on the back of the house, the back door opens, and Betty steps out. As petty as it is, I pretend to ignore her and continue dropping handfuls of leaves, acorns, oak pollen, and other detritus into the wheelbarrow below me, then grab more in my clumsy, gloved hands.

"You shouldn't use the ladder alone," she says, setting the baby monitor on the back patio table so we can hear if Georgia stirs from her nap. Then she crosses the grass to hold the base of the ladder for me.

"I'm fine," I mumble. "Almost done."

She gazes up at me for a while before saying, "You know, I had no idea things were so bad for you at work. I ask you every night how your day is, and you say, 'Fine,' then turn all your attention to Georgia."

"I was starting to annoy myself, saying the same things every day about that... that asshole," I explain, descending the rungs and returning to the ground.

She steps back from the ladder and grabs the rake resting against the house. "I'm here for you, though. You used to tell me everything." She picks up the remnants of the gutter garbage in the grass, the stuff that missed the wheelbarrow, and flings it on top of the stuff I've already deposited. "I thought you guys were getting along better, since I hadn't heard anything about him in weeks. And you've always made the problems between the two of you sound like a petty personality clash."

"Some days, it feels like it is. Then I witness him botch yet another encounter with a patient or a parent, and I'm reminded it has nothing to do with liking or disliking the guy. It's better that I *don't* like him. Because it would be hard to be as tough as I need to be with him if he were likable."

"I wish you would have said something sooner."

For the first time since she's joined me, I stop what I'm doing and look her fully in the eye. "Why? What would you do about it? Besides worry."

"I don't know. Probably nothing. But I'd still want to know. Because we... we're supposed to be a team. We used to be."

I consider that for a few seconds, then lift the handles of the wheelbarrow and push it toward the compost heap. "We still are," I say confidently.

She follows me. "No, we're not. You're withdrawn, and I'm paranoid. It's all going downhill so fast."

Neither of us says anything more as I empty the wheelbarrow into the compost heap. Nor do we speak while she grabs the rake, and I take down the ladder, collapse it to its storage size, and carry it back to the garage, where we store the yard tools in their proper places. The silence prevails as we wash our hands at the kitchen sink and make our way down the hallway into the bedroom. I shed my dirty clothes and strip down to my underwear.

Finally, I say, "Close the door," so our voices won't carry down the hall and wake Georgia.

Betty grants my request, but before I can say anything, she cuts in. "I'm sorry. About everything. Including the stuff that's not my fault. I'm sorry you're going through it. I'm sorry about your parents and the stuff at work. And I'm sorry that I'm adding to your stress, because I can't seem to recover from the one part of this nightmare that directly involves me."

I put my hands on my hips and look down at the floor,

sensing there's more, despite her long pause, and not wanting to interrupt her train of thought.

Sure enough, she continues, "But you have to stop trying to deal with all of this alone. You have to *talk* to me, even when you don't want to. Or when you feel like I might already know what you're going to say. Because chances are, I don't. And when you don't talk, I fill in the blanks—usually with the wrong information."

"So, everything is *my* fault?"

"Absolutely not. That's not what I'm saying. If anything, I'm saying the opposite. It's my fault for falling to pieces and becoming the type of person you feel like you need to shelter." She walks closer to me and picks a fleck of dried leaf from my hair. "I need you to lean on me more. You can't do it all. You're going to have a nervous breakdown."

When I say nothing to that, because I'm afraid she may be right, she murmurs at my chest, "You know, we joke about how miserable it was when you were Frank, and we spent every weekend in bookstores and libraries, but I'm starting to look back on those times more fondly. We made it fun."

I contemplate that for a few seconds, then finally say, "That was a departure from real life, though. And it was an absurd situation."

She looks into my face. "It was real to us. We were living it, no matter how bizarre it was."

"You want me to dress like a hipster and act like a smug douche on the weekends again? Is that what will fix this?" I smile slightly and pull her against me. "Bring me my phone. I'll order a pair of those glasses, some sweet skinny jeans and flannel shirts, plus a few scarves—don't forget the scarves..."

"Stop." Her lips twitch upward.

"Georgia will be confused at first, but babies are adaptable.

Hmm... how would Frank act around a baby? Aloof? Not sure I could pull that one off."

When her shoulders shake with suppressed laughter, I'm encouraged to continue.

"Maybe we can call Frankie and get her in on it, have her check in to verbally abuse us every so often, really take us back there."

"You're being ridiculous, Nathaniel."

"But you're smiling."

"Because you're a dork."

"A tired dork."

"Me too." She looks at me through her lashes. "I hate when we fight."

"Real couples fight. And it's not like we were arguing about what color to paint the living room."

"I keep telling you, gray would look amazing."

"Too dark!"

She narrows her eyes in a mock glare.

I kiss her knuckles.

Suddenly serious again, she states quietly, "This is the first time you've touched me in here in months." She tilts down her chin, so there's no mistaking her meaning.

I close my eyes then offer up as a lame defense, "You've been on pelvic rest."

"That's been over for a while, and you know it."

"Okay, but..." I tuck a piece of her hair behind her ear. "You haven't seemed... interested—and that's totally okay!"

"Because you don't want to have sex with me anyway." Her small voice chips off a piece of my heart.

"That's not true. At all. I didn't want to rush you or make you feel bad about not being able to—at first—then not being into it."

"It feels like *you're* the one not into it."

"Betts—"

"Don't 'Betts' me. Please." She raises her eyes but sits on the foot of the bed, turning her back to me. "I have felt so ugly and undesirable and... and... gross. Like you can't look at me without seeing... that."

I sit next to her and grip her shoulders, looking around them to see her face. "I swear, it's nothing like that."

"It feels like... like I'm losing you. I lost our baby, and now I'm losing you."

Before her emotions can overwhelm her, I whisper, "Never." I kiss her neck. When she turns to face me, I take her face in my hands and search her eyes. "When I look at you, I see the woman I love. The only woman I love. My partner in life. My best friend. Strong, smart, funny, no-nonsense, sexy, beautiful you."

She blushes.

"And I want you so bad right now, but... I smell like a rotting compost heap."

Her laughter shakes loose a tear that I blot from her face with the back of my hand. She pulls away from me and stands but immediately grabs one of my hands and pulls on it, moving in the direction of the bathroom. "Let's get you cleaned up then."

I gladly let her lead the way.

18

PLAY NICE

No matter how off-base (I hope?) Betty's suspicions are about Lynette's feelings for me, seeing my friend at work today will still be awkward. After all, I *did* catch her drunk ass in my kitchen. And I *did* see her nipples. (Yes, I looked! Duh! They were right there! I may read chick lit, but I'm still a heterosexual male. Our eyes have nipple-lock.)

But I'm determined for it to be business as usual. I'm going to pretend like Saturday night never happened. None of it. That's for the best, all-around.

Unfortunately, Janet corners me in the staff room before the morning meeting and lets me know that's not going to be possible. "On the way home Saturday night, Lynette told me what happened in your kitchen."

"Nothing happened," I insist, rinsing out my travel mug.

"She's mortified."

I turn off the water. "It's embarrassing to trip in front of someone else. It happens, though. No biggie."

"She said Betty walked in and thought you guys were... you know. She said Betty was piiiiissed."

Since my co-worker looks inordinately gleeful about that, I

say firmly while pulling a paper towel from the dispenser above the sink, "Betty knows nothing inappropriate was going on, and she's over it."

"You should definitely tell Lynette that. She's freaking out."

"How about since I just told you, *you* tell Lynette?" I wipe the water droplets from the inside of my mug with a paper towel and smile tightly.

"I think she'd rather hear it from you. That way, she'll know everything really is okay. But don't tell her I told you."

Tossing the paper towel into the trash can, I sigh, "What is this, high school?"

"She didn't want you to know she'd told anyone else. Especially since she asked you to show her if you were going commando under your costume." She glances down at my crotch, and I reflexively move my hand and coffee mug in front of it.

"She didn't ask me to show her my junk; she asked me to show her my underwear, to prove I was wearing it."

"What's the difference?"

"If it had been the other way around, I would have been decidedly uncomfortable. The way it went down, it was silly. Anyway, I refused, so it's irrelevant."

"Fine. Sheesh. You don't have to get all defensive about it."

"I'm not. I'm trying to nip this out-of-control story in the bud, because I can tell this has the potential to get stupid in a hurry. Its highly unreliable narrator was drunk at the time, tripped in her ridiculous platform shoes, and spilled some beer on herself. I caught her and was checking to make sure her ankle wasn't sprained or broken when Betty came in and saw us close together, alone, with Lynette's wig all crooked, and her wet shirt showing... some things. In the heat of the moment, Betty misinterpreted what was going on, but everything's been sorted out since. Questions?"

She narrows her eyes at me. "Yeah. Remember when you used to be nice?"

I throw my hands in the air. "I *am* nice!"

"No, you're not. You're a crabby jerk."

And there goes all my hard work of the past few weeks. Wellness Week? What's that?

She spins away from me and flounces into a chair, pulling out her phone and glaring at it while she waits for everyone else to arrive for the meeting.

I lower myself into the seat directly in front of her, sitting sideways and draping my arm over the back of the chair. "Listen. I'm sorry. I'm glad you told me how upset Lynette is, so I can talk to her, and we can all forget about it."

"You're welcome."

"And I'm sorry I'm a crabby jerk. I'm trying to be better about that."

"So far today, fail."

I can't help but laugh at the accuracy of her assessment. "I deserve that. Apology accepted?"

She looks up from her phone and smiles. "I guess. Nobody can stay mad at you, you know. You have that face..."

I wish that were true.

* * *

LYNETTE DOES a passable job of avoiding me for most of the morning, but when we nearly bump into each other as I'm leaving an exam room after an appointment and she's walking back to the front desk, I snag her arm. And pull her out of traffic in the hallway.

"Hey."

She looks down and edges away. I follow her, step for step.

"Stop," I tell her. "I just wanted to say—it's okay."

She laughs nervously. "What are you talking about?"

I grin. "Oh, I see. Good. Yeah. Let's forget the whole thing."

Her cheeks redden. "Except the part where Betty hates me. Because that won't be forgotten."

"Betty doesn't hate you."

"She—"

"She was mad in the moment. But she's fine now." *LIAR!!!!*

"Are you sure?"

"Yes. We talked about it. At length. Trust me."

Looking like she's about to cry, she says, "I'm soooo sorry. It's..." She pauses as Mary-Kate and a patient and parent walk by, then nods toward the staff room. "You mind stepping in there?"

I have to admit, despite my insistence that nothing has happened, is happening, or will ever happen between the two of us, being alone with her gives me pause like it never did before the party.

"Uh..."

"Only for a second," she promises. "I don't care if someone walks in while we're talking, but I don't want any kids or parents to hear us."

I signal my agreement by ducking into the staff room behind her.

She hops onto the counter next to the sink and swings her legs. "Okay. Here's the thing. I was drunk."

"Yes. We've established this."

"I was drunk before I ever got to your house. I had to *get* drunk to make myself go to the party at all." When I tilt my head, she says, "Never mind. I wanted you to know that I didn't get smashed at your party, if that makes any difference."

"Okay."

"I'm—" She stops and grips the edge of the counter. "I'm

kind of a mess right now. In general. There's something—
someone—who's sort of doing my head in."

Heart pounding, stomach churning, I rush to say, "You
don't have to explain anything to me."

"I feel like I do, though."

"Nope. I needed to tell you not to worry about what
happened Saturday night in the kitchen. Now, we're good."

She smiles sadly. "Oh. Great. That *is* a relief. I like Betty. I
would never—" She stops and takes a huge breath. "I really did
just trip."

"I know. We both know."

Hopping down from the counter, she dusts off her hands.
"Excellent."

"I think so." I walk to the door, but she calls my name to
stop me.

Facing her, I raise my eyebrows expectantly.

"Are we still dressing like Mario and Princess Peach on
Wednesday? For Halloween?"

My gut sinks, especially when I notice how hopeful she
looks while she waits for my answer, which unfortunately has
to be, "That's probably not a great idea."

Her face falls. "Oh. I see. Betty's *not* okay with me, still. I
get it."

"No! She's—" I sigh, not sure where to go from here. It's
obviously important to Betty that I preserve our privacy and
not say too much, but my need to fix *this* is seriously at odds
with that goal. Finally, I simply say, "It's too soon, that's all.
She's a bit sensitive."

Lynette nods at her feet. "That's... Well, that's fair."

"Sorry. If *you* want to be Mario, I can bring my costume
tomorrow. I'll pick something else."

She laughs at first but points at me. "You know, I might

take you up on that. I'm not in the mood to think any more about Halloween costumes."

"It's a deal." I jab my thumb over my shoulder. "Well, I better get back to it."

"Yeah. Of course." She takes a deep breath. "Thanks, Nate. You're... Well, you're one of a kind."

I laugh off her compliment, which seems like more than a casual remark. "There's at least one person who's mighty glad of that. And speaking of, he's waiting for me. If Dr. Dou— Dan arrives in an exam room before me, he starts without me, which can be disastrous."

She waves me off. "Get back to work, you slacker."

19

IN THE DOGHOUSE

IN CASE YOU THINK I'VE FORGOTTEN ABOUT MY EFFED-UP extended family in all of this, don't worry. They're still hanging on the periphery, waiting to pop up when it's least convenient, to add a few more complications into my already complicated mess of a life.

As a matter of fact, I have a dinner date with my dad tonight, but I couldn't face another meal where I count his beers while half-listening to him alternate between some version of "I'm fine" and "I have no reason to live anymore," so I turned it into a wider invitation, including Betty and Georgia. This way, Dad will get to see his granddaughter and daughter-in-law, and Betty will see that I really am hanging out with my dad once a week.

Yes, I went there. Because she may say she trusts me, but someone who trusts someone else doesn't mention—repeatedly—that she may be dumb for trusting that person. Nor does she have such specific examples of when I may be lying to her. "Jogging," "working late," and "meeting up with your dad" may as well have been in sarcastic air quotes when she said them after the Halloween party. Now every time I do one of those things, I realize at least a tiny part of her is wondering. And we can't have that.

Plus, Dad needs to start moderating his behavior. It's natural to go off the rails when your wife of nearly four decades leaves you and has a guy younger than either of your sons waiting to take your place. However, at some point, you have to get on with your life. Or at least confine your craziest behavior to the privacy of your own home. Getting drunk at The Cheesehead and booming about "That bitch!" week after week is unacceptable. He won't pull that crap around Betty or Georgia.

I hope.

Unfortunately, I'm running late, which means I'm rushing around the clinic to close out my day and get out the door. Moving with urgency as the end of the day approaches always alerts Dr. Douche to slow down, pile more work on me, or force me to talk to him. Or all of the above, like tonight.

"Yo, Nate!" he calls as we pass in the hallway about twenty minutes after our last, excruciating appointment, where yet again I almost had to physically insert myself between him and a dad. Turns out, tone is important when you're pointing out a child's nervous tics, some of which are commonly associated with autism. It's not that my colleague was wrong to inquire when he noticed them, but as usual, his blunt, accusatory delivery put the parent immediately on the defensive. I stepped in and directed Dr. Douche's attention to the boy's chart, which contained a note about a previous screening for spectrum disorders that yielded a negative diagnosis.

Now, without slowing, I reply, "What's up?"

He does a U-turn and catches up to me, trailing on my heels like an annoying little brother. "Did you notice the jars of tongue depressors and cotton balls are getting low in some of the exam rooms?"

"Can't say I did," I say, logging onto a computer at the nurse's station. When I spy the time in the bottom right corner of the display, I nearly groan out loud. But that will only antagonize him. On the counter next to me, I slap the list of the day's specialist referrals to enter before I can leave.

"Well, they are," he says, resting his hip against the counter and crossing his arms over his chest. "And I was thinking—"

"Lynette's still around here somewhere."

"Nah. She left a while ago. Had a hot date, or something."

I snort at that. "Right. Well, track down Mary-Kate or Janet. They're supposed to keep up with that stuff."

"Everyone's gone. Nobody here but us guys."

Typing as fast as I can, I look back and forth from the list to the screen. "Those supplies are in the closet, where we keep everything else. Feel free to top off the jars."

He chuckles. "Good one, Nate." When he pats me on the shoulder, it's hard enough to knock my hands from the keys, throwing off my stroke and causing me to type a bunch of gibberish.

Sighing, I hit "backspace" about ten times and re-enter the text so it no longer reads, "Patient exhibits symptoms of chronic oinkoingyt," which sounds like a disease common to pigs in the Ukraine.

"It's my and Veronica's anniversary."

"Happy anniversary."

"Thanks. But I'm late to meet her for dinner, so... I gotta get a move on. No time to play nurse, if you get my drift."

"Uh-huh. Well, I'll make sure someone takes care of it first thing in the morning. Or you can mention it in the staff meeting."

"It'll only take a minute to do it now, though. Why wait?"

I type the last entry and log off the computer, then cross to the cabinet where we file each day's referrals. Over the metallic slide and clank of the drawer, I say, "Because I have somewhere to be too."

"Five minutes isn't going to kill you."

Yeah, well, Betty might if I leave her alone with my dad.

"In the time it's taken for you to argue with me about this, you could have done it," he points out, pushing against the back staff door. "Make sure you do it before you leave, m'kay? I'll be here early tomorrow, and I'll be checking to make sure we're all good to go."

"But I—"

"Good night!"

The door bangs behind him. I spend a few precious seconds considering my options and finally decide to simply do what the guy wants, in the interest of playing nice and ensuring he can never accuse me of being uncooperative. And because I don't want to hear him bitch about it in the morning if the stupid jars haven't been refilled by the time he gets in.

Despite sprinting through the exam rooms like my life depends on restocking the tongue depressors and cotton balls in record time, I'm twenty minutes behind schedule when I set the building alarm and rush from the clinic.

Halfway home, I receive a text from Betty. *Where are you?*

I don't text while driving, but I have no problem speeding to get to my destination so I can reply to a text I've received while driving. Something tells me that's not quite what law enforcement has in mind, but whatever. They can't have everything. Jerking the car to a stop in the driveway, I grab my phone and thumb, *Be right there. Running late. See you in 30.*

Minutes??? We're waiting for you!

Don't. Go ahead and order. I'll have the veggie burger. XO

I vault from the car and burst into the house, shedding clothes and stuffing them into the washer, then racing naked through the house to the master bathroom, where I hop in the shower without waiting for the water to heat up.

I sing an amazing soprano rendition of "Ave Maria" as the cold water hits my babymaker, adding a few English lyrics I'm pretty sure were never in the original song about Jesus' mother.

Heart pounding, I lather and rinse in the bare minimum amount of time it would take for me to get clean. The water has just reached the perfect temperature when I yank the handle to the "off" position and jump, shivering, onto the bath mat to scrub myself dry with the same towel I used yesterday, ignoring the faintly mildewy scent it holds when I rub it against my hair as I rush into the bedroom and throw open the closet.

I yank jeans from a shelf and spin to the dresser to pull an undershirt, boxer briefs, socks, and a sweater from its drawers. Keeping Betty waiting alone to entertain a toddler and a father-in-law who sometimes acts like a toddler isn't going to do much to repair my image.

"Shitshitshitshitshit," I hiss.

Reba waddles into the bedroom doorway as I'm ready to exit the room. "Move it, Rebes," I say, keeping my tone light so the command at least doesn't sound rude.

She ignores it, anyway, stretching with her butt in the air and her head closer to the floor than it already normally is. I'd step over her, but experience has shown she'll choose that moment to stand at her full height, and I'll go tripping down the hallway. It's better to simply wait.

She yawns, farts, and rises.

"Nice. Do you mind moving now?"

Continuing her doggy calisthenics, she shakes herself from her ears to her stubby tail, then whines and leads me down the hall.

"Yeah, yeah. Of course, you need to go out. And this will be one of your leisurely shits, I'm sure, because I'M IN A HURRY!" I pull open the back door and usher her outside with a sweep of my arm, mumbling about her possibly being in cahoots with a certain pediatrician.

While she does her business, I pace, dashing off another text to Betty. *Almost out the door. Reba's crapping.*

Your dad's in the bathroom. Crying. Is he always like this?

Yes.

Should I get him another beer or cut him off?

Cut him off. He'll get worse, the more he drinks.

Great. Get your ass here.

I'm trying!

Through the back door glass, I see Reba moseying her way toward the house, so I swing open the door. "Good girl! C'mon! You can do it. A little faster..."

Nothin'.

I tap my toe and watch my slow-motion dog approach me on her stubby legs like she's shooting a romantic dog food commercial. I'm seriously in the dog *house* with my wife—again —and the Corgi ain't helping matters.

Finally, she makes it up the back steps and through the door. I rub her between the ears and lob her a biscuit from the tin in the pantry. "No parties while we're out. We won't be late."

I lock the back door, rush through the house to the front door, lock the knob from the inside, then pull it closed. When I reach in my pocket for my keys to lock the deadbolt, there's nothing to grasp.

"No. Nonononono!" I bang my forehead against the green-painted panel next to the tiny stained-glass window in the center of the door. My keys and wallet are still inside, possibly in my scrubs... in the washer, which I thankfully forgot to start after my shower. But still. My stuff is in *there*, and I'm out *here*. Locked out.

Not for the first time, I rue taking out that doggy door. I would have no reservations crawling through that thing right now. (With my luck, though, I'd get stuck.)

At least I still have my phone.

Locked out of house.

You're joking.

I wish.

Call your brother.

Good idea.

I dial Nick's cell number, which goes straight to voicemail. Seriously? Is it legal for a surgeon to not be reachable 24/7? I dial Heidi's cell. She answers right before I despair that she never will.

"Hello?" she says breathlessly.

"Heidi? Hey. It's Nate."

"Nate…"

"Not a bad time, I hope."

"Considering your brother left me home alone with two wound-up boys so he could have a nice, quiet dinner with you and your dad tonight, it's not what I'd call a *good* time."

I swallow. "Wh-wha…? Hm. Well. That wasn't very nice of him. Shoot. I, uh… The thing is, I've locked myself out of the house—"

"How the heck did you do that?"

"Long story. And I'm supposed to be at The Cheesehead, oh… forever ago, so I was hoping Nick could bring the spare key he has and save my bacon."

"Why didn't you call *his* cell?"

"I did. It went straight to voicemail. Phone must be dead. Or something."

"I wish I could help you, Nate, but Nick's the one with

your key. And anyway, you could break in by the time I chase the boys down, load them in the SUV, and get to your house."

"Yeah. I get it. No, don't worry. I'll figure out something else. Um, good luck with the rest of your evening."

"Whatever. Massi! Get down from there! Oh, my gosh!"

She hangs up in my ear after deafening it.

Quickly, I call Betty. "Hello?" If murder has a voice, it's hers.

"Hey. Uh, Nick's not there, is he?" I ask, cringing while I anticipate her answer.

"NO! Why would I tell you to call him to unlock our door, if he was sitting right here? Are you drunk, Nathaniel?"

"Just checking. I did call Nick, but his phone went straight to voicemail, so I called Heidi. He told her he was having dinner with Dad and me. She's home alone with the boys, and none too pleased about it."

"Oh, gosh." Her voice softens marginally but still holds an edge of annoyance. "I hope he's okay. Maybe he was in an accident."

Since I hadn't considered that, it makes me pause. For a second. But I remember the conversation in the summer, in his front yard, and instantly dismiss it as unlikely. "He's hiding. Lying about where he is, because having dinner with Dad and me is more noble and acceptable—slightly—than sitting in a bar watching Monday Night Football."

"For real? That's shitty."

"Are you surprised, though?"

"I guess not. So, what does this mean for us tonight? Are you going to get here, or what?"

"I don't... Wait!" I run to my car and try the driver's door. Sure enough, I forgot to lock the car in my haste to get into the house and shower. "Eureka!"

"You did not say that."

I hit the button to raise the garage door and let myself into the house. Reba lifts her head from her position on the couch, her blinks conveying her utter boredom at my frantic state.

"I blame you," I grumble at her on my way past.

"Excuse me?"

"I was talking to Reba," I quickly explain.

No need to make things worse than they already are.

In the laundry room, I reach into the washer and pull out my scrubs bottoms, jabbing my hand into their pockets to retrieve my keys and wallet. "I'm on my way for real this time. And I'm so, so, so, so, so sorry."

"Save it."

"Okay. I'll, uh, make it up to you later?"

"I accept chocolate, shoes, and jewelry."

"I was thinking about something more... romantic."

"Wine works, too. Get. Here."

20

DREADSGIVING

EVERYONE SEEMS TO HAVE HAD THE SAME IDEA WE'VE HAD on this unseasonably melty Saturday afternoon. The park is packed with parents who have decided their Halloween-candy-fueled kids need some fresh air and exercise. The wind is still cold, but the temperature is above freezing, and the sun is trying to peek from behind the clouds. That's all the invitation Wisconsinites require in early November.

After waiting several minutes for a toddler swing, I display zero shame running for the one that's just opened up. Betty follows closely with a bundled Georgia, whose snowsuit-encased legs fit snugly through the holes in the seat.

"Ten minutes, George," I warn her as I pull back on the swing. "Others are waiting their turns." I let go, and she shriek-giggles at the flying sensation.

We delight in her joy for a while, then Betty turns to me and says, "I'm sorry I was so irritated at you for being late to dinner with your dad."

Her out-of-the-blue apology five days after the fact surprises me, but I reply truthfully, "I don't blame you for being annoyed."

"I do. It's been bothering me all week. I tell you we're a team, but I act all put out when you need me to pick up the slack."

"That was some pretty big slack."

"It shouldn't matter."

I shoot her a cheesy smile between pushes. "Please. Don't worry about it."

"He was scaring me. I've never seen him like that before. I've never seen anyone like that before. And you say that's how he is every week?"

"From what you've described, you got the subdued version." Noticing Georgia's getting too high from my frequent nudges, I step back and let her coast, tucking my hands in my coat pockets to give them some relief from the biting breeze. "He didn't shout any obscenities or bang his fist on the table, did he?"

"No! Oh, my gosh. I would have died."

"And he never put his head down on the table and sobbed, right?"

"No! He did get weepy. That's when he excused himself to the bathroom."

"I'm sure he didn't want you to see him that way."

"But I already had! It was awful."

"Consider yourself lucky. Sounds like he was on his best behavior for you."

Georgia kicks her feet when her swing stops providing enough of a thrill for her liking. Betty takes up the pushing. "I had no idea. I can't believe you subject yourself to that once a week."

"He's my dad."

"He's Nick's dad, too, but you don't see *him* providing a shoulder for your dad to cry on."

I scrunch my neck down into my scarf. "Nick and Dad

don't have that sort of relationship. They're all about doing manly things together, things that don't require the sharing of feelings, things that lend themselves more to competition and opportunities to make each other proud or humiliate one another. That's how it's always been."

"Doesn't stop Nick from *pretending* he's participating in the emotional support you're offering now. I can't believe him! Lying to Heidi like that…"

"It's cute that you're so shocked and outraged."

"Don't patronize me, Nathaniel."

I wink at her. "I don't know if you've noticed this about my older brother, but he's an a-hole. Nicer than he used to be, and every once in a while he does or says something to redeem himself—but still an a-hole."

She laughs. "I definitely got the better brother."

"Thanks." I glance over my shoulder at the line of toddlers on parents' laps. The two kids who were swinging before we got our turn are still going strong next to us, their dads too wrapped up in their talk about football to notice—or care—that others are waiting.

Speaking of a-holes…

At the risk of provoking a serious tantrum, I step forward and grab hold of Georgia's seat back the next time she swings toward us. Sure enough, she squawks and bucks when the apparatus stops. Ignoring her protests, I lift her, turn her around to face me, and say near her ear, "C'mon. Let's go on the slide."

She head-butts me in reply.

Clenching my teeth, I carry her toward the toddler climbing area, Betty laughing behind us.

When she catches up to us, she asks. "Are you okay? Where'd she get you?"

"I'm fine." I detour to a bench, where I balance the baby

on my knee and bounce her a couple of times to try to calm her, then examine her forehead, where it met my cheekbone. There's a red smudge but no bump. "You gotta be careful, baby girl."

She does her best to continue to show me her tonsils, so I grab her hands and jounce her harder and faster. "Hang on! Whoa, horsey! Oh, my gosh! It's out of control!"

She slides back and forth on my knee, her cries soon merging with tearful giggles.

Betty chuckles next to us. "You're going to scramble her brains!"

The "horse" canters, then trots, then slows to a walk. "Whoa," I say, stopping it altogether. "Whew. That was some ride."

Betty reaches over with a tissue and wipes snot and tears from the baby's face.

"Hawsey!" Georgia digs her spurs into my legs.

"Horsey's tired," I say, petting my thigh and nickering. "Good horsey."

She pats it, too.

"Slide?" I ask her.

"Hawsey!"

"Slide," I insist, standing and "flying" her to the playset before she can get too bent out of shape about the end of horsey time.

I plunk her down at my shoulders' height on the unoccupied slide, keeping a grip on her waist and zooming her down the chute. At the bottom, I lift her and swing her into the air in a wide arc, then back against my chest.

"Daddy!" she screeches, making me laugh. I hold her close while I catch my breath and wait for some bigger kids to take their turns. Then I repeat the process a couple more times before realizing how physically exhausting it is and needing a more prolonged break.

We return to the bench, where Betty's chosen to stay and watch us from afar. I drop Georgia into her mother's lap and collapse onto the seat, hooking my elbows over the cold metal backrest to open my airways.

"You two are nuts," Betty declares affectionately, kissing Georgia's rosy cheeks and pulling her knit hat more fully over her ears.

Before I have enough breath to confirm or deny the accusation, she asks, "Hey. Out of curiosity, on a scale of one to catastrophic, how bad is your parents' Thanksgiving plan?"

Switching gears, I squint into the overcast glare and tuck my chin toward my chest. "Oh, you mean where we all still get together like nothing's happened, *except* Ry-Guy will be there as a constant reminder that we're effed up beyond all recognition?"

"Yes, that plan."

"Your scale doesn't go high enough."

"Dang it. That's what I thought."

"Don't worry about it."

"I'm not, because I'm thinking we should take a vacation at that time and skip it altogether." She wraps her arms around the baby and squeezes her. "Maybe... Jamaica?"

"Don't tease me, woman, with your impossible fantasies."

"Why is it impossible? Let's do it."

"I can't do that to my dad. Plus, if I'm not there to try to keep the peace..." I shudder. "I don't want to imagine what we'd come back to."

She sighs. "Fine. Be all noble and good."

I laugh. "Someone has to *try*. And nobody else is volunteering for the job in my family right now, so..."

"Maybe if my parents accept your parents' invitation,

everyone will play nice, because there will be two people there who normally aren't."

I groan at the idea of more of my family's dysfunction on display for Kitty and Witt. "Do we have to pass along that invitation to your mom and Witt? Can't we spend Thanksgiving with my family and Christmas with yours and ruin both holidays, like normal people?"

"Or we can get it over with on Thanksgiving and go to Jamaica for Christmas," she proposes.

"Sold."

She grins and claps Georgia's hands. "Yay! And..." She hesitates.

I wait.

"Maybe we can go, just the two of us?"

Snorting, I say, "And do what with George? Board her at a kennel? Have the neighbors come by twice a day and check on her?"

She pushes on my shoulder. "No! Leave her with family. Your brother. My parents. Your mom or dad. I don't know! I haven't thought that far ahead. I'm brainstorming here."

"Right. Well, none of those options seem viable. Heidi would be the one stuck with all the extra work, and she'll be about to burst by then. We can't do that to her. Your parents? Ha. Dad? No way. And my mom? I don't think a baby fits into her current lifestyle." I tap Georgia's nose. "Plus, a week away from George? I don't know..."

"It would be hard," she concedes, then tacks on quietly, toward her lap, "but maybe we need it."

I study her profile for a while, seriously considering her proposition. "Maybe," I finally say. "Let's see how Thanksgiving goes."

She looks up at me and smiles. "Really?"

"Yeah. It *would* be nice."

Leaning over, she rests her head on my shoulder and sighs contentedly while Georgia's palms slap against her arms. "I think so, too. Really nice."

* * *

WHAT AM I THANKFUL FOR? First, that it was a short week at work. I never used to care much about short work weeks or long weekends; now I live for them. I'm also thankful I'm still walking free, having resisted the urge to kill a certain man-tanned pediatrician. After all, I figure if I'm patient enough, one of the parents will do it for me. Why should I get my hands dirty? And finally, I'm thankful that things seem to be stabilizing at home and that I'm one month closer to being on a white sand beach with my wife.

Until then, my plan is to pretend like everything's hunky dory on all fronts, because that's what you do at this time of year. You gush about how wonderful everything is and how blessed you are. Then you use the following Christmas season to fill the voids you've been in denial about for the past month with material goods. Exactly like God intended.

On Turkey Day, I'm bent over, trying to organize the myriad pots, pans, foil-covered dishes, and small appliances in the back of my car and prioritize their transfer inside Nick's house when someone grabs my hips from behind and grinds his crotch against my butt.

He laughs and says, "Hi, I'm Ryan. Nice to meet you."

"Cut it out," I growl at my brother, "and help me carry this stuff in. Mom has the turkey going already, right?" I hand back the heavy pan of dressing that will be cooked separate from the stuff in the bird and pull forward the dish of deviled eggs that slid against the backseat during the short drive from my house to his.

"Bro, I don't know! This is your show."

"Nothing about this is my show, Dr. Seuss. I'm merely the caterer. In fact, I would prefer to be at my house right now, pretending today is a random mercy day away from Dr. Douche. So shut up and schlep."

With both of us providing transport, it only takes a couple of trips to get all the food inside. On my way to the kitchen, I survey my surroundings, and the other people gathered. Suddenly, being busy in the kitchen all day doesn't seem so bad. At least I don't have to make awkward small-talk.

Betty joins me in front of the oven after greeting her parents. "Everything okay in here? Anything still need to be carried in from the car?"

"No. Nick and I got it. Everything's under control, I think. Oh, shoot. Where are the potatoes? I already had them soaking in salty water in a stock pot..."

She points to the stove. "Uh... would that be them?"

I sigh, and my shoulders slump.

"Relax. This is a family dinner."

"Yeah. Family. Plus one."

"Well, if it makes you feel better, your dad seems fine."

"He's already drunk, isn't he?"

She winces. "Maybe. But he's happy-drunk, as opposed to The Cheesehead-drunk."

I continue to fuss over the food, plugging in the slow cooker that's holding my sweet potato casserole and keeping it warm. "Awesome."

"It's going to be okay. Your parents have promised to be on their best behavior—"

"Not a meaningful promise, considering."

I shove the green bean casserole in the top oven to get it out of the way, momentarily. If showing up without it wouldn't have caused a mutiny, I would have skipped making it. Disgusting.

Pressing the button to turn on the light in the bottom oven, I inspect the turkey, which looks like it could use some attention. "Mom!" I bellow. "When's the last time you basted this thing?"

Mom sashays into the kitchen. "Well, Happy Thanksgiving to you, too, Nathan," she replies with a kiss on my cheek. She opens the oven door and grabs the baster from the nearby counter. While she sucks the drippings from the pan and squirts them over the curve of the bird, she smiles and glances at the other dishes around us. "Mmm... looks good. You've outdone yourself, as usual."

It's all I can do not to laugh at the sight of her. Or cry. Or something. Dressed in black from her suede ankle boots to her skinny jeans to her high-collared, fitted, square-shouldered shirt (I guess that's what you'd call that thing, with its random buckles and decorative straps), she looks like a cross between the Dread Pirate Roberts and Janet Jackson during her "Rhythm Nation" days of yore. The only thing missing is headgear.

Then again, her hair makes up for the lack of hat. The curls that usually fall in tamed waves stand at attention all around her head, like Medusa's snakes. Only wilder.

I resist laughing by asking her the second-most pressing question on my mind, after *"What hell are you wearing?"* "What time did you start this thing? It doesn't look like it's going to be done in time."

"It'll be fine. We're not on a strict schedule, are we? If we eat slightly later than planned, it's not the end of the—"

I glare at her.

"Okay. Never mind. We're eating at one, whether the bird is cooked or not, apparently."

Before I can say, "As you wish," Betty smacks my chest with the back of her hand but pairs it with a smile. "Lighten up, Nathaniel. It's Thanksgiving."

"Sorry," I mumble, peeking under the covers of my dishes to ascertain what goes in the fridge, what stays out on the counter, and what needs to be cooked or heated. Humming (great, now I have "Rhythm Nation" in my head), I clear some counter space by sliding stuff into the refrigerator, swap the green bean casserole for the stuffing, turn on the oven, and set the timer. "I was hoping the turkey would be done soon so I could use that bottom oven for other things."

"You should have said something," Mom chides. "I would have made the turkey in my roaster to free up the oven."

"I didn't think about it until just now."

"Oh. Well, that's hardly my fault."

"I'm not saying it's anyone's fault, Janet."

"Who's Janet?"

Betty, getting my reference, snorts, but I'm already regretting saying anything, so I wave off Mom's question. "Never mind."

"And actually, it *is* your fault for not thinking ahead."

"Why am I the one who has to think of everything?"

"You have a better idea of the menu, as a whole. I'm only in charge of the turkey."

"Must be nice," I mumble.

Mom closes the oven, returns the baster to the paper towel on the counter, and watches me turn on the burner under the potatoes to bring them to a boil. I scoot the large pot to the side to make sure the burner's working, then re-center the cookware, shaking it gently to jar the potatoes loose from the bottom.

"Are you going to be like this all day?" she asks.

Betty makes a move for the exit, but Mom holds her in place with a raised hand. "It's okay. You don't have to go."

"But I... want to?"

Ignoring their exchange, I answer my mom's question with my own. "Like what? Tense because this giant meal is my responsibility? Yes. Next time, do it yourself. I'm sure Ryan would love to be your sous chef."

She clicks her tongue. "Ah. I see. This isn't about the food at all."

"Please, do not psychoanalyze me today."

So much for being the peacemaker. Is it too late to hop a plane to Jamaica and leave these guys to it?

"You know, it's perfectly understandable for you to feel uncomfortable when faced with evidence of my still-burgeoning sexuality, but—"

"Well, there goes *my* appetite."

"I thought you and your brother could handle this. I thought perhaps my happiness would take precedence over your discomfort."

"Your happiness takes precedence in enough people's lives right now." I stir the quartered potatoes with a wooden spoon. After tapping the excess water from the utensil, I lay it on a rest next to the stove, then make eye contact with my mom for the first time today. For the first time in months, more accurately. "I thought you were happy with Dad."

"Well, I wasn't. Just because you want that to be true doesn't mean it was. Get over it."

I scoff. "Is that what you tell your patients?"

"You're not my patient; you're my son."

"Yeah, I am. And I'm older than your boyfriend."

"You're *acting* about the same age as Georgia—throwing a fit, because you're not getting your way."

Betty steps between us. "Hey. Let's... bring it down a bit,

okay?" She glances nervously through the archway that leads to the dining room, which flows into the living room. The conversation out there is still going strong and loud, and none of us in the kitchen have raised our voices, so I'm not worried about making a scene. I suddenly only care about going on the record.

Gently, I place the lid on the pot of potatoes and step away from the stove, lifting my chin to meet my mother's accusation. Grasping Betty's hand, I weave my fingers through hers and pull her to my side so I can better see Mom when I tell her, "It's rich that you're accusing me of acting like a child, of being only concerned with my own interests, considering the life choices you've recently made. It also proves you don't know anything. That you prefer to be ignorant of the facts, because that's how you sleep at night. I guess. I try not to think about what you do at night, to be honest." I swallow down another wave of nausea and clear my throat.

Betty lets go of my hand and transfers hers to the back of my neck, her palm cool against my searing skin.

"You know how I spend at least one evening of every week?" I ask.

Mom blinks listlessly and sighs, but I don't let her apparent disinterest deter me from continuing.

"I spend it across a table from Dad at The Cheesehead, listening to him vent his misery. Some days, he's so angry at you, I wonder if I should call you and warn you. I worry about your safety. Until I remember it's Dad, and he's all talk. Other nights, he sobs into his beer. Literally. He doesn't say anything, just cries. And sometimes, I get to watch him torture himself with the 'if only's. 'If only I'd been a better husband...' 'If only I'd taken her on more trips...' 'If only I'd told her more often how much I love her...'" I shake my head at my shoes, then look up, chuckling bitterly. "You don't know shit, Mom." More to hide my filling eyes than to check the time, I glance at the clock on the microwave. "Now, if you don't mind, I have a meal to finish cooking, so..."

Without a word, she leaves the kitchen.

"Good," I mumble to myself while I shake the rolls from their bakery bags into a basket. "Go make someone walk the plank. I'll handle everything from here. Flaunt your new boyfriend in front of everyone and try not to think about what a fool you're making of yourself and us."

While I set the strainer in the sink, ready to drain the potatoes as soon as they're fork-tender, Betty follows me around the room with her eyes.

"Stop staring at me."

"I'm proud of you."

"Because I ruined my mom's Thanksgiving? Proud moment for me, too."

"No, because you told her what you needed to say."

"That wasn't the half of it. I'm saving the good stuff for the dinner table."

She laughs. "You joke, but it wasn't easy for you to tell her that stuff about your dad. You're much more comfortable smoothing everything over."

"We'd have an easier time flattening her hair today." I open the oven, turn the stuffing pan sideways, and place the green bean casserole dish next to it, then close the door and bump up the temperature a few degrees.

When the beeping ceases, Betty asks, "Are you okay?"

Before I can answer, Georgia screeches from the other room. Betty ventures halfway into the dining room, to a point where she can see into the living room, then hurries back to tell me, "I'd better go in there. Mom's holding Georgia and staring at her like she's an alien. See? Nobody's mom is perfect."

"I'd settle for normal."

"Me, too—once we figure out what the heck that is." She edges toward the crying. "I'll try to get back soon to help you out in here."

"I've got it. Go rescue our daughter." *And break the cycle of maternal ineptitude that's suddenly one of our saddest family legacies.*

21

HOLIDAY HULLABALOO

BETTY DOESN'T MAKE IT BACK TO THE KITCHEN, BUT SHE sends an ambassador in her stead. Heidi reports for duty as I'm pouring the drained potatoes into a mixing bowl for whipping. My assistant can't get closer than a foot away from any surface in front of her, however, so she's been relegated to arranging the crudités and keeping me company. Which is fine, since cooking isn't her strong suit.

After Heidi stops for the third time and rubs the small of her back, I nudge a bar stool from the island closer to her with my foot.

"Take a load off, mama."

"I'm almost finished here," she answers, gesturing to the jar of olives she's emptying onto the plate.

"You can do that sitting down too, you know."

She takes my advice and perches on the stool, moves her head in a circle on her neck, and closes her eyes.

"You okay?" I ask. She's not that close to her due date (although you wouldn't know it to look at her), but I'm suddenly worried she's in more than the usual seventh gestational month discomfort.

"Just tense, that's all," she murmurs, returning to chasing the olives down a few at a time from the jar. I want to tell her she can drain the liquid and dump them all at once, but micro-managing the relish tray seems a tad over-the-top, even for me.

"Yeah, this whole thing with Mom and Dad is awful. I bet you're wishing it was the year to be with your side of the family."

She smiles sadly. "Maybe. But your mom and dad are doing okay out there. And Ryan's not a bad guy, once you get to know him."

I snort. "I'll pass."

"We've had him and your mom over a couple of times, and—"

"What? Seriously?"

She lifts one shoulder, keeping her eyes down on her work. "Yeah. Your mom wanted to see the boys, and Ryan was with her, so..."

"Wow."

"It's happening, whether you like it or not."

"I choose 'not,' and I don't have to condone it."

"The kids always behave better when other people are around. I needed the break."

I let that statement hang in the air while I whip the pota-toes with an electric hand mixer. When the spuds reach the right consistency, I turn off the device, eject the beaters, and tap them on the side of the mixing bowl. "Do you have a serving dish you want me to transfer these to?"

She points to a cabinet almost too high for me to reach, but the stretch does my tight muscles some good. Returning to the island, I scoop the silky potatoes from one bowl to another, glancing at my sister-in-law through my lashes every once in a while when she sighs or grunts on the other side of the work surface.

She looks... bad, for lack of a better word. And I don't mean that in a superficial, ugh-the-girl-needs-to-be-more-diligent-with-her-skincare-regimen way. She looks unhealthy. Her hair is lank, and her eyes have bluish rings around them. Incidentally, her skin *is* dull, too, and her chin hosts an acne breakout. Unheard of in Heidi Land. And her posture... She's practically lying across the counter. Or she would be if she weren't about a thousand months pregnant and could get closer than she is.

I can't help but repeat my earlier question. "Are you okay?"

She sits straighter on her seat. "Why do you keep asking me that?"

"Because you seem... not okay."

"I'm tired."

"Oh. Well, I guess that's to be expected."

She shakes her head. "It's not only about being pregnant. I'm tired. Of a lot of things." Placing the final olive with its other juiceless friends on the platter, she drops the spoon in the jar with a clang and looks up at me. "I think Nick's having an affair."

I gulp.

"There. I said it out loud," she says, her voice brighter than it's been since she joined me.

I stare down into the mound of starch in the bowl in front of me. Having had that same accusation leveled at me recently, it's horrible to suspect it of anyone else, especially my brother, but I have to admit, it makes sense, in his case. Still, I press, "Uh, what makes you think that?"

She hops from the stool and waddles around the island, placing the pickle and olive jars along the back of the counter by the sink. "Stuff."

"Like?" I check the turkey and baste it some more, not sure

if the sweat popping on my face is from the oven's heat or the topic of conversation. Maybe both.

Leaning her lower back against the counter, she crosses her feet at her ankles and absently rubs her enormous belly. "He's never home, for one thing. He's always 'working late,' or 'hanging with Dad and Nate,' or whatever. And when he *is* home, he putters around the yard, doing everything he can to avoid spending any time with me."

I close the oven and face her, baster aloft. "I'm sure it's not that," I say, not sure at all.

"What other explanation is there? What has he told you?"

Fuuuuuuuuuuuuuuuck. I set down the glorified bulb syringe (a.k.a., "booger sucker") as if it's made of crystal, stare at it, and then turn away to check the green bean casserole and stuffing through the top oven's window. The fried onions on top of the casserole have browned nicely, so I open the tempered glass door and slide the dish from the metal rack, then place it on some waiting hot pads on the counter. While covering it with a towel to trap in the heat, I say, "Nothing."

"Is he with you when he says he is?"

"When does he say he is?"

"When is he with you?"

The answer is *"Never."* I haven't hung out with Nick outside of his own house in ages. I've hardly seen him at all, as a matter of fact, since Halloween. I can't say that, though. Unfortunately, I don't need to say it for Heidi to know it's true.

"See? I knew it. And when he's not home, he turns off his cell phone. If I try to call him about anything, it goes straight to voicemail. What if I went into labor, Nate? What... what if there was an emergency with one of our crazy kids?"

I cross the kitchen to hug her, but her belly stops me several inches from my destination. I pat it, then put my hands on her shoulders, my arms nearly straight to reach them from where I'm standing. "Hey. If anything like that happens, and you can't get in touch with him, you call me. Understood?"

Blinking and sniffling, she nods. "Okay. But that still doesn't tell me where *he* is, what *he's* doing."

I sigh, wishing Nick were in here right now, so I could kick him in the crotch or squirt him in the face with hot turkey juice. "Listen. If you want to know what I think..." I pause, and she waits expectantly, dabbing her eyes, so I continue, "he's probably hanging out at a sports bar, watching the game—whichever sport is in season—and drinking beer."

"He doesn't come home smelling like a bar. And if he was drinking beer in a bar that often, he'd be getting"—she glances down at my midriff—"paunchy." While I try not to take offense at that description (I'm *not* paunchy!), she continues, "He's still as fit as ever, and I'm..." She covers her face with both hands.

"You're beautiful, Heidi Irene Plotzler... er, Bingham." I step to her side so I can wrap my arm around her shoulders and squeeze her to me in a side hug. "You're beautiful, inside and out."

"That's what everyone says to fat, ugly people."

Someone beautiful on the inside wouldn't refer to anyone as "fat and ugly," but I'll cut her some slack, since she's having a moment.

After a few seconds, she lowers her hands. I grab a paper towel from the under-cabinet roll by the sink and hand it to her. While she's mopping her face, I rub her back.

"I didn't want to have another baby," she says at a near-whisper.

I keep rubbing, not wanting to do anything to give away my surprise at this information.

"I was on birth control, and everything! I wanted to focus on Massi and Cruz. And Nick. Lose all that pregnancy weight and be the woman he fell in love with." She swipes under her lashes, inspects the mascara streak on the paper towel, and sniffs. "I didn't feel like myself, still wearing some of my maternity clothes, always so run down and tired, usually asleep by the time Nick came to bed. So, you know, I started to make more of an effort. I got a babysitter to come by three times a week so I could go to the gym. And it was working. I had energy. I could wear some of my normal clothes. I felt pretty. Nick still didn't seem all that into... things, and the co-sleeping wasn't helping, but..."

I try to block out the memory of my brother's version of this same story, conveyed so crudely to me at the baseball game last summer. The last thing I want to do is blurt something like, *"Maybe you should shave your legs more often,"* or anything else that would give away this isn't the first time I'm hearing about the strain in her sex life.

"Then *this* happened." She pats the proof.

I rest my hand on the bump and receive a greeting kick that makes us both smile, albeit sadly.

"It's going to be okay," I tell her.

She nods resolutely, but her face quickly falls. "I don't know. Another boy, Nate. How? How am I—"

"You just will. They won't be babies forever."

"I know. And it's awful that I wish they'd grow up and be gone. That's not me. I wanted a big family. Always have, you know. You and I talked about it all the time. One of the few things we could agree on." She smiles sadly at me, and I tamp down the hundreds of poignant emotions her expression elicits in that one instant.

"Anyway..." I move away from her. "It's okay to be overwhelmed, you know. To be scared. And I'm sure that's all it is with Nick, too. He escapes and turns off his phone, because he's in over his head with you and the boys. And he's not used to that feeling, right? He's normally the guy with all the answers."

"You don't think he's having an affair, then?"

"Definitely not having an affair. Who would cheat on you?"

She shrugs, but I can tell that argument doesn't hold up with someone who feels so inadequate. Unfortunately, I don't have any other reassurances to offer.

I cross to the oven to turn on the light and check on the turkey again, then turn up the heat when I see that annoying little red button still hasn't popped. "Do you have a meat thermometer?"

"Somewhere around here. It would be in a drawer."

I root through a few before I find one. Setting the roasting pan on the stove, I shove the thermometer between the turkey's thigh, above the drumstick, pretending the bird is my brother.

That dodo bird and I are going to have a talk later.

* * *

SINCE I DID all of the cooking, I'm excused from the cleanup effort, but when Betty and I find out the crew consists of one person, Heidi, we exchange pointed looks and say together, "We've got it!"

On my way into the kitchen with a stack of plates, I stop in front of my brother, who's thumbing a text message into his phone for about the fiftieth time today.

"Here. Grab some dishes and make yourself useful," I say, thrusting the dirty dinnerware into his chest and abdomen. His choices are to receive the plates in his arms or drop them on his sparkling real-wood floor. He makes the choice I was betting on.

"Hey! I'm kind of in the middle of something here!"

"Yeah. Cleanup. Put your phone away."

"How do you know I'm not on a consultation?"

"It's Thanksgiving, and a consultation wouldn't put that stupid grin on your face."

I grab more dishes and pile cutlery on top of them, then prod him in the back toward the kitchen. In there, I suggest that Heidi and Betty leave it to the guys and go catch up.

Betty shoots me a semi-panicked expression, since hanging with Heidi isn't her favorite thing to do, but I pretend not to notice. I need to have a heart-to-heart with my brother, and I don't want an audience for this one. There are some things I plan to say that neither of our wives needs to hear.

Heidi smiles. "Okay. If you insist."

"I do. Out."

As soon as the women are gone, Nick groans. "You have no idea what you've done. Look at this mess! We could be throwing the football right now."

Ignoring his childish whining, I return to the dining room and retrieve the glasses. When all of the dishes are lined up on the counter, I open the dishwasher and start loading it after rinsing each item.

"It's not all gonna fit, you know?"

"Duh. We're going to do more than one load. And hand-wash some of this stuff."

"Hand-wash? I haven't done that since... ever."

"I know. You're a spoiled cock."

"Geez."

"Just telling it like it is."

"You've been in a foul mood all day. Get it? *Fowl* mood?" He elbows me in the back, then crosses to the fridge and drops a gallon bag full of white meat into a deep drawer.

Over the sound of the running water, I say, "I'm in a foul

mood, because a couple of people in my family seem to have lost their minds."

"Who? It seems to me like everyone's been pretty well-behaved, considering. We both deserve credit for not laughing out loud when Betty's mom asked Ryan what he does for a living, and he thought he was being ironic when he answered that he still isn't sure what he wants to be when he grows up."

"I didn't laugh because I didn't think it was funny. It's humiliating."

"Oh, lighten up, man. Mom's midlife crisis isn't a reflection of us."

"She should have had and been over her midlife crisis by now."

"Maybe she's a late bloomer."

"Maybe you guys can compare crises."

He laughs. "Whatever, bro. I'm not having a midlife crisis. I'm too damn young for that."

"All the signs are there."

"Whatever."

"See, a guy on the verge of turning forty shouldn't say, 'Whatever,' like a sorority sister."

He slops the final spoonful of potatoes into a plastic container and snaps on the lid, then slides it down the counter, closer to the fridge, and moves on to the green bean casserole. The bean, cheese, and soup mixture oozes from the glass dish into the waiting Tupperware. "Don't jump all over me because you're in a bad mood."

"I'm in a bad mood partly because of the way you've been treating your wife lately." When he stares blankly at me, I explain, "She told me all about it before dinner."

"Why's she crying on *your* shoulder?"

Slotting a plate into the last open space in the bottom rack of the dishwasher, I move to fill the top rack with cups and glasses. "I don't know! I was a captive audience in here, I guess. By the way, her version of things in your marriage is a bit different—and more believable—than what you've told me."

"She talked about our sex life to you?!"

"Not as graphically as you did, but she hinted at some things."

"I'm sure it was a short tale, because there's hardly any of that going on."

"She's about to pop!"

"Not for another two months."

"Still. Can't you try to understand how miserable she is right now?"

He peers into the slow cooker at my overdone sweet potatoes. Wrinkling his nose, he says, "Let's chuck this. Nobody's going to want something that looks like this."

"Is that your answer to everything? When things aren't as attractive as you'd like, you cast them aside?"

"Are you comparing my wife to dried-out sweet potato casserole? And anyway, who says she's not attractive? She's still damn fine! Tastes better than this crap, too," he adds on a mutter.

I roll my eyes. "What a touching, heartfelt declaration."

"Listen, bro. I don't know what she told you, but—"

"She told me that you're a moody jerk when you *are* home, which isn't often, because you're either working late or 'hanging out with Dad and Nate.'"

His face pales.

I turn off the water, then place a detergent cube in the dishwasher and close it with a click. After pressing the button to start the appliance, I lean a hip against it and lower my voice so my brother has to come closer to hear me. "I sort of covered for you, man."

"What do you mean, 'sort of'?" He shifts from one foot to the other and stares intently into my face.

"I didn't come right out and confirm her suspicions that you're a liar."

"She doesn't believe me?"

"She thinks you're having an affair."

He blinks at me for a few seconds, then pinches his eyes and runs his hand down the side of his face. "Oh, man."

"Yeah, dumbass. You tell her you're somewhere that you're not, you turn off your phone so she can't reach you... Shit! I know you're not that stupid, but even I'm having a hard time thinking of other reasonable explanations, and I'm not thirty-two weeks pregnant and overloaded with hormones. What do you expect her to think?"

"Well, you reassured her that I'm not. Having an affair, that is."

"Why is it *my* job to reassure her? *You* should be doing that. Or better yet, stop making her suspicious."

"Yeah, yeah. Whatever. What did you tell her?"

I lick my lips. "I told her you were probably hanging out at some bar, watching sports, because you're overwhelmed right now and need some alone time."

"Hey, that's a good one. Good thinking on your feet."

"Because that *is* what's going on, right?"

"Close enough." He pats my upper arm and steps away to return to leftovers packaging. "You're the man."

I follow him across the kitchen and stand next to him, so close my chest rubs against his arm.

He glances nervously at me. "Bro, a little room here."

"No. Tell me I'm not an accomplice to something horrible."

"Don't worry about it, man. It's none of your business, anyway."

"But it *is*, because she told me about it, and I stood up for you. Plus I'm her damn emergency contact now, because she can't reach you half the time. What the hell? Why are you turning off your phone?"

"It's like you said. I need some time to myself, and hearing her ringtone makes my stomach hurt."

"Then change her ringtone."

"It's not the stupid ring—"

"I know!" I push him with both hands, and he slops sweet potatoes across the counter.

"Look what you did now, you idiot."

I refuse to look. I'm too busy boring a hole in the side of his face with my laser eyes. "Tell me what's going on."

"Nothing! It's nothing." He reaches for the nearest towel and smears the sweet potatoes across the counter. "Aw, shit. That made it worse."

"Stop ignoring me."

"Grab a paper towel and wet it for me, will ya?"

"First tell me." When he opens his mouth to continue claiming it's "nothing," I persist. "I'll be the judge of that. Just tell me."

"No. Back the hell off. And get me a paper towel."

I step back but reply, "Get it your damn self. I'm finished doing you any favors."

He rolls his eyes, steps across the kitchen, and rips a sheet from the roll, then dampens it under the tap. "I never asked you to lie for me."

"But *you* lied, using me as your alibi, knowing that if Heidi asked me about it, I'd cover for you enough for you to come up with a plausible story of your own."

"That's what brothers do for each other, all right? I've told you what's going on here—"

"You made it sound like she was a harpy, and the kids were

crazy, and that everyone was getting what they wanted except *you*. But that's not the case, is it? Heidi's just as disappointed as you are at the current state of things, but she doesn't have the luxury of going AWOL. You guys are supposed to weather this stuff together, be in it together."

"Like you and Betty?"

I pull up and answer uncertainly, "Yes..."

"Because something tells me you're not practicing what you preach. But I guess that shouldn't come as a surprise."

"What are you talking about?"

"I hear things."

"From who?!" A series of traitorous faces flashes through my head in a split second.

"People. People who know that you guys aren't the perfect couple you want everyone to believe you are."

"We've never claimed to be per—"

"And another thing. Your days of being Heidi's hero are over, pal, so step off."

I blink and flex my jaw. "What are you— Seriously? You think I'm making a move on your wife?"

"I think that, once again, I have what you want—"

"You've lost your freaking mind."

"Have I?"

"Yes. I'm beginning to think you're on drugs. Which would explain a lot."

"I'm perfectly clean and sober. And I'm sorry you and Betty can't have more kids—that must be terrible for you—but my wife is off limits, no matter what your history is with her. It's just that: history."

"What did you say?"

"I said my wife is off limits."

"Before that. You're sorry Betty and I can't have more kids? What the...? Where did you get that?"

"I told you, I hear things."

"You're hearing things, all right. Your source is wrong."

"My source heard it from someone who heard it straight from your wife."

"They're lying."

He throws his hands in front of himself when I take a threatening step toward him. "I'm only repeating what I've heard, bro."

"Why don't you shut the hell up and stop talking about things you don't understand?"

Dad slips into the room and bumps his hip against the counter on his way in. "Hey, guys. What's going on? Allva sudden, it started to sound kinda tense and loud in here. You guys havin' a brotherly disagreement?"

I avert my eyes, then turn my back on him completely and say down to the nearest counter, "Dad, you're drunk."

"'Course I am! How else you think I'm gonna get through this day? Now, what'sa problem in here? Maybe you guys could use a drink or two."

Nick shoves the last of the leftovers into the refrigerator and bumps it closed with his elbow. "Is the game on yet?" He steers Dad from the room by his shoulders. "Let's go watch the Lions get their butts kicked."

I stare at the sink of dishes still waiting to go in the dishwasher. The thing is, I don't want to stand around long enough for the machine to clean the first batch, but I'll be damned if I leave the rest for Heidi to do. Lord knows my useless brother's not going to do them. I stride to the sink and turn on the hot water, full-blast, then squirt a liberal amount of dish soap into the stream.

I just want to get this done and go home.

22
DAMAGE CONTROL

WHILE I DID THE REMAINING DISHES BY HAND LAST NIGHT, Betty accepted an invitation from her mother to spend the rest of the long (long, long, long) weekend at her parents' cabin... with them. Except for throwing my own clothes in the overnight bag and loading up the car with the thirty tons of crap we tend to have to take with us when we travel anywhere overnight, I've taken Betty at her word that this weekend will be her show. I'm determined to simply go along for the ride.

Not that I've had much of a choice. My mind and body are spent. If I tried to drive us, we'd end up in a snowbank, I'm sure, during one of my frequent space-outs. Betty's better at driving on snow than I am, anyway, but it doesn't matter, because the roads are clear. The worst we'll encounter will be the cabin's driveway, but Witt promised Betty he'd try to get someone out there to grade it before we arrived.

That means all I have to do for the next two hours is sit here in the passenger seat and try not to think too much.

After the first thirty miles, it's obvious that's not going to be possible.

How could he? How *could* my defensive, lying bastard of a

brother turn everything around on me, after I defended him to his wife, made excuses for his bad behavior, and stuck my neck out for him? He repays me by repeating a terrible rumor, supposedly started by my own wife, about something so personal, so painful? If Dad hadn't walked in, I'm not sure what I would have done.

The last time I was that angry, I head-butted a vamp-lit author and gave us both concussions. Not sure I would have gotten off that easily if I'd attacked Nick. He's a bit more solid than Yardley Cummins. Doesn't mean I wouldn't have done it, though, and lived—or not—to regret it.

Remembering that crazy day at the romance writers' conference leads me to think—naturally—about the rest of that trip, including the night when Georgia was conceived, the night that changed my life forever.

The only constant in my adult life has been the desire to be a dad. When Betty told me I was going to be one, it was a bonus that I'd also get to marry my best friend and raise that baby with her. And although I told Betty our ambivalence at finding out we were going to have another baby didn't cause the miscarriage, medically, that doesn't mean I don't hate myself every day for taking that baby for granted. If I'd only known.

If I'd known that was my last chance at something I foolishly assumed I'd experience at least a couple more times, I would have cherished it more.

Not that it would have changed the outcome. If anything, it would have made the loss more painful. Or at least painful in other ways.

And Georgia... I love that girl more than I ever thought it was possible to love someone. Knowing she's going to be my one and only makes her that much more precious, too. It's almost not fair to her, to have that much of one person's love foisted on her. What if there *is* such a thing as too much love? What if an overabundance of it becomes oppressive and stifling? Is that how I'm going to screw up my kid? By loving her too intensely?

That thought leads me back to the rumor Nick repeated to me. I take about five miles to weigh the pros and cons of mentioning it to Betty, then ten, or so, more miles to figure out how to discuss it without it turning into an argument. Since there's no way to guarantee that, and I still *need* to get this off my chest, I peek into the backseat at a dozing Georgia and take the plunge.

"Hey. I, uh, want to ask you something."

"No, your butt doesn't look big in snow pants."

Confused, I look down at my jeans.

Keeping her eyes on the road, Betty laughs. "In case you were ever wondering."

"Okay..."

"Your butt looks good in anything."

"Good to know. Thanks."

"That *is* what you wanted to ask, right?"

I chuckle and scratch the bridge of my nose. "Yes. Definitely. Now I can rest easy every time I wear them. Which will be never, if I have anything to say about it." I rub my chin. "But there was something else—much more minor—that I sort of wanted to know about."

"Do you want me to guess? Because I'm apparently pretty good at that."

Smiling, I look at her profile. "No. I'll just ask it, if that's okay with you."

"Fire away."

My stomach flips. "And I'd like to preface it with the statement that I'm not mad, and I don't want this to turn into an argument."

She mutters something under her breath that sounds suspiciously like the f-word but keeps her smile in place, albeit tighter now.

When that's the only encouragement I receive to continue, I take it. "All right. So. Um... Did you tell anyone that we can't have more kids?"

Her smile drops from her mouth altogether, and there's no doubt which word she hisses this time. And it's all the answer I need.

"Why?" I ask, keeping my tone neutral, not betraying any of the befuddlement or dismay behind my question.

She makes a big show of checking the mirrors, even though we're one of the only cars out here at the moment, then lifts her right shoulder toward her ear.

"Can I tell you something, and you won't think I'm the most horrible person in the world?"

Hello, loaded question. It's still pretty safe that I could never think she's the most horrible person in the world, unless this is her confession that when she's supposedly on business trips, she's acting out her double life as a serial killer. (I recently binge-watched *The Fall*... alone... while she was away. Mistake.)

Since she's asking in response to my question, though, I feel fairly safe replying, "Of course."

"I realize you're not thrilled about my friendship with Veronica..."

Must keep neutral expression.

"...but she and I have a good time together. We shop and laugh and... I'm remembering what it's like to have a girlfriend. And I've missed it."

Swallowing my objections to her specific choice in friend, I simply say, "I'm glad you have a new friend," *even if she does stir the pot and make you suspicious of my perfectly innocent friendships.*

"And—this is the part that's really bad." She blushes.

Geez. What the hell?

She glances at me but immediately returns her eyes to the road. "I don't feel like as much of a failure when I'm around her. Because... Oh, my gosh, this is so awful, and I can't believe I'm about to admit this out loud."

I reach over and pat her thigh. "It's okay."

She chuckles. "No, it's not, but I have to tell someone." Deep breath. "I don't feel like as much of a failure, because at least I was able to have one baby." She catches herself. "Well, two. But one that she knows of."

"She doesn't know about the one you gave up for adoption?"

Shaking her head, she raises her eyebrow and pulls her mouth sideways. "Are you nuts? No."

"Oh. I thought... maybe it came up in conversation, or something."

"She may be all about over-sharing, but that's not my thing."

"But she does know about...?"

"The miscarriage? Yeah, I told her that. I felt like I had to. She was talking to me about her and Dan's struggle with infertility, and she was so upset, and it... it seemed mean to sit there, pretending like I had no idea what she was going through, like I'm some fertility phenom. I didn't go into detail, or anything, but I mentioned we'd had our own issue recently. It seemed to make her feel better, not so alone, maybe."

"That was nice. And I'm sure it was hard to share that."

She shrugs. "I felt like I was talking about someone else. Later, though... Later, I felt worse for having told her, like... like... it was my way of throwing her a bone so I didn't have to feel so bad anymore about feeling superior."

"Oh."

"Because it might not be her fault."

Yeah, low sperm count or limited motility seem like givens for Dr. Douche. Filter, filter, filter.

"It's probably *not* her fault. Or if it does have something to do with her, physically, that's still not something she can control. It could be there's nothing wrong with either of them, but they're not reproductively compatible." *There. Doesn't get more diplomatic than that.*

She shoots me a look. "Forget the medical lecture. What I'm saying is, she mostly talks about how stressful the IVF is. But it's like they're obsessed with trying, despite giving up hope that it will ever be successful. They've already tried six times. Can you imagine?"

I move my hand up to her shoulder and squeeze it. "Hey. None of that makes you a bad person. It makes you a *human* person. You sympathize with her. It's not like you're rooting for them to keep failing. And I bet if you examined your feelings more—and were less critical of yourself—you'd realize that you're not feeling superior; you're feeling lucky. If she called you today and told you she was pregnant, you'd be happy for her."

She shakes off my hand.

"Right?" I check.

Resting her elbow against the window, she leans her head against her hand and pinches her temple. "That's the worst part. I don't know."

I stare at her profile while her lips tremble, and her chin wrinkles.

Near a whisper, she croaks, "I'd be happy for her, but I'd be sad for me, and that's so selfish, so—"

"Human."

"Humans suck." She darts a sad smile my way.

"Jealousy is a terrible feeling. It's a physical presence, here."

I gesture to my gut. "You want me to tell you what I sometimes think and feel when Heidi and Nick are around?"

She smiles. "Nothing I haven't thought or felt myself, I'm
sure."

"When you think someone isn't appreciating something
they have that you'd give nearly anything to have... it hurts.
And it makes you think terrible things, things you wish you
weren't capable of thinking."

"Yes!"

"But that still doesn't answer my original question. Why
did you lie and tell her we can't have more kids? Because we
can, but we *won't*... apparently."

*Oh, shit. That last word wasn't supposed to slip out. Especially not
in that resentful way.*

Betty either doesn't catch it (doubtful) or chooses to ignore
it (more likely) (and mercifully). "I told you I didn't go into
details with her. I said I had a miscarriage and that we
wouldn't be having any more children. She must have
inferred..."

For the first time in two days, my shoulders relax. "Oh. You
didn't tell a tiny white lie so you guys would have one more
thing in common, and you wouldn't have to feel bad that your
situation is by choice, while hers isn't?"

Her jaw tightens, and she answers through clenched teeth,
"No."

The ice is definitely cracking under my feet at this point,
so I retreat to the shore. "Okay. That's, uh, all I wanted to
know."

"What brings this up, anyway?"

*Well, I'm glad you asked, because it turns out your new "friend" is a
bitchy blabbermouth who repeated what you said to her in confidence
to someone else—most likely her douchey husband—you know, my
boss?—who then told someone else, and so on, until it got to my*

brother, who's filed it away as more evidence that I'm pathetic and inherently jealous of him, because I'm inferior to him in every way, including potency. In other words, it's all over the Green Bay medical community, and I'm surprised we haven't been inundated with sympathy cards and casseroles.

In the interest of keeping things simple—and non-incendiary—I reply, "Because somehow her inference made its way to my brother. And he asked me about it yesterday."

Yeah, that almost describes that train-wreck of a conversation. Close enough.

"Oh."

"Yeah."

"I'm sorry. Like I said, I didn't want to go into the gory details with her, so…"

"Whatever. It's not your fault."

"It feels like it is," she says quietly. "All of it." She bangs her palm against the steering wheel. "I can't believe Veronica repeated what I told her."

Although I want to say, *"I can,"* I reply, instead, "Only to her husband, probably. You've told me the things she's said to you. The only difference is, I'm a decent human being and would never repeat it to anyone, much less someone I work with, who also works with Dan. But hey, different strokes."

She moves her left hand from her temple to the steering wheel, which frees up her right hand to reach across and grab one of mine, limp in my lap. "Nate, I'm sorry."

I wave away her apology and stare out the window at the white, rural landscape flying past us. "It's no biggie."

"Yes, it is."

"Well, it's done. There's nothing either of us can do about it."

"I'm never telling her anything again."

"That might be a good plan going forward. Is there

anything else you've already told her that I should know?" I scrape my upper lip with my bottom teeth while I wait.

Finally, she mutters, "I may have said things have been... rougher than usual between us."

"Ah. Yes. Well, that explains the other thing Nick said."

"About what?"

"About us not being the perfect couple we want everyone to believe we are."

She flicks a glance over at me to verify I'm being serious, then grunts indignantly. "We don't try to act like something we're not! Maybe he's getting us confused with him and Heidi."

"Maybe."

"Oh, gosh. I feel sick."

That gets my attention in a hurry. I crack the windows and study her pale face. "Are you going to puke?"

She shakes her head. "No. But I do want to cry."

"Then pull over."

"No. I'm okay."

While she returns both hands to the wheel, blinks furiously, and breathes slowly and evenly, I reach over and tuck a piece of hair behind her ear. "Hey, it's okay."

"It's not, though."

"It's just gossip.

"Gossip sucks."

"It does. And it blows to be the subject of it. But as long as we know the truth, who cares what other people are saying?"

"I care. A little bit. Maybe that makes me a superficial person. But I care."

I examine my feelings on it for a second, then say, "Yeah, I do, too. Not because I care about their opinions of me, of us. Only because I'd prefer not to have my co-workers know that much about my private life, good *or* bad. When I'm at work,

I'm a nurse, I'm their colleague, and I'm their friend, to a certain point. My personal life is not a soap opera for them to follow. It's a distraction from what we're there to do."

She nods and sniffles.

"I didn't mean to make you cry again."

"It happens constantly. Don't think you're so special that you do it so well. I'm a mess."

"Your mess is my mess, and I love it and wouldn't give it up for anything, no matter what the gossipers say."

"I love you, too. I'm sorry I'm so horrible at showing it lately."

"We both have some improvement areas. Stop being so mean to my wife."

She pokes a finger into the tears collecting at the corner of her eye, stanching the flow down her face before it starts. "I'll try."

"I only asked about all of this because if you'd told someone we *can't* have more children, I wanted to know why. I wanted to understand, that's all."

She clears her throat and sits taller behind the wheel. "No, I... I'm not ashamed of the truth. I don't like talking about it, but I don't cover it up or try to pretend it's something it's not."

"Good. See? That's all I needed to know. I didn't want it hanging over my head all weekend."

"You were right to ask. I'm glad you did. And I'm glad you told me what's going on."

A few weeks ago, I wouldn't have. I would have stewed all weekend. I would have imagined all sorts of conversations between her and any number of people, including Dr. Douche, himself. And I would have worked myself into a rage at all of the possibilities, most of them absurd and not at all in character for her. My sullenness would have ruined these days off, days we both desperately need to recharge and reset. And all along, it would have been something that could have been cleared up with one conversation. Not a particularly fun conversation. But not as bad as the blow-up that would inevitably result from my being an ass-face for as long as it took Betty to get to the bottom of my lousy mood.

After a few minutes of riding along with the radio providing the only sound in the car, other than the occasional sniffs from my companion as she recovers, I take a deep breath and say, "So! Big weekend at the lake with Kitty and Witt, huh?"

"Yep. Should be interesting."

"Hopefully not as interesting as the first time we did this, when we were first married."

She laughs through her last straggling tears. "In hindsight, I guess it *was* dumb to take the bedroom right next to theirs, when there were so many to choose from."

"Who knew that the walls were so thin in such a fancy house?"

She giggles again. "Oh, man! I felt like a caught-out teenager when that banging started on the wall next to our heads. I thought we were being quiet!"

"We were newlyweds. Why couldn't they put their pillows over their ears and deal with it? It's not like we were settling in for a marathon."

"I guess they didn't know that. Either way, it would have been uncomfortable for them the next morning at the break-fast table."

I rest my hand on the side of my face when I remember, "It didn't help when I called them Titty and Titt over our scrambled eggs."

Her howling pitches her forward against the steering wheel, honking the horn. "Oh, my gosh! I forgot that part. The best was the context, though. 'What do Titty and Titt

Kate like to do for fun?' Like you were a smarmy game show host with strippers as contestants."

Around my chortles, and while reaching into the backseat to soothe a startled Georgia, I defend myself. "Hey! My brain and my tongue got confused. I was nervous! I hardly knew them, but I'd knocked up their daughter before I married her, and the night before, I'd been informed most abruptly that our private party wasn't so private. I was trying to make polite conversation so we could all move past... everything. I think it worked."

"How do you figure *that*?"

Having successfully distracted the baby with one of her favorite plush toys, I drop it in her lap and face completely forward once more, adjusting my seatbelt across my chest. "They went from thinking I *might* be a boob to knowing it for sure."

"Baaaaaaaaahahahaha!"

When we've both recovered from our giggles, I sigh. "I wish I could say I've changed their minds in the past couple of years, but... No. I'm pretty sure I confirm it in some way every time we're together. As recently as yesterday. Witt asked me during dinner if I was always in charge of big family meals, and I said, 'Oh, I'm a regular Martha Stewart. Minus the felony conviction. Although there was that one time... but my attorney got it downgraded to a misdemeanor.' And his eyes about bugged out of his head, so I had to say, real quick, 'Kidding!' But I could tell he still wasn't sure."

"Oh, my gosh. You *are* a boob."

"It'll be interesting to see how creatively I can humiliate myself in the next two days."

"You know, we should totally brainstorm what you got busted for."

"No. I don't need your stepfather thinking I'm a criminal, on top of everything else."

"C'mon! Let's have fun with it. Bamboozling people was our specialty, once upon a time. Plus, Witt's used to my teasing. I'll make sure he knows—eventually—that it's a joke."

I consider it for a second and decide there's no harm in it. It'll at least give us something to talk about.

"No sex crimes. They already think I'm a horny deviant."

"No, no. Nothing like that. Let me think about it for a while. Do you mind if I surprise you? Will you play along?"

I shake my head at my foolishness for entertaining the idea but chuckle and say, "Yeah, sure. I trust you."

"Sweet." She winks at me. "Hey, Nathaniel?"

"What?"

"Let's make this weekend our bitch, huh?"

"Let's."

23

OLD SINS DIE HARD

By Saturday evening, I figure Betty's forgotten her practical joke or has decided against it, either of which is okay by me. As soon as Georgia's in bed, we hunker in the living room for the Tates' favorite activity: ignoring each other.

This is the second night of this routine. Witt reads a stack of financial magazines and newspapers, Kitty works on sudoku or crossword puzzles, and Betty and I read books or look at our phones, occasionally glancing up at one another and making faces at how unbelievably silent and boring her parents are.

I'd suggest we go for a walk, but the snow is deep, the night is dark, and the wind is painful. Some butt-flattering snow pants might come in handy right now. But alas, I only packed jeans and sweatshirts.

Kitty startles me by saying to no one in particular as she scratches numbers into grids in the course-papered booklet in her lap, "I never knew until this weekend how early you put Georgia to bed." The wrinkled nose at the end tells us exactly how she feels about that.

"She goes to bed early," I confirm, setting my e-reader on the arm of the couch next to me. *Since she's a baby, and all.*

"But that means she's also up early in the morning."

I nod. "Yep."

"When Betty was little, I let her stay up late so she'd sleep late."

"Hmmm."

Betty pipes up, "We put her to bed early because she's usually tired and cranky, and Nate and I like to have some time to ourselves in the evening. Having her sleep late in the morning doesn't do us any good, since we have to be up early, anyway, for work."

"It's not only about convenience for our schedules, either," I add to our defense. "She needs at least twelve hours of sleep, and we have to be out the door by 7:30 every morning."

Kitty frowns. "I suppose that makes sense on weekdays. But on weekends like this..."

"It's easier to maintain the routine. Some weekends we fudge it, but we usually pay for it."

Witt rustles his paper and clears his throat. Taking that as a sign he'd like us to shut up, I return to my Graeme Simsion book.

But Kitty doesn't care what Witt prefers and, looking over her half-moon glasses at me, smirks and says, "It's amusing to see Betty forced to be an early riser. She was always a night owl and a late sleeper. Sometimes in the summer, she wouldn't stumble out to the kitchen until after noon! And then only to eat some cereal before going back to bed."

"There was nothing else to do," Betty defends herself. "And I wasn't always hibernating. Sometimes I'd read or watch TV."

"Sounds like hibernating to me." Again, Kitty directs her remarks at me. "We thought she was on drugs."

I blink at the matter-of-fact way she says it. "And? What did you do about that, when you suspected it?"

She waves at the air in front of her. "Nothing. It's not like we were ever seriously worried. Before we could do anything about it, she was over that phase and back to being a social butterfly. *Too* social, sometimes."

I wiggle my eyebrows at my wife. "Were you a party animal?"

She lifts her chin. "Don't act like it's a surprise... or like you didn't do the same things."

"I was an angel."

With a twinkle in her eyes, she drops, "Until college, that is, when you set up that little business venture from your dorm room."

"Huh?"

"Oh, don't play innocent, Nathaniel. Kitty and Witt aren't going to be scandalized by a little pot distribution."

Witt's paper rustles to his lap, and his forehead wrinkles. "Tell me you're kidding."

Before I can give up the joke, Betty butts in. "It wasn't that big of a deal. Just a way to make some cash between classes... until he got caught. Ratted out by his own roommate."

"Good for your roommate," Witt says with a sniff. "You were expelled, I take it?"

Betty laughs. "Is this the first time you're hearing of this? I thought Nate told you about it a long time ago."

Kitty snaps her pencil against her puzzle book and whips off her glasses. "No! Not a word!"

"He hinted at it at Thanksgiving dinner, but he said he was joking," Witt replies.

I smile sheepishly. "It's not something everyone can easily overlook."

Witt folds his paper and drops it on the floor next to him.

"I'd think not! How did you get a job in pediatrics with a drug conviction on your record?"

Oh, that. I shoot a meaningful glare at Betty to let her know now would be a good time to let her parents in on the joke, but she widens her eyes, blinks, and waits eagerly for my answer, exactly like she used to do when readers at book signings would ask Frank bizarre questions, and I'd have to spout unrehearsed responses on the fly.

I click my tongue, lick my lips, and say, "Hm. Well. The thing is, my parents hired a crack—uh, no pun intended—lawyer who not only had the charges reduced to a misdemeanor but also had it expunged from my record."

"He must have been a magician!"

"I don't know, honestly. I was a stupid college kid. I didn't understand at the time how much trouble I was in or how it could affect my future." In danger of laughing, I cover my mouth with my hand and rub, like I'm considering the seriousness of it now.

Kitty shakes her head. "What moral ground will you have to stand on if Georgia ever experiments with drugs? None! And you!" She points to Betty. "You were already going to have a time of it when it came to teaching her about safe sex, thanks to *your* little stunt."

The laughter that was so close to the surface fizzles in my chest, replaced by horror.

Betty's smile fades. Swallowing, she looks down at her hands in her lap. After what feels like an eternity, she says, "I made sure I wouldn't have to feel ashamed to tell any of my future children what happened."

Kitty snorts. "You have a son out there—I have a grandson —who we've never met. Who doesn't know us."

"That's how I wanted it to be. I wanted him to only know one mother; the one who wanted him."

"Is that supposed to make Georgia feel good? That she was lucky enough to come along when you wanted her?"

Betty's breath hitches in her chest when she inhales to answer, so her words come out pinched as she stands and says, "I don't feel well." She strides for the downstairs room where we're staying, flinging back at us on the way, "Nate never dealt pot. We were only kidding."

My in-laws turn their full attention to me. Further head-shaking ensues, like they're more disappointed in me for being part of the prank than they were when they thought I was a former drug dealer.

Witt picks up a glossy magazine on the end table at his elbow, licks his forefinger to gain traction, and turns the first page. "What a stupid thing to joke about," he mutters before looking down at the publication, effectively dismissing me.

Kitty returns to her puzzles. "I hope you're happy."

I grunt and sigh. "We were goofing off! You're the one who had to go too far and bring up *that*."

"You can't even bring yourself to say it."

I rise. "I'm truncating, because we all know what we're talking about. And anyway, you're the one who wanted her to have an abortion. There. I can say *that* word. Can you?"

Unfazed by my challenge, she lifts her head, tilts it, and replies coolly, "I encouraged her to take care of it before it became another person affected by her stupidity."

My stomach turns. "I suddenly don't feel very well, either."

Without a good night, I snatch my e-reader from the couch and follow in Betty's footsteps.

* * *

EXPECTING to encounter a tearful wife when I reach our room, I'm surprised—and somewhat more worried—when that's not the case. Instead, I find her painting her toenails. On the spotless white duvet. But her hands are steady as she strokes the turquoise polish onto her dainty toes. Only the way she jabs the tiny brush in and out of the bottle belies her true emotional state.

"Um, so, that kind of backfired," I begin, leaning against the wall by the door.

Her tongue sticking from the corner of her mouth as she paints her baby toenail, she merely grunts. When she's finished, she stabs the brush into the bottle and yanks it out again, then starts on her other foot. "I refuse to let her upset me. I should have known better than to give her the opening. It's her favorite topic: 'How Betty messed up that one time.'"

"Maybe I should give her some material to add to her list, so she's not so fixated on that one thing?"

She sneers at me. "Thanks."

"No problem. I'm here to help." I watch her for another minute. As she blows on her feet to dry the first coat, I say, "Seriously, though, are you okay? That... She was really cold. I mean... what's wrong with her?"

"It was the one time I defied her."

"The only time?"

"Of course, I did things I knew she wouldn't approve of, necessarily. All the time. But she never knew about them, so she never expressly forbade me, and those didn't count. In that one case, though, she made it clear what she wanted—expected—me to do, and I refused, and she... she's never forgiven me. And she capitalizes on every opportunity to remind me about it."

"You did the right thing."

"I know I did. For me. Maybe it wouldn't have been the right decision for someone else, but it was right for me. And it was right for that baby."

"I'm glad you haven't let her change your mind about that."

"Hell, no." She starts on her topcoat.

"Make sure you get some of that stuff on the bed, too."

She laughs and rolls her eyes. "I've been doing this for a while; it'll be okay."

"Set it down next to you, and I'll pretend I didn't see it and plop on the bed and knock over the bottle." I cover my mouth and widen my eyes. "Whoops."

"You're so passive-aggressive sometimes." Her tone chides, but her expression admires.

"You know, it's a miracle, given our respective parents, that we're normal, functioning human beings."

"Is that what we are?"

I shrug. "Closest there is to it anymore, I guess."

"Neither of us is the type to blame our parents for our issues. Then we'd also have to give them credit for our triumphs. Screw that." She smiles cheekily, looking up at me through her eyelashes.

"You're not mad at them?"

"No. I'm used to it."

"Because I sort of am. Definitely am. Your mom... Betts, I don't like her!"

She grins at the revelatory yet apologetic tone of my statement. "Okay. Fine. You're not hurting my feelings by saying it."

"Witt's a dullard, and a bit gruff and old-fashioned and emotionless, but your mom... She's mean!"

"She can be."

"Maybe it's for the best that Georgia doesn't spend much time around them. I... I can't be responsible for what I'd do if your mom said something derogatory about you to our daughter. And I can totally imagine her doing that."

"It's not worth getting yourself all worked up."

"Yes, it is!"

Her tongue pokes out and touches the middle of her upper lip. "Let me guess. After I left, she called me stupid. Or something."

I refuse to verbally confirm it, but my silence is confirmation enough.

She nods and bites her lower lip. "Mmm-hmm. Typical."

"It's amazing to me how you can be so casual about this."

"I've been dealing with it for, like, fifteen years. It's old hat."

"Man." I shake my head and look down at my feet. "That's... Well, good for you. You're tough. Tougher than I am."

"Plus, you're pissed off enough for both of us."

"It appears that way."

"Only this time..." She pauses and edges along the inside of her big toenail with her thumbnail, wiping from her skin some excess lacquer. "Well, saying what she did about Georgia, that was new. And that hurt. Because it hit too close to the truth."

"What, that you were readier and more prepared and willing to raise a child in your thirties than while you were still in college? Well, duh."

She blinks but says nothing, simply keeps painting.

"Another big difference: you had *my* support and cooperation."

She blows me a saucy kiss, and I notice her eyes aren't as dry—nor her attitude as blasé—as they were a few minutes ago. She slides the brush into the bottle for the last time and screws it tightly into place. "What hurt wasn't about Georgia, though. It was about—" Setting the polish on the bedside table with a faint clack against the wood, she takes a shaky breath. "It made me think. I've never gotten pregnant on purpose. I've never said to someone after careful thinking and planning, 'Hey, let's do this. Don't you think it'll be great?'

Instead, I've always—after the fact—counted the weeks, gotten that sinking feeling in my stomach, and peed on a stick alone, praying it wouldn't give me that damn positive result." She pulls her legs up to her chest and wraps her arms around them. "It's like, what the hell is wrong with me? Why do I keep getting that part of it wrong?"

"It's not wrong; it's typical. Most people share that experience with you, with *us*. And in our case, we've recovered well, and things have worked out."

"Not every time."

I step to the bed and sit on the edge, my back facing the side of her bent legs. "You know what I'm saying, though."

"I... I wish I had gotten it right, just once. To prove that I'm not still as... as... clueless as that stupid college girl who believed that asshole when he said it was only one time, and nothing would come of it, and if it did, he'd be there for me."

I reach behind me for her hand, grab it, and squeeze. "You're not stupid. You were never stupid."

"Easy for you to say. The worst thing you ever did in college was sell a bunch of pot from your dorm room."

I roll my eyes toward my forehead. "That never happened, remember?"

"Says who? I'm rewriting history."

"Trust me, I did plenty of other stupid things in college— and beyond. Hello, do you remember my dressing in skinny jeans, scarves, and fake glasses, weekend after weekend? I was well in my thirties then. What excuse did I have?"

"Temporary insanity?"

Laughing, I say, "Or love. Same thing."

"Ew. Let's not talk about your love for Frankie."

"I wasn't; I was talking about *you*. I never did any of that for her."

"That makes it somehow more insane."

"Maybe. But look where it got me. I'd do it all over again."

"More evidence of your mental instability."

I swivel at the waist and scoot closer to her, resting my hand on the other side of her body and leaning against her legs. I kiss her knee. "Every stupid thing we ever did got us here. And there's presumably a teenager out there, free to make his own stupid decisions, who wouldn't be alive to make them if it wasn't for you."

She nods and whispers, "Yeah."

"So, screw your mom."

"Nathaniel!"

I laugh at her shock. "What do you expect from a former drug dealer?" Quickly, though, I sober and return to my original point. "You're a thousand times the mother she'll ever be. Because you care. You made the harder decision, in my book. You didn't just have a baby; you created an entire family where there wasn't one before."

Her hands fall from her legs, which she straightens. Sitting forward, she kisses my forehead, then my nose, then my mouth. Touching her nose to mine, she says, "I love you so much for saying that."

I stare into her eyes, studying the light blue marbling in the dark blue, almost black, rings at the edges of her irises. "It's the truth. And you've done it twice. I'm so glad for that second time."

"You're going to make me cry." Sure enough, the whites of her eyes pink, and her long lashes clap together repeatedly.

"No more crying," I murmur, bringing my other hand to the back of her head and holding her steady while I try to distract her from her emotional reflex. Between increasingly frantic kisses, I say, "I love you," as often as I can, to make up for all of the times I've thought it but didn't voice it, for all of the times she didn't hear it from the others who owed it to her.

For the next several minutes, I pour that sentiment into everything I do, until she clings to me and cries out my name. And I don't care who hears us.

THE ULTIMATUM

TODAY, INSTEAD OF SPENDING THE MAJORITY OF THE DAY AT the cabin, as planned, we loaded up first thing in the morning and said our strained goodbyes to Witt and Kitty. When I thought the three of us were going to leave the house together, Betty said quietly to me, "I'll meet you in the car, okay?"

A few minutes later, she slid behind the wheel and said, "DJ, play my favorite songs."

I cued up a playlist on her phone and set it to repeat play, but since it was still snowing, Betty needed to focus on driving, so I didn't force her to tell me what happened or what she said to her parents, although I was dying to know. I figure she'd tell me when she was ready, hopefully not making me wait too long.

But life has been... life... since we've been home, so we haven't had a chance to talk about it.

Reba was pissed we left her here for two days with only occasional visits, food refills, and potty breaks courtesy of our next door neighbors. She greatly prefers when Lynette stays at the house, but... that wasn't happening this time around, since it was too short of notice. *Yeah, that was the reason.*

Therefore, we found several fun surprises, like the office Reba ransacked by strewing the trash from the wastepaper basket and knocking over the shredder, the lid of which popped off and released approximately thirty tons of cross-cut confetti. And two biohazardous presents, one that I almost stepped on in the hallway when we first got home, the other I touched with my bare hands while scooping up a mound of shredded paper.

Later, with the cleanup complete and guest room window open to eradicate any lingering smells, I listened to Georgia perform a grouchy concert from her high chair, while I washed my hands for the third time at the kitchen sink. We didn't have to wonder long what her problem was, as she proceeded to poop out everything we fed her for the rest of the afternoon and evening and spiked a fever.

Now, it's time to make The Decision.

"Who's staying home with her tomorrow?" I ask while smearing diaper rash cream on Georgia's irritated under-carriage.

Betty bites her lip. "Well, I have this thing in the morning, and I'm low on personal days, but I can work from home in the afternoon, if you want to salvage your afternoon appointments."

I consider it, then shake my head. "Nah. You know what? It's about time Dr. Douche takes on his own patient load, without me serving as his sidekick."

"Is that wise?"

Diaper fastened and ready to receive its next load, Georgia kicks her feet and babbles while I change her into warm pajamas.

"It's crunch time," I declare while cleaning my hands on an antibacterial wipe and dropping it in the diaper pail. "Anyway, it's best if I'm not there the first day he goes solo. I'll be a nervous wreck, wondering how badly he's screwing things up. Being home with a cranky baby will be a decent distraction."

"If you're sure..."

"Yep. I'll call it in right now."

"You're the best." She rubs my arm.

"I'll do the graveyard shift, too."

I zip Georgia's footie pajamas to her neck and snap the flap that covers the plastic zipper. Lifting her from the changing table, I wave her hand at Betty. "Good night, Mommy."

Betty kisses my bicep. "Really? I feel kind of bad."

With my continued assistance, Georgia blows kisses. "Don't. Leave it to the professional and get some sleep."

She steps forward, kisses the baby's forehead, and tries to smooth her flyaway hair. "Okay. I guess. Come get me if you need anything. Or if she gets worse. I want to know."

"She's cutting a tooth. Not a big deal. I'm going to keep her clean, comfortable, and hydrated. Right, George?"

High on a full dose of fever reducer and pain reliever, she grins at me, grabs my face, and plants an open-mouthed kiss on my cheek, shaking her head back and forth for maximum slobber effect.

Betty laughs. "Okay. But if she does get worse..."

"You'll be the third one to know." I wipe baby drool from my face and hold her out for one more snuggle from her mom. "Good night."

After Betty leaves with a worried look over her shoulder, I carry Georgia to the overstuffed chair in the corner of her room, by her overflowing bookshelf under the window, and lower us into it, settling her in the crook of my arm. "Now, what's it going to be? The classic, *Goodnight, Moon*, or are you feeling adventurous?"

She smacks my forearm and blows raspberries.

"Both, huh? Okay, here we go..."

* * *

I JERK awake several hours later and subtly shift my stiff muscles. I have no idea what time it is, but before I fell asleep, the clock was creeping toward two a.m., not an hour I relish seeing.

Careful not to wake Georgia, who finally appears to be sleeping soundly for the first time all night, I keep the arm holding her as still as I can while I straighten in the chair. Reba lifts her head from her position on the floor by the door. She weaseled her way back into my good graces earlier by letting me use her as a foot warmer, but she's since crept closer to the exit, making a break for it every time another dirty diaper has presented itself.

Blinking in the soft lamplight, I rub my neck with my free hand, then look down at the slumbering baby. A quick touch of my fingers to her forehead suggests her latest dose of medication hasn't worn off, which is also part of the reason she's so conked. I study the shadow of her lashes against the curve of her cheek. Her bottom center teeth glint through the tiny space between her top and bottom rosebud lips, chapped due to a combination of the cold, dry weather and her fever. Smiling, I sweep her fine hair from her forehead and tuck another strand behind her ear.

I should put her in her crib and move to my own bed—which would feel so good right now—to salvage a couple of hours' sleep, but I'm hesitant to move, despite not being one hundred percent comfortable. It's easier to keep track of her fever while holding her, anyway. She's safe and secure; that's all that matters.

The whisper of bare feet on the wood floor is the next sound to wake me. Reba's collar jingles as she raises her head from her paws. Betty crouches next to the arm of the chair and studies Georgia. "How's she doing?"

"Restless sometimes, but no fever at the moment."

"Has it broken completely?"

"Not yet, but the medicine is keeping her temperature down."

"Come to bed."

"I'm afraid she'll wake up if I move her. Or her fever will spike, and I won't know."

"She'll let us know." She rises. "C'mon."

Still unconvinced, I don't move.

Betty rests her hand on my shoulder. "I'll get up and check on her in a couple of hours, if she hasn't woken up by then. It's my turn to take a shift, anyway. Or she can sleep in our bed. It's just one night," she tacks on hastily when I reflexively shoot her "the look." Co-sleeping works for many of my patients' families, but it's not something I want to institute. Our bed is sacred, one of the few places in the house I'm allowed to be alone with my wife. It's bad enough the dog sometimes takes her own liberties.

However, on this night, it might be a perfect compromise. I can keep tabs on Georgia's fever and sleeping while also getting some rest in a position that won't leave me crippled in the morning. I'm not as young as I used to be and can't sleep standing in a corner or sprawled on the floor... or propped in an armchair.

"Okay," I relent, earning a grateful smile and a kiss.

Betty lifts Georgia from my arms (one of which has fallen asleep) and rests our daughter's head on her shoulder, shushing and bouncing the baby when she whimpers. "Let's go," Betty whispers.

It takes a couple of tries, but I'm finally able to rise from the chair and hobble behind her. In our room, I change into a sweatshirt and gym shorts, then do a half-assed job of brushing my teeth before sliding into bed, suppressing the moan at the slice of ecstasy that is my half (or slightly less) of the mattress.

But now I'm wide awake. Figures.

In the darkness, the only sound for a while is Georgia enthusiastically sucking her thumb, until I reach over and gently pull the digit from her mouth. Betty, who I thought was asleep, startles me by saying, "Give her a break. She doesn't feel well."

"I did. I let her do it for longer than I usually do." I half-sit, reach into my nightstand, and pull out one of many stowed-away binkies. I push it into Georgia's still-moving mouth. "There."

"You're, like, magic."

Closing my eyes, I smile. "Yeah. That's me."

As I'm drifting off to sleep, Betty murmurs, "I told them—well, Mom, anyway—that if she ever brought it up again, in order to humiliate or upset me, that would be the last time she saw us."

At first, I wonder if I'm dreaming. Then, when Betty says my name, checking that I'm awake and heard her, I grunt to stall for time and digest what she's said.

She helps by adding, "You know, when we were leaving, and I told you to wait for me in the car?"

"Yeah. I, uh... yeah. What did she say to that?"

"She rolled her eyes at me and called me 'melodramatic.' When I said I wasn't kidding, she said, 'Fine, fine, if it's that important to you,' like we were talking about ham versus turkey at Christmas, or something equally petty." I hear her swallow in the dark. "She managed to make me feel like an idiot. Again."

I raise my arm and extend it across our pillows, resting my palm on Betty's head. It's the best I can do with a baby between us. (See? This is why kids have their own beds.)

She reaches up and squeezes my fingers, then continues, "I said I didn't need her reminding me of him all the time, that I think about him every day, that even if I wanted to forget about him—which I don't—I'm never allowed to. There's a damn book about the whole thing out there, for heaven's sake!"

Ah, yes. The book. Frankie's fictionalized account of Betty's experience: *Girl Noir.* There's nothing like having an author immortalize one of the most difficult experiences of your life and—even better—turn it into a romantic comedy with a happily-ever-after mother-son reunion that never happened.

"Like I told Mom, I don't want to forget, but I don't want what happened to be a source of shame, either."

"Exactly."

"It was too much, wasn't it? The ultimatum? It's a threat I'm not willing to follow through on, so now, if she calls my bluff…"

"I don't think she will."

"It's not like she cares about seeing me most of the time, anyway."

I want to be able to refute that, but "caring" and "Kitty" don't go all that well together, and I have to admit, she does seem apathetic when it comes to being around us, Georgia included.

Threading my fingers through hers, I murmur, "I'm proud of you for saying something."

"It was dumb. I should have let it go."

"No. You've done that enough, always thinking it's the last

time she'll rub your face in it, like you're a naughty dog who crapped in the hallway."

She chuckles at the comparison to which we can relate too well today.

"It was time for you to tell her enough is enough."

Nodding, she turns on her side and, still holding onto my fingers, pulls them down to her mouth to brush her lips against my knuckles. "Okay. Thanks for helping me see it that way."

"And I'm glad you told me, so I can help you follow through. If that's what you want to do."

"I hope I don't have to."

"Me, too."

"She's my mom, you know?"

"I do."

"I can't keep cutting people from my life because they don't act the way I want them to. Pretty soon, I'll have no one."

"You'll always have me."

"I don't know... You keep squeezing the toothpaste tube from the middle..."

"If that's the worst complaint you have with me, I'm doing something right."

"You do a lot of things right, Nathaniel."

"I try."

Wide awake, I stare at the shadows on the ceiling and listen to Betty's deepening breaths and Georgia's squeaking pacifier.

Before Betty falls asleep for good, I rush to tell her, "You don't have to tolerate abuse. Ever. Not from friends, not from family, not from anyone."

"I know," she mumbles sleepily, her breath warming my fingers. "Thanks for the reminder, though."

It's a sucky reminder to have to deliver. I close my eyes and tamp down the heart-quickening rage at the list of people who have made it necessary. And despite her joke about the toothpaste, I vow to never be one of those jerks.

25

CLINIC SHOWDOWN

AFTER THE FOUR-DAY WEEKEND AND TWO ADDITIONAL DAYS home with Georgia, I return to work, feeling like I've been gone for longer than six days. My schedule reflects it, too. When I ask Lynette why I'm so light, she explains it away with, "We weren't sure when you'd be back, so we shifted as many appointments as possible to the doctors."

It sounds reasonable enough, and I'm admittedly relieved not to come back to a balls-to-the-wall day, so I tamp down any paranoia about sagging patient load and decide, instead, to catch up on what happened with the patients I was supposed to see on Monday and Tuesday.

Coffee in hand at the currently empty nurses' station, I straddle a stool, roll over to one of the computers, and log on. I click into each appointment from the past two days and read the patient notes, coming across the usual cold-weather diagnoses of strep, flu, and colds that lead to complications like pink eye, sinus infections, and walking pneumonia. All standard stuff. Until...

I hit a well-child checkup that I'm about to skim over when I see the red note at the bottom: *Patient transfer requested.*

Send file to Dr. Hews at... I trail off at the name and address of the clinic but go back and read it when the delusional moron that still occasionally rides around in my head hypothesizes the patient's family may be moving, requiring a closer doctor (although everything in this town is a fifteen minute drive, no matter what).

No. No change of address noted. No reason given for the transfer request, either.

Taking another sip of coffee that joins a now-bubbling brew in my stomach, I push forward through the other patient files. The bubbling intensifies when I run across another transfer request, then another. Soon, I'm no longer reading the notes for diagnoses; I'm exclusively scrolling down, looking for the dreaded red lettering.

After the fifth one, I set down my mug with a clonk that attracts Janet's attention as she sidles up to type something into the computer next to mine.

"Everything all right there?" she asks lightly, her tongue poking from the corner of her mouth as she transcribes something from the chart in her arms to the screen in front of her.

I swivel my head slowly and say to her profile, "No. Are you noticing an uptick in transfer requests?"

She hits "enter," clicks her mouse a few times to save, close, and log out, and faces me. "Now that you mention it, I guess so."

"You guess so? Now that I mention it? Someone has to mention it to you for you to notice?"

She raises her eyebrows. "Maybe you should cut back on the coffee."

"This has nothing to do with my caffeine intake. This... this... Are Dr. Reitman's patients asking for transfers, too?"

"Oh, yeah. But that's been going on ever since we sent out the letters about her retirement."

"What?"

"That's to be expected, though."

"Why? Why is that to be expected? What we should expect is that people feel comfortable enough with the practice, as a whole, that it shouldn't matter who their kid sees when they're here, because we're all great. We're all like... like family to them."

She laughs. "C'mon. Isn't that kind of—"

"What? A given?"

"No. I was going to say, 'naïve.'" She stands. "Gotta get a move on. But if you're worried, you should talk to Dr. Dan or Dr. Reitman about this. I'm sure they're not worried, so you shouldn't be, either."

I spin on the stool to follow her progress from the area and say, before she gets so far away that I have to raise my voice, "My—*our* patients are running from this place like it's on fire."

"You might be exaggerating a tad bit." With that, she smiles indulgently at me, dumps the chart in the "to be filed" tray on the counter, and walks toward the door to the waiting area to call the next patient.

If there are any out there to call.

I turn back to the computer, log off, and snatch my mug by its handle, hurrying to the break room to put it in the dishwasher. Bursting into the front desk area, I startle both Lynette and Mindy, who appear to be having a leisurely chat over their own steaming cups.

Glancing beyond their heads into the nearly empty waiting room (I *knew* it!), I say through clenched teeth, "I need to see the doctors' schedules."

Lynette blinks at me. "Okay."

"Now!"

"Fine, geez. Wearing Angry Birds scrubs doesn't mean you have to be an angry bird yourself."

"Just print the schedules for me, please."

While she clicks around on the computer, I ignore Mindy's open-mouthed, semi-incredulous stare. As soon as the papers slide from the printer, I grab them one-by-one, scan the grids, and grab the next sheet, still warm from the machine. The fourth page confirms my suspicions.

"Were the schedules like this Monday and yesterday?" I ask nobody in particular, my eyes still glued to the print-outs.

Neither of them answers at first, so I look up, but since my eyes shift from Lynette to Mindy, they still don't know who's expected to talk.

"Anyone!" I snap.

Lynette adjusts her headset. "What do you mean by 'like this'?"

I shake the sheets. "*This*. Not fully booked."

"It's been a slow week," she replies. "Busy on Monday, but nobody was double-booked, if that's what you're asking."

"Nobody was double-booked, and we were down a person."

She thinks about it, then shrugs. "Yeah. I guess. It was nice."

On a mutter, I repeat her last word, take a deep breath, then ask, "And call volume? Up or down since then?"

"I don't count the calls."

"Are the phones ringing or not?"

"Not. As much," she hurries to add. "But it's the week after a holiday—"

"Which is usually busier than ever!"

"If it's any consolation, things have picked up today. Parents are glad you're back." She flutters her eyelashes at me, as if flattery is going to fix this. The phone rings on the counter behind her. "See?" She taps the button next to her ear. "Pediatrics. How may I direct your call?"

While Lynette serves the caller (hopefully not someone

requesting a referral to a different doctor) and Mindy deals with a patient who's arrived for her date with Dr. Reitman, I clutch the doctors' schedules in one hand and run my other one through my hair. Closing my eyes, I turn my back to the waiting area.

There's no resisting the panic now. We're dying. Quickly. It's happening. And I'm either the only one who notices or the only one who cares.

The faces of the patients whose charts contained those red transfer notes flash behind my eyelids. Some of them I met when their parents brought them in for their very first checkup, mere days after birth. I've known them longer than my own daughter. I'm familiar with their likes and dislikes, their fears, their allergies, their medical histories... I've held their parents' hands through emergencies or after long, sleepless, worry-filled nights. I've laughed at the outrageous things they've said without knowing they're saying anything funny at all, when they're being their unique, wonderful selves.

I've also silently cursed a few of the more spoiled, precocious ones—I'll admit it. But that's part of any job where you come in contact with different personalities, especially kids. Some you like, some you like less. At the end of the day, though, I've served them all, and I've felt lucky to have made a difference, even if that difference is as small as making silly faces or telling a dumb knock-knock joke to get someone to stop crying after a shot.

They've collectively been a part of my daily life for the better part of a decade. And I guess since they've been such an important part of *my* life, I've fallen into the trap of overestimating my importance in theirs. In fact, I'm merely another member of the service industry, dispensing medication and advice and bandages. And when they stop receiving the service they've come to expect, they go elsewhere.

It sucks that the service the majority of us provide has never faltered; yet we'll be punished along with the offender. We're like an outstanding waitstaff with a shitty chef. It doesn't matter how attentive we are; as long as the product coming from the kitchen sucks, people aren't going to return.

Lynette's phone call winds down, so I take a deep breath and shuffle through the schedules once more, looking for an open appointment time in both doctors' days that coincides with an open time in mine. It's depressingly easy.

Spinning, I say to Lynette, "Block off the 2:30 slot for all three of us."

"What's the magic word?"

We stare each other down. I'm the first to blink. Shoulders sagging, I concede, "Please."

"That's better." She types and clicks, all the while muttering something about "your brother," but I can't be sure, and I don't care, to be honest.

Maybe I *am* acting like Nick. But maybe being a bit of a dick is what this situation calls for. Being nice is getting me—and this clinic—nowhere.

* * *

HE'S LATE. Of course he is. He's never on time for patients, so why should he be on time for this appointment? Dr. Reitman and I have been chatting for ten minutes while we wait for Dr. Douche to make his entrance.

"There's something about that DNA that presses the panic button that's so rarely triggered in an exam room with someone else's child," I'm saying now, referring to my time at home with Georgia the past two days. "I knew it was most likely a tooth—or two or three teeth—but I still couldn't stop myself wondering, 'What if?' and coming up with horrible diagnoses, like meningitis."

Dr. Reitman chuckles. "One time, when my youngest was about ten, I forced her into an ice bath when—based on touch —I swore she was burning up with fever. I was about to call 911, because my husband was out of town on business and I didn't trust myself to drive with what I was sure was about to be a comatose kid in the backseat of my minivan. Turns out, her fever had broken hours earlier, and she forgot to tell me she'd been snuggled under an electric blanket since then. She was crying so hard in that bathtub, because it was painfully cold, that it took forever through her blue lips to give me all the information I needed. I felt like such an amateur! She's in college, and she *still* brings that up. 'Remember the time Mom tried to give me hypothermia?'"

We're laughing about that, and I'm filing it away as another "What Not to Do," when Dr. Douche breezes in, coffee in one hand, powdered donut in the other.

He flicks the wrist of his donut hand to spin his watch around and get a good look at it, sprinkling white sugar and crumbs onto the floor in the process. Instead of apologizing for being late (and making a mess), he says, shifting a huge bite to free up one side of his mouth, "How long is this going to take? I have a patient in fifteen minutes."

I watch a crumb launch from his lips and land on the carpet. Focusing on that morsel, I moderate my response.

Dr. Reitman steps into the silence. "I'm not sure, since I didn't schedule this meeting. Nate?"

All of the diplomatic things I've rehearsed in my head until now disappear, as I look up from the crumb on the floor to the one balanced on his upper lip and blurt, "You're killing us."

"Wha...?" he muffles through another mouthful while still standing in the open doorway.

"Can you come in here all the way, please, and shut the door?"

He complies, pops the last bite between his lips, and washes it down with coffee. "What the heck is all this about?"

"Sit."

"I'd rather not."

"Fine." I lean forward in my chair, rest my elbows on my knees, and try to draw courage from my shoes when I ask, "Have either of you noticed a drastic decrease in patient volume?"

Silence.

Dr. Reitman finally says, "Well, yes. But for obvious reasons. I figured it was a result of my impending retirement, that Lynette and Mindy were scheduling more patients with you two and fewer with me."

I look at Dr. Douche to get his answer. "Don't look at me!" he says. "I wouldn't have any means of comparison. Seems like I'm busier than ever."

Yeah, with your four patients a day, as opposed to two.

Before I can point that out, Dr. Reitman says, "I take it you're experiencing a decline?"

"Yes. A dramatic decline."

"Sounds like a 'you' problem," Dr. Douche mutters.

My hands fly to the wooden arms of the chair, and my back straightens. "Excuse me? Before you came along, I was booked solid. Double-booked. Every single day."

"Oh, I see. This is my fault."

"Pretty much."

"You're delusional!"

"You're incompetent!"

"Guys, guys!" Dr. Reitman stands behind her desk and slaps the surface to get our attention. When we both stop shouting at each other and look at her, she says, "Whoa. How is this helping anything?"

"You can't cure a disease until you diagnose it," I say.

"We are going to speak respectfully to each other." Her tone is gentle, but the criticism is there nonetheless.

"You're going to take his side? Seriously? He's wrecking what you've spent your entire career building."

Dr. Douche snorts. "This guy..."

I keep my eyes on Dr. Reitman, because her opinion is the only one that matters to me. I need her to believe me. And she does. I see it. She knows I'm right. She *knows*. Yet she's been standing by, watching it happen, watching the rest of us play out the beginning of the end and hoping she's long gone before Greenbrier pulls the plug on us.

If I were in her shoes, would I do the same? She's retiring; it's out of her hands. Does she have to let it go, move on with her life, and accept that it's not her battle anymore? Is it a defense mechanism? Do I fault her and resent her for it?

Yes. Yes, I do. And I'm not going to let her off the hook.

"I'm working my ass off, trying to keep this place afloat," I say, rising to my feet. "I've endured months of shadowing this doofus"—I jab my thumb in said doofus's direction—"not that it's done any good. He's still as hopeless as he was on the first damn day."

"I'm right here, you know."

I glare at him. "Yeah. Unfortunately."

"Listen, pal, like it or not, I'm this clinic's doctor."

"It doesn't matter what I like or don't like. It matters what the patients—and their caregivers—like. And they don't like *you*."

Dr. Reitman sighs. "Nate, let's not make this personal."

"It *is* personal, though. It's been personal since Day One, when he called me out in front of everyone in the morning staff meeting."

"You're *still* whining about that? Jesus H.—"

"I'm not whining about it. I'm stating a fact. You've had it in for me."

"In other words, I'm destroying this practice to stick it to you? Is that your self-important, paranoid theory?"

"What? No! I'm just saying..." I take a deep breath and collect my thoughts. They both wait. Finally, when I'm sure I'm not going to mortify myself by crying, I continue, "I take all of this personally. Because it's more than my livelihood; it's my"—I blush and swallow— "passion. All right? And you may not think the stakes are high, Dan, but they are."

"You think I want to fail?"

"You know it's impossible to fail."

"What's that supposed to mean?"

"It means that after you drive this place into the ground, Greenbrier will find somewhere else to put you, because you're... you. The rest of us won't have it so easy. Beulah, who's raising her grandkids—not sure if you knew that or cared—will be looking for a job for the first time in nearly thirty years. Janet's also a single mom. And Mindy will have to find another way to supplement her student loans to pay for college. Maybe her boyfriend can sell his motorcycle."

"For crying out—"

"Or how about Lynette?"

He smirks. "What about her? I know you have a soft spot for her—"

"Don't start with that bullshit rumor that you and your wife have been trying to spread—"

"Veronica and I haven't said a word!"

"Yes, you have. To my wife."

"I've never had a private conversation with your wife about anything, much less about your brother's piece on the side."

I close my mouth on the retort I had ready and shift my weight to my other foot, shake my head, and say, "Excuse me?"

"What?" He looks from Dr. Reitman to me. "Don't tell me you didn't know about Nick and Lynette." He laughs—nay, giggles. "Hot damn. You had no clue."

"Shut up. You're lying."

Placing his free hand on his heart (or where that organ would be if he had one), he blinks rapidly. "With God as my witness... Dude. I thought everyone already knew, so there was no point repeating it."

Mouth dry, I turn to Dr. Reitman and tilt my head.

She looks down at her desktop.

"You're— This is a sick joke, right?" My tone beseeches her to answer affirmatively.

Instead, she says, "We've strayed a bit off-topic. And we need to get back to work, so..."

I curl my hands into fists at my side. "Yeah. Well. I..."

Clearing her throat, she suggests, "Maybe we can all brainstorm over the next few days and come back Monday morning with some ideas for boosting our numbers. Referral incentives, or something. A banner in front of the office that says we're accepting new patients?"

I can hardly focus on what she's saying, because I'm suddenly unable to think of anything else but my brother and Lynette. Mental flashes of them... When? Where? An echo of Lynette's voice the Monday after the Halloween party: *"I had to get drunk to make myself go to the party at all.... I'm kind of a mess right now.... There's something—* someone—*who's sort of doing my head in."*

And I'd stopped her. Because, like an idiot, I'd worried she might have been talking about *me*, and I didn't want to be responsible for that information. But it wasn't me. It was Nick.

That rat bastard. I'm going to kill him.

I say that last sentence out loud as I stride from the room, yanking the door open in the middle of Dr. Reitman's musing over our Monday schedules, trying to figure out when the three of us can reconvene to discuss recruiting new patients and retaining the ones we have.

That can wait.

On my way to the staff door leading to the back parking lot, I claw my phone from my pocket and, with shaking hands, text my brother, *You. Me. The Cheesehead. Tonight. 6:00.*

He fires back. *No can do, bro. Already got something else going on.*

After crashing through the door, I lean against the brick wall and suck in huge gulps of painful, icy air. When I've contained my rage, I tap, *I'll tell Lynette your plans have changed.*

Nothing comes back for several minutes. By the time I get a response, I've been out here long enough to start shivering in my thin scrubs. Teeth chattering, I read, *OK. See you at 6:00.*

I want to throw my phone, but this thing wasn't cheap, and I'm not due for an upgrade for at least a year. Instead, I bang the flat of my hand against the brick wall, reveling in the sting that distracts me from the nausea my brother's utter lack of denial induces. Clenching my tingling hand in front of my mouth, I blow into it, wondering how I'm going to go back inside and face Lynette, much less the rest of my day.

The cold—and my few remaining patients—give me no choice, however. I pocket my phone, rub my arms, and implore myself to pull it together, then jerk the door open and step back inside.

26

CHEESEHEAD CHEATERS

BY SOME MIRACLE, I SUCCESSFULLY AVOID LYNETTE FOR THE rest of the afternoon. Or maybe she avoids me. After all, I'm sure Nick isn't relying on me to tell her about their change of evening plans; he must have gotten word to her that I know about them.

Oh, gosh. There's a "them." Eff me.

Anyway, between the few appointments I have from in the last two hours of the day, I cloister myself at the nurses' station and stay clear of the front desk. And as soon as the hands hit the five and the twelve on the clock, I don't give anyone a chance to delay me. I need to get home, take a shower, change my clothes, and get the heck back out of the house before Betty and Georgia arrive.

It's one thing to text Betty from work to let her know I'm going to spend the evening with Nick—just two brothers catching up and shootin' the breeze. It would be a whole other thing to try to pull off that story straight to her face. I couldn't do it. I'd have to tell her the whole sorry tale, and I don't have the time—or the stomach—for that. Plus, I'd work myself into such a rage relaying it to her that there'd be a real danger of my killing Nick when I see him.

All goes smoothly, and well before six, I'm bellied up to the bar, waiting for my scumbag brother. Fifteen minutes later, I'm still waiting. For once, though, I don't mind that he's late for our rendezvous. It gives me time to finish my second Guinness. That doesn't mean I don't give him crap when he finally does slide onto the bar stool next to mine.

"What's with doctors, anyway? You guys purposely set your clocks, watches, and phones ten minutes slow so you can assert your authority by making everyone wait for you?"

He signals to the bartender and orders one of those trendy "ultra" beers that taste like watered-down urine (I imagine) but promise a less bulky calorie count.

"Oh, right," I say, staring at the lacy foam stuck to the side of my stein. "Gotta maintain that sleek figure the ladies love."

"You're pissed at me," he states, receiving his beer and taking three long swallows.

"Pissed? At you? Nah. Why would I be?"

He licks his lips and stifles a burp. "C'mon, bro. Just give it to me."

"I'll leave that to my co-workers, thanks."

"It was one time."

I laugh and get the bartender's attention. I'm going to need another drink or seven. "Sure. Tell me another good one."

"It was!"

"And now you guys meet up in secret to talk about your feelings and your hopes for the future? Futures that don't include each other?"

He says nothing; merely stares into his half-full drink.

I turn my head and stare at him until he lifts his green eyes —so like our mother's (and mine)—and stares down. "What the hell are you thinking?" I ask.

"I—"

"Have you lost your mind?"

"If you'd let me—"

"Because less than a week ago, you looked me straight in the face and told me you weren't having an affair. You swore I wasn't lying to Heidi when I told her that exact thing. And now I find out—from Dan Chancellor, of all people—that you not only lied to *me*, but you've been lying to your wife—your *pregnant* wife—and having an affair with someone I work with every day."

"This isn't about you, all right?"

I take a swig of my newly delivered beer, swallow, then say, "Fair enough. But you still haven't answered my question. What the hell?"

He frowns, looking exactly like his older son when he craps his pants and doesn't have an answer for why he didn't ask to go to the toilet. "I dunno. Nothing. It doesn't mean anything. It's just an escape." Over my muttering, he continues, "I— It just happened."

"No! No clichés! I don't want to hear the version you're going to tell Heidi when she finds out."

His head bounces up. "You're not going to tell her, are you?"

"What? Hell, no! But she's going to find out from someone. Apparently, I was the last person in the Green Bay medical community to find out."

He sighs. "She's not going to find out, because it's over."

"Oh, like that, huh?" I scoff and snap my fingers. "Because you don't need that 'escape' anymore?"

"Because it's wrong. But Lynette's so... uncomplicated. And fun. And cute. And... and tight."

I nearly spray beer all over the bar but hold it in at the last second and dribble it into my glass.

"Sorry," he mumbles. "But it's true."

"Stop it," I say through gritted teeth. "Just stop. Your wife has had two of your children and is expecting another."

"Exactly! It's not the same as it used to be."

I shake my head and stare at the ceiling, hoping something up there will distract me from the urge to punch my only brother until his face is unrecognizable. So much for that happy drunk I usually am. Or maybe I would have killed him by now if I were completely sober.

Finally, I growl, "You are such an asshole."

"I know."

"No, I mean, you are in a class of asshole I thought only existed in stupid guy movies about hot tub time travel and epic hangovers."

"I know!"

"Stop saying that!"

"Why? Because I refuse to argue with you? I'm robbing you of your self-righteousness?"

"No, because if you know, that makes it *more* unacceptable."

"I know."

I groan at his insistence upon torturing me with those two words. After a few more swallows of beer, I ask, "How? How the hell did this happen?"

He chuckles. "I see. You want to know details."

"No, I don't. Not *those* details. I want to know... How did you two even... It's not like you travel in the same social circles."

"How would you know?"

I lower my chin and shoot him a look. "Please. Let's not pretend a twenty-something receptionist is in the same social class as a successful thoracic surgeon. She's not invited to formal charity benefits; she doesn't have season tickets to the symphony and opera. Let's be real. For once."

He holds my eye contact for a while, then blinks and concedes, "Fine. You're right. We didn't bump into each other at a social function, or anything like that."

"Okay. Then?"

"It was... uh..." He shifts on his bar stool. Dread builds in my sloshy stomach. "Promise you won't punch me."

"Since when are you physically afraid of me?"

"Since the answer I'm going to tell you may push you to a place you've never been."

Suspecting I'll regret it, I nevertheless promise, "I won't hurt you."

"She was dog-sitting for you one weekend when you and Betty were up at the lake last March. I couldn't remember if you'd asked me to check in on the dog, so I drove by, just in case. Lynette was there."

"Oh. Oh, no. No, no, no."

"Yeah. I saw her car in the driveway and was going to keep driving, but it was one of those days, you know? The thought of going home..."

"Why didn't you come here, then? Or go to Mom and Dad's? Meet up with a friend? Why, why, why did you stop at my house?"

"I didn't plan to do anything wrong. I planned to hang out for a few minutes, maybe laugh about you behind your back."

I snort.

"But she invited me in, and she was most of the way through a bottle of wine and a private viewing of that movie with the dude who does nasty things to that girl in the pain room, or whatever. And like... I wanted to have something—to *do* something—for me, for once. And it's only sex."

I stare incredulously at him.

"Purely a physical thing. I love Heidi."

"Chocolates and wine. That's how you prove you love your wife. Not by banging your brother's dog-sitting co-worker—"

"We didn't do it on your bed or anything, if that's what you're worried about. It all happened on the living room floor, which proves it was an impulsive, crazy, irresistible urge."

I stagger to my feet and fling some money on the bar to cover my tab. "I have to go."

"Wait!" Nick grabs my arm. I clench my teeth but don't shake him off, as much as I want to. "Nate, I'm sorry. By doing that at your house, I implicated you."

"I have nothing to do with your impulse control issues. Or your God complex. Or your lax morals."

"True. But I still feel bad."

"No, you don't. If I hadn't found out about this, and if I hadn't insisted we meet here tonight, you'd be with her right now, wouldn't you?"

He lets go of my arm and rubs his palm across his chin. "Yes."

"Then the only thing you're sorry about is that I found out and you feel ashamed enough about it now to stop."

"No, that's not true. I swear it."

On my way past him, I lean closer to his ear. "Your vows mean dick."

He drops his head.

I rush to the doors and out onto the cold sidewalk, still feeling as sober as when I arrived. But that means nothing when it comes to my blood alcohol content.

At my car, I call Dad. He owes me a few dozen rides.

* * *

DAD *AND* MOM pick me up. I'm too irate (and the beers are

catching up to me) to question this strange new development. Anyway, it works to my advantage, because with two sober people in attendance, one of them drives my car home and saves me the trip out here early tomorrow morning before work with an annoyed wife (and a hangover).

Fortunately, they don't ask what my problem is—other than being a lightweight who can get too drunk to drive on three measly beers—and I don't volunteer the information. It's not my place to tell them one of their sons is a cheating jerk-wad. Like they'd care. Consider my audience. Mom might be proud that she's set such a lovely, you-only-live-once example.

But Dad and I don't talk at all. As a matter of fact, even though we're the only two in the car, since Mom's following in mine, I choose to sit in the backseat like a moody teenager, watching the snowy city pass by my window and trying not to get too carsick on the short ride.

When we arrive at my house, I thank them but don't invite them in for so much as a coffee. I'm not in a hosting mood. If they mind, they don't let on. I don't stick around long enough in the driveway to allow them to voice any displeasure or disappointment. Rude? Sure. Do I care? No. I'm past the point of caring what these people think. They obviously don't give a damn about my opinions—on anything lately.

Betty's surprised to see me home so early. She's more surprised when I give her a terse "Good night" and am in bed in my underwear before she can react and follow me.

"You gonna tell me what the heck is going on?" she asks, silhouetted in the bedroom doorway, backlit by the hall light.

Perhaps I answer, "Nick and Lynette screwed each other on our living room floor," but then again, I may merely be thinking that—complete with a drunken slur in my inner voice —before I pass out.

When I wake a few hours later, the sugar in the alcohol

making its way through my system and jolting me from my temporary, dreamless booze coma, Betty's sound asleep next to me. After a quick trip to the bathroom, then a longer visit to the kitchen for rehydration, I rejoin her to experience a restless slumber filled with nightmares about my family members' adulterous sex lives.

This morning, Betty wakes me from above with a shake to my shoulder. "Your alarm's been going off for thirty minutes."

"Huh?" I slurp drool from the corner of my mouth and wipe the excess from my cheek on my bare shoulder, having forgotten I'm not wearing a shirt. The result is too much "sexy" before seven a.m.

"Are you going to get up and go to work, or what?"

Work. Lynette. Nick. Beer.

I flip to my front and bury my still-damp face in my pillow, where I grumble an obscenity.

The mattress sags next to me, rolling my hip against Betty's. She traces lazy circles on my back that don't help with the morning wood I'm sporting.

"You want to elaborate on that teaser you gave me last night in your family's continuing telenovela?"

"No time," I muffle but don't move.

"I've filled in most of the blanks myself, because I'm a smart girl, but... when did this happen?"

Turning my head so I'm no longer breathing my own morning breath, recycled through the fibers of my pillow, I keep my eyes closed and answer, "Last spring. When we went to the lake, and Lynette stayed here with Reba. Nick was making sure he wasn't dropping the ball on dog-sitting duties, and instead of driving past when he saw Lynette's car, he thought, 'Hey, I know. I'll stop in and do it doggy-style with someone who's not my wife. That'll be fun.'"

Betty slaps my shoulder. "This isn't funny."

"I'm being flippant so I don't barf."

"And he admitted this to you, out of the blue, at The Cheesehead last night?"

"No, I found out about it from Dr. Douche." I groan at the memory. "He was delighted to be the bearer of that news, let me tell ya."

She leans down and kisses my ear, then whispers next to it, "I'm so sorry."

"Betts, you're making me seriously horny right now."

She backs away and slaps my butt (which also doesn't help things). "How can you think about sex right now?"

"Seems like that's all *anyone* in my family can think about... ever. I guess I need to stop fighting it. This is what Binghams are, apparently. Sex maniacs."

"Well, I need to get Georgia up and ready, and you need to stop sulking about stuff you can't control and get on with the things you can."

"Your tough love is so hot." I roll onto my back so she can see how effective it is.

She laughs and rises from the bed, saying over her shoulder, "Work it off in the shower, Nathaniel. You're going to be late."

I flap my lips, then yawn. Time to get on with the things I can control. That list is depressingly short, unfortunately.

* * *

FOR THE REST of the week, I'm granted a reprieve from seeing and working with Lynette, since she calls in sick on Thursday and Friday. Monday, however, she's back. Fortunately, I'm a bit distracted by my light schedule and the brainstorming session, designed to address our dwindling patient load, to dwell on the obvious tension between the two of us. I have bigger problems, believe it or not, than who my brother's been sticking it to behind my sister-in-law's back. As a matter of fact, that issue's becoming old hat in my family. I'm desensitized to the dishonesty and deception.

Again, Dr. Reitman, Dr. Chancellor, and I meet in Dr. Reitman's office, since it's the largest private room in the building. It's quickly obvious that none of us have come up with a magic solution to the problem since we last spoke, so we decide to try Dr. Reitman's original idea of patient referral incentives. We're also going to spring for a professionally printed banner in the front lawn of the clinic, where people can easily see it as they drive past on one of the town's busiest thoroughfares. It will shout, *"Now accepting new patients!"* like we're doing *them* a favor.

Now, we have to figure out what the referral incentives will be—and how we're going to fund them.

Dr. Reitman pipes up, "I've seen Greenbrier do this with other clinics. They'll have a ready-made plan for us, if we tell them we want to use it."

I shift in my chair. "See, that's the part I'm not so wild about: the humiliating ourselves and admitting we need their help."

She looks across the table at Dr. Douche. "Well, that's where Dan comes in."

"Me?"

"Yes, you. Since you have connections on the Board."

He laughs mirthlessly. "What? No."

"Yes," she and I say together.

"Why?" he whines.

Before I can say, *"Because this is all your fault, you dumbass,"* Dr. Reitman answers more diplomatically, "Because you're this clinic's doctor. You said so yourself last week. And it was a valid point."

I sit back in my chair, cross my arms over my chest, and try not to laugh out loud. I don't attempt to hide my grin, though.

He glowers at me. "You can wipe that smug smile off your face, because I'm not doing it."

"Yeah, you are," I reply, standing and crossing to the door. "Well, this was a good, productive chat. I'll take care of the banner. You two can reimburse me for your share whenever. I look forward to hearing what Greenbrier recommends, incentive-wise."

In the hallway, I'm still chuckling at the memory of the horrified, mutinous expression on Dr. Douche's face when I come face-to-face with Lynette, who's rounding the corner from the staff room.

She straightens her headset and steps past me, muttering, "Excuse me."

"Is this how it's going to be from now on?" I ask before I realize I'm going to say it.

She stops shy of pushing on the swinging door to take her back to the front desk. Face inches from the wooden paneling in front of her, she says, "I guess."

Checking to make sure there are no little ears or parents of little ears around, I say, "That sucks."

"I figure you're pretty mad at me."

"I am."

"And I don't blame you."

"I'll get over it. It's not my place to be mad at you. I'm not the injured party here."

Tapping her finger on the door, she allows, "I guess not, but..."

"I do love the person you're hurting."

She nods but says, "Listen, can we not talk about this here? It's... it's uncomfortable and inappropriate."

"So... what? We never talk about it? We pretend it never happened, that it isn't happening?"

"It's not happening anymore, okay? Drop it." Now she does push through and leaves me in the hall, getting intermittent, increasingly brief glimpses of her taking her seat as the door swings back and forth in shorter bursts, until it finally comes to rest in its frame.

I stare at the dark wood for several seconds, torn between feeling bad for Lynette, relieved that Nick finally did the right thing (better late then never, I suppose), and worried about what's still to come for Heidi.

27

HOUSE OF HORROR

Bundled in the pale pink snowsuit and bunting she lives in five months out of the year in this godforsaken area, Georgia blinks out at me, the epitome of tolerance and patience. It helps that I've decided "in the car" is another acceptable place for binky-sucking, so she probably sees this immobilizing get-up as a means to an end. The pacifier quivers in a way her arms and legs can't.

I sweat from the effort of getting her into the suit, then strapped into the bunting-encapsulated carrier. Since Betty's at yet another boondoggle this week, this is my life twice a day, morning and evening. I stand back and examine my work (and catch my breath).

I wipe my forehead. My sweaty bangs stand up in spikes. I brush them down again, then place my hands on my hips to further open my airways. "You're getting too big for this thing, George," I refer to the carrier. "This weekend, it's time to make the switch. A true rite of passage. We'll say a few words and retire this old thing. Get you a proper big-girl's car seat." My bright tone belies my heartbreak at the zooming passage of time.

Squeak, squeak, squeak.

"I knew you'd agree."

Behind the wheel, I fasten my seatbelt and take a moment to let the car heat up (and catch my breath again). I'm pathetically out of shape, although I still wouldn't describe myself as "paunchy." More like... unconditioned.

Speaking of... "What do you say we drop by Pop-Pop's house for a visit tonight? One squeak for 'yes,' two squeaks for 'no.'"

Several squeaks float from the backseat.

"Actually, I was only asking to be polite; you're not in charge here. Let's go."

Dad was quiet on Monday night at our usual meet-up at The Cheesehead. I wasn't particularly chatty, either, considering the only thing I can think about lately is my jerk brother, and I'm not allowed to talk about that. Nor do I want to. I just wish I could stop thinking about it.

Dad and I ate mostly in silence, grunting a few things here and there about work. At first, I thought that was a good thing, that he'd turned a corner and had finally exhausted the topics centered around Mom's infidelity and how lonely he is. Yay. Improvement.

But the more I've thought about it this week, the more his subdued manner has niggled at me. Like the eerie stillness before all hell breaks loose in a summer storm. Plus, there's a difference between acceptance and resignation. If he's accepting his new life, that's great. That means he's healing and moving on and ready for the next phase, whatever it may be. Resignation is another story. People resign themselves to their lot in life. Then they commit suicide.

And now I'm obsessed with that awful idea. It's bloomed in the last couple of days, too, as I've called and texted him and received no response. None. That's unheard of.

I'd consult with Nick—and get him to go check on Dad, or at least come with me—but since we're still not talking, by mutual agreement, that's not an option. Anyway, I don't need to talk to my brother to know exactly what he'd say. He'd explain Dad's silence with "Maybe he's finally getting laid again," or reassure me, "The housekeeper would have found his body by now."

I've come up with a few less crass and traumatic explanations, myself. Like, maybe he lost his phone. Or perhaps he's at a psychiatry conference that he failed to mention—or mentioned when I wasn't listening. But that wouldn't prevent him from replying to a text. Or returning a call... eventually.

So, at the risk of finding something gruesome, Georgia and I are going to check things out. I keep telling myself she's too young to remember anything horrible she might see. And I'll simply have to add it to the list of psychologically damaging issues from my past year.

Just in case, I dial my dad's number. Because it would be so much better if he picked up his phone right now. I could take Georgia straight home, and we could eat a nice, quiet dinner (as quiet as a dinner with a toddler and dog can be), then settle into the bedtime routine. And oh, yeah... my dad wouldn't be dead.

Again, my call—and another text (*I'm starting to worry about you. Text me back a sign of life. LOL... not really laughing*)—goes unanswered.

Now I'm convinced.

And no amount of acting like this is a normal visit to "Pop-Pop's" is going to change that.

The best I can hope for is that he chose a clean exit plan. Pills. Or a hose from the tailpipe through the driver's window of his car. Please not hanging. Or wrist-slitting. He doesn't own a gun, so unless he recently bought one... Oh, gosh, anything but that.

For the entire fifteen-minute drive from daycare to Dad's, I pray. Hard. Not merely, "Oh, dear Lord, please don't let me find a bloody mess." Like, for real praying. The Lord's Prayer, the Serenity Prayer, Hail Mary (and I'm not Catholic), the Apostles Creed, the Nicene Creed. Songs by Creed (but that's not at all helpful, so I double back and start over again with the Lord's Prayer). I'm throwing every prayer I possibly can at this situation. I even go freestyle for a while at a particularly long stoplight, punctuating my pleas with plenty of "Oh Lord"s and "Jesus"es, like an enthusiastic evangelical.

At Dad's, I park in the empty driveway and take some shaky breaths while I contemplate my strategy. Do I leave Georgia out here in the car? No, that would be irresponsible. I'm going to have to trust that everything my parents taught me about memories was true, and she won't remember this day, no matter how traumatic it turns out to be.

I ring the doorbell. Nothing.

I look down my arm at Georgia. My breath billows between us when I say, "Okay, here's the deal. We're going in. But I'm setting you down by the front door while I look around."

I unlock the front door, step inside, and close it quietly behind us. Because I'd hate to disturb any dead dads in here.

After setting Georgia down, I say, "Suck your pacifier and think happy thoughts. I'll be right back. Hopefully."

Squeak, squeak, squeak.

I take a few steps, then backtrack and lock the front door. No use tempting fate to make this a worse experience than it already is. "Don't move."

I realize who I'm saying that to and almost laugh, but I

may be physically incapable of that right now. Instead, I try to lick some moisture into my dry mouth and lips.

Inexplicably, I tiptoe from room to room, peeking around doorways and corners, holding my breath at each new threshold. I hear a thump overhead, so I turn away from the short hallway leading from the mudroom, abandoning my impulse to check the garage for idling cars or bodies.

Now, climbing the stairs, I keep quiet so I can hear what's going on up here. Moaning. Combined with that rhythmic thumping, I'm sure Dad's fallen in the shower, broken something (most likely, his hip, given his age), and is writhing in pain, possibly bleeding from a head wound, maybe going into shock, depending on how long he's been incapacitated. Without hesitating, I burst through his mostly closed bedroom door, determined to run to the bathroom and use my nursing skills to save the day.

"I'm here!" I call, the final word dying like a deflating balloon when I take in the scene in front of me. On the bed. Limbs. So many limbs. Too many, it seems, for two bodies. But there are only two heads, one of which belongs to that familiar-yet-I-can't-believe-what-I'm-seeing woman. Who looks like... Oh, shit. It *is* my mom.

She screams and rolls onto her back in one motion, her legs flying in opposite directions, so I get a horrifying, detailed view of a part I haven't seen in more than thirty-five years and wouldn't have been able to pick out in a lineup... until today.

"Holyhellwhatthefuck?" I gasp, slapping my palms over my eyes and spinning around to face the exit. I don't need to look again to recognize the black-sock-clad feet attached to the pasty, sun-spotted legs I briefly spied under my mom.

"Nathan! What are you doing?!" she screeches.

"What am *I* doing? What are you...? Never mind; don't answer that. I... I thought Dad was dead. And I was coming to find him. But I heard moaning and thumping and thought he was up here, hurt!"

"Ever thought of calling?" Mom asks, still breathless but not as upset as before.

"I've been calling for days! And I rang the doorbell! Is everyone dressed?"

"No!" they say in unison behind me.

It doesn't matter. I'm sure if I opened my eyes, I'd find myself hysterically blind.

I'm glad my dad responded to my question, because I was starting to think my initial suspicion was correct, and something even kinkier and sicker than what's actually happening was going on between my mom and my dad's corpse.

"Please, tell me this isn't happening, and I'm going to wake up any second now, covered in sweat, sick to my stomach, and unable to look either of you in the eye for a couple of weeks, but still, not as messed up as I'm going to be if this is reality."

"This is happening. And you can turn around. We're decent."

That's debatable.

Without a single glance at them, I walk to and through the door, then down the hall, to the closest safe place I can think of right now: my old bedroom. No sex ever happened in that room. It's a fact that used to haunt me, that Nick used against me more times than I can count, but for which I am so thankful right now, I could cry.

Inside the sexless sanctuary, I close the door, push in the lame doorknob lock, and sag against the wood slab. Before I realize what I'm doing, I see my shaky fingers punching the buttons on my phone screen, calling my brother.

"I see you've decided to stop being a pissy pussy and call me, huh?"

"Oh, crap on a cracker. Don't say 'puss—' that word."

"You're more repressed than a nun from a planet of nuns who reproduces asexually using eyelashes and an atom splitter."

"Shhh... Shut up! I walked in on Mom and Dad."

"Walked in on them? Doing...? Oh!" He laughs. "Bro. No way."

"Yes way!" I pant, then focus on slowing down my breathing so I don't hyperventilate.

"At their house? What the heck were you doing there?"

"I was looking for dad's body."

"What?"

Impatiently, I explain, "I haven't been able to get in touch with him for a couple of days, so I was worried he... he was dead, or something."

"Only you would jump straight to that conclusion."

"I figured the worst thing I'd see tonight was his lifeless body, perhaps some blood... some brains."

"That's sick."

"Well, this was so much worse!"

"C'mon, be real. Where are they now?"

"I don't know!" I listen for a second to what may be going on in the hallway behind my back but hear nothing but my ragged breathing. "Hopefully registering for the witness protection program, where I'll never be able to find them, not that I'm interested in searching for them."

"Where's Georgia?"

That I do know. "Oh, shit. I left her in her carrier by the front door."

"Man up and go get her. And face the music."

"I can't. I need a minute. She'll be fine. But I won't be. I saw Mom's—" I gulp and shiver at the mental images. "Oh, gosh."

"How the hell did you get *that* close to the action before

realizing what was going on? And bro, enough with the details. I'd rather not know."

"Too bad! This should be you! You should be the one here."

"Me? Why me?"

"Because you're a bad person, and you deserve to have bad things happen to you."

"Wow. Thanks."

He doesn't sound all that hurt, so I don't feel bad insisting, "You are! And I'm a good person. I don't cheat on my wife or treat my co-workers like crap..." *Well... most of the time...* "...or call people 'bro.'"

"It makes me a bad person that I call you 'bro'? You're the only one I call that. Because you're my brother."

"I don't avoid hanging out with my kid."

"Where is your daughter right now, again?"

"That's different! And I recycle! And compost. And I drive a hybrid, so I'm good to the planet, too. I drop money in the red Christmas kettles every time I pass one on my way in or out of a store. I also always tip fifteen percent—or round up to twenty when the math is hard—and... and... I rescued a dog from a shelter!"

"What the hell is your point, br— man?"

Having moved on from traumatized to truly pissed, I snarl, "My point is, why does this nasty shit happen to me? If there was any justice in this world, crap like this would only happen to scumbags like you."

"Hey, don't hold back."

"It's no secret that's what you are. It's not like you're trying to hide it, for the most part. *I* have all the evidence, anyway. Maybe you've fooled others—for now—into thinking you're a stand-up guy, but I know the truth." I press my hand to my chest. My heart knocks against my palm. "God knows I wish I didn't. I wish I was still as in the dark about it as your wife, maybe suspecting something's off but not having the proof, therefore blissfully able to go about my business, not thinking about what you've been up to lately in your 'spare time.'"

"That's over. I ended it. You going to throw it back in my face for the rest of my life?"

"Maybe. Isn't that what you deserve? Shouldn't you have thought of that before you ever did what you did?"

"I thought it was a one-time thing. And that nobody would ever find out."

I scoff. "Oh, that makes it okay, then. My bad for calling you a scumbag."

"Apology accepted."

"I'm not apologizing, you idiot!"

"I'm going to cut you some slack and pretend like you are, though. Because you're having some kind of psychotic episode, triggered by what you saw, like you're the only person who's ever had this happen to him. If it makes you feel better, I *have* walked in on Mom and Dad before."

"Recently?"

"God, no! I was a kid."

My heart sinks. "Not the same."

"Still horrible."

"Not even close."

"It's traumatic, no matter how old you are."

I picture what I just saw through the eyes of a child and argue, "You had no idea what you were seeing until years later. And by then, it was a foggy memory. I will never forget this. I know *exactly* what they were doing, and now I'll never be able to do that to my own wife again."

"You and Dad share some moves, eh? How long did you stand there and watch, anyway?"

"A half-second, maybe. Too long! And then there was

screaming and flailing limbs and—" I gag and squeeze my eyes shut.

"It's going to be okay," he calmly reassures, then brightens. "Hey, silver lining: looks like they're getting back together. This should make you happy."

"Oh, yeah. Seeing Mom and Dad bump uglies would make any guy happy. What's wrong with me?"

"You're always focused on the negative."

"I'd like you to get your positive ass over here, see what I saw, and tell me how happy you are."

"No thanks. But this is entertaining, listening to you flip out about it."

A knocking behind my shoulder makes me flinch away from the door, then lunge at it again to make sure it's truly locked.

"Nathan?" my mom calls through the wood. "Who are you talking to?"

I slide down the door, sit on the floor, and hug my knees. "Nobody. I'm so scarred, I've taken to talking to myself."

"Dadadadadadada!"

"Go put Georgia back in her carrier, please."

"She was burning up in that thing."

"Tell me you didn't undress her." Good sign: I can still worry about the extra work of stuffing my kid back in that damn fleece snowsuit, so I must not be completely gone.

"I unstrapped her and took her out of the bunting, that's all. But she still doesn't seem comfortable."

"Don't worry about it; we're not staying. Put her back, and go somewhere in the house where I won't see you or Dad on my way out. Please."

"Now don't be ridiculous. We're all adults here."

"Yeah, we're all adults here," Nick chimes in from my hand. "Listen, if you're finished treating me like shit to make yourself feel better, I have to go. Heidi and I have a big brothers' class to take the boys to."

"How cozy."

"I'm trying, all right? Stop busting my balls."

"Does she know?"

His silence is the answer.

Of course not. Because if she did know, he wouldn't have any balls for me to bust. They'd be in a baggie in Heidi's purse, where she could take them out whenever she wanted and smack them against the nearest hard surface.

"Of course not. Anyway, I have to go." I stab at the button on the phone to hang up on him, wondering why I ever called him in the first place.

Damn reflex. Stinking co-dependent bullshit, always needing to commiserate with him when our parents do or say something crazy. I wish I'd been thinking clearly enough to remember I despise him, and I never want to speak to him again, no matter how many times I see our parents doing *that*. And it better be zero more times.

As a matter of fact, when I get home, I'm going online to research time travel, and the first thing I'm doing is going back to that moment in the daycare parking lot and deciding I *don't* care if the housekeeper is the one to find my dad's decaying body.

"Nathan? Sweetie?"

"Mom! Why are you still out there? You should be hiding."

"I'm not going to hide from you. That's silly."

"Then I'm never coming out. Or I'll leave by the window. Please put Georgia on the front porch."

There's a clicking and scraping at a point directly above my head, which I realize too late is one of those stupid lock-springing sticks she and Dad used to employ when we were teenagers. ("We don't lock doors in this house." No shit.

Maybe we should rethink that policy, huh?) The door smacks me in the back, then slams again when I fall against it, digging my heels in the carpet.

Georgia cries at the loud bang.

"Nathan, you're upsetting the baby."

"*You're* upsetting her. And me."

"Come out here and let's talk."

"Let's not. Why can't you do what I tell you to do and let us leave?"

"I'm not going to put her down now; she's crying."

"Give her her pacifier. Then hand her in here." I scoot away from the door to give it clearance to swing into the room. It cracks open, and Georgia waddles through the space and into my lap. I quickly lean against the door again to close it before getting so much as a glimpse of my mother.

And yes, I'm aware I'm being childish, but I'm being much more communicative than I want to be. I want to lie on the floor in the fetal position and rock until I fall asleep, hopefully not to dream about anything I've seen or heard or thought about in the past six months.

Instead, I scoop up Georgia, hug her to my chest, and rock *her*. Because I'm not a child; I'm a dad. And a husband. And a brother. And a son to a pair of weirdos who are perfect for each other and should have never looked for happiness with anyone else and should answer their damn cell phones. If Dad had only answered his phone—or the door—none of this would be happening.

I press my lips to the baby's temple. "Shhhh, it's okay. I'm sorry. This is weird, I know. Beyond weird. I'm supposed to protect you from dumb stuff like this. But I suck." I try to push her binky into her mouth, but she grabs it in her chubby hand and holds it aloft so she can continue crying.

"Gamma!"

"She sucks, too. Although, thank God I didn't see that literally. What I did see was bad enough. And when we get home—if Gamma ever stops holding us hostage—I'm going to install several locks on Mommy and Daddy's bedroom door, so you never ever ever have to experience what I just did. Of course, I may never want to have sex again, so I guess the locks won't be necessary. But you can never be too safe."

Georgia reaches up and shoves the pacifier into my mouth. "Shhhh," she hisses.

I clamp the rubber nipple between my teeth, close my eyes, and laugh. "Got it," I say around the binky. "Suck on this and think happy thoughts, right?"

28

URGE TO FLEE

DESPITE HOW I REACTED, I *AM* AN ADULT. IN THE TWENTY-four hours since walking in on my parents 'reuniting,' I've regained at least twenty of my nearly thirty-six years. I recognize they're two adults who love each other (still, I suppose, despite what they told us five months ago), who are married (since their divorce isn't final yet), and who have obviously enjoyed physical intimacy with each other for decades (la-la-la-la-la-la). And all that was fine when it was theoretical. I've never begrudged them any of it. Until I came face to... whatever... with it.

I'm not proud of how I handled myself, either, but I can't take it back. And realistically, I'm not sure how else I could have responded to that experience. I know too much, I saw too much, and I may never be the same again.

Nick can claim he's suffered the same trauma, but he hasn't. He hasn't. It obviously didn't make an impression on him, or he would have mentioned it before now. And it would have been a joke from the time we both got "the talk" from our parents. Lord knows that was traumatic enough. But it's funny now. At least, we've laughed about it enough over the years that it's become funny.

What happened yesterday... that's never going to be funny.

I just want my wife to come home. I kept Georgia awake later than usual tonight, justifying it by telling myself I was keeping her up so Betty could see her. In fact, I knew by the updates Betty was sending about delays that there was no way Georgia would be able to last long enough to welcome her mom home. I wasn't worried about her not getting enough sleep, because tomorrow is Saturday, so she'll get her twelve hours, no matter what, but she was tugging at her ears, crabbing at her stuffed toys, and whining at the things I did that usually make her giggle until she has trouble breathing. My selfish need to delay the moment I'd be alone, left to my own devices with no distractions and nothing to occupy me and my thoughts, bordered on cruelty as exhaustion settled in. I finally admitted to myself that I was being a pathetic jerk and put the poor child to bed.

Since then, I've tried reading, watching TV, and sleeping. But I'm wide awake. And my thoughts are pinging in all directions, but they bounce back to one place: I want to get out of here. Out of this town, out of this state, out of this mess.

And I'm not talking about Jamaica at Christmas, either. I'm talking: Out. Of. Here. Permanently.

Is this merely an urge to run away from my problems? Hell, yes. I'm not pretending it's anything else. A fresh start is what I need. It's what *we* need. Who cares what the impetus is?

That's why I'm looking at real estate in coastal, southern areas when Betty finally arrives home. After our initial hellos, she plops down on the couch, still in her coat, snagging my beer on her way down. She swigs the drink, then drops her head to the back of the couch.

"I thought I'd never get home."

"I thought you'd never get home."

"Connecting through Chicago is a nightmare. And this stupid winter weather doesn't help."

"Winter sucks."

"Two weeks until I unleash my pasty white skin on the corneas of those poor, unsuspecting Jamaicans."

"They won't know what hit them. Seeing one minute; blind the next."

She laughs weakly and gulps the rest of my beer. For the first time since sitting down, she tilts her chin down to view the laptop on the coffee table. "What are you working on?"

"Busting us out of this joint."

"Right."

"I'm serious."

Pursing her lips, she sets the empty bottle next to the computer and says, "So, what did I miss?"

"I walked in on my parents having sex."

She gasps and covers her mouth. "Oh, my gosh. That's terribahahahahaha!" Clamping her hand more tightly against her face, she cuts off the flow of her laughter and muffles, "I'm sorry."

"It's not funny."

Her hand drops. "No, I'm sure it wasn't." She bites her lip and flares her nostrils while she struggles to contain another giggling fit. Eyes watering but under control once more, she grabs my hand. "Tell me what happened."

I start with Dad's weird behavior at The Cheesehead on Monday night, which led me to jump to such dramatic conclusions about his wellbeing to begin with. When I get to the most crucial, life-altering part of the story, she drops my hand and rubs her palms up and down her thighs, grunting and rocking with the effort not to laugh. It only gets worse from there, so I don't give her a word-for-word recall of my conversation with Nick.

Therefore, she has no idea she's echoing him—and saying the wrong thing—when I stop, and she says, "Well, does this mean they're getting back together? Because if they are, that's great!"

I stare at her for a beat, then snap, "That's so beside the point!"

"No, it's not. Bottom line—"

"Don't mention bottoms."

"Their happiness is what matters."

"Knowing how messed up my family is right now, it was a booty call for old times' sake. Maybe they've worked 'friends with benefits' into their divorce settlement. How... amicable."

"Wait a minute. You mean, you didn't ask them if they're getting back together?"

"I asked them to stay hidden while I left their house, so there'd be no chance of having to look at them after seeing what I saw. That's the extent of what I asked."

"Oh, dear. You didn't handle things well at all."

"How was I supposed to handle things?" I explode. "'Hey, guys! Good to know that's still going to be possible a couple of decades from now. Mom, you might want to make an appointment to get that Brazilian touched up. And Dad, some friendly advice: socks off, man. Anyway, glad you're alive! I'll show myself out. See you at brunch on Sunday'? Like that?"

"Well, that's a bit much, but... Do we really have brunch with them on Sunday?"

Her whiny dismay at the prospect makes me laugh, the sound of which surprises me. She chuckles nervously. Our laughter builds, and soon we're clutching at each other, wheezing and shaking. Holding to the lapels of her wool coat,

I press my forehead against her clavicle, then howl until my cheeks hurt and my abdomen aches.

She recovers first and, sniffling while she catches her breath, dabs at her mirthful tears with one hand while cupping the back of my head with her other. I let go of her coat but wrap my arms around her and turn my head to rest my ear against her chest.

"See? It *is* sort of funny," she manages, her voice still choked with simmering giggles. "But we don't have brunch on Sunday, right?"

I blink and stare at the arm of the couch, directly in my eye line. "No."

"Oh, good. Too soon."

Suddenly, with her running her fingers through my hair, I'm exhausted, in danger of falling asleep right here, trapping her under me. She doesn't seem in any hurry to move, so I stay put. I wish we could stay like this forever, laughing at the rest of the world, at our problems, at life, but not expected to do anything about them.

After a few minutes, her voice vibrates against my ear as she says, "So you thought, 'Now that I've seen my parents doing the nasty, let's get out of here'? Where are you planning to move?"

"Anywhere," I slur, my voice rusty. I clear my throat. "Well, I've purposely researched places that don't have an NFL franchise. And I want to go far enough south that we don't need to bring the snow blower with us. It would be nice to live near a beach."

"Do I get a say in this?"

I pretend to think about it for a second. "I guess. But I've already done all the hard thinking."

"I simply have to show up, huh?"

"Yeah."

"How nice of you. You know, beaches are nice to visit. But living on or near one? Unless you're wealthy enough to have a private beach—which we're not, in case checking the bank balance didn't fit into your plotting—out-of-towners are a big, inconvenient part of your life for much of the year."

"I'm not related to them, though. Score one for the tourists."

"Okay, fine. And you say you want to live away from the cold, but you're not a fan of hot weather, either. You bitch as much in the summer when the temperatures spike higher than eighty-five."

"I like to complain."

"And sand. You're so OCD. Sand would drive you crazy. It gets everywhere, no matter how careful you are."

"We don't have to live *on* the water. A two-hour drive—like the distance to your parents' cabin—would be fine."

"Why are we talking about this?"

I lift my head and brace my weight against the back of the couch, my hands on either side of her body. Locking eyes with her, I answer, "Because I need to. I need to get out of here."

"Because you caught your parents in the act?"

"No! Yes! No. It's not just that. It's everything. It's them, it's my brother, it's the job I used to love but don't anymore, it's—"

"It's winter. Everyone goes slightly stir-crazy up here at this time of year. It'll pass."

"You can say that, because you've been able to escape nearly every week."

"That hasn't been my choice."

"But it's still true. You're in Chicago one week, New York the next, San Diego after that. You got to go to Miami!"

"It wasn't all that."

"Liar."

She sighs. "Fine. I'm not feeling as restless as you are. But that's why I can see this... this... urge of yours for what it is. Trust me; you'll feel so much better after our week in Jamaica. Sun, sand, surf, sleep... sex."

I shake my head and close my eyes. "Don't say 'sex.'"

She laughs but there's a nervous edge to it. "'Don't say 'sex'? Who are you and what have you done to Nathaniel?"

Pushing away from her, I sit with my legs spread, my elbows on my knees, the heels of my hands pushed into my eye sockets. "That's what I'm trying to tell you. All of this... everything... is turning me into this black-and-white, two-dimensional, lame version of who I used to be, of who I always thought I was. With every new disappointment, with every new stressor, I'm fading, letting go, giving up."

"Don't say that." Her hand falls on my back, between my shoulder blades.

"It's true. I'm sorry if it's hard to hear. I'm sorry if it freaks you out. Try feeling it happen to yourself."

"And you think moving away from everyone you know, every*thing* you've ever known, is going to fix it?"

"Maybe."

"People who live near beaches have problems, too."

"I want to trade these problems for a new set, that's all. I want a change of scenery and to meet new people and to enjoy waking up to go to work. I don't want to feel this way anymore."

"You should talk to Dr. Reitman about prescribing you something—"

"I don't need drugs!"

"A lot of people around here do, especially this time of year."

"This is not seasonal depression, Betts. I don't have that problem."

"Why? Because you're so much better than that?"

The bitterness in her voice makes me drop my hands and look at her when I say, "No! You know I don't feel that way. But it's not the issue here."

"Self-diagnosis doesn't work."

"In this case, I don't need a diagnosis. This isn't the winter blahs. It's been like this since last summer."

As if a manic movie's unreeling between us, I see flashes of Dr. Douche's smirk and my dad "toasting" us at the lake and blood-filled toilets and Betty Rubble's tear-streaked cheeks and Heidi's dark-rimmed eyes and Nick's defiant jaw and Lynette's pale, drawn face. And finally, the film freezes in my parents' bedroom. I jam my hands in my eyes again. "Oh, God," I groan. "All of it happened *here*."

She traces her finger across my forehead and taps my temple. "And now it lives *here*. You can move to Outer Mongolia, and all of that stuff will travel with you."

"Mongolia's too cold anyway."

She ignores my pedantic statement. "Nate."

Again, I uncover my red eyes and train them on her.

"I'd go anywhere with you—"

"Then let's go," I whisper, my throat, chest, and chin aching with my desperation and pent-up tears. "Please." I scrape my hand against my trembling mouth.

"C'mere." She opens her arms, and I fall against her, resting my chin on her shoulder. I immediately feel stronger, less like I'm going to break into a million pieces. It's as if she's holding me together, fusing all of those cracks with the gentlest of embraces. When I stop trembling, she rests her hand on the back of my neck and squeezes. "All right?" she checks.

I nod, my evening facial growth rasping against her coat.

Her chin bumps against my shoulder when she says, "You don't cut and run in the middle of a job. That's not you. And you're in the middle of some stuff here. A lot of stuff. Stuff that's not fun. Stuff that sucks. But stuff that people are depending on you to see to the end. Whatever that end is."

"The clinic will be fine." *If I keep telling myself that, maybe it'll be true.*

"I'm not just talking about the clinic." She pushes away from me and moves her hands to my upper arms. Straight into my face, she says, "I'm talking about everything. People need you."

"No, they don't."

"Yes, they do. And they need you *here*."

"I don't want their problems anymore, though. I want to focus on us."

"They *are* us."

"Betts, I—"

She presses her fingers to my lips, then trails them down my chin and neck. "Soon, okay? It always looks the worst before it gets better. You know that's how healing works."

"It's how dying works, too."

"You're right. But you have to see it through to either of those conclusions before you can move on."

I take a deep, shuddering breath. "Soon, though?"

She nods and smiles. "Sure. Doing something new—with you—sounds exciting. And fun." She brushes her lips against mine. "Be patient."

29

TORCH-PASSING

With every day that passes that I don't act on my impulse to take my family and get the heck out of my home-town, the more firmly entrenched I realize I am. Trapped. With no options; merely the illusion of options. However, the emotion that fed the desire that night as I looked at real estate online pulses stronger than ever. The difference is, it feels like a silly, impossible fantasy. The only way I'm getting out of here is on a plane to Jamaica in a couple of weeks. That's going to have to do. Until then, I'm in survival mode, trying to get through the usual pre-holiday madness.

So far this season, I've attended four parties—one for the clinic staff, one for patients, one for Betty's work, and an open house for Georgia's daycare—and now, I'm at the event I've been dreading for months: Dr. Reitman's retirement party.

Betty is tonight's designated driver, but despite having a chauffeur, I've decided I'm not going to go any further than "pleasantly buzzed," because I'm all about moderation, and that will make for a much nicer Saturday morning than if I get hammered here. There's also less chance of doing or saying something I'll most definitely regret if I stay reasonably in command of my impulses.

Unlike the staff holiday party, which was an adults-only formal affair at an insufferably pretentious venue (Dr. Douche's country club), tonight's event is casual and family-friendly, set at one of those loud pizza buffets attached to a massive arcade, including a go-cart track and laser tag course. (Yes, I'm looking forward to shooting Dr. Douche later.)

Our party is tucked in a private room with its own bar, so conversation is possible, but I'd be okay with spending the entire time in the frenzied gaming area, playing skee-ball and collecting a bunch of tickets for one of Beulah's grandkids or Janet's kid. I kick ass at skee-ball, even after several drinks.

Unfortunately, there are ceremonies to attend to before we can all eat, drink, and play away our feelings. The guest of honor would like to address the assembly, but she feels duty-bound to wait for a certain jerk—who's late, as usual.

After Dr. Reitman's much more diplomatic announcement to that effect, I hand Georgia to Betty and nod toward the bar. "This may call for more alcohol than I anticipated," I mutter, rising from the table where we've already claimed two chairs.

She laughs. "Try not to get 'I'm-awesome-at-karaoke' drunk."

To my credit, that only happened once, and it was in front of complete strangers. To my discredit, it was on our honeymoon, and I sang "Total Eclipse of the Heart," complete with hand motions, which upset my equilibrium and almost caused me to fall off the stage. My pregnant wife had to drag me from the bar and support me on a three-block walk back to our hotel room, which then whirled around me for several hours. Not going to repeat that... ever.

"Don't worry," I tell her now. "I'm just taking the edge off."

It's a moderate-sized edge, but she doesn't need to know

the details as long as I don't make it her problem later. And I won't. I'll drink here at the bar with the other lushes.

The only empty stool is next to Lynette, but we're adults, so I act like it's no big deal to be shoulder-to-shoulder with my brother's former (I hope) lov— lov— special friend. I can do this. I order a pale ale, determined to stay away from hard liquor truth serums.

Lynette is the first to speak. "Dick move, being late to your predecessor's retirement party." She runs her finger along the rim of her martini glass.

I take the first sip of my beer, lick my teeth, and reply, "Right?" This turnaround in her opinion of Dr. Douche should be a welcome change, but I can't help wondering how much of it reflects Nick's opinion. Which leads me to resent the fact that my jerk-ass brother holds more sway with her than someone who's been her friend and colleague for years. But whatever.

Take another drink, Nate.

"If I were Dr. Reitman, I'd start without him," Lynette declares. "It's her day."

"Her day, her choice. She obviously wants him here."

Lynette lowers her voice, now filled with glee. "Oooh... maybe she's going to tell him off in her farewell speech!"

I can't help but smile at the idea. "That would be epic. She's too classy for that, though."

"Yeah... Damn."

"I'd totally do it. There would be no worries about burned bridges, so why not?"

"You'd do it here, in front of everyone?"

I consider it for a second, then sigh. "I guess not. There are kids here."

We quietly contemplate our drinks—and our new boss—

for a few minutes before I say, "Hey, I saw you brought a date. That's..."

...an improvement.

...interesting.

...a relief.

"...cool."

She laughs at my lame finish. "Something like that. He's just a guy. You know, a rebound. He'll do."

"You're suddenly quite cosmopolitan," I tease. "What's this rebound guy's name? What does he do? Is he a good guy?"

"Does it matter?"

"Absolutely. He's dating one of my best friends. I need to vet him."

"His name is Will."

"Good start, knowing his name."

She leans to her left, bumping me. I hold firm to avoid knocking into the person on the other side of me. Mindy's biker boyfriend might not take too kindly to being part of our human Newton's cradle. I smile, though, and prod, "And?"

"He's an electrical engineer. And that's about all I know about him. We've been on two dates, including this one."

"This is your second date?"

"Yeah."

"And you're sitting up here at the bar without him?"

"You're up here without Betty."

"That's different; we're married and have seen each other do things that have shattered all illusions we may have had about one another. Plus, she and George are no doubt surrounded by a bunch of people by now." I glance over my shoulder to verify this suspicion (and that I haven't actually abandoned my wife like a beer-guzzling jerk). "See? So, where's this Will guy of yours?"

"Since he doesn't know anyone here, I told him to go ahead

into the arcade, and I'd meet him in there after all of this depressing business is over."

"If something doesn't happen soon, I might join him."

As if to save me from following through on my threat, Dr. Reitman takes her place at the front of the room, which quiets.

* * *

"I THINK we're all here now," the doctor begins lightly, "so I want to say a few words—short and sweet and not too mushy, I promise—before we all do what we're here to do: have fun!"

Polite laughter flutters through the room. Betty waves me back to the table, so I give a quick "See ya" to Lynette and hurry to my original spot, bringing my half-full beer with me. Something tells me I may wind up crying in it. Or throwing it in someone's face. But probably just gulping it.

Settled in my chair, I drape my arm over the back of Betty's and lean back, resting my ankle on my knee. Georgia flirts with me over her mom's shoulder. I flirt back, shooting her a wink, then sticking out my tongue at her.

I'm paying much more attention to this activity than what Dr. Reitman is saying until I hear, "My youngest daughter is transferring next semester to the University of South Carolina and will be going to medical school there, so it seemed right to stick close to her. No more Wisconsin winters for me. I'm trading blizzards for hurricanes."

My face slackens. Betty half-turns toward me and says, "Lucky lady."

The doctor waits through the chuckles, then continues, "There are many of you here tonight, though, who took time out of your busy schedules to say goodbye, and I appreciate that. I hope you have a great time. Some of you currently work

at the clinic; others are faces from the past, faces I'm glad to
see again one more time before I head east. And in case I
don't get a chance to talk to you before you scatter, I wanted
you to know that I've enjoyed working with each and every
one of you. I've considered it an honor and privilege."

She pulls some notecards from her back pocket. "To prove
it, I've written down my favorite memory of each of you, a
sentence or two that sums up our relationship, and I'd like to
share those now. I might even get through most of these
without crying."

Aw, no. Aw, hell no!

I sit up taller and whip my head from side to side, like a
trapped bank robber looking for the exits. Betty swivels to see
what all my fidgeting is about.

"I need to go to the bathroom," I hiss, leaning forward to
get up.

Betty places her hand on my thigh and squeezes. "Don't
you dare, Nathaniel. She put a ton of thought into this; you
owe it to her to listen."

"But—"

"It's okay if you cry."

Normally, I'd agree. But not here. Not now. Not around
these people.

"Park it," Betty insists through clenched teeth.

By now, Dr. Reitman's made it through half a dozen people,
none of whom I recognize. It seems she's going chronologi-
cally through her career, and due to the number of people
from her early days who couldn't make it tonight, she's quickly
approaching the current clinic staff. I'm starting to recognize
nurses' names. Now she's mentioning people who were still
around when I started.

My leg bounces under the table.

She recalls the first time Beulah ever had to change the

toner in the copier, and it exploded all over her and the work room. And how Janet never forgets a staff member's birthday and brings in their favorite homemade treat, without fail. And how Mary-Kate, the immunization ninja, can give a shot so fast the kid doesn't have time to cry. And how the most contagious thing in the clinic is never a virus; it's Lynette's laugh. And how Mindy started out as a patient, then became a summer-intern-turned-part-time-employee, and is now working on her nursing degree. "Mindy, you're going to make a great nurse someday. Even Nate says so."

Hey, why is everyone laughing so hard at that? They act like I'm stingy with compliments or something. Sure, I like things done well, but I'll be the first to admit there's always more than one right way to do something, and I give people credit all the time, when they deserve it. Still, I laugh along with everyone, because... Well, they have a point. I hold the nurses at the clinic—myself included—to a high standard. And I'm pretty proud of that.

Dr. Reitman lets the laughter die down completely and stares at her cards for a few seconds into the silence before taking a deep breath and saying, "Which brings me to the first and only self-described 'murse' I ever worked with, Nurse Nate, the owner of, hands down, the largest collection of novelty scrubs in the state of Wisconsin. I'm sure of it."

"Yep," Betty confirms under her breath. "They have their own closet."

I tap the back of her head. "Shush."

Although nobody can hear us, including Dr. Reitman, she laughs at our antics. "I remember when Greenbrier placed him in the clinic, I spent the first month he worked there trying to figure out what his angle was. I asked him about a hundred times, 'Pediatrics, huh? You're not using this as a stepping stone for hospital work?' He always answered matter-of-factly and never lost his patience with me, when he could have, several times, said, 'No, woman! What's your deal?' But it didn't take long to see he was exactly where he was supposed to be.

"The thing is—and I'm going to sound incredibly sexist and show my age when I say this—it's been rare, in my experience, to come across a guy as effortlessly nurturing as he is, with such an instinct for what young patients—and their parents—need in any given situation. I've been doing this long enough to know how extraordinary it is—in *any* medical professional, male or female. Bedside manner is often the hardest thing for any of us to master. Some of us never do, especially not to that level. And I can't speak for anyone else, but there have been countless times I've been jealous—but thankful—he's been able to get kids to do things I can't."

She looks straight at me now. "Which has nothing to do, of course, with the fact that you're a man and everything to do with the fact that you're plain good at what you do."

I nod and mouth, *"Thanks,"* wishing the floor would open up and swallow me, preferably before I start blubbering. Which is about to happen in three seconds, tops.

Addressing the entire group once more, she blinks rapidly and says, "I have about a hundred Nurse Nate stories, most of them involving him charming every last ounce of resistance from an uncooperative patient or their caregiver, but I've already gone on long enough. Seriously." She laughs and holds up her note cards so we can see the one on top. "Look here. It says, 'murse' and 'novelty scrubs collection.' That's all I was going to say. But in the end, I guess that felt inadequate." She chuckles and blushes at herself. "Moving on!"

I dash my fingers across my eyes, which I roll toward the ceiling to distribute the tears before they leak down my face.

Damn. Damn, damn, damn. Why'd she have to go and say

all that? "Murse" and "scrubs" would have been perfectly adequate and would have made everyone laugh. Now they're all going to think I'm her favorite, or something stupid. Something worse, possibly. Plus, she made me effing cry!

Like that, I'm in fifth grade again, the teacher's pet, not by design, but by chance, because I turned in that dumb poem that blew my teacher away when she thought it was about mortality. In fact, it was about my favorite video game, *Mortal Kombat*. Only my mom made me take out the name of the game (in hindsight, she totally set me up), so it was never specifically mentioned, and therefore, *did* sound deeper than it was.

My teacher read the poem aloud and gushed about it in front of the entire class, and I got teased mercilessly for months. Until I finally put a peanut butter slathered whoopie cushion in her chair and signed the back of it so everyone would know it was me. That after-school detention earned back enough street cred to stop the recess bullying, and I had people to sit with at lunch again. It was totally worth it.

What am I supposed to do here, though? Nick took a pair of scissors to my whoopie cushion after I used it on him in front of a girl when we were teenagers. And I can't very well pants Dr. Reitman in front of everyone to show I didn't put her up to telling everyone how wonderful I am. She gets the benefit of the doubt, since I believe her that she didn't plan to go on and on. But in the end, she did go on and on. And on.

While I've been composing myself, the doctor has continued with her memories of Zach, the clinic's janitor, and the current lab techs we routinely partner with. Then she tucks her cards into her back jeans pocket and says, "There's only one person left, and that's my successor, Dr. Dan Chancellor, or 'Dr. Dan,' to those in the know. And I haven't worked with Dan long, so I don't have any anecdotes about him..."

Do we have a few hours? Because I could bring the house down with just a small selection of the buffoonery I've witnessed the past few months.

"...but I will tell you all this." She pauses for effect. "The clinic will never be the same again."

I hide my "ha!" in a cough behind my hand. Leave it to Dr. Reitman, the most diplomatic person I've ever known, to find a way to zing the guy and make it sound like a compliment. And give him no recourse but to thank her or risk looking like a defensive jerk.

Dr. Douche smiles tightly as he makes his way to the front of the room. When he arrives, he says, "Thank you, Pat. Let's all give her a hand for such thoughtful tributes to us and for her years of service."

The room erupts in applause, leading to a standing ovation that lets him know we're clapping because we want to, not because he told us to.

After we return to our seats, he smiles smarmily at us. "It's time now to deliver on our true purpose for being here today, and that's to honor the decades Pat Reitman has dedicated to children's health in this community. As she mentioned, we haven't worked together long, but her reputation precedes her, so I have plenty to say."

Oh, great. And my beer's all gone.

He proceeds to recite the doctor's résumé, like a funeral director eulogizing someone he doesn't know. Or worse, a preacher forced to speak in generalities about someone nobody else liked, in order to convince the people assembled, *"She wasn't all that bad, after all. Everyone's redeemable."*

Plus, he keeps calling her "Pat," which is going all through me. Every time he says it, I have to remind myself who he's talking about. None of us here know her as that. It's like calling a person by their first name when all their life, they went by their middle name or a nickname. All you can think every time you hear the name is, *This numb nuts doesn't know a damn thing.*

Ten minutes into Dr. Douche's speech, I shift in my chair for about the fiftieth time and sigh so audibly that several people around me turn to see where the noise originated. Betty shoots me a glare and hands an equally squirmy Georgia to me, like a mom handing a toy to a restless child in church. *"Here, play with this and shut up."*

That's fine by me. I welcome the distraction from this inadequate piece of public speaking drivel. Who decided it would be a good idea to put this joker in charge of the appreciation speech, anyway? Greenbrier couldn't spare anyone else or ask someone like Beulah, who's worked with Dr. Reitman for nearly thirty years, to say a few words that actually mean something? After all, Dr. Reitman gave everyone she's ever worked with—the ones here, anyway—thirty seconds (or more, in some cases... ahem) of carefully selected stories from our time together, and this is what she gets in return? The living-person equivalent of, *"She loved her country and was a hard worker"*?

Eff that.

I almost say it out loud, but since my toddler daughter is standing in my lap, facing me, I hold back... barely.

After what Dr. Reitman said about me, I can't let a reading of her professional bio stand as the final word on her career. Of course, after what she said about me, I'm also hesitant to draw more attention to myself. But this isn't about me; it's about someone who's shaped the health and lives of countless kids, not to mention the careers of everyone she's worked with.

I let Dr. Dan finish his boring "tribute," because to interrupt him might be perceived as dismissive of the information he's conveying, but as soon as he's finished, I push down my nerves and embarrassment at making a spectacle of myself and stand.

With Georgia still in my arms, I say, "Thanks, Dr. D-Dan." *Whew... Close one!* "Can I just... I'd like to say a few words, if that's okay."

He nods grudgingly and steps back from the podium to give me the mic, but I stay where I am.

"We've always been impressed by Dr. Reitman's résumé; it's one of the reasons she was such a popular choice for pediatric staff placements during her tenure with Greenbrier. But, uh, it was only one of the reasons. And—at least for me—the smallest one, to be perfectly honest. So... I don't know. I thought, well, this is it, right? This is goodbye, so—"

Georgia saves the day—and what's left of my dignity—by waving her hand and saying, "Buh-bye," making everyone, including me, laugh, not cry.

"Exactly. And since we're here to honor one person, we don't need note cards or to think all that hard to come up with our own examples of why working with Dr. Reitman was so amazing. So, if you feel comfortable doing so, I think it would be appropriate, and only right, to go around the room and share that with her. Because she deserves to know. And because she didn't cry once during her speeches about us, and that's not fair."

While my colleagues laugh, I quickly think about what I want to say before I sit down and don't say another word for the rest of the night. Because skee-ball doesn't require talking. And I plan to park myself in front of one of those lanes and not speak to another soul as soon as this is over.

"Anyway, this is going to sound completely lame after Dr. Reitman delivered what could go on an application for my sainthood, but I remember what she referred to a few minutes ago, how she used to ask me—nearly daily, my first month working with her—if I was sure I wanted to work in a pediatric clinic. At that point, I was used to being asked at social gatherings, 'Are you still *just* a male nurse'?" I smile so everyone knows it's okay to laugh with me. "Always 'male nurse,' too. Like we're an exotic breed or something. And I guess we are, somewhat, since I'm the only one in this room.

"But Dr. Reitman was different. For one thing, she refused to call me a 'murse,' so I'm surprised she mentioned it here tonight. And when I'd tell her I was sure about my career choice, the grin I'd get in return was one of the most satisfying parts of my day. It was an affirmation that I'd made the right choice. She was checking that I was going to stick around and be a long-term part of our patients' mental and physical development. That was *always* her first concern. Always." I risk looking at her now. "And that's what made working with you—for me, anyway—the most rewarding. So... thanks."

"Fanks! Buh-bye!" Georgia weighs in as I sit down.

"Good job," I whisper to her, too giddy with relief that it's over to give into any other prevalent emotions.

For the next several minutes, I come down from my adrenaline high, hopefully putting on a good show that I'm listening closely to everyone else's speeches, but I'm merely trying to get through this. And Georgia's no longer helping, either. Being the center of attention must have worn her out, because she's since stilled, and now a peek at her face, rested on my shoulder, confirms she's seconds from nodding off.

Looks like defending my skee-ball title's going to have to wait.

30

ROLE MODEL

THE TIMING COULDN'T BE WORSE, BUT WHEN I GET A TEXT from my brother with an address and the word, "Important!" on my way home from my last Urgent Care shift before Betty and I leave for Jamaica, I don't hesitate to head that direction before calling my wife to let her know what's going on and that I don't know when I'll be home.

When I arrive at my destination, what appears to be an indoor driving range, I worry the mapping app has led me astray, but sure enough, Nick's car is one of two in the snow-banked parking lot. Immediately, I assume he's here with Dad, who's had a heart attack, or something, but why wouldn't Nick call an ambulance and have me meet them at the hospital? I don't waste time speculating; I run into the place, looking around for my brother's familiar figure in the massive, empty place.

"Hey, Nate!" a somewhat familiar voice says from the check-in desk to my right.

I recognize a former high school classmate, Scott Walters, dressed in khakis, golf shoes, and a polo shirt with the name of the range embroidered above his shirt pocket. I haven't seen him since Nick's wedding, but like most guys, we don't make a big deal about it; rather, we act like we see each other all the time.

After some distracted (on my part) chit-chat, I ask if he knows where I can find Nick and Dad, explaining, "My brother told me to meet him here, that it was an emergency."

Scott's brow wrinkles. "Hmm, that's weird. Your dad's not here. Just Nick. And he stepped into the bathroom, saying he wanted to hit the head before you got here. Seemed fine to me."

He points the way, and I jog over there, still worried about what I may find. Maybe Nick was having chest pains, but he didn't want to freak out Scott, so he didn't let on. Before I even clear the door, though, I hear a flush, and my brother steps from a stall at the same time I enter the sink area.

He grins while adjusting his pants. "Oh, hey. You found it."

"I, uh...yes. What's wrong?"

"Nothing," he says, scrubbing his hands as vigorously as he would prior to performing surgery.

"But you said it was an emergency."

"No, I said it was 'important.' You wouldn't answer my calls or my texts, so I had to resort to desperate measures."

"What? So, you're fine?"

"Yes, but you're leaving for vacation tomorrow, and I need to talk to you. You won't be around at Christmas. And when you get back, it'll be crazy, getting ready for the new baby, and then he'll be here, and who knows what fresh hell... er, temporary chaos that's going to bring, so this seemed like the last chance for a while for us to talk."

I stare at his back and shoulders.

He turns and grabs two paper towels from the automatic dispenser on the wall, his smile now sheepish. "Sorry, bro. I didn't mean to scare you."

"Yes, you did."

"I wanted you to respond, that's all. And Scott offered to open the place up for me tonight so I could give it a test run before his grand opening next week. Thought it would be the perfect opportunity for you and me to talk, man to man."

"Unbelievable," I mutter, my heart finally returning to its normal rate.

"Right? This place is kick-ass!" Dropping the towels into the gleaming trash can, he slaps my back and steers me from the bathroom. "C'mon. You're wound pretty tight. Let's get Scotty to dip into his beer supply and loosen you up."

"I can't stay long," I say, following close on his heels to what looks like a 1950s soda shop counter. "I'm supposed to be at home, packing."

Nick bellies up to the bar and looks around for Scott. "Who's taking care of Reba while you're gone?"

I narrow my eyes at him. "Mom and Dad. Why?"

His hands fly up in front of his chest, and his eyes widen. "Not for that reason, all right? I was just wondering. You know, we would have been glad to keep her for the week. The boys love her."

Instead of pointing out that we'd come home to a dog ready for a padded dog house if she stayed with him for a full week, I more diplomatically state, "Yeah, but having Reba around would be an unnecessary complication if Heidi goes into labor while we're gone."

"It's a bit early for that."

"It happens, though."

"Yeah. Anyway..." He slaps the counter. "Scotty! Where'd you go, man? We need to wet our whistles!" While we wait for the range owner to reappear, Nick nods to a remote lane marked with a #16 on a large fiberglass golf ball on a tee. "I'm over there. You can take Lane #15. I already got you a bucket of balls. I have a brand new driver you can use, too."

Goody. I like golf almost as much as I like football. But it's one of the few sports Dad forced Nick and me to learn. I put up with it because it meant spending time with my dad and brother, but despite eventually becoming a passable player, I never learned to love it as much as they do.

After Scott twists open two aluminum bottles and hands them to us, he waves us on and tells us to make ourselves at home while he takes care of some last-minute pre-opening tasks at the front desk. "Keep the beers at the bar, though. I don't want anything spilled on the turf before I open the place."

Nick gives Scott a smart-ass salute. "You got it, man." Then he proceeds to drain his entire bottle. I drink half of mine and set it next to his empty, hurrying to keep up with him when he strides to the driving area.

He slides a Titleist from his upright bag and holds it out to me on his open palms, as if it's Excalibur, not a golf club. He throws me some gloves. "Here's my extra pair."

"Uh, thanks." I drop a ball in the tee-off circle and stare down at it. It's been forever since I've done this.

Nick's a lefty, and I'm a righty, so we face each other as we settle into our stances. Testing his range of motion, he takes some gentle practice swings, following all the way through, the stem of the driver resting against his shoulder and back. He's the first one to take a real shot. His ball floats toward the netting placed about a hundred yards away and drops gently before hitting it.

"Nice," I approve, taking my own swing, dismayed—but not surprised—at how much shorter mine falls.

After a few more hits each, Nick says, "You guys are going to have so much fun in Jamaica. Heidi and I... Our honeymoon was amazing. And Georgia's going to love the water and the sand."

"She's actually going to stay here with Mom and Dad," I say, watching my longest hit so far.

"Oh. Dang. Then it's going to be better than I thought. I'm seriously jealous, bro."

I take more care than I need to take, positioning my next ball with the toe of my shoe.

"Does this mean you've patched things up with Mom and Dad?" he asks.

I grunt, not wanting to get into describing the awkward dinner they forced me into attending—sans blindfold, as was my original request—so they could officially announce their reconciliation. "They insisted on watching her for us to try to make up for everything. And Betty and I need this time alone more than we need to be with Georgia every second of the next week."

"It's smart of you to recognize that. You'll be fine, once you guys get down there and get a few drinks in you. You're always just fine."

Not sure what he means, if anything, by that, I wait, adjusting my grip on the driver, like Dad showed me so many years ago.

Nick rewards my silence and patience with a clearing of his throat and, "So, uh, I wanted to thank you for the Christmas gift."

My innards clench. Not that it's a big deal I have no idea what he's talking about. It's simply awkward that Betty went rogue on me and gave him something "from both of us" that I had absolutely no part in. This could be awesome; or a disaster. Since his thank you seems sincere, I'm guessing it's more of the former than the latter.

"Um, sure. You're welcome. Glad you liked it."

He smirks and glances up at me, then back at the ball on the ground in front of him. "You have no clue what I'm talking about, do you?"

"Sure, I do. The... thing. That, uh... we got you..." I sigh and confess, "No. I thought we'd exchange gifts when we got back. I was planning to get something for you down there."

"A beach trinket?"

I blush and bluff, "No. Something nice. That will fit in my suitcase."

"A bottle of rum from the duty-free shop at the airport?"

"Maybe. But the good stuff." I produce a satisfying *thwock* with my latest hit, and the ball hits the far net, hard.

"Damn. Nailed that one. Anyway, rum's cool. I don't need more shit, that's for sure."

"Well, now it's not going to be a surprise, so I'm glad we got you something else, something nice."

He rolls his eyes. "Do I have to spell everything out for you, man? I'm not talking about an actual wrapped present; I'm talking about my marriage."

"Huh? I didn't—"

"That night at The Cheesehead, you told me what I needed to hear. You were pissed off at me and disappointed and disgusted, but you were... you were right. I'd been the worst type of asshole, the type who"—he glances over his shoulder and, seeing Scott engrossed on the phone, continues in a lower voice—"cheats and not only makes excuses for it but blames his pregnant wife for it. I don't know what got into me."

"You've always been kind of a prick," I interject, to lighten the mood.

I wish Betty were here now. She'd know how to make this less awful. She'd settle it with one or two sentences and pull me toward the door so we could drive home and get on with our evening. But that's not possible. I'll have to make do with channeling her and doing it myself, especially when my brother looks crestfallen in the wake of my joke about him being a jerk his whole life.

"Hey, I was kidding," I reassure him.

"But it's true, too. Everything, until now, came so easily to me. I didn't have to study in high school or college. I was always part of the popular, cool crowd, mostly because I was good at sports. Again, not that I worked at it."

I take a break, resting the club across my shoulders and draping my wrists over it while I wait for him to get to his point. If he has one.

Positioning his next ball, he avoids my eyes. "That's just it, though. Because so many things have come easily to me, when something does require me to work—because it's not in my nature—I don't know what the hell to do. And it's not like you can study how to be a good man." He underscores that with a mighty swing that doesn't result in as long of a drive as it should.

Then he turns to face me and smiles sadly. "I'm trying harder at home, though, and Heidi's... responding to that. So are the boys. They actually listen to me. The house is less crazy. And that's great. I'm not saying things are perfect, but they're better. They're good enough. And I'm sure they'll get better every day. Thanks to you."

"I didn't tell you anything you didn't already know."

He looks down at his feet. "Knowing what needed to be done and having a clue how to do it are two different things. And I would have been screwed, except... I had a pretty damn good example to follow, right in front of me." He raises his eyes. "That would be you, bro."

"Oh. Um, okay..."

"You're never going to win any contests for being cool,

but... I dunno. At this point in our lives, being a good husband and a dad and being happy at home *is* cool. You know?" He blinks rapidly, and his Adam's apple bobs. "I want to be like you. You're happy with your life."

This misconception makes me twitch. I lower the club and knock the head of it against my tennis shoe. "Well, not always. Everyone has some things they wouldn't mind changing."

"Yeah, but you love the big things: your wife and your kid and your dog. And your career." He belts a drive that would continue going for several yards if not for that pesky net and wall. "You're happy with who you are, and you don't care what anyone else thinks."

"I care!"

"Nah. Someone who cares about public opinion doesn't drive the car you drive and wear the clothes you wear. And your hair... bro, 2003 called and wants its little boy cut back."

I pat my hair self-consciously. "There's nothing wrong with my hair!"

"There's nothing *wrong* with it. But you've had the same haircut your whole life! Look in our school yearbooks and family photo albums, and you'll see I'm right."

"Whatever."

"Anyway, that's what makes you so awesome, though. You're consistent. Everyone knows what to expect from you—"

"Boring, nerdy, uncool, unstylish me, you mean?"

"C'mon, don't get all butt hurt about it! I'm trying to compliment you, and you're turning it around and making it sound insulting! Let me finish, all right?"

"You're not done?"

He shakes his head. "No."

I flatten my lips and flare my nostrils, determined not to say anything else, to hear him out, to not be a defensive jerk.

When he's sure I'm going to stay silent, he crosses one leg over the other, plunks the toe of his fancy golf shoe into the AstroTurf, leans on his driver, and continues, "More guys should be like you. You have your priorities in order. You always have."

I swallow. "That's... That's the nicest thing you've ever said to me."

"Heidi would have been much better off with you." When I pull back the corners of my mouth in a grimace, he laughs. "I'm sorry. I don't mean to make you feel uncomfortable, but you should know I'm fully aware of it."

"She's with the person she's supposed to be with; the person she loves. I am, too."

"Her life would have been better if she had stayed in love with you, if *you* were the one she was supposed to be with."

"There's a reason things didn't work out between the two of us."

"Oh, yeah. I know *that*, but—"

"And you know what else? You have the power to make her life better."

"I'm working on it."

"Good." I rub the back of my neck and walk to the row of chairs behind the safety line. He follows, and we sit side-by-side. It strikes me that two such similar-looking guys couldn't be more different. "Listen, Nick. I didn't do anything that any other brother wouldn't do."

"Not true. A lot of guys would have looked the other way and claimed it was none of their business. You're a role model."

"Great." *Is this conversation over yet?* "I'm glad we got that settled, and I'm glad things are better for you at home. But..."

No. No, no, no! Why did I say "but"? This talk needs to end... thirty minutes ago. How did that pesky word slip out?!

"But?"

Despite kicking myself repeatedly and firmly in the ass, I say, "I may not be in love with Heidi anymore— I'm not," I quickly clarify. "But I do still care about her. Like a sister. And you hurt her. You can't erase that by kissing my ass and telling me what a great—albeit nerdy—guy I am. I'll never be around Heidi again without thinking about what you did—in *my house,* among other places—and how I know about it, and she doesn't. She still doesn't, right?" I check.

He shakes his head and looks down at his hands, poking at the raised outline of his wedding ring through his golfing glove.

"Not to mention, one of my best friends and co-workers—" I stop. It's not my place to tell him how heartbroken Lynette seems. Quickly, I cover, "I can't forget what you did because I see her almost every day. And I can't avoid seeing her because I work with her."

"I'm sorry. I told you, it wasn't a calculated thing."

"Yeah, well your miscalculations have made a huge mess for more than just the two of you."

His only audible response is a gulp.

"I appreciate this gesture, and I'm glad we had this talk"— *for the most part*—"but if you're seeking some sort of absolution from me, you're not going to get it. It's not mine to give."

"I'm not apologizing; I'm thanking you for bringing me to my senses."

"You're welcome, then."

"I've already apologized to Lynette."

"And Heidi?"

"How can I tell her how sorry I am without telling her everything? She'd hate me. She'd regret marrying me. She'd... she'd leave me."

"Maybe. Maybe not."

He pinches the bridge of his nose. "I'm not brave enough to find out. Would you be?"

"That's something I plan never to have to worry about" almost falls from my lips, but at the last second, I choose the less judgmental, "I don't know."

"Well, I do. I know I can't. I can only do the next best thing: try to make it up to her."

"And hope she never finds out some other way." When he shoots me a murderous glare, I quickly clarify, "Not from me! Never from me. I couldn't do that to her."

"Neither could I."

I rise, suddenly worried about how late I am getting home, and how much I have to do when I get there. "You already did, though; she just doesn't know."

"You know what I'm saying."

"Yeah, and I get it. But so help me God, Nick..." I stand in front of him, towering over him for once, and jab the driver into his chest. "You ever pull another stunt like that again, and I'll make sure she finds out. I won't let you be some serial philanderer who disrespects his wife whenever he gets bored or feels like he's not getting enough attention at home."

"It won't happen again."

"Better not." Jamming the club back into the bag, I peel off my gloves and rest them on top of the metal heads. "I gotta get going. Merry Christmas."

31

THE DEALBREAKER

JAMAICA WAS... WELL, IT WAS JAMAICA IN DECEMBER. Which means it wasn't Green Bay in December. Which means it was amazing. And leaving Georgia with my parents was one of the smartest things Betty and I have ever done as parents— or as a couple. It's not that we didn't miss her. But we missed her just enough to give us an incentive to come back. Otherwise, we might still be down there, having chucked our careers to sell seashells by the seashore.

Most importantly, Betty and I rediscovered what brought us together in the first place (other than lying to the general public about my identity): our close friendship. We needed that more than anything. The sun, water... and other things... were nice bonuses.

That was nearly five months ago. The mundane pleasures have taken pride of place again in my day, but I've attacked life with a new vigor and attitude, determined to hang onto the energy provided by our short time away. As far as other people's problems go, I have a new motto: *Not my business; not my problem*. My life is far from perfect and problem-free. I have plenty to handle. Why borrow other people's problems, too? I need to focus on my marriage, my child, and my job.

More resolved than ever to save the clinic from death, I've made the referral program my bitch, signing on more new patients than any other staff member. As a result, I've been fully booked for nearly all five months since Dr. Reitman's retirement.

This is both good and bad. Good, of course, because that means this place may survive in the post-Reitman era. I'm moving on, finally accepting that she's not coming back and Dr. Dan is here to stay... which is the bad news. Kidding. That is, he *is* here to stay, but I refuse to give up hope that it will eventually be a good thing. Or at the very least, a "normal" thing.

Also on the negative side, I miss many of our former patients, and it's hard to start all over again with new ones. That can be rewarding in its own way, though, and I keep reminding myself that if we do our jobs well, these new patients will eventually be old friends.

I finish my physical examination of one such potential new friend, Tyler Gregson, my last patient of the day, and wash my hands. While the water runs over my soapy knuckles, I make small talk with the first grader but surreptitiously study his mom. In addition to the lines in her forehead and the down-turn at the corners of her mouth, the dark circles under her eyes tell a story of sleepless nights, a series of them, either dealing with the current issue for which she's brought in her son, or lying awake, worried about it.

Tyler doesn't seem too at ease, either. He mumbles his responses to my light inquiries about school, his upcoming summer plans, friends, and his favorite video games. His fingernails are bitten to the quick—and look none too clean.

Sitting upright on the exam table with his legs dangling over the side seems like it's taking more energy than he has.

I turn off the water by releasing the foot pedal, grab two paper towels from the dispenser on the wall, and rub my hands dry before flinging the damp, wadded sheets into the trash can for non-biohazardous waste.

At first, I perch on the rolling stool reserved for me, as usual, but I quickly change my mind, feeling like that's putting up one more barrier we don't need. I stand next to the exam table and ask, "Mind if I sit next to you?"

Tyler shakes his head. I make a big show of dragging my old body into position, groaning, then finally settling after putting down his chart behind me, out of my way. Mirroring his slumped posture, I fold my hands between my spread knees and say, "It says in your file that you're quite the heavy sleeper."

He shrugs.

"So heavy that sometimes your body doesn't tell you to wake up when it needs to use the bathroom."

His only answer is a blush.

"That's a bummer, dude."

"None of my friends pee the bed."

Knowing what I do about nocturnal enuresis, or bed-wetting, both statistically and from personal experience, I reply, "I wouldn't be too sure about that, bud. Lots of kids your age—especially boys—have trouble waking up in the middle of the night to go." I pause, then add conspiratorially, while leaning closer to him, "I did."

His head swivels so quickly to look at me that I worry about whiplash. "You did?"

"Uh... yeah!" I say, as if that's what all the cool kids do. "Not last week, or anything. But definitely when I was your age."

He laughs, showing me a mouth that looks a lot like Georgia's, only his teeth are a mixture of big and little, and the gummy gaps between them probably netted him some decent tooth fairy money.

"When I was your age, I'd sleep through almost anything. Then I'd wake up wet, sometimes in the middle of the night, and I'd have to get my mom and dad to help me change my sheets. Then I'd have to change my clothes and clean myself up, too."

"I hate that part. But I don't want to wear diapers."

Nodding, I scrape my bottom teeth on my top lip, then drop my head back to look at the ceiling. After a few seconds of thinking about that, I say, still not looking directly at him but watching him from the corner of my eye, "Here's the thing. There's this chemical—a hormone—in your body that tells your kidneys"—I affect a high-pitched voice—"'Hey, I'm going to sleep now; make less pee!'"

Tyler giggles.

I lower my chin and look more directly at him. "Some people don't have enough of that hormone, so they can't get through the night without their bladder filling. Combine that with a small bladder or someone who's a deep sleeper, and you have a problem. The good news is, someday, you'll make enough of that hormone. We're going to give your body some help by telling it in other ways how you expect it to behave."

"With diapers?"

"Nah. Diapers aren't the way to go. But what about a sleeping bag?"

He wrinkles his nose at my idea.

"No? It might sound weird, but think about it. Sleeping bags are waterproof on the outside, right? That means your bed won't get wet if you have an accident. *Plus*, if you wake up and realize you've wet yourself, all you have to do is unzip the sleeping bag, take off your clothes, and throw all of it into the washing machine. Easy peasy!"

I wink at Tyler's mom when her son says, "Oh, yeah."

"Good idea," she seconds.

I smile and admit, "I've given this advice a few times." Shifting, I straighten my back. "Cuz here's the thing, folks: this is really common. And let's get something out in the open right now." I point to him. "It's not your fault." I point to her. "And it's not yours, either."

Her eyes puddle. "Okay."

I pretend not to notice. The last thing she needs is me fawning all over her and making a big deal about her crying when she might not know why she's so emotional right now. Instead, I continue ruling out anything serious, asking her about strange colors or odors to his urine.

When she answers my questions satisfactorily, I say, "Okay, so here's what we should do." Holding up my hand, I tick off on my fingers: "No drinks after 6 p.m., empty your bladder right before bed, go to bed at the same time every night, sleep in a sleeping bag, get a night light so you can see your way to the toilet... I think that's it for now. Let's be consistent with what we've talked about today and see how that goes."

"And if that doesn't work?" Mrs. Gregson asks, looking unconvinced.

"If he's still having accidents in three months, we can talk other options. Sound like a plan?"

They both nod vigorously.

I hop down from the table, grab his chart, and slap him playfully on the head with it. "Great. I'll go grab some hand-outs that discuss everything we've talked about here, so you don't have to try to remember it all."

It takes a few minutes to gather the right papers, and since I'm about to take the last one in the stack about rewards for dry nights, I spare a minute to make a few copies to replenish our supply. When I return to the room, I hear Dr. Douche's voice on the other side of the partially open door, so I pause.

What the fu—?

"...it works!"

Mrs. Gregson replies, "Nate didn't say anything about those other methods. He said we should try these basic strategies first. And I have to say, a loud alarm that senses wetness on a mattress sounds traumatic, not to mention expensive. And drugs? Hypnosis? I'm just not sure."

I can hear the smirk in Dr. Douche's voice when he says, "Nate's a good nurse, but he's definitely a product of his upbringing. He thinks everything has psychological ramifications. His parents sent him to college and nursing school on that baloney."

I knock lightly, then push open the door, using every last ounce of restraint—and acting skill—to pretend I didn't hear what was said in my "absence." With a grin, I hand over the papers to Mrs. Gregson. "There you go." As an aside, and a form of dismissal, I say, "Hey, Dr. Dan! Thanks for checking in and introducing yourself to one of our new patients."

He stands straighter. "Absolutely. Wanted to make sure they had a good experience."

"I'll be sure to send them a survey." Turning away from him, I address Mrs. Gregson. "Those are the papers I told you about, outlining the strategies we discussed. Patience and persistence. Works nearly every time."

"But not *every* time," Dr. Douche points out smugly. "Whereas—"

"Nothing does," I state firmly. Again, trying to ignore him, I physically edge in front of him and show him my back while I wrap up the Gregsons' visit. "You have any questions or concerns, you call me. At any time. Day or night. The answering service can get in touch with me 24/7, and I'll get right back to you."

"Sounds like he's volunteering to come over and change those sheets for you. Of course, you wouldn't need to take him up on it if you skipped all this other malarkey and went straight to the surefire solution. I could guarantee you'll never deal with urine-soaked bedding or an upset child again."

"No, he can't," I say when his ridiculous claim sparks heart-breaking hope in both mother's and son's eyes. "Dr. Dan, thanks for your input. I'll take it from here, and if further intervention is required, I'm sure Mrs. Gregson will be in touch." I face him and step forward, forcing him to either collide with me or step back and out of the way.

Conceding, he raises his hands in front of his chest and says, "Suit yourself. Just calling it like I see it," and exits the room, leaving us with, "Have a nice evening! It was good to meet you!"

As I turn to usher my patient and his mother to the check-out desk, Mrs. Gregson holds firm in the middle of the exam room. "Are those other methods really that effective?"

I cross my arms over my chest. "Listen. If you want the quick fix, that's fine. It's not going to hurt my feelings. Like Dr. Dan so bluntly pointed out, I'm not the one doing your laundry. I'm sorry you've suddenly been put in such an awkward position."

She bites her lip. "No. Don't be silly. Please don't apologize. The advice you gave was good. We'll definitely try it first."

"If you're sure..."

"I am."

I usher mother and son to the check-out desk. While Mrs. Gregson schedules a follow-up appointment (miracle of miracles) for three months from now, I make light conversation with Tyler about his favorite summertime activities, then say goodbye to the two of them.

And march straight down to Dr. Douche's office.

* * *

INSIDE THE DOOR, I stand, waiting for him to acknowledge my presence. While I wait, I look around at what used to be Dr. Reitman's peaceful, classy (yet functional) office. In the five months since Le Douche has assumed residency, it's undergone a huge transformation. And by "transformation," I mean like the "before and after" posters you see of normal people who have been addicted to meth for a while. The soul has been sucked from the place. If it had eyes, they'd be vacant and lifeless, but every once in a while, you'd see a flash of awareness, a memory of what it used to be. I can also still see the dents in the floor where her heavy, dark-wood desk and bookshelves rested. The divots stand out like pockmarks in a ravaged face.

Part of the problem is Dr. Douche's hideous, too-modern furniture. It's like he repurposed a bunch of the fixtures from the stark, sterile exam rooms and plunked them any old way in this space, which swallows it all. His white acrylic-and-stainless steel desk looks lost and dwarfed by his stupid Dr. Evil leather chair. He has no chairs for guests, either, which is just as well, since nobody wants to come in here to talk to him, anyway; and if they do, they don't ever want to stay long enough to sit.

Right now is no exception. After nearly a minute of him ignoring me, I say, still standing in the doorway, "May I speak with you for a second?"

He deigns to look at me but doesn't accept or deny my request, so I take initiative. "What the hell was that about with the Gregsons?"

Steepling his fingers under his chin, he replies, "I was introducing myself to them, familiarizing myself with Taylor's health concerns."

"Tyler. You can't even get the kid's name right?"

"Taylor, Tyler; whatever. I met him once, so give me a break."

I resist pointing out that I've only met the kid once, too, since I don't want to get bogged down in any petty details when there are so many *huge* things to discuss here. He doesn't give me a chance to speak, anyway.

"Then I find out you've given her all these namby-pamby suggestions, things I'm sure any idiot would have tried before making an appointment with a doctor—Oh, sorry. A nurse."

I grit my teeth but refuse to react to his goading.

He scratches his chin, then clicks open an email that's loudly arrived in his inbox. Distractedly, he continues, "What was I supposed to do? Blindly back you up, despite disagreeing with your proposed solution?"

"Yes!"

He snorts. "Hardly!"

"I've been doing it on nearly every recommendation you've made for the past year! Because it's unprofessional to contradict each other in front of patients and their caregivers, unless it's absolutely unavoidable and in the interest of the patient's health and safety. Which in this case, it wasn't."

"Are you suggesting, then, that the advice our patients receive varies depending on who they see at this clinic? They go to you and get one story; they go to me and get another?"

"On some things, yes. We have fundamental ideological differences. On many things."

"That's not acceptable."

"That's pretty standard. Dr. Reitman and I didn't agree on everything, either."

"That's not the impression I got."

I ignore his snide tone. "Those drugs you recommended to Mrs. Gregson are expensive and can have serious side effects. That alarm scares the bejeezus out of kids and attaches additional anxiety to an already-humiliating issue."

When he merely blinks laconically at me, unmoved by my argument, I segue to the secondary issue regarding his most recent interference. "And another thing. When I want or need your input on something, I'll ask for it. I always seek out your professional opinion, when it's warranted. This wasn't one of those cases."

"Oh, yes. About that... you don't need to have me sign off on every specialist or surgical referral. I'm getting hand cramps from all of the hand-holding I'm doing in the form of my signature."

My blood pressure edges higher, making my ears ring. "You're the doctor! I'm not asking you to blindly sign off on things. When a parent mentions surgical remedies—most of which I believe are unnecessary—and I pull you in for a second opinion, I'm asking you to review the case and make a thoughtful determination."

"Don't feel bad; you're not the only one who seeks out my constant approval. The front office girls can't order toilet paper or office supplies without my signature. I need to get a stamp."

"You need to get over yourself and just do what needs to be done. Because you should do *something* around here."

"How dare you?"

"How dare *you*? Sometimes it's not about what solves the problem the fastest; it's about what solves the problem while also doing the least amount of harm. But these are just other people's kids you're toying with, right?"

"You're out of line, Nate. I suggest you cool it."

Too irate to care that I've gone too far, I rage blindly

forward. "I'll cool it when you offer one piece of responsible, sensible advice in my presence. That's something I've yet to witness."

"That's subjective."

"Fuck subjective. We're men of science."

He rises and leans forward, bracing himself on his fingertips against his desktop. "Well, I guess you won't have to worry about it anymore, because it's obvious you and I are at an impasse. Get your things."

I shift my weight to my other foot, swallow, and blink at him. "You're kidding me."

He stands taller, straightening his white jacket and adjusting his neck with a faint crack. "No, I'm not. There's obviously not enough mutual respect between us to continue to work together. We're working at cross-purposes, always at odds, and that's not fair to our patients."

"You don't have the authority to fire me."

"You have a contract?"

My heart races when I have to admit, "No," but I calm myself by pointing out, "There's a procedure and a review process for every termination, though."

"Very well. But I do have the authority to write you up and send you home while the review is pending."

"You're suspending me?"

"Yes. And that's not going to look good on your spotless, saintly record." He arranges his face into a fake pout that makes me want to vault over his Erector Set desk and slap the shit out of him.

I laugh mirthlessly. "You—" Before I say something that will surely go in the record and not do me any favors when it comes to finding future employment, I stop. Boring a hole through his wrinkled forehead with my glare, I say, "Don't bother with all that hand-cramping paperwork. Because I quit."

"Wait a minute." Beulah's voice rings out behind me, making both the doctor and me flinch and turn toward the door. Without our realizing it, our co-workers have crowded behind me in the hallway. "If Nate goes, I do too."

"No!" I object.

"Me too," says Lynette immediately.

"Same here," Mary-Kate chirps.

"I'm totally there as well," Mindy agrees.

Janet looks at the others and rolls her eyes. "Okay, fine. Count me in too."

"Guys, no. This is bad enough, as it is. Don't make it worse," I plead.

Lynette inspects her fingernails like we're gathered to discuss what brand of printer paper to use. "This place wouldn't be the same without you, anyway. Not worth staying."

"I think I speak for all the 'front office girls' when I say our answer is final," Beulah adds with a head-bob that confirms just how much of the argument they heard.

"You can't all quit," Dr. Douche says, pale as the surface of his desk.

"Yes, we can," Lynette counters. "And we will, if Nate walks out that door today without his job."

Color returns to the doctor's face in the form of angry red stress blotches in the hollows of his cheeks. "I dare you."

"Everyone, wait!" I shoo them from the office and farther into the hall, toward the nurses' station. "I need a minute alone with him, okay?" I murmur. "Trust me."

When I'm sure they're going to stay put, I return to Dr. Douche's office, close the door, and say, "Here's the deal. I'm going to give you what you've wanted—for whatever reason—

from the minute you walked through the sliding doors of this clinic: I'm leaving."

"None of you will work for Greenbrier. Ever again. I'll see to it."

"That's where you're wrong. Because I'm going, but they're staying."

"But they said—"

"I'll make sure they don't walk out with me today, without notice. But you have to promise me you'll honor their transfer requests or write glowing recommendations for every last one of them if they ask for them."

"Why should I?"

"Because I'll go quietly, and you'll still have some staff to work with while Greenbrier shifts some personnel around. Then nobody but me is out of a job, and you're not up Shit Creek trying to run this place by yourself. Considering you can't be bothered to refill the cotton swabs and tongue depressors, I'd say you better take my offer."

He sighs. "Fine. Whatever. Just go."

Sick to my stomach, I nevertheless nod. "Okay, then. I'm out."

"And when I come in tomorrow, you swear they'll all be here?"

"I promise."

Considering it for a few seconds, his eyes narrowed as if I might be leading him into a trap he's simply too stupid to foresee, he mumbles, "If they're not, the deal is off, and I'll write up every last one of you."

"Fair enough."

And like that, I'm free.

32

PACKING IT IN

WHEN I RETURN TO THE NURSE'S STATION, I SHOOT everyone assembled a shaky smile.

Lynette speaks first. "Let's go."

I hold up my trembling hands. "Guys, I appreciate the gesture—"

"It's not a gesture. We mean it!"

"Yeah, well, here's the thing." I clear my throat. "I don't have a choice. It's walk or be fired. Either way, I'm gone."

"Then so are we."

I unhook my pen from the V-neck of my scrubs and pitch it on the counter at the nurse's station. My ID badge and lanyard join it, and I look around for any of my personal effects, including a framed picture of Betty and me from Jamaica, Georgia's newborn hospital photo, and a few hand-drawn pictures and trinkets from patients. "Okay, but not today, all right? You can ask for transfer requests or give your two weeks' notice."

"No way!" Lynette explodes.

"Screw him!" Mary-Kate agrees.

"Shhh... Listen, it's not about him," I say, tucking my treasures into the crook of my left arm. "I need you guys to stay. I realize it's a huge thing to ask, but if he wasn't going to write me up and have me fired—God knows he has enough ammunition, and that's my fault—then I'd suck it up and stay, too."

"What? After everything he's—"

"I'd stay for our patients."

It's so silent I can hear Beulah's watch tick.

"See what I'm saying? If we all leave at once, who suffers? Him, sure, because he'd be screwed. But the ones who would suffer the most would be the patients we're deserting. I need you guys to stay and cover for me."

Janet looks relieved. "You've got it, Nate."

"How can we work with him after all this? He'll make our lives hell!" Lynette says.

"If he does, you tell me, and I'll take care of it. In the meantime, look for new jobs. Don't leave him high and dry—give him a respectable notice or go through the proper transfer channels through Greenbrier."

"Now that you're leaving, there's no way this place is going to last," Lynette says, and Mindy nods her agreement. "We make the appointments. Nobody wants to see him. They all ask for you."

"That has less to do with me and more to do with him, fortunately. Otherwise, I'd feel worse than I already do."

"You have nothing to feel bad about," Beulah insists. "You did everything you could—and then some."

"If I thought reporting him would do any good, I'd drive to headquarters in Madison tomorrow and do it, but... he's entrenched. After he kills this place, Greenbrier will find another clinic to put him in."

"It better not be the one they transfer me to," Mary-Kate mumbles.

"Transfer again," I suggest. "Well, I better get out of here.

Please... I told him you'd all be here tomorrow, because I knew you'd care more about the patients than making your point. But if any of you don't show up, he's going to write up every last one of us."

"What a dick!" Mindy says on a sigh.

I can't help but laugh. "Well, I don't call him Dr. Douche for nothing." I sigh and lift my free arm, waving them closer to me for hugs. "I guess this is it. No mushy stuff now. Everything's going to be fine."

"What are you going to do?" Lynette asks, her frown deepening.

I wave away her wobbly question. "Ah. Don't worry about me. I'll figure something out. I've been trying to find a way to bust out of this joint for months."

They laugh at what they think is a joke, and a slight pang of guilt tweaks my guts, but it's greatly overtaken by a much more powerful duo of emotions. Elation and relief conceive one of the most sincere grins I've produced in months. "Guys, it's been mostly awesome."

Pulling each of them to my side in turn, I say, "Take care of those kiddos," to Beulah; "Tell Damian I want a full report when that new Avengers movie comes out," to Janet; "If you don't call me for a reference when you apply for nursing school, I'll be hurt," to Mindy; and "Doctors Hews, Parsons, Weggman, and Valenti are all pretty cool, so if they come up on your transfer request, you're golden," to Mary-Kate.

When Lynette steps up to me, she gives me a rough hug, then almost instantly lets go and shifts on her feet, blinking at the floor. "Get out of here."

I pat the top of her head. "Take care of yourself and stay out of trouble. No more asswipe surgeons, got it? You deserve better than that."

"Yeah, well, I learned my lesson."

"Good." I take a deep breath and repeat, louder, "Good. Tell Dr. Douche I said *adios*. Something tells me he'd prefer to skip the hug."

With their sniffly laughter behind me, I raise my hand in a blind wave and push through the back door to the parking lot, drenched in early evening orange light. I take a deep breath, but instead of baked blacktop, car exhaust, and new grass, I smell one thing: freedom.

* * *

I DRIVE HOME, my fingers twitching and itching the entire way, but I don't break my rule about not using my cell phone while driving. At home, I park the car, turn it off, and scroll through my contacts, my shaky hands making me miss the entry I want three times before I get it. Holding the phone to my ear, I scratch at the skin between my nose and upper lip while I wait through the rings.

"Please answer," I whisper, then decide leaving a message might not be the worst thing. Maybe it's foolish of me to talk to anyone about this before my wife knows I'm jobless.

Then again, I want to have a solution in place before I tell her. I have to be able to say, "Everything will be okay," and believe it. Until I talk to this person, I can't say that.

"Nate!" Dr. Reitman's cheerful voice greets me as I'm scrambling to think of what to say to the voicemail I fear is about to pick up.

I suck in a breath and choke on my spit but quickly recover after a subtle cough. "Hey!" I reply, as if I call her every day. As if this isn't weird. As if I haven't just been fired (effectively) for the first time in my life. As if I'm not terrified. As if I'm not equally elated. As if I haven't lost my mind. "How's retirement treating you?"

Yeah... that's *why I'm calling.*

She pauses but replies in a sunny tone that matches mine, "Great! It's... great!"

"Great. That's... great."

"And how are you? Keeping up with those strong women, at home and at work?"

"We're great. They're great."

Okay, now that we've established everything and everyone is effing great...

"So, what's up?" she asks after another awkward silence.

"Not much, not much," I lie, tapping the steering wheel to a silent beat. "Uh... Well, I guess a few things are happening. Small things." I chuckle, as if what I'm about to say is going to make her laugh, too. "Like... I, um, just walked out of the clinic for the last time." I glance at the small pile of my personal effects on the passenger seat, then quickly refocus my attention on the closed garage door through the windshield.

Quietly, without an ounce of surprise in her voice, Dr. Reitman asks, "What happened?"

Although she can't see me, I shrug, then answer, "Oh, the specifics aren't important. Yet another disagreement between Dr. Chancellor and me, only I wasn't as good at keeping my temper in check this time and said some things. Then he said some things, one of which was to get my stuff and get out of there."

She laughs. "He can't do that, Nate."

"Oh, I know." I exhale loudly. "I made sure he knew, too. Then I quit."

"I see."

Those two words reflect the same underlying disappointment I have with myself, so I groan, press my forehead against the steering wheel, and say, "God, I'd had it. It didn't matter that he didn't have the authority to fire me; I wish he did. Because it would mean I wouldn't have to be the quitter."

I briefly describe white-knuckling it since her departure, mostly in denial about my inevitable failure but getting enough flashes of honesty, in unguarded moments, to know I wasn't going to be able to sustain that working arrangement long-term.

"The best I could have hoped for was waiting him out, hoping he'd do something stupid enough—preferably not at the expense of some poor kid's health—to get himself in trouble with the higher-ups. Or that he would kill the practice before I reached my limit. Damn. Can you imagine wanting either of those things to happen?"

"That must have been horrible."

"It's been a nightmare. The guilt..." I lean back and tilt my head up, staring unseeing at the ceiling a few inches from my nose. "This is just as bad, though. I've jumped ship, deserted those kids and parents... and my friends. By choice." I pinch my eyes, my fingers sliding to the bridge of my nose and squeezing painfully hard. "And the worst thing is, the relief overshadows the guilt. More than anything, I'm glad to be out of there. I care more about not having to work with that idiot than I care about the kids I've abandoned to his incompetent care, and that sucks. That's the opposite of what a good nurse does. You don't put your own interests ahead of—"

"Nate."

"—your patients' wellbeing!"

"Nate!"

I stop, hold my breath, then squeak, "What?"

"Calm down." The smile is strong in her voice.

Suddenly embarrassed by my unfiltered rant, I say, "Oh, man. I'm sorry. I didn't mean to unload on you. I called to ask you for a reference and maybe some leads on doctors in private practice who might be interested in a dependable FNP as a backup." I let go of my face and drop my hand to my lap. "I don't want Betty to worry."

"She won't worry. She trusts you. You have this under control."

I laugh. "But I don't."

"Sure you do." When I don't have the energy to argue with her anymore, she continues, "And I'd be glad to provide a reference for you."

"Thanks."

"I'm also glad to hear you're ready to leave Greenbrier behind and explore the private practice realm."

"Not sure I have a choice there." I trace the outline of a rocket ship on my leg. "Probably burned that bridge pretty good."

"Well, I have the perfect doctor for you."

I scoot my hips back and perk up. "You do?"

"Yes. I'm so glad you called. Because I've been working up the nerve to call and tell you about this. But I didn't want to complicate your life with an opportunity that you might not be willing to consider."

"It's plenty uncomplicated now, huh?" I quip. "Lay it on me. Who's this doctor?"

"She's an experienced pediatrician, just getting into private practice. Big believer in teamwork and collaboration but also understands the importance of a strong hierarchy. She's genuine and dedicated and expects the same from those around her."

"Sounds refreshing."

"And knowing her and you, you'd be an amazing team. She's already familiar with you and likes what she knows."

I blush. "Seriously?"

"Here's the catch, though."

She takes a deep breath, and my heart sinks. Damn. A catch. I don't like catches. Then again, I don't have much room to be picky here.

"You'd have to relocate. To South Carolina."

I freeze. No moving, no breathing, no speaking, only thinking. My heart palpitates when I realize just who we're talking about. *Damn. I want that so bad.* Still, I play dumb. Licking my lips, I say, "Hmm... I see."

She clears her throat. "Retirement is overrated. The first three months were amazing. But now? I'm bored. So bored that for the past two months I've done nothing but try to figure out how to get back to work... here. Because I love it here. I don't like being idle, though."

"I can see how that would be difficult for you."

"It has been. So, I'm buying out a retiring doctor's practice. Which means—unless their parents decide to take them else-where—his patients are part of the deal." Into my expectant silence, she says, "And I guess what I'm trying to ask is if—now that you're so conveniently free—you'll come here and be my FNP."

I chew the inside of my cheek to prevent blurting a yes to her proposal.

"Well?"

"I'll have to talk to Betty."

"Of course. That goes without saying."

"And she's going to want to know what happens when you decide to retire for real in a few years."

"Valid question, and one I've already considered."

"And?"

"I don't see myself retiring—again—any time soon, but when I do, if you haven't already left me for something bigger and better..."

I snort.

"...I'll put the practice up for sale, and you and I will choose my replacement. Together."

Looking down at my knees, I scratch my eyebrow. "I could fly out there, see how much of a risk this would be."

"It's not as risky as you'd think, Nate."

"How so?" *Please. Convince me. Tell me something, anything, that makes this possible, that would make it seem like a no-brainer to Betty, too.*

"Private practices are huge down here. People don't want to take their kids to a corporate-run clinic in a nondescript building that looks like all the other clinics. They like having their doctors in the middle of quaint neighborhoods, five minutes away for middle-of-the-night house calls. They want to see their doctors in the pew at church and at the meat counter at the grocery store. It's all very retro."

"Sounds awesome," I have to admit, my hard-to-get act slipping.

"And the medical community takes care of each other. They step up when one of them is too busy or on vacation or is retiring. Everyone keeps in touch. They've welcomed me."

"I can see that. Sounds like you've made some connections and are fitting in well in your new community."

"I have. I am." She pauses, then after a deep breath, says, "Listen, I'm sorry I left you—and the Green Bay clinic—with such a mess. At the time, I felt I had no choice. I had to do what was right for me, for my family, for my life. And I guess I don't regret it too much, because it's led to this opportunity, but I'm sorry you've been so miserable."

"It's really not your fault," I reply magnanimously, although it gives me great satisfaction to hear her take *some* responsibility.

"Maybe not," she says quietly after a few seconds. "But I'd like to try to make it up to you, anyway. And moving you here to help me set up and run my new practice is the closest thing to a sure thing I can offer. Nothing comes without *some* risk. But you have to admit, this is an amazingly convenient, serendipitous arrangement. We couldn't have scripted it better. And I'm confident we can do this, Nate."

I exhale, trying to harness the excitement and hope that's become so foreign to me in recent months. Movement to my left catches my eye, and I turn my head to see Betty pull up next to me in the driveway.

"Oh, gosh. I have to go. Betty's home."

Dr. Reitman says, "Okay. Right. So, you'll discuss it with her?"

"Yes. Definitely."

"I'll let you go then. I'll email you an official offer, so you have salary details to discuss with her, but no rush, no pressure. I'm going to do this no matter what. It would be such a relief to have a dependable, familiar partner, though."

I feel exactly the same way. Here's hoping my *life* partner, who's looking decidedly confused by my current behavior, likes the idea as much as we do.

* * *

NEARLY TWO HOURS LATER, while Betty's sitting on the edge of the bathtub, giving Georgia a bath before bed, I finally get up the nerve to tell my wife about my eventful day. When I get to the end of the story and drop the news about no longer having a job—here in Green Bay, anyway—she reaches blindly for the towel rack next to her on the wall. Her eyelids flutter.

I grab her shoulders before she falls into the tub on top of our daughter. "Don't pass out!"

"You can't command someone not to pass out," she grumbles weakly.

"I'm telling you not to, because everything is going to be fine."

I help her to the closed toilet, take over the baby bathing duties, and quickly recap my conversation with Dr. Reitman.

When I finish, she looks like I must have looked through the windshield of my car when she first came home. After several blinks but no words from her, I say, "I told her I had to talk to you, but... C'mon. I'm taking it, right? It's perfect."

She places her hands on top of her head and asks, "I'm supposed to quit my job and drop everything and... and..."

"Well... I... uh... That's why I told her we'd have to talk about it, but we already *have* talked about getting out of here in the past, so..." My heart pounds while I wait for her to respond some other way than by staring at me with her mouth clamped shut and her nostrils flared. "You come home all the time, threatening to quit your job. Now you can."

"Everyone says that when they're fed up at work! Following through is another story." She looks down at her legs, picks at her pants, and sighs.

"But in this case, it's really okay. Because we can get by on one income, and—"

Her head snaps up. "It's not just about money, Nate!"

Rookie mistake, Bingham. Time to do some major damage control. "I know! I totally get that. I—"

"I have a career. And I've worked just as hard to get where I am as you did to get where you are. The difference is, *I* still have a job."

Ouch. But fair. "Yes. Absolutely. I—"

"So don't toss it aside like it's a cute little hobby that gets me out of the house and funds my shoe shopping habit."

"I didn't—" I take a deep breath and flinch when Georgia slaps the surface of the bath water, sending a shower onto my chest and lap. Closing my eyes, I count to five but push on before Betty interrupts me again. "That isn't what I was imply-ing. I only meant that we won't have to worry about money, so you can take your time finding the perfect job to replace the one you'd be leaving here."

"You talked money with Dr. Reitman? Specific figures?"

"Not on the phone, no. But I can show you the official offer letter she emailed to me. My salary would be comparable to what I make here."

"'Comparable' as in 'more,' or 'comparable' as in, 'less, but close'?"

"Factoring in the higher cost of living, about the same."

"It costs more to live there?"

"A little," I concede.

Her forehead still full of worry, she leans down to check the temperature of Georgia's cooling bath water then squeaks a rubber ducky at the baby, who giggles and grabs the toy. "South Carolina, huh? Have you researched schools? Crime rates? I mean, we know nothing about this place, other than where it is geographically. Which brings me to my next point: hurricanes."

"Unbelievable," I mutter.

"What? I'm thinking about the big picture here!"

"Where we'd be moving isn't on the coast," I quickly point out, grabbing a towel. "Quite a way inland. But still close enough for fun weekends at the beach. As for your other concerns, I honestly don't know, Betts. I've had the job offer for all of two hours. I haven't had time to do the research yet. But I'm sure everything will be fine."

"I don't know... What about your family?"

Snorting, I stand and reply, "What about them?" as I lift Georgia from the tub and fold her into a towel, nestling her in the crook of my right arm. "I'd still be a phone call or text or email away. I don't need to live right down the street. Are you worried about leaving your parents?"

"No. They're rarely here, and when they are..." She rises and edges close to me. I wrap my free arm around her. She snakes one arm behind my back and the other one around Georgia, who squeals and flails her rubbery arms and legs.

"Then let's go," I murmur, my lips against Betty's cheek. "You know you want to."

Her face lifts against my mouth as she smiles. "I do, but..."

Moving my chin to the top of her head, I say, "It's an amazing opportunity to do something *we* want to do. In a brand new place. Just you, me, Georgia, and Reba. And Dr. Reitman."

She chuckles while twirling a strand of the baby's wet hair around her finger. "Clean slate, right?"

"Yep. Think of how much fun it'll be."

"We'll need to come up with an organized, detailed plan before you give Dr. Reitman a final answer."

"I suddenly have a lot of free time to help with that, so plan away. I'd expect nothing less."

Pulling back so she can look up at me with a quiet smile while she rubs Georgia dry, she says, "Okay. Let's do it."

33

THE ULTIMATE PLANNER

BEING THIS HAPPY MAY BE ILLEGAL IN SOME STATES, BUT I have a feeling this will be the new norm, after just one draining day here.

Perma-grins plastered in place, we loll on the living room floor of our new house, surrounded by carefully labeled boxes and the furniture we're eschewing, because we're dusty and sweaty and dirty... and loving it. A half bottle of wine sits between us. I lift a red plastic cup toward my wife in a toast.

"To one room down, too many to think about to go," I say, having recently finished setting up Georgia's bedroom to put her down for the night.

Betty drinks to that, then sets down her cup, rolls halfway onto her stomach, and pulls a twice-folded sheet of paper from her back pocket. "It's okay. I have a plan."

Of course, she does. Once she warmed to the idea of leaving Green Bay and moving to South Carolina, she threw herself into the moving process. First, though, she made me play hardball with my negotiations with Dr. Reitman.

"This salary is unacceptable," she declared, reading the offer email.

I looked over her shoulder. "What do you mean? It's more than I make now."

"True, but she needs to factor in a few things other than cost of living."

"Like?"

"Moving expenses. The fact that, for a while at least, you'll be our only income. Private schools."

"Private schools?"

She shrugged. "I did some research while you were putting Georgia to bed—how many stories did you read tonight, anyway?—and while the public schools in South Carolina aren't the worst in the country, they're not the best."

"So? Wisconsin schools aren't the best, either."

"Better than South Carolina."

I sigh. "We have a while before we have to think about that."

"It'll be here before you know it."

"I can negotiate a raise when the time comes."

"Don't bet on it."

"Hey!"

She laughed. "I'm just saying, Dr. Reitman's willing to fork it over now, to get you there. Once you're there, if finances are tighter than she anticipated, she'll have already factored your salary into the budget, and she'll be hesitant to raise it."

"She's not like that."

"It's nothing personal. But she's a business owner now. She has to worry more about the bottom line." Betty hit "reply" so a blank email message opened. Typing in an embarrassing figure, she said, "There. That's more like it."

"No way!" I reached for the backspace key, but she pulled the laptop out of my reach.

"Yes way. Trust me. I Googled average FNP salaries in that area, and *this*"—she pointed to the number she'd typed—"is median. Don't be a weenie, Nathaniel. This is our life we're talking about. A major change. A huge risk, no matter what anyone says. Don't get all sentimental on me."

"Betts..."

"We're doing her a favor. But it's not going to come cheap."

"That sounds so mercenary."

"It *is*. We're not doing this out of the goodness of our hearts. We're doing it to improve our lives, too. And part of that improvement is monetary. That's just how it goes."

I convinced her to come down a couple thousand on the salary but agreed to ask for the doctor to pay for our moving expenses. "With a professional mover," Betty specified. "I'm not loading up and driving a U-Haul cross-country. Organizing everything is going to be headache enough."

And maybe it has been, for her. But it's been shamefully easy for me so far. The worst part was hitting "send" on that counter-offer. Since Dr. Reitman's swift acceptance, I've hardly had to do anything but show up. Betty's coordinated everything. Sure, I helped pack, and I'm sure I'll be instrumental in unpacking everything. But all the other hassles have been Betty's projects. She wouldn't have it any other way, either.

Now, the thought of seeing, written out in black and white, everything we have yet to do to get settled almost kills my dopey grin, but I bravely take the list from her as she returns to her reclined position on her elbow. Prepared to tease her for what's sure to be a thirty-part itemized list in Roman numeral outlining, I'm shocked to find only three things neatly printed on the paper.

"Wow. Three things. That's totally doable."

With a mouthful of wine, I skim over them. And nearly do a spit-take. And sputter. And read them again. Then drop the list and push myself to an upright position more conducive to... not dying.

Betty scoots closer to me and pats my back. "Oh, my gosh. I'm sorry. I didn't mean to almost kill you."

Eyes filling for more than one reason, I accept her ministrations while desperately trying to suck in enough air with each choking breath. When I finally recover, I retrieve the paper from the floor and read it again. And again. And again. Until I'm only looking at one line in Betty's neat, precise printing.

"Well?" she nudges.

Still blinking away tears, I move my eyes from the paper to her face and nod. In a choked voice due more to aspirated wine than emotion—for once—I reply, "Are you already— I mean, is it...?" I nod toward her abdomen.

She follows my gesture, looking confused, then laughs. "Oh! No. Not yet." Pointing to the list, she explains, "That's my carefully considered plan. 'Unpack; Be Happy; and Have Another Baby.' It's rough, but... Well... " She winks at me.

With a knowing smile, I say, "We can fill in the missing steps. C'mere." I press my forehead to hers. "I love you. And I love this plan. It's perfectly simple."

"I love you, too. And this plan allows me to say something I've always wanted to say."

I wait, my throat tightening sympathetically when, suddenly emotional, she whispers, "Hey, let's do this. Don't you think it'll be great?"

I wipe a tear from her cheek with my thumb and whisper back, "The greatest."

I wonder if our youngest child will ever know he or she may have been conceived on the living room floor the day we moved more than a thousand miles away from everything and almost everyone we knew, to start over. It's a great story, one that begs to be told.

But personal experience tells me the poor kid could be

traumatized by that information. And there's no way to prove this is when it truly happens. Many attempts will be made in the next several hours, days, and weeks. Therefore, as tempting as it is to pass down the most romantic version, science, accuracy, and our child's mental wellness forbid it.

And I'm more than good with that.

For real.